RELIANCE,
ILLINOIS

ALSO BY MARY VOLMER

Crown of Dust

RELIANCE, ILLINOIS

MARY VOLMER

SOHO

Published by
Soho Press, Inc.
853 Broadway
New York, NY 10003

Library of Congress Cataloging-in-Publication Data

Volmer, Mary
Reliance, Illinois / Mary Volmer.

ISBN 978-1-61695-672-1
eISBN 978-1-61695-673-8

1. Teenage girls—Fiction. 2. City and town life—Illinois—History—
19th century—Fiction. I. Title
PS3622.O645 R45 2016
DDC 813.6—dc23 2015041329

Interior design by Janine Agro, Soho Press, Inc.

Printed in the United States of America

10 9 8 7 6 5 4 3 2 1

For Chris

When a government makes reasonable acts criminal, reasonable people commit criminal acts. —LORENA FRENCH

Our job is not to make young women grateful. It is to make them ungrateful so they keep going. —SUSAN B. ANTHONY

RELIANCE,
ILLINOIS

PART I
1874

1

I was three months from thirteen when Mama and I stepped off the carriage in the Mississippi River town of Reliance. We carried between us one tattered carpetbag and a hatbox of balding crushed velvet filled with lace-making and sewing notions. And we carried a marriage proposal from a Mr. Lyman Dryfus.

Two other passengers, a consumptive old farmer and a woman in a foreign looking dress, heaved their trunks and disappeared into the arms and wagons of loved ones. The coachman hissed low obscenities to his team; then he, too, continued up Grafton Road, leaving Mama and me alone together on the outskirts of a brick-and-mortar town that looked ready to tumble from the limestone bluffs above. A white haze veiled the sun. Farmland yawned westward while the river pressing south seemed to me the source and end of all the changing colors quilting the Illinois shore.

"Read it to me again," Mama said. Upriver, a cannon boomed from a trolling steamer, all but its twin stacks, hidden by a thin, tree-lined island. "Madelyn."

"Said wait by the river road. Don't see no other river. No other road."

"Don't be smart." Mama coiled a strand of hair around one finger, sucked the split ends to a point; she gave her skirts and petticoats a shake as one would freshen long-shelved linen, and then we both became conscious of the figure hulking in the shade of a nearby oak. He was wide through the eyes, his chin studded with soft blond whiskers and angry red blemishes, and his long arms and legs had a dumb restless look about them. I slipped behind Mama, pulled my bonnet low.

"Miss Rebecca Branch?" he asked.

Beautiful women, like Mama, only pretend to be unconscious of the effect their looks have upon men. On the train to Alton, her practiced scowl warded off uninvited attention, and the smile she gave this man—no, boy, a great big boy, slumping into the light—strained Mama's neck and shoulders. We had been expecting a man with a *steady business and dependable income*, so his age and the frayed legs of his trousers were suspect.

The cannon boomed. The boy, recovering himself, nodded toward the steam trail. "A girl's gone missing."

"That's terrible," she said. The boy shrugged.

"If she drowned, they're looking too far up current." He deliberated, craning his neck to see me. "Isn't there only meant to be one of you?"

But Mama, stepping quickly forward, captured his full attention. "And you are Mr—?"

The boy blushed. "It's Hanley. Just Hanley. Mr. Dryfus's devil. Work for him. But I'm joining to fight out west, soon as I'm old enough."

"Hanley, then," she said and taking him by the sleeve, left me to mind the bags. "Take us to Mr. Dryfus."

EVEN WITH HER HUMBLE TROUSSEAU, Mama maintained the entire journey a desperate, hopeful pride, which earned at once the slack-jawed admiration of men and the denigration of women—and made her even more a mystery to me than normal. In the days that must surely precede her wedding, she planned to stitch every scrap of lace she'd made about the collar and cuffs of her Sunday dress, in the hope that Mr. Dryfus would find her attire frugal, as opposed to poor. For in correspondence with Mr. Dryfus, Mama (that is to say I, because Mama never learned to read or write well) led him to believe she stood to inherit a respectable sum and a modest estate from an aged aunt, who, unfortunately for all involved, did not exist. Except for her hands—square, and callused as a man's—Mama could pass for twenty. But there was no benevolent aunt, no money, no land.

And of course, I did not exist in the mind of Mr. Dryfus.

No other advertisements in the *Matrimonial Times* featured mother with daughter, though plenty featured mutually attractive sisters, their hands full of daisies or knitting needles, sometimes a Bible. Mama decided. We both agreed. Better to make explanations as they became necessary. At the time, I'd thought little about omitting myself from the page, and nothing of the fact that Lyman Dryfus had included no photograph of himself when Mama had submitted two, a profile and portrait at great expense. His ad read simply:

254—A man of advancing age, adequate height, & weight, with a steady business and dependable income, seeks energetic wife, fit and healthy, with a strong physiognomy. No Catholics.

He was a man. He owned a house, a business. I liked the sound of his name, Lyman Dryfus. Neither of us had known the meaning of the word *physiognomy*. Dot, the widow with whom we had been living—and very much a mother to us both—decided it must mean beauty, a "strong beauty," especially since there had been no other mention of appearances. Her dying wish was that we stay this side of the Mississippi, as if that muddy gash separating East from West would prove, even for her spirit, insurmountable, farther away than the spirit realm where Dot's husband, Sam, had waited with far more patience, she said, than he'd ever managed in life.

Dot needn't have worried. Ads from men living in the ethereal West promised riches with a brand of reckless confidence that made Mama wary. It was his letters, so passionate and generous next to that ad, which convinced me that Mama should, by all means, fall in love with Mr. Lyman Dryfus.

I hope you too, he had written, *might one day learn to care for the river, to love the current's heavy pull, its murky unreflective face, hiding alike her deeps and shallows.*

And in another: *After the first snow in Reliance, but few leaves stop the eye short of the horizon. Plucked cornfields reveal blackened, old-woman skin, flaking and fallow. Color drifts downriver and after the shallows have frozen, before ice locks the riverbanks, the eagles come.*

Such a curious contradiction, the ice-locked riverbank, and the fierce free flight of those eagles . . .

He wrote about the sycamores in spring, the wind through the reeds, and I, who was then exceptionally sentimental, found it all terribly romantic—albeit unlike any of Dot's yellow covered literature. I, nevertheless, felt confident in my reply.

My Dear Mr. Dryfus, I wrote. *My soul is sobbing and lamenting at the thought of our great distant and I have been praying our separation willn't destroy my tinter hart.*

I tipped my nose for the scent of mud earth as Mr. Dryfus had described it, but smelled only the cannon's sulfur leavings. I listened in vain for the soft whisper of his river reeds and could not differentiate sycamore from maple. I had expected the river to fit neatly into his descriptions, but his words had become no more than stacked stones, and the river—its changing colors, its breadth and constant motion—a living thing quite apart.

It made me afraid to meet him.

MAIN STREET, REFUSING TO REMAIN loyal to the meandering contours of the Mississippi, cut straight up the hill. Redbrick buildings, two and three stories tall, presented themselves in formal rows, and the streets they lined imposed a cage over the crumbling bluffs. I could see, beyond a steep green, the columned portico of a courthouse, shaded by a giant oak alive with blackbirds. From all directions up the hill, competing church bells chimed the noon hour. I felt glances but kept my face covered, my eyes on Mama's boots until we turned down Union Street, an older part of the town I guessed from the blackened brick and frayed trellises.

Here the clatter of Main Street softened. A trio of old men, all knees and elbows, perched like vultures on a bench before the post office, staring openly. I might have ignored them except that we stopped next door, before a narrow brick shop built, like the post office, into the side of the hill. No awning here, no flourish. Painted boldly across the shop window: THE RELIANCE REGISTER. Below in smaller lettering: DRYFUS'S PRINT SHOP AND JOBBING PRESS. And there in the lower left corner of the window, a curious thing: a broadsheet with the outline of a human head divided into a series of irregular quadrants like a county map.

Mama's breath grew shallow, but she did not waver, even when we heard a scuffing behind the door. A body stopped the gold pinprick of light through the peephole. The shop bell jangled. The door creaked open to a tubby old woman. A film clouded her left eye and her head bobbed, in greeting I thought, until I realized she had no control over the action. In one long look, the old woman cataloged our worldly belongings. Her head stilled. She frowned, stuck her neck out, sniffed.

Mama straightened herself. "Here for Mr. Lyman Dryfus," she said.

"I told them there was only meant to be one of them," said Hanley.

But the woman had shuffled inside, mumbling and gesturing non-sense, I thought, until Hanley answered in the same language and hurried away through a passage under the elbow of an unlit staircase. On the left, the hallway opened to a shop counter, thick with dust, branded with the grimacing shadows of the stenciled window. With a gesture and grunt, the old woman bade us wait by a door on the right and went in. We heard voices through the door, then nothing, and my stomach made a fist inside me.

"I want to go. Mama, hear me? Let's go."

"Where we going to go?"

The voices inside matched the pitch of our own.

"Don't care."

But the old woman opened the door, and from the set of Mama's shoulders, I knew I could do nothing but follow.

"Mr. Dryfus," Mama said, stepping into the room. She bent in an awkward curtsy, and though I would have preferred to stay hidden behind her indefinitely, I needed to see the man who had written so lovingly of a river.

What I found was a nervous-looking fellow, tall and thin, with a mousy, mustached face, propping himself against the scuffed corner of a large writing desk. He wore a clerk's vest. Ink spots stained the collar and cuffs of his blouse, but not one hair on his blond head defied that pale, white part. "You," he steadied himself. Nimble fingers fumbled for the pipe in his breast pocket and gripping it, calmed.

"You are Miss Rebecca Branch?"

His voice proved deeper than I imagined from looking at him, but neither this nor his thick Germanic vowels seemed to surprise Mama. They considered one another, his eyebrows remarkably active for a man whose face appeared otherwise void of expression.

"I told them," said Hanley through the door behind us. "I said there's only meant to be one of them."

Mama's hand fished behind her, and when I did not take it, she stepped back, linked her arm with mine, and forced her urgency into the shape of a smile. "Say hello, Madelyn."

"Hello, Madelyn," I said.

"I think she must be dumb," said Hanley.

"I'm not dumb!"

"Madelyn, please," and judging this a time when explanations had become necessary, Mama plunged into our tale: how aunty passed so very recently, how she couldn't leave me, her *sister*, behind alone. "If there was anyone else," she said, "anyone else in the world, I would have left her."

All of this we'd practiced, of course, but practice never made such a hole inside me. Maybe what struck me so hard was the way nerves thickened the Kentucky in Mama's voice, but in the pregnant silence that followed, the lilting cadence buzzed like flies between my ears and fell dead at my feet.

"You spoke nothing of a sister," said Mr. Dryfus.

"Mr. Dryfus, I . . ."

But Mr. Dryfus, aided by that copper-headed cane, turned his back. Doing so seemed to give him confidence. He limped toward the bookcase and set his hand atop a hollow-eyed ceramic bust, the skull of which, like the flyer in the shop window, was divided by lines into quadrants.

"Some say, Miss Branch, that the eyes are the windows of a man's soul. Aristotle believed it was the nose. A beak or a snout, he thought, might indicate the insensitivity of a pig, the irascibility of a dog, or the impudence of a crow. We are mirrors of our animal characteristics— animals, except for our ability to reason." He turned. "And to lie."

"Mr. Dryfus, she won't be no problem. She—"

"She will have to eat, will she not?" Neither his color nor his voice rose, but Mama and I both jumped. "I would be support- ing her, would I not? At least," he said, and I did not like the way his voice pitched to a question, "At least until you come into your inheritance, Miss Branch?"

He looked significantly at Mama.

"Aristotle also thought the brain's function was to cool the blood. But science advances. Our understanding grows." He paused. "I do not mean to frighten you, Miss Branch. What I mean to say . . ."

At this he took from his pocket one of the photographs we'd sent: Mama in profile, hair curled, dressed in taffeta, a lace collar, holding Dot's Bible to her chest. The corners of the photograph had been rubbed smooth and he stared as if the image were infinitely more substantial than the woman, flesh and blood, before him.

"What I mean to say is that I might have predicted something like this would occur."

Something like what? Like me?

"What I mean to say is that your organs of Ideality, Industry, and Secretiveness are remarkably developed."

He circled with his pipe distinct regions of the ceramic bust and the corresponding regions on Mama's photograph, then looked up at her as if this had settled something between them. "But great strength often reciprocates in some great weakness. The phenomenon is the same in domesticated animals."

Mama bristled. "Animals?"

"*Domesticated* animals," Dryfus corrected, warming to his subject. "Human beings are domesticated animals, Miss Branch, no less than cattle or dogs. Consider the German shepherd, no the Pekinese, bred for the lap and nothing more, but excellent for their purpose."

"Purpose, Mr. Dryfus?"

From the angle of her chin more than the tone of her voice, I could tell that fear and indignation were turning to anger. Mr. Dryfus noticed nothing. In fact, he showed little trace of his previous nervousness; for the first time, he allowed his eyes to sweep Mama's person. The old woman said something. "Turn," said Mr. Dryfus. Mama turned once around, arms held at a doll-like funny angle; she stared nowhere in front of her. The three of them—Mr. Dryfus, Hanley, the old woman—watched, swallowing Mama whole, her small frame, her full chest, her dark curls framing tragic brown eyes. She seemed to me then like someone else, a character in a book, the beautiful heroine who must be saved. I felt like stepping in front of her, shouting at them. "Stop looking at her like that!"

But I didn't move, didn't say a thing.

It was the old woman who spoke again.

"Now your hands," Dryfus said. "We will see your hands."

Mama stiffened.

"Was I not clear?" He looked from Hanley to the old woman.

Mama offered her callused man-hands for inspection and my insides cracked and bled for her. The old woman bared a yellow smile.

"What purpose, Mr. Dryfus?" Mama asked tightly, holding her hands to her chest. "Mr. Dryfus, you said something about . . . What purpose, Mr. Dryfus?"

"I know, Miss Branch, that I am not a young man. Nor do I possess requisite attributes, which might impress a lady of any standing or stature.

"You"—he eyed our paltry belongings—"you are not a rich woman. Nor are you likely to be. Am I right? Am I? And from your letters, neither are you well educated."

Mama's hand dug into my arm for silence. Oh my letters! My beautiful letters!

"So, you will forgive me for observing that your prospects in civil society, lovely as you may be, are *limited*." Inclining his head at the last word, he took a step back to examine her again, this time with a removed, clinical interest, and began to pace crook-step with his cane, the double row of ink-drawn portraits on the wall as much his audience as we.

"I venture to guess factory work would prove fatal. You might meet some young farmer on whose bleak acreage you would labor the harsh seasons, yourself becoming as used as the land. Or perhaps you might find your way to San Francisco, where your beauty might win the arm of some rich magnate. But—" He stopped. He turned. He pointed his cane at her. "The uncertainty, Miss Branch. The desperation and uncertainty remains, does it not?"

He tapped his cane twice like a gavel and even the old woman jumped.

"You need a husband you may rely upon for shelter and sustenance; I, a wife to see Mutter and me comfortably through our latter years." The old woman, brightening, placed a possessive claw on Mama's shoulder. "And, of course, a man of a certain age desires, well," he said, looking down at the bare scuffed floor, "companion-ship."

I almost scoffed at this—companionship was not, in my expe-rience, what men desired of Mama—but now he turned those pinprick eyes upon me.

"Which leaves only one question. Your sister."

I held tight the hem of Mama's skirt. Of all of our lies, he chose to believe this one? Mr. Dryfus peered closer. "What are we to do with you?"

I won't do without her. I made a mistake. We'll go. We'll go together.

This is what Mama should have said. With so many of our lies in pieces on the ground, she should have told him this one truth.

"She can work. She's a very good worker." I let go of her skirt. It was another lie. I was easily bored with tedious tasks; she said herself I was ungrateful and undisciplined, with no desire to be otherwise.

"I would like to see her face," he said.

"No," I said. The boy and the shaking old lady barred the door.

"Young lady," said Mr. Dryfus, "you are not in a position to dis-obey."

Mama turned me round. Please, she mouthed. Even as I shook my head, she was peeling the bonnet brim from my face. I let her. I stood there exposed before them—until I unbuttoned my skin and rose up and out of myself to where I might not feel but only see.

Taken in parts unrelated to one another, I am not unattractive. Both of my eyes are well shaped, though they do not share the same shape, my left being slightly fuller and higher than the right; my left earlobe hangs long. I possess a distinguished overbite, a version of which I've seen in *Harper's* sketches of the Irish, and I chew my lower lip when nervous, like now.

But none of these features, which to some extent have softened with time, compelled me to hide behind that atrocious oversize bon-net. I owed this particular modesty to the port-wine-stain birthmark coloring my left side, from forehead to thigh. It was—it is—a lovely shade of red, I think. Lovely for a wine, a rose, a fine Indian silk . . .

"I see," he said, "why you might not mention her."

I pulled my bonnet back down, thought nothing, felt nothing.

"She'll be no problem to you. She's a good worker. It would be," Mama said, gathering herself, "charitable."

That word hurt Mama. She considered begging worse than steal-ing, wouldn't beg to save her life or mine, and had a deacon's scorn for anyone who did.

Mr. Dryfus dismissed the word entirely. "No one gives without expecting something in return." He snatched his hat from the hat tree. "But we can, we *will* discuss this later, find more suitable accom-modations. You are ready?"

"Ready, sir?"

"To be married."

"Now?"

"I see no reason to wait."

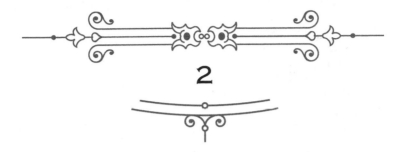

2

No lace, no church, no preacher. Mama was married in her traveling dress in the courthouse above the town green, by a paunchy
little magistrate more intent on his lunch than the proceedings. That
night, as Mama and I lay together on a cot in a cramped sloping
attic where I was banished until *more suitable accommodations* could be
found, I had already given up on Mr. Dryfus and on Reliance, and
could hardly believe Mama did not feel the same.

"He can't be what you imagined," I said, fitting myself into her
hollows; her breath came quick and her nerves buzzed straight
through me.

"Didn't let myself imagine."

I didn't believe her. I had done nothing for the last six weeks but
dream about the man who'd written those letters and neither his
pinched little mousy face nor his nervous limping footsteps below
matched the man I'd constructed—not rich or romantic. Not at all
handsome.

In the attic were a few pieces of furniture draped in winding
sheets, a pair of traveling trunks, stacks of newspapers nearly as tall
as the ceiling, a vanity mirror with a long river-shaped crack down

the center. Mama's expression, visible in the two halves, revealed nothing.

"We could go," I said. "Mama?"

"It's not that simple."

"You think *he'd* be able to stop us?"

"Not what I mean."

"What do you mean?"

Wind rattled the dormer window. She combed her fingers through my hair. "You need a nightcap. Did you see today, the ladies in their dresses?"

"We could stow away on a steamer."

"Stop! Stop now, listen to me." She turned me round and cold filled the space between us. Words packed her dark eyes, but she said nothing.

"What, Mama?"

"Mind Mr. Dryfus, and his mother."

"Mama—"

"There's nowhere else to go. Hear? Mr. Dryfus, he's right. Nothing's worth desperation. You got no idea. Be grateful you got no idea. No, now look at me! Things are different now."

"*How* different?" Back in Kentucky, before Mr. Dryfus's reply, before Dot died, the husband featured only nominally into our plans. If he, whoever he might be, did not suit us, well, we'd thieve him and run. Looking around, I didn't see much worth thieving.

"I mean to start over here," Mama said. "I mean to be a lady." The word *lady* like a shoe she was trying to fit. "We got to make ourselves necessary. Hear me? Make yourself necessary. Indispensable."

She heaved the attic door's iron ring and, catching her divided reflection in the cracked glass, put one hand to her stomach, forced her shoulders level, smoothed her hair and dress.

"I got to go to him."

"Mama."

"Call me Rebecca, Madelyn. You got to remember."

I watched, frustrated, sick with an apprehension I couldn't name, as she climbed down the ladder away from me.

"BE GRATEFUL YOU GOT NO idea," she said. Well, I wasn't grateful. How could I be if I didn't know what I was being grateful for? I wanted to know, but Mama had always been a silent woman, and the part of her past she'd closed to words had, since Dot died, begun to anger me, and the anger felt, not good exactly, but filling in a way Mr. Dryfus's wedding supper of coarse brown bread had not. Outside a dog howled. Insects, silent for an instant, pitched into their next throbbing chorus. Knotty eyes glared at me from boxes and stacked barrels; the slanted rafters became the roof of a great toothless mouth fixing to swallow me. I scooted from the cot to the dormer window and opened my scrapbook, my one treasure.

It was nothing special. No cover or binding to speak of, just a cured goatskin shell. Dot had shown me how to sew sheets of foolscap together to make a book; it hurt me to leave my other scrapbooks behind, for I was sure John's wife must have burned them. John was Dot's son. For as long as I could remember, he had been sending lithographed letter sheets with pictures of buildings and views of California and had written almost exclusively about foods I had never tasted and could barely imagine: Pineapple. Mango. Banana. Dot called them hungry letters. "No one getting their fill," she said, "writes so much about food."

She needn't have worried. It was no thin hungry man but a giant who arrived in May of that year. His wife was Mexican and Chinese and something else besides. I flipped through to the page in my scrapbook that said: *Juanita digs her fingernails into her palm when John looks at Mama.* I wasn't sure what made me write this down or why, that night, I found myself staring at those words.

Inside my scrapbook, I kept all sorts: Mr. Dryfus's letters, of course (there were three of them); also a four-leaf clover, a dragonfly's wing with silver veins webbing the transparent skin, a yellowing piece of cigarette paper, a blade of grass, a torn Confederate note, nine silver fish scales arranged in a circle. None of the lilacs I'd pressed remained intact. They left behind rust-colored impressions of a stem, a leaf. I'd glued a braided clump of Dot's hair behind the cover, but this hadn't preserved Dot either, not her voice, which I was already forgetting, or her spirit, nothing. I knew this, but still that fragmented hodge-podge remained necessary to me without qualification—remained, I suppose, a reflection as true as any I found in a mirror, and the only record I had of the past.

Mama, who could spend hours hunched over her lace making, teasing patterns from hopeless tangles of thread, spoke little of her people or her past. Dot blamed the war for her silence. She blamed the war for everything else as well, and when I was old enough to consider such things, I remember thinking the whole of human history must be divided into three distinct eras: before the war, during the war, after the war. The war itself was a knot joining the before and after. When you think about it like that, without the war to bind them, the past and the future might never have met at all but remained part of two different ropes, two different stories, two different countries.

I do know that I was born in the middle of that knot in a wattle-and-daub house a mile outside of Susanville, Kentucky—that's south-southwest of Somerset, if you're looking on a map. My father's name was Landis Wilcox. He was the middle son of Abel Wilcox, on whose land Mama's family cropped, alongside free Negroes and hired-out slaves. Mama, she thought Landis was going to marry and make a lady of her, but he went away to fight alongside his brother and daddy a good while before Mama came to figure it was a baby ailing her. Landis's mama, Mrs. Abel Wilcox, called her something filthy and turned her away, which was bad, but made some sense to me. What didn't was how Mama's own family could have turned her out, or how they managed to use God as the reason. She was thirteen years old.

I don't know how, by luck or providence, but it was Dot's house Mama stumbled upon the night I was born. There'd been fighting. Dot had been crouched for hours behind an upturned table, holding a single-shot blunderbuss, listening to artillery thunder and men and horses screaming. Given the date, the skirmish might well have been part of Zollicoffer's Fall. But Dot wouldn't have cared for such details; she'd already lost a brother to one side and a husband to the other and had stopped searching for her son in soldier's faces. When she heard pounding on her door, she fired. Instead of a soldier dead on the porch, she found Mama in a rag dress and peacoat, writhing in birth pain. The bullet only grazed her shoulder.

Dot, she didn't think either of us would see morning, tried not to care. But five hours into the labor, she began calling Mama "baby," at ten began negotiating with God. Fifteen hours and she'd given up tobacco, sorghum, mulled wine, swearing, lustful dreams, and novels; after twenty she was bargaining with her own life, and it was this exchange that apparently proved acceptable. She liked to complain that her life had been given in service of burdensome blessings, but she never made me feel anything but a blessing.

WHEN SHE WAS WELL ENOUGH, Mama ran away and left me with Dot. Where she'd gone, why she'd gone, what she'd done to survive those years, I didn't know, though I liked to imagine she was still out looking for my father, Landis. After a certain age, I stopped asking. Doing so brought a pale blankness to Dot's eyes that frightened me from the answer; I hadn't missed her that I know of. I don't remember having been aware she was gone, until she returned a skeleton woman, eyes wild with more kinds of hunger than I could name. And so beautiful. Even I, a child of four, who had never considered such a thing as beauty, was struck by those spooked dark eyes, darting and catlike, those lips, red as radishes. Full lips that suggested an invitation Mama did not intend and combated with a frown, which became the shape of her face at rest. Dot peeled me from her leg, and pushed me toward her. "This your Mama," she said, but for many years, Mama was a name, like Susana or Mary; *Dot* carried the meaning, and in Dot's wrinkled, blotchy face I saw myself.

That is until my eighth year, when I endured a half term of formal education in the Susanville School. Here I learned, in no uncertain terms, that I bore a face distinctly my own. In three months I got into a half dozen fights with town girls who looked at me funny, and had my fingers rapped by Mr. Lynd for standing atop my chair during class. Mr. Lynd, a one-armed veteran—himself known to provoke older boys, then wallop them, just to prove he could—made a point never to look at me. Standing on the chair was the only way I could think to get his attention, and it worked. He threw me out.

For years Dot's son, John, sent nothing but promises from California. Dot took in sewing. Mama sold her lace and made collars from patterns out of a battered *Harper's Bazaar*. A Negro named Isaiah and his family cultivated most of Dot's twenty acres, but cotton had soured the soil and prices were too low for profit. We would have survived fine with the goats and the garden, but we ate well for other reasons. The first, and my favorite, was Hiram Cassidy Main.

We lived only a mile from town, but off the county road; you had to mean to come or, like Mama, stumble blind on the place. Hiram was a traveling agent for the Methodist Book Concern, a polite, taciturn man, hairy all over, with a burned red nose and yellow teeth. In addition to Bibles and Baxter's *Call to the Unconverted*, Hiram sold dime novels and certain other tracts that guaranteed his customers would be in need of holy forgiveness. Every few weeks, Hiram happened by with a lesson or copybook for me (which is how I taught myself my letters) and a romance novel for Dot, not to mention a dozen eggs or a side of pork or a bushel of new potatoes or a shovel.

"Why Hiram Cassidy," Dot would say, "you really shouldn't have. But what a shame we got no sugar to go with them berries. Rebecca'd make you a pie." Then she'd send me outside while Mama took Hiram in the back room Dot kept tidy for the purpose. I didn't question this. Seemed the most natural thing in the world at the time. It was the same for all of the backroom men who made their way to Dot's house: "Why Hiram, why John, why Wilson, Albert . . . you shouldn't have, but what a shame we got no flour, salt, cinnamon . . ."

To Dot's dismay, Mama did nothing to encourage these men. She thanked them as if they were offering groceries only for smiles, took them in the back room, and came out looking all the more disinterested for their reddened faces.

"Think beauty lasts?" Dot asked one night after a small, muscled farrier, name of Bindle McDaniel, left only one gristled leg of lamb. Mama was squatting in a pot of herb water in the kitchen, cleaning herself. "No sir," said Dot. "Then where will we be? Better grab one of those backroom men, show some interest. What's wrong with

Hiram, now?" She slapped the meat upon the cutting board. "Or what? You waiting for love?"

That wasn't it. Mama scoffed at the love stories I read aloud with Dot, just as she scoffed at unicorns or fairies or any other made-up things found in books. At the time, we had enough to eat and a place to live; she had no reason to get married.

Until that spring, when Dot's son John came back and brought his own wife.

I remember the warmth in the air carried a honeysuckle sweetness and the moon was sharp and brittle through the window. I was standing before the fire reading to Dot from *The Lamplighter*, a story adhering, more or less, to my favorite formula: pretty, pious, unloved orphan is rescued by a kind, downtrodden man, who finds her a rich benefactor, who transforms her into a lady worthy of adoration, so that she might be loved. (That I was not orphan, pious, or pretty never prevented me from imagining myself as one of these heroines.) "'No one loved her,'" I cried, "'and she loved no one; no one treated her kindly; no one tried to make her happy, or cared whether she were so. She was but eight years old, and alone in the world.'"

At which point, Dot was meant to offer a hearty "Poor, poor dear!"

Dot's attentions were not properly directed upon me, but beyond to a husky lout peering through the window. Mama, who'd been in the barn milking goats, came at him from behind with a pitchfork, but he roughed it away, held her by the neck between me and the blunderbuss I'd grabbed from the hearth. Still Dot did nothing but stare as if he were but an overgrown pumpkin, with awe and not a little bit of horror. "Hi, Mama," he said.

Neither he nor his wife settled in nicely. In spite of his letters, he was very much a stranger. Dot, who for so long had spoken of her son in a dreamy hopeless way, didn't seem at all comfortable speaking with him. She ignored his half-breed wife completely. She would never admit to it, but I think having John back, not as the skinny, hairless boy she remembered but as the overgrown stranger time and war had shaped, made her sadder, reminded her of all she'd lost and distracted her from all she had—that is, Mama and me. I don't think it was brain fever, after all, but disappointment that killed her.

I closed my eyes on the thought of Dot and on the tears welling there and tried to imagine my way back to the river. Nine rungs down the attic ladder. Ten steps down the hall. Fourteen down the stairs. Eight out the front door. How many through town? How many to the river? How many would Mama take with me?

3

Mr. Dryfus's mama, Clara, was squat as a winter squash and solid enough to fill a doorway. Even I, late to growth, stood a hand taller. Her stomach nearly overwhelmed the muslin folds of her dress; she had squeezed into a pair of shapeless leather slippers, and when she shifted one leg to another, floorboards moaned recognition. It was this, coupled with the endless bob of her head and her mothering tone, that disarmed me, though I had little idea what she said even after my ears began to wrap themselves around the few English words I recognized.

Not that it mattered. When she handed me a knife and pointed me toward the vegetables on the kitchen table, there was little doubt what she wanted. And there was little doubt of her satisfaction when Mama appeared through the kitchen door with the empty chicken slop, set it down and left again with the coal scuttle. Footsteps sounded in the hall. Clara's palsied face broke into a smile. *Indispensable*, I thought, bending to my task. Here I am, Mr. Dryfus, indispensable.

But another, younger fellow, bearded, rough looking as a back-room man with mud on his boots and a dark halo of curly hair, ducked through the doorway. He hugged Clara from behind.

"Mutti," he said, teasing his whiskery chin across the top of her head. When he caught me staring, he did not, as I expected, look away. From a face like mine, you see, everyone, even Hiram Cassidy, who was used to seeing me, looked away. Instead, a smile crossed his lips, and as if we had shared the same amusing thought, he winked.

"You." He slumped into a chair across the table from me as Mr. Dryfus limped into the room, a stack of newspapers under one arm. "You are not Miss Rebecca Branch."

"*That*," said Mr. Dryfus, "is the sister."

"There was meant to be a sister?"

"Madelyn," I managed. *Sister* irked me. "I'm not dumb."

"I can see that." The young man stretched his legs under the table. His fingers, too, were long and restless, with peculiar black stains on pointer, ring, and thumb.

"And you will be mindful, William," said Mr. Dryfus, levering himself carefully into a chair, "that Miss Branch is Mrs. Lyman Dryfus now."

"Oh yes, I heard. Everyone has heard. Off the carriage and into the courthouse, Lyman?" Then to me. "Did he even give your sister time to brush the dust from her skirts?"

"I saw no reason to wait," said Mr. Dryfus stiffly.

"Didn't you? Well. One thing is sure. You'll have no need to place a marriage notice in the *Register*." Again adopting me as audience and ally, he leaned forward, smelling faintly of mud and not so faintly of sweat, apples, and whiskey, his deep voice becoming soft and playfully urgent, as though imparting great confidences. "Many a willing widow calls this a dark day," he said. "And now look at him."

Mr. Dryfus looked no different to me than he had the day before, except maybe less nervous. He folded his broadsheet sharply.

"And now he's off to the courthouse I suppose?" said William. "Today Lyman? No rest for the . . ."

It was then that Mama, coal smudged, scuttle in hand, opened the backdoor. I was sure mucking the scuttle had been her idea, but appreciated, nonetheless, the accusing expression the young man gave Mr. Dryfus. Mama had never been particularly obedient; Mr. Dryfus and Clara would learn this. She was making herself useful, and besides, she preferred work to leisure. Even at night, with all necessary labor complete, she took up her tatting. "Busy hands make a quiet mind," Dot used to say. She also used to say, "Ain't coming to see your lace, Rebecca," when she must have known as well as I, Mama didn't make lace for backroom men. Something else, maybe a lingering romance with the big, white Wilcox house, drove the compulsion. She admired beautiful things.

The young man, recovering himself, bowed, sweeping an arm over his head and down like a gallant. "Miss Branch," he said. "I mean, of course, Mrs. Lyman Dryfus." But upon rising and looking full upon her, his manner altered, as did his waggish tone.

"The photographs lie, I see," he said with utmost earnestness. "Your beauty far exceeds your likeness."

Let me assure you that no backroom man had ever managed such a phrase. No one, I thought, would ever spend such a phrase on me.

Mr. Dryfus sat up straight.

"You might have met last night, had you returned at a decent hour."

The young man's eyes had not left Mama's face. She glanced between the two men, carefully unmoved. I might as well have vanished from the room.

Said Dryfus: "I have spoken to you about roving nights."

"Yes, yes," said the young man softly, his eyes not leaving Mama. "You have spoken."

"Your mother would not have—"

"My mother?" He jolted to his feet, bumping the table. Mama took a step back, but the violent change in him took everyone by surprise. Everyone except maybe Mr. Dryfus, who I'm sure meant to rile him.

"Wilhelm," said Clara edging toward him.

"My *mother* cared not what I did with my time so long as I did not interfere with her painting."

"'Tisn't beneficial in any case," said Mr. Dryfus without seeming to notice Clara glaring nails at him. "Neither to the health." He creased the broadsheet. "Nor to the mental faculties."

"Lyman!" said Clara. The pot bubbled. Outside a chicken cackled, quieted, but I hardly heard it. I was watching William. We were all, even Mr. Dryfus behind his paper, watching William, who, before she could pull away, took Mama's coal-blackened hand and placed on her palm a slow, deliberate kiss. Then looking up at Mr. Dryfus, he walked out.

I ADMIT IT. I HAVE always envied men their facial hair, would have liked to grow some myself. Receding chins, flaccid cheeks, all manner of blemish or stain could be hidden beneath without notice; the whole of a man's appearance might change with one trip to the barber.

Blemish or not, the young man, William, was hiding something. I'd been sure of that even before Mr. Dryfus's insinuation, which I didn't understand but found easy to resent on William's behalf. When Mama sent me upstairs for the linen, I decided that if I discovered anything of Mr. Dryfus's worth thieving—anything rich enough to tempt Mama away from Reliance—I'd have no qualms taking it. But the parlor held nothing of obvious worth, nor did the room Mama shared with Mr. Dryfus. My first glimpse through William's door, the last on the right, was no more encouraging.

Barn swallows streaked tight shadows across the broadcloth curtain; the window was closed, the air thick and stale, and there was nothing at all on the walls, which seemed odd if his mama was a painter. (I gathered from the talk she was gone, maybe dead, and found out later she was.) Even Mr. Dryfus had hung pictures: a portrait of a young man, his father maybe, standing beside a cushioned chair and a cross-stitch of oak tree in a field. This set me wondering what Mr. Dryfus and William were to each other—cousins? Surely Mr. Dryfus was not old enough to be his father, though I knew better than to assume.

I put the laundry basket down by the bed, ran my hand up the catches and hooks of a faded purple afghan bunched at the base. Under the bed I found nothing more than dust and a threadbare sock. On the rolltop desk adjacent the window were blackened pen nubs, two smooth, green river rocks, scraps of paper. Nothing of worth. Only the drawers offered a brief, false hope, when opening the second on the right, I found a cigar box the size of a Bible with long-necked river birds carved in relief on the lid.

Inside, though, were only photographs of women. Plump, bare-breasted women draped over couches, and lounging on chairs with their legs wide open. Their eyes, soft as their bodies, and their open mouths made them look like infants, passing gas. Another girl might have been, but I was hardly shocked, for they were of much the same persuasion as the pictures Hiram Cassidy hid under copies of *Call to the Unconverted*. I didn't think they'd fetch much, and

I did not think them beautiful—until I imagined William looking at them too, and heard his voice in my head. *Your beauty far exceeds your likeness.*

Then another voice. "Hey."

I whipped around, holding the case behind me, and there, filling up the doorway, was the big boy, Hanley.

"Nothing," I said. "The linen."

But of course the bed was still made, and anyway, he hadn't asked what I was doing. He wasn't going away, either. Apart from the long parade of backroom men, three eventful months at Susanville School represented my only experience with the male species. Unless, of course, you counted the pageant of handsome lovers traipsing through the novels I'd read aloud to Dot.

He stood watching me.

"What?" I said, looking down to hide my face beneath my bonnet. Probably the impulse made me even more suspicious.

"In books," said Hanley, "ugly means dumb."

"Yeah?" I said. "Well, so does big."

Kick him in the jewels and run. That's what Dot told me to do if ever a backroom man got ideas. What Hanley did surprised me more. He laughed, the grin on his bristled face as disarming as the lolling tongue of a great, friendly dog.

"I guess so," he said, but still didn't budge. I heard Mama call. I really did need to collect the linen. "You know the girl that went missing?" he said finally. I nodded, though in truth I hadn't given that girl a second thought. "They're not going to look anymore. I just," he scuffed his big foot against the door frame. "I don't know. I thought you'd want to know."

"Okay." I wasn't sure what else to say, and stood there staring at the floor until finally Hanley turned to go. I waited for his footsteps on the stairwell before I put back the cigar box of naked ladies, gathered the linen, and joined Mama in the backyard.

"I BEEN THINKING ON IT," I said, dumping more potash into the wash boiler with the linen. Already lye was cracking my fingertips. "I don't think Mr. Dryfus wrote those letters he sent."

Mama frowned over one of Mr. Dryfus's shirts. "We go'n to need chalk to lift this ink."

"Didn't cross his *t*s or his *f*s," I persisted. "They look more like *l*'s."

She motioned me to get busy. I did, for a few minutes, but it was sticky hot, the sun glaring sideways at us over the fence of a yard twice as long as it was wide. At the far end, near a coop made of apple crates, three chickens picked through a browning garden patch. Somewhere close a dog was barking, a child screamed, gulped for breath, screamed again, and a woman called "Jacob? Jacob, leave that be now!" So many people so close did not seem natural. I glanced again at Mama. I'd had my monthlies, considered myself all but grown (certainly I understood more about life than many a young woman on her wedding night), but I couldn't understand how Mama could be as resigned to this place as she pretended.

"Well," I said. "Don't *you* think Mr. Dryfus the kind of man to cross his *t*s?"

"Not sure as I know what kind of man he is." She looked at me crossly. Hanley stepped from the kitchen to the side alley for a smoke. Mama lowered her voice.

"Anyway it don't matter now." She dunked a pair of skivvies. "We are staying where we are. Mr. Dryfus and me, we legally wed and he got to provide for us now, by law he got to, so don't go upsetting a good thing."

"Good thing," I scoffed.

"Everything settled." She scrubbed. "Everything go'n be settled. Tonight."

I had been watching a dappled tom slink through a hole in the fence and looked up to find the bafflement and the hint of fear in her voice, mirrored on her face. Dot had been her confidant as well as mine. We were not in the habit of confiding in each other, so, it was a moment before I understood what she was saying.

"What? You mean to tell me he ain't—"

"Lower your voice—"

"Well, can't he?"

From what I had observed in Susanville, through the knothole in the backroom wall, what was required was a purely mechanical act easily accomplished by some of the dullest specimens ever to wear trousers. Mama's role took no active participation at all, unless you counted cleaning herself after. He was able, she said. That was obvious enough. And she could tell restraint pained him. Well, this baffled the both of us. Could it be? Was he being considerate? Was he giving Mama, the supposed virgin, time? Was *he* the virgin?

I laughed out loud. Mama did not. Maybe Clara spoke with him? Maybe it bothered him to think his hasty marriage had been publicly misconstrued as other than it must have been in his mind: a pragmatic use of his only free afternoon that week. How was he to know that pragmatism served Mama better than consideration? Consideration was not an obstacle Mama was regularly forced to overcome. If he expected her to be grateful, she was not. They lay awake for hours, both miserable.

Somehow I didn't guess William would be burdened with the same scruples. And really I didn't see what difference it could make, what they did or did not do now. She said herself they were legally wed.

"It'll be settled tonight," Mama said with a force of will I recognized and knew to trust. Then she pointed at me, hands dripping, as if the failed consummation were my fault. "You just stay out of his way."

Later, in my more generous mood, I allowed that, although she might have been shaped by circumstances cruel and indifferent, Mama was not by nature cruel or indifferent; she was not without the capacity for surprising, if rare, tenderness. Hiram Cassidy Main, the traveling agent who brought us books, once placed in my hand a white-brown shell the size of a good throwing rock and bade me be still and silent even when something spiny began prickling. Soon I was staring at a sand-colored crab testing its legs against the warm planes of my palm. I used to think of Mama like that crab, hunkering down inside a shell, venturing out tentatively, and never for very long.

When I was little, she knitted me caps and embroidered dresses. She called me darling! My *darling* Madelyn, like we were both fancy ladies. Sometimes I'd imagine for her a joyous reunion with my father, Landis Wilcox—or rather a reunion between Mama and a handsomely nondescript man in a gray peacoat. I never dreamed myself between them, remained a stranger to them both, an observer, because . . .

Well, I guess I'd always suspected that I was the tragedy of Mama's life. No one had ever said this, but I could feel it deep down, and now along with the accustomed, almost comfortable guilt this fear brought, came an exhilarating resentment.

"Well," I said. "You can't tell me what to do, can you? You ain't my mama, right?"

The sweet venom with which I'd spoken soured in the next long moment of silence. Hanley lumbered back through the kitchen door. In the distance I could hear shouts of the children at the school off Main Street. Mama had not stopped scrubbing, but her shoulders had squared, her eyes set on the suds bucket as if it held some great curiosity.

"Need lemon juice to bleach," she said finally.

"Mama?" I whispered, full of useless remorse.

"Vinegar might do," she said.

4

Mama's marital purgatory lasted a full three weeks. I know because she informed me of each successive failure with a baffled little shake of her head. Another, more expressive, woman might have fretted. Mama transferred all anxiety into effort, that is, into housekeeping, and had no qualms conscripting me into service.

We washed and aired the linen, mended bedspreads, darned socks, scoured floors, polished silver (a quick job, to be sure), and this in the first four days. The shop, like all shops along Union Street, had been built into the side of the bluff. Spiders colonized every corner, closet, and window frame. At night when I lay down to sleep, I could feel the tickle of the webs I swept daily and the prick of tiny legs down my skin. Before long whatever romantic notions I'd entertained of the life we'd encounter in Reliance were soundly crushed, for it truly appeared I helped buy Mama the title of wife with all my remaining claims to freedom.

I began to dream in food: poached eggs, chicken livers fried in lard with onions, sow's-foot stew with broth thick enough to hold a penny—any number of tasties might have made the toil acceptable. I might even have taken some satisfaction in the labor. As it was, I shat out most of Mr. Dryfus's graham bread and healthful fare, and Mama's guts suffered terribly.

"Mrs. Dryfus," said Mr. Dryfus one night as we sat, the very likeness of a family: Mama with her tatting, Dryfus with a book, in the dismal little corner parlor. "If Nature had not intended the body to expel its noxious emanations, She would not have made it thus painful to refrain."

Then he promptly set an example.

Frankly, I was impressed by this and more by the fact that he'd noticed Mama's discomfort at all. Mama was mortified. Her expression alone could have torn holes in the brickwork. She walked out, leaving her tatting like a reprimand on the armchair, and me on the floor pretending great interest in Bewick's *History of British Birds*, one of few books in the shop that wasn't in German. You see, Mama could not speak or write like a lady; nor had she yet ventured to the shops among real ladies "and their dresses." But by God, she felt she had the makings, and ladies did not pass gas. Not, at least, in parlors.

I might even have told Dryfus this, if he'd asked me, which he didn't. Really, I'm not sure what he would have made of it if I had. Not much probably. I don't think he wanted Mama to be a lady. Would have been just as happy to have a maid in the house as a wife. Except he didn't have to pay a wife, and it was obvious, by now, how much he'd overstated matters when he promised a steady income.

The *Register*, one of three weeklies in town—the only to publish in English and German—sold by subscription, which few had money to buy. The small amount of scrip he did receive was all but worthless, issued by banks that no longer existed. People paid by other means: in corn or apples or hazelnuts and such. Once I opened the door to a toothy little man with a dead goose under one arm, which, to my horror, Dryfus passed on to the bank clerk in payment for other debts.

Refusing meat was a matter of health to Mr. Dryfus; eggs, a matter of principle. He charted his own bowel movements as a captain charts the sea and would have done the same with Mama, I think, had he the wherewithal to insist. Besides heads, he read books in three languages and championed all kinds of principles and theories, and while he never asserted himself physically, he thrust his opinions forward with an authority that only William, on that street of craftsmen, clerks, and grocers, seemed to doubt. A good number of people in town, even Hanley—who, as devil, endured the brunt of his criticisms—seemed to respect, even to like him.

Every Monday night, for example, he hosted the Reliance Phrenological Society, which from what I could see was six men drinking Wallendorf's Beer, reading aloud scholarly articles, and offering asides and solemn nods when a pause seemed to make such responses appropriate. They deferred to Mr. Dryfus whenever a dispute arose. Mr. Le Duc, the cobbler, called him Herr Professor. William, when feeling contentious (he often felt contentious) did the same.

William's every exchange with Mr. Dryfus, even the simplest, was prickly. And I could tell Mr. Dryfus didn't like, any more than I did, how William watched Mama, how he did things for her like open doors and pull out chairs, and other niceties I'd read about in books. (It was William who'd written those letters Mr. Dryfus had sent Mama—I was almost sure of it. He'd written, in effect, to me and I to him and the knowledge, frankly, thrilled me.) Still, I guessed more than Mama stood between them; from the way they avoided the subject since that first day, I had an idea it was to do with William's mother. Or maybe with Clara, who, from what Hanley told me, as much as raised the both of them, though they weren't cousins, or in any way related like I'd guessed. Hanley reckoned William was a good number of years younger, not yet thirty at any rate.

Clara, I learned, had been William's nurse in Saint Louis before William went off to the war. Hanley knew because his mama and older sister had been maids of all work in the same house. William's mama had been Willa Stark. "The portrait painter," Hanley said in such a way I knew the name should have meant something to me. "She died, after the war. Cholera. Lots a folks died." Then added, thoughtful more than sad: "My mama, too."

Two years before Mama and I arrived, Clara brought William to Reliance to live with Mr. Dryfus, which was also when Mr. Dryfus took Hanley on. (Hanley didn't think that was Dryfus's idea either.) Now William rented a photography shop across the street above the tobacconist and made lithograph plates for the *Register*. The only thing that linked them all, as far as Hanley knew, was they had all come to Saint Louis from a part of Prussia with its own slow-moving muddy river.

To be sure, my interest in all of this remained, at first, very much a fancy to pass the time before Mama and I left Reliance. Because things could *not* go on as they were. After Mama walked out of the parlor that night, she and Mr. Dryfus hardly said a word to each other. When he had anything to say, he told Clara, who communicated, in her way, with me. Depending on my mood, I might or might not tell Mama, and she ignored anything she did not want to hear. Every night she buried herself in her tatting, he in a book, and the tense, watchful silence made me want to stand up and shout every last curse word the backroom men had taught me. Surely they couldn't go on like this. Surely Mama would have to listen to reason and run away with me, away from this place, away from Reliance.

But one morning in the third week, I saw a change between

them. Mr. Dryfus sat for a long time at the kitchen table after breakfast, meerschaum pipe cocked between his teeth, watching Mama cube parsnips as if he'd never before seen the task done. Mama, catching my eye, gave a sober little nod, the grim look in her eye replaced by pride, almost. Relief, certainly.

After that, Mr. Dryfus said no more about finding me a more suitable accommodation, and Mama would hear no more of leaving.

5

I was dull indeed with all that work and no dreams of escape to sustain me. Really it's no wonder I took refuge in another growing obsession: William. William, who looked at me; William, who winked.

Already I'd learned his letters by heart, not just the words, but each sweeping accent of his pen. Now I began collecting what I imagined to be pieces of William—broken pen nibs, a cuff link, strands of curly black hair—happily conjuring from these fragments a William who suited me. Wasn't so hard. I'd had long practice ignoring vices (those photographs of plump women, for example) and imposing virtues on backroom men who visited Mama: men, I see now, who tolerated my needy admiration as they did the cost of admission.

Each afternoon, I'd find reason to loiter in the kitchen when William brought Clara fruit-filled stollen, and warm meat pies called *bierocks*, from the German ward. (Clara did not share Dryfus's passion for self-denial, but his willing ignorance on this account allowed for a variety of unspoken compromises between them.) Clara and William would sit, heads bent over a tasty, solving, for all I knew—they spoke German—the problems of the known world. "Is this not what you were thinking?" William might say, glancing over at me, confident of my unmitigated approval. "You see, Mutti? Madelyn agrees." Otherwise they ignored me.

Until one day, not long after Mama finally bedded Dryfus, I looked up from some idle task, to find William and Clara watching.

"Hanley says you broke his foot," said William. "Is that true?"

Coffee beans crackled in a pan on the stove; a crock of fermenting cabbage frothed by the larder. It took me a second to find my voice.

"I didn't *break* it," I said.

"How do you know?" Hanley called from the composition room. "Nothing crunched, did it?"

It was Hanley's fault, anyway, brushing up so close, that morning, trying to steal the bonnet off my head. He was lucky I'd aimed for his foot.

Honestly, I still wasn't sure what to make of the boy. He could read and write English and German, for one thing—a fact that mightily impressed me, though I would never say so. And he hummed more than seemed natural. Not just grog-shop jingles, either, but tunes fit for the Turner Hall, his voice higher than you'd expect, given his size, always the first thing I noticed about him, then the bruises, fresh ones every day that he earned playing war and fisticuffs with the boys he ran with. That's what I assumed.

He looked a brute, no question. But sometimes it seemed to me there was this smaller, gentler boy trapped inside him, his bulk like a badly knit sweater, his arms so long he was never sure what his hands were up to on the end of them. Made him clumsy. In the shop especially. He was constantly misplacing his *b*'s, *d*'s, *p*'s and *q*'s—not hard, given the size of the type and the fact that he was meant to

place letters upside down and backward. It drove Mr. Dryfus to con-
niptions. "Mind your *p*'s and *q*'s, Hanley. How many times do I have
to tell you?"

It bothered me, some, the way Dryfus nagged Hanley, but I wasn't
feeling much pity for him at the moment.

I could feel William's eye upon me.

"He," I hesitated, "he stood too close."

"I'll remember not to do that." William stepped back. "Look
there, Mutti. She smiles."

Grinned like a fool, more like it.

"And he. He wanted a look at me. Under my bonnet."

"Ah." William nodded gravely. He straddled his chair and, resting
his bearded chin on the back, regarded me with far more scrutiny
than I was used to. "And his interest frightened you?"

"Frightened? No! Hanley doesn't frighten me," I said, which
was mostly true. I could hear the thump of the Washington Press
through the kitchen wall.

"But you do not wish to be looked upon?" said William softly.

"To be mocked!" I said.

"You think they are the same? You think one rises inevitably from
the other?"

"Now you're mocking me."

"I've seen you at night." William sat back again. The shop bell
rang, and Hanley, in the next room, stopped the press to see about it.
"I've seen you watching me through the baluster when I come in."

I looked away from him to the mud-grimed soles of his boots. "I
don't. I mean I can't sleep." I wasn't used to sleeping without another
body close. Without Mama.

"I never sleep," he said, and I, unsure sure how to read his tone,
ventured a sideways glance.

"Not at all?"

"Church." He said this softly, winking at Clara, which told me he was teasing her. "I sleep on Sundays."

"Oh, I'm not much on church, neither. But Dot and I, we go every spring to get saved in Hudson's Creek."

I blurted this, was embarrassed and a little relieved by his amused expression. Truth was, I wasn't much on camp meetings either. All that talk of washing sin's stain made me anxious. What about a face? Could sin stain a face as it did a soul? Had Mama's sin stained me like the girls at Susanville School said? Could Reverend Meyers, with his toxic goiter, wash my stain away, make me beautiful?

In the end I never could commit myself. Far more terrible than the thought of standing nearly naked in the creek before all of those people was the fear that I'd emerge unchanged, unlovable. I needed to believe. I needed to believe love and transformation possible. And though I had no clear notions what form this transformation would take, its end, I knew, would be beauty.

Beauty, the key that opened hearts. Beauty turned men's heads, turned William's head, to Mama. Beauty must be the key, for if it were not . . . Well, if it were not, I would be forced to entertain the possibility that no such key existed.

"Dot, your aunt?" asked William. "You must miss her very much."

The care in his voice, the tenderness; I couldn't say anything without tearing up. Clara stirred the coffee beans and that sharp, dark scent, combined with what William said next, brought me back to myself.

"Your sister," he said. "She must miss her, too. She doesn't smile much."

"My *sister* is a married woman." He looked surprised I would say this. "And don't talk to me like—"

"Like what?"

"Like I'm dumb, or slow. I'm not dumb or slow. Only—"

"What? You are only what? Do you watch me every night? It's okay. I don't mind. You have become my"—he paused thoughtfully—"my apparition. My midnight apparition."

Clara, eyeing me, said something. A buzzing, black fly appeared, vanished, and appeared again through streamers of dusty light. "There are many ways of looking," said William. "Many ways to watch, to see, and to be seen."

"Sounds like preaching to me," I said, though in truth I was thinking about those photographs I'd found in his room.

Clara said something more.

"What?" I demanded. "What is she saying?"

"She said . . ." But the smile had left his face. He seemed to collect himself. "She said Willa would have loved to look at you." He looked away. "She's right. My mother would have painted you."

WHAT WAS THAT SUPPOSED TO mean? And who was he, anyway, to talk about looking and being seen when his face was masked in hair? One thing was sure, the William I'd conjured did not ask so many pointed questions, though he was right, I did watch him. The very fact he'd noticed felt, more and more as the day went on, a kind of validation. That afternoon—what with Hanley and me still at odds and Mama inside mucking the larder—I abandoned the wet laundry in the tub and followed two chattering young women across the street to Stark Photography, where I'd not ventured before.

To hear William's name on their lips didn't surprise me. He could be charming when he wanted, and there was, even thinking on it now, something mesmerizing about him, a whiff of mystery, maybe, which kept him on the lips of women at the water pump as well. (It didn't hurt, of course, that there remained, since the war, a shortage of marriageable men, much less men with a business and all of their limbs. "Me," Dot used to say, "I'd take a bruised apple over no apple at all.")

The shop was above the tobacconist, accessible by a wobbly alley-way staircase clinging to blackened brick. I paused at the bottom, hand on the rail, until I heard the door above close on their voices, then climbed, quiet as I could, and cracked the door to a stagger-ing brightness. For a disconcerting moment I could see nothing but brightness, which radiated, not from the windows, as you might expect, or lamps, but from eight rectangular glass panes built into the ceiling.

I thought it the strangest thing I ever saw, and foolish with no breeze and the sun hot enough to bake a pie. Across the glass were fabrics of various thicknesses, strung on parallel rods, so that rather than hanging down like curtains, the fabric lay flush with the ceiling. This made even less sense. Why put a window in a ceiling? Why put a window in a ceiling only to cover it up? I could make nothing of it until I eased the door wide enough to peer fully into the room.

At the far end, the two young women, one tall and slouching, the other no bigger than a girl, stood watching William pull a layer of thin fabric over the glass with a sheep prod, thereby training the light upon a small raised stage. He wore a linen jacket of a kind I'd never seen, sweat stained under the arms, curious for its great length (it extended well past his knees) and for the mismatched pockets bulg-ing with unimaginable necessities. He beckoned the smaller woman to the stage, and she stood there beside a pronged iron rod, somewhat like a hat rack. Then he stepped back to look, his hand flat against his cheek, as if the woman were clay to fashion.

A white wooden trellis framed her. A bowl of wax grapes and a ceramic floral vase sat atop a round table to her right. A mishmash of podiums, fancy chairs, vases, and a maple wardrobe had been banished to the wings with the tall woman, who was beating the air furiously with a little Chinese fan.

"Mr. Stockwell," the tall woman was saying, "he calls Miss Rose a base moral influence just because she was in the theater." That William's attention remained so fixed upon the other woman obviously displeased her. She held the fan still. "Well, *I* don't care about that. No one else has brought excitement to this forgotten little town. It is forgotten! My father says if the bid for the railroad had been successful, well, we'd be living now in a metropolis. A *metropolis*! As big as Chicago! Imagine!" She breathed in the wonder of the loss. "Theaters, an opera. Imagine. Well, is there any reason we cannot at least be civilized?"

"I'm not sure Mr. Stockwell would agree with your definition of the word, Nora," said William without turning.

"Jackson says she's for suffrage," said the small woman. "'No bigger stage than politics,' he says."

"What about you, William? Hmm?" Nora asked. "What do you think of the *woman* question?"

"No more than I have to," said William, which Nora found incredibly funny.

"Well, I hear she has invited Mr. Emerson to the next soiree. He has been two weeks in Saint Louis, and one of the maids at the manor told the baker's wife, who told my Susie, that he has accepted. They will be serving flan." Nora beat the air. "Have you ever tasted flan? William?"

Of this Miss Rose I knew little and might have cared less, except to wonder what William had to do with her. I'd seen her black hansom about town, of course, and the ads she took in the *Register* for these soirees. Hanley told me she lived in the mysterious Werner Manor, high on the northern bluff overlooking the docks. I didn't understand, then, what a novelty she still was (having arrived only the year before), much less what a force she would become.

William had eased the small woman into place on the iron stand, then stripped another layer of fabric from the ceiling, exposing her to a sharp, naked light. Bound there, beneath his considered gaze, she seemed to fill a space much larger than before.

"How is it, Angela?" William asked her. "Does it pinch? Tell me, for any discomfort will show in the photograph."

"It does pinch, a little."

"Where?"

She pointed to the softness under her ear. The two stood close as a breath, and my breath caught. When he beckoned her forward, I felt myself edge into the room. He pulled a strip of silk from one of his pockets to pad the iron prongs, then molded the small woman back into place.

"Flan," he said over his shoulder, "is a refined taste. I think it may be a disappointment to you, Nora." Then to the small woman, "Better?"

"Yes," we said, our breath short, shallow. He rolled the camera forward, slotted the glass plate, and, raising the felt skirting, ducked his head beneath. When he spoke again, his voice was muffled, distant, thrilling.

"When I raise my arm," he said, "you will breathe out, one, two, three. Beautiful."

And that is when the small woman, Angela, still pinned to the iron stand, saw me.

"William. Is that . . . ?"

He emerged before I gained wits enough to run.

"Oh! My apparition."

"Assistant, you say?" said the smaller woman, stepping down. "Oh, William, you are a dear."

"It's the *sister*," said Nora, for some reason finding it necessary to say this behind her hand.

"I am not the *sister*!" I managed.

"She's *not* the sister?" Nora asked William.

He turned to me. "What is it, Madelyn?"

But I had no reason to be there. Nothing to give or ask of him. I felt the ladies' eyes.

"Well." William plucked a pencil from one of his many pockets and turned back to them. "Thursday? You will want to see the samples and decide the number you wish."

Go. Stay. I wasn't sure what to do. I wanted to stay but had no excuse. The ladies passed by me out the door, their skirts stirring the tobacco air.

"Madelyn," said William. Two camera lengths separated us. I stared at a spot at my feet until his silence defeated me and I looked up.

"Are you always so angry?" he asked.

"I'm not angry!" At least not at him, anymore, I didn't think. I'd never stood this close to him. He had a tiny cut above his right cheek, and his eyes were plain brown, not hazel as I had thought. I looked away and blurted the first daft thing that came to me.

"You have windows in your ceiling."

He squinted upward, tugged his beard as if baffled.

"By God. You're right!" Then held up his hands. "Okay. Alright. I get it. Don't tease Miss Maddy. Yes, there are windows in my ceiling. A photographer traps light as a sailor harnesses the wind."

"Traps light?" Was he still mocking me? He draped his arm over the bulky camera.

"In a manner. Do you really want to know?"

I did. I really did, but it didn't matter, for the door banged open and his attention was taken. I turned to find Mama.

"Rebecca," said William. Not even Mr. Dryfus called her Rebecca. Mama ignored him.

"Madelyn. All that scrubbing and then you leave the wet laundry for chickens to—"

"I mean, of course, Mrs. Lyman Dryfus," William interrupted, stepping around the camera, holding both hands before him. "I owe you an apology."

He did? Mama blinked.

"What do you mean?" she asked. She was very pretty when suspicious.

"I needed some assistance, you see. I asked Madelyn to help— begged, really, didn't I, Madelyn?" His expression placating, amused. Mama's, nothing of the sort. "And what could she do but abandon the laundry?"

Not until she and I were safely in the alleyway did Mama turn me to face her. "What were you doing up there?" she demanded. "Madelyn."

I hadn't been *doing* anything, and I didn't see why she had to be so rude to him. If ladies admired him, why was she treating him no better than a backroom man?

"Madelyn."

"Assisting!" I pulled away. "*I* am his *assistant*."

Which, of course wasn't even nominally true. Still, that hopeful little fabrication earned William the burden of my gratitude and, every day after, my company.

6

His assistant, his apparition, I haunted him. Tuesdays and Fridays, when the packet boat docked, I'd fetch his mail and watch as he picked through it with tense interest—he had been waiting for word, he said, about a friend—then feel a small but bitter sense of failure each time he discarded the lot. Mostly I loitered, silent in the back of the studio, watching him adjust the angle of a man's hat, the light through those curious ceiling windows, the train of a lady's skirt.

Most of his customers were ladies. I saw how their eyes followed him, vulnerable, full of hope, waiting perhaps, as I waited each time his head dipped beneath the camera's felt skirting. Waiting for him to say, "Beautiful."

Usually he said nothing at all, and still, I could tell, the women were left feeling, if not beautiful, then significant in ways they hadn't before. They walked out fluffed up, glowing. It was how he looked at them, I think, the way he arranged them on the stage, then stood back and silently looked. His face, masked in hair, remained the same, but his eyes would light as if to say, "Oh, there you are!" and then he would take the picture. Sometimes I'd stand beside him, try to see what it was he saw, but the women didn't much like this,

probably thought me some kind of dumb, piteous chaperone, lurking in the back, which was fine because I knew that when they left,
William would cast aside his charm as if it were a pack he'd strapped
on, slump into the rocker, and for a time be mine.

If he found me tiresome, well, he never said so; I still like to
think he enjoyed my company. After all, what young man can
resist the adoration of a girl, however ugly, who has no real claim
on him? At any rate, he humored me, showed me portraits and
landscapes he'd made and various panoramas of the Saint Louis
docks, which were three, sometimes four, photographs glued
together on long pieces of card stock. He spoke fervently of silver gelatin, dry-plate collodion, exposure times, fixing agent—it
was the fixing agent that turned his fingers black. I enjoyed setting the stage. Loved standing close to him, excruciatingly close,
within the felt-curtained closet he used to develop his pictures,
feeling the heat of him, watching faces emerge as if by magic on
albumen paper and copper plate.

"There are those," he said, "who believe photography merely a
science, or a craft, not an art. There is no art without craft, Maddy,
no art without the science that makes the medium possible. I am an
artist, even if not a painter."

And then, smiling down on me with a playful benevolence I was
happy to call affection, "Shall we travel the world together? Take
photographs, my apparition? London, Paris, Rome? Shall we capture
the world?"

For a month or so, this went on, too short a time for the great
space it takes in my memory. He gave me a place to go each day for
an hour or so, and a nickname: My Apparition. Later, he gave me
Miss Rose, and he didn't have to do that. Even in the midst of one
of his troubled moods, which descended, sometimes, in the space of

a breath, he was kind to me, and to this day I am grateful. Grateful even knowing all that I know now.

ONE DAY, ESCAPING MAMA'S CONSTANT demands, I climbed the stairs to the photography shop and, finding William alone, threw myself barefoot and graceless into the rocking chair. Only then did I became aware of a breathless tension in the room and the dim, strangled light through the shrouded ceiling glass. He did not look up to greet me but sat cross-legged on the floor amid a scattering of photographs from a box I'd never seen. His linen jacket lay crumpled on the stage. His brow was damp with sweat. I knew his moods well enough to keep my distance, but when finally he looked up, he smiled and beckoned me closer.

I came, wary at first. He was placing in careful rows before him photographs of soldiers, dozens of them, young and old, posed arms crossed or holding guns or bent over maps. I picked up the image of a young man, a boy really, ghostly, a hint of a smile, hat at a rakish angle.

"You took all these?" I asked.

"During the war. I was too young to fight, at first. But I knew how to make pictures. So that's what I did. Before the battle. And the aftermath."

I didn't see any afters.

"Don't need pictures to remember that," he said.

"Why not?"

"I don't know. I guess maybe I felt. Maybe I feel . . ."

He took the photograph, placed it with its fellows, and the hair on the back of my neck stood up. Nobody I knew ever talked about how they felt. "What?" I said. I couldn't help it. "William?"

"I don't know." He sat on his heels. "Responsible, maybe."

I considered this. "But you only took their pictures."

"Took their pictures, fixed their shadows, fixed the shades of men whose souls are fleeting on this earth."

Forgive me, but I thought it wonderful when he said things like this, so poetic, so bafflingly melancholic. It reminded so much of his letters that I wasn't at all prepared when, after gathering the photographs back into the box, he turned and said. "May I ask? Your mother?"

"Mama?" I said, that heavy complicated word. We never spoke of mothers.

"What happened to her?"

I flopped back into the rocking chair. "She died," I said to end it.

"I'm sorry."

He looked so sorry that I was sorry.

"She ran away." William cocked his head. "She ran away, and then she died."

"Oh. Oh, Maddy. When?" It was not grief but his pity that brought tears to my eyes.

"When I was born. She died having me. It was during the war."

"That must have been very hard for your sister."

I said nothing, the chair groaning as I rocked. William put a lid on the box of photos, but did not, as I hoped, discard the subject. "Something happened to her?" He said this carefully. "During the war?"

"She doesn't talk about it."

William nodded, spent a thoughtful moment staring at the stage. I was thinking about the way he held the door for Mama, bowed to her, thinking maybe he did this with more purpose than to raise Mr. Dryfus's gorge.

"Do you remember what you told me?" he asked. "That you thought about the war like a knot in a rope? Well, some of us, Maddy.

Some of us have a hard time finding our way out of that knot. Some of us, I don't think, ever find a way out."

"You want to take a picture of my sister," I said and, when no answer was forthcoming, looked up to find him staring at me as if I had spoken in tongues. "You don't think my sister is a beautiful woman?"

"Yes, Maddy," he said. "Your sister is a beautiful woman."

I'd annoyed him. I didn't know how, but I'd annoyed him. I wished, suddenly, I'd worn my shoes; I felt so exposed sitting there before him, and still I could not stop the next question.

"Do you want to take a picture of me?"

I had stopped rocking, stopped breathing. I could feel his eyes but did not look at him.

"Do you want me to take a picture of you?"

"No!" Which was and was not true.

"Well then, my apparition." He rubbed black-tipped fingers down his beard. "What are we talking about?"

Really, I wasn't sure anymore. But that night when I woke to a tapping and opened the attic door to find Clara's palsied face, lamp lit in the hallway, I knew we were going for him, for William. Can't say how I knew, any more than I could say how Clara guessed his need or where to find him—by that queasy deep-down kind of knowing Dot called "gut sense," I suppose, because by the time I'd slipped on my dress and Mama's old shawl and climbed down, my guts were tangled.

No one stirred in the room Mama and Mr. Dryfus shared. Clara stopped my mouth with a finger and, leaning heavily on my arm, pointed out the door, into a cold and ghastly silence that seemed to hold us back, until we turned off Union Street to Main and headed toward the Patch.

The Patch, with its scruffy boarding houses crawling with cats and ragged children, was poor and mostly Catholic. In Reliance this meant Irish—during the day that is. At night, after the brewery and the glass factory southeast of the German ward closed, the grog shops and brothels of the Patch came alive; all manner of man could be found there: Irish, Germans, Jews (all but Negroes, who stayed clear).

Still, it wasn't men I saw when first we turned off Main Street, past the Catholic church, and onto McClatchey Road. First I saw bonfires, then men drinking around them, some missing arms or legs, others holding themselves like something had been cut off inside. Yellow flames obscured their faces. They sniggered. They laughed and sang, and the brick walls, unable to contain their monstrous shadows, grew smaller.

I wasn't sure I wanted to find William among them.

"Clara?" I said, tugging her arm. Her palsy now shook us both, but her will was steady. She drew her shawl tight, made a twisting path through the men until we stood before a weather-battered hotel, sign posted, THE LILY WHITE. A woman's high cackling laugh pierced the belly of the place and a man, shirtless, in overalls, staggered through the swinging doors, sicked over the rail of a wraparound deck, and passed out, head lolling like a rag doll.

I had no wish to go in, but Clara lifted her skirts over the mess, and I followed, up the stairs, through the doors into a rush of smoke. It stank of piss and liquor and unwashed bodies. At the piano, a little man in a tattered bowler mashed out a dance-hall tune, but the only dancer, a bawdy woman from her dress, hugged herself in the center of the room and swayed to a song of her own. I was holding tight to Clara now, my bonnet low, bracing myself, but no one paid us any mind at all. No one but a man leaning on the bar's far end, and as his eyes found us they shifted over our shoulders. I turned to see two women, shrieking down the stairs, holding trousers aloft between them. The owner, a sweaty balding young man, undershirt tenting over his cock, clambered down after.

"Friedrick?" Clara called, her voice lower and stronger than I'd ever heard it. The music stopped, heads turned, and the young man ducked behind the baluster and stared down between the slats. *"Wo ist Wilhelm?"* she demanded.

He pointed to the bar, I thought, until I spotted a door just beyond. Soon we stood outside in a narrow, piss-stinking alley.

"Wilhelm?" Clara called. She poked a groaning form with her foot. *"Wilhelm?"* Then stepped over the man, pulling me with her down the alley, toward the dock, across the road. Behind us, the piano hushed and razzed again. The air dense and cold. The moon over the horizon painted a long white finger shore to shore.

That's when I saw him.

That is, I saw a man face down on the dock, as if pinned by the tip of that finger. Dead? He twitched. Clara called his name. William lay staring at his reflection in the moonlit water, and when our reflections joined his, he pushed himself to his knees, crying softly, swaying. His nose had been broken; blood and sick chunked in his beard. He retched again, over the side of the dock, lay back against the bollard and smiled up at us.

"Who is this? And what is here?" Then grabbing hold of Clara's ankles, he began to whisper over and over again. "I am half sick of shadows. I am half sick of shadows."

MAMA AND MR. DRYFUS WERE up, the shop brightly lit by the time Clara found two men sober enough to drag William home and up to his room. Mama sent me for hot water and towels; when

I returned, William was sprawled as he had been on the dock, face tipping over the bedside. Mama had stripped his shirt. Clara was working on his boots. He smelled of rum and sweat and rotting apples, and his thin broad shoulders were whitewash pale; each island of bone marking his spine looked sharp enough to pierce the skin. I wanted to touch each one in turn, to touch him.

Mama put the water by the bed, set one towel on the lowboy, another on his back, and grabbed the leg of his trousers.

"Get now, Madelyn." She looked over at me. "Do as I say."

I sank down outside the door, hugging my knees, and knew I wouldn't sleep for the jealous ember lodged in my throat.

PROBABLY I WAS NOT THE only one who felt this way, because a few days later, after William had taken off downriver with his camera and bedroll—much against Clara's wishes—Mr. Dryfus limped into the kitchen and stood stiff as a cleric in the doorway, watching Mama and I scrape greens from a pair of head-size rutabagas. He addressed himself to Mama, but it was first Clara, then the room at large to which he spoke.

"It has been *suggested*," he said, punctuating "suggested" with a slight incline of the head, "that I have been *insensitive* to your needs. That I have been *demanding* and *unkind*. I cannot agree. I have, in fact, *recognized* and *appreciated* your efforts, even if I have said nothing to that effect."

Clara, pretending no interest, had begun to hum a low unsteady song. Herb jars mustered across her shelves; scoured pots hung ready on the flanks as Mr. Dryfus soldiered on.

"You must understand," he said raising himself to his full slender height. "What I mean to say is that you *will* forgive me if, sometimes, I fail to anticipate needs beyond my own."

"Men have no needs beyond their own." Mama surprised herself. Dot used to say that. That was Dot speaking. But Mr. Dryfus glanced between Clara and Mama as if the two had colluded against him. Impossible. I remained intermediary between Mama and Clara, and I was sure no such collusion had occurred. It was an honest relief when Hanley broke the moment, yelling "Mr. Dryfus!" from the alleyway, saving him from a response, though Dryfus did his best to appear inconvenienced by the interruption.

"Hat, Hanley!" he said. Shirttails dangled out the back of Hanley's trousers. A shiner blackened his left eye and part of his nose. He swiped his hat from his head.

"Listen now, Mr. Dryfus. I know I'm late, but . . ."

"A man, Hanley, is judged first by his punctuality, then by his character."

"I know, but, Mr. Dryfus . . ."

"A man does not arrive late. A man—"

"But they've arrested Miss Rose!" Hanley couldn't help himself. He grinned. "She and that other woman, French. They say they mean to vote!"

WHEN MR. DRYFUS RETURNED, LONG after supper, he sat talking with Clara at the kitchen table. Mama had gone to bed, and I, restless and lonely, sat in the dark hall listening to the German words scratch the backs of their throats. After a time, Clara hefted herself and, holding her son's cheek with quaking hands, laughed at the urgent thing he'd said.

"Mutti—" said Mr. Dryfus, but she stopped him with a kiss on his narrow forehead and shuffled away to the little servant's bedroom she kept by the kitchen.

For weeks I had been trying to hate Mr. Dryfus and be done with it, but my hatreds have always been fickle, and a good deal about the man had begun to intrigue me: the meticulous way he filled, tamped, and cleaned his pipe; the strained focus on his face when he smoked it. Even the phrenological bust staring blindly into his study intrigued me—especially since he appeared content with conclusions he'd drawn on our first encounter and gave no indication he planned to subject my skull to closer scrutiny. I wonder, now, what conclusions he might have drawn reading his own physiognomy.

Next to William, who was not yet thirty, Mr. Dryfus seemed very old, though he could not have been much over forty—younger than I am now. On the rare occasions he stood straight, he was taller than William. His skin, pale and stretchy looking, was smooth about his deep-set eyes, and his head floated on a pencil-thin neck. He was not warm or jovial, did not tell jokes like other men, or laugh at them. Most of the time, he was either bound up tight as a pork barrel or floating far away in his own mind. Even setting type, his attention divided between what he was doing and some other, greater thought poised in the offing. Maybe this ponderousness had to do with his leg? Or the war? I didn't know.

I did think he owed Clara more than the glimmers of gratitude he gave her. For what specifically? For being a mother to him, I suppose. For loving him. For doing so without resentment. I think there should be a better word, a bigger word than *gratitude*—a word that stretches a full page of type and takes at least ten minutes and a lifetime of practice to properly say.

At least, this is how *I* would have felt about Clara if she were *my* mother. Gratitude so enormous it overwhelmed the words at hand.

I did not like the way Mr. Dryfus persisted in looking at Mama, or rather, at her fingers. In the day, they burrowed into separate work, but evenings, as Mama hunched over her lace pillow in the parlor, Mr. Dryfus watched her hands. I was not accustomed to this kind of focus. Like dogs bolting food, men's eyes swallowed Mama whole, leaving me to covet the oddments. (William looked at her this way.) Mama offered herself to them as dutifully as she mucked the coal scuttle; I allowed her to do so.

But Mama's fingers were mine.

Her rosebud ears, mine. The pink hollow at the base of her neck, the shadowy recess of her collarbones, the tiny branching scars on her right knee, the smooth pale mountain of her ankle-bone—mine. Mine. Mine. Mr. Dryfus had no right to look so at her hands!

But that night as I watched him sitting there alone, a funny thing happened. Everything that had become familiar about him became strange in a brand-new way that's hard to describe. It was like when you stare at a simple, ordinary word so long it stops meaning what it used to mean—stops meaning anything a word can say, at any rate. That happened as I watched Mr. Dryfus. His pipe had gone out. He cupped the bowl in his palm as you might cup a chick to keep it warm. His body bent like a question mark over the table. Lamplight cast shadows across his face, and his eyes, grasping at some worry or thought, glazed. He seemed so fragile, so unsure, and alone, which was pretty much how I felt most of the time; I wanted to reassure him somehow, or maybe just hold him in my mind just as I saw him at that moment, like a photograph. Whatever the case, I felt my heart reach out with tender recognition that vanished when I heard his voice. "Young lady?"

I froze.

"Young lady, I know you are there. A word?" He cleared his throat. *"Please."*

I slipped to the doorway, but no closer.

"I would like to know. I would like to ask. Your *sister* . . ." He stopped.

"My sister?" I said more harshly than I intended. Whatever deal Mama had made to make him keep me was not binding. I knew he could still get rid of me.

"I wonder. I must know." He examined his pipe; heat from the dampened coals prickled my skin.

"Must know what?" I asked, then added. "Sir."

"Is she happy?"

Happy was not a word I associated with Mama.

"With the arrangements as they stand," he revised. "I have noticed." He stopped. "Well, she does not smile much. I suppose I mean to say, would anything *make* her happy?"

"You mean a gift, sir?"

"A gift! Why yes, of course, a gift," he said, trying on what was obviously a novel idea to him. "Does she want anything?"

"Like what, sir?"

"Flowers? A dress? Anything, within reason. Flowers?" he supplied when I did not answer fast enough.

"No, a dress," I said. "She would like to make a lady's dress."

"And this will make her happy? Well." Relief washed his face. "And your sister, would she—"

"Mr. Dryfus? What happened with Miss Rose?"

"Miss Rose?" He blinked. "Why does it matter to you?"

Really, it didn't. Miss Rose meant nothing to me, at the time. I had no inkling she ever would. It was just, well, I suppose I no longer wished to speak of Mama's happiness.

"Nothing *happened*. Nothing of *consequence*. They threatened to throw her in the jailhouse. She demanded it, in fact. But they did not. She is a demonstrative woman." There was, I think, looking back, a hint of admiration there. "But New York is more forgiving of suffragettes and spectacles." He stopped. "A dress, you say?"

7

Two days later, with a warm breeze nuzzling the rims of our bonnets, Mama and I followed Hanley down Main Street to the dock market, where cloth and ribbon would be cheaper than in the shops. William was still away. I looked south in the direction he'd walked but saw only the river, like a line-drawn profile, stretching away from me. The leaves were turning. The Missouri fields, shorn to stubble, were bare, but the carts that passed were full of sweet-smelling apples and squash of every imaginable variety; the last days of fall seemed to balance there between this bleakness and bounty like an egg on a high, cambered roof.

"Samuel Fromme," said Hanley happily, "lost both feet above the ankle. Richard Hansel lost an eye; Ansel Willerby, a leg. And pinkie finger." He held up his pinkie, tried to poke me in the side and I gave him a shove.

"Madelyn," said Mama as Hanley pointed out another house of crumbling brick, sagging between two neighbors. Actually he was pointing to the grate beneath the porch steps. "Down there," he said, "that's where Mrs. Gandershan keeps—"

"Gandershan?" It was one of Hanley's chums, Adam, coming

up behind us. What I knew of Adam Harrison I didn't much like. Cocksure little runt. His daddy worked at the brewery with Hanley's sister's husband, a man named Robey, whom Hanley lived with but never talked about—which was funny given that Hanley talked so much about everything else. Adam was always smirking at Mama and bossing Hanley like he had a right. I suspected the bulk of Hanley's bruises had been won defending Adam's big mouth. Hanley never seemed to notice he was being bossed. But then, nothing much ever seemed to bother Hanley.

"Keeps her son down there," Adam said, finishing Hanley's sentence. "I heard he eats raw oysters, shell and all. Crunches them up with his back teeth. Lost his front to shrapnel."

"Don't believe a word you say," I told Adam, but all this talk of lost limbs made me wonder. "What about Mr. Dryfus?" I asked Hanley.

"What about him?"

"Was it the war? Did he hurt his leg in the war?"

"Mr. Dryfus? Nah," he said. "He never fought."

"Then what happened to his leg?"

"Don't know. Born that way I think. William went to war."

I knew this but saw there was more in the look that passed between Hanley and Adam. "There's talk . . ." Hanley said, looking sheepish.

"What talk?" asked Mama. She rarely addressed Hanley for any reason, and I think this shocked him into a quicker answer than he might have given.

"That he tried to kill himself. After the war. I don't know what happened. He was in a prison camp south of Cayro. Then his mama died. Cholera, you know."

"Not the way I heard it," said Adam.

"Yeah?" I said. "What'd you hear?"

"Me? Don't believe a word I say, do you?"

I didn't press because I could see from the mean little gleam in his eye I didn't have to.

"I hear he killed his mama," he said. "Snapped her neck like a chicken." Looking right at me, he mimicked the action, and made a cracking noise.

"Nah!" I said, trying to make light, but Adam wasn't done.

"Then he fills his pockets with stones and jumps off the bluff into the river. Niggers found him in the levy pilings near Carondelet. Then he got thrown in with the lunatics."

"I never did believe that," said Hanley.

But he'd heard it, I thought. It wasn't just the details that gave weight to Adam's story. I remembered Clara's worried face when William walked away downriver with his camera, alone. And I saw him again, saw him wretched and face down on the levy pier.

Adam pulled him away toward a ball game raising dust beyond the warehouses. Mama stood watching them go. I stood watching Mama, a heavy lump in my gut.

"I don't trust that boy enough to spit at him," I said, but something in Mama's expression made me work to keep hold of my doubt.

"You stay away from William," she said. I said nothing. "Madelyn, hear me?"

"Why? You don't believe ..."

She turned, looked me in the eye. "Doesn't matter what I believe. We ain't talking about that. Listen to me, now. Never was no good trusting a man who ain't the same man one day to the next. One minute to the next. Look at me," she said. "Now I seen you sashaying around him. You got no idea what—"

"I don't sashay!"

"Madelyn," she said, but walked on. Lace curtains heaved through open windows; sun glanced red off the muddy river. We rounded the bend overlooking Market Street; voices and shouts rose with the stink of charred meat, apples, bundled lavender. Every tall bearded man I saw was William. William unloading pumpkins and squash from buckboard wagons; William throwing dice against an abandoned warehouse wall and lounging on flatboats bobbing off the docks.

"Because you like him, is why," I mumbled, when I caught up to her, then again, louder. "Because you like him."

"You got no idea what you're talking about. Behave now."

What she meant was "don't draw attention, don't embarrass me." Trips through Susanville had been tense affairs. Her reputation preceded her, whispers and dark stares followed. She used to walk then as she was walking now, as if one misplaced step would crack the earth in two.

Dogs and small children scavenged underfoot; glass-factory boys, scrawny and fierce, rolled dice for chew; near the butcher's block, a happily oblivious hog munched slops. A little black boy mounded dust at the feet of a woman selling fortunes and cut pearl buttons. I saw William trying on a hat, William carrying a saddle, William admiring the young women whispering confidences behind Chinese fans.

Mama's eyes followed these women. She pulled me close enough to link elbows, as if we, too, were but friendly intimates.

Atop a packing crate, a man sang the virtues of temperance to an audience of lubricated naysayers. I was keen to stop—it had been a year since I'd heard a good stumping—when the spice of cooked meat erased every other hunger. "Sausage!" I tugged Mama back.

"Not now."

The German butcher, his great belly challenging his trouser seams, had the biggest, whitest teeth I'd ever seen.

"Why not now?" Because I'd suggested it, was why. Because I was supposed to follow her, to stay off her dress one minute, link arms like friends the next, as suited her.

"Later," she said, tugging me forward.

"When later?"

"Later, later. Don't be difficult."

"Aren't you hungry?" Mama was always hungry. And I was more difficult when hungry. I stood my ground. She was tired all the time, and I felt in her now a different species of silence than I was used to, a deliberate and directed silence that scared me, and made me mad.

Mama said nothing, for we had arrived at a lace-and-ribbon stand, manned by a frowning fat woman with bright red cheeks.

"May I help you?" She sounded doubtful.

The stand, really more of a canvas tent, housed hinged display cases with drawers to store ribbons and lace and hooks on which to display the reels. I could tell she thought us inferior to the establishment.

"No, Ma'am," said Mama. "Thank you."

Red Cheeks was no more a Ma'am than Mama was.

"Why don't you wear your lace?" I asked her.

"I'm saving it."

"For what?" I said.

She stared into the mirror. Red Cheeks hovered like an old hen.

"You could sell it. Yours is nicer," I said pointedly. "I bet we could make it all the way to New Orleans on the money."

Mama tucked a strand of hair behind her ear, tried on three different smiles.

"Or New York or California. Or Rome," I said.

She spoke without turning. "Am I pretty?"

It was the fact she asked, no less than the *way* she asked, with urgent, worried eyes that stunned me silent. She had never asked me before. The answer, so obvious.

"Madelyn?" She turned, her eyes gleaming, the dark hair framing her face backlit by the sun. I could feel tears rising with the word on my lips, and didn't know why.

"Beautiful," I whispered.

She turned back to the mirror. "Yes, well, course that's what you'd say."

"Fine!" I said, tears vanishing in a rage whose source was just as mysterious to me. "Fine! Then I won't. I won't ever say it again." And picking up a bit of lace, I roughed my fingers over the webbed pattern. Red Cheeks bristled. Two young women giggled into the tent. "If you don't want me saying it, I won't say it, not ever."

"Madelyn!" Mama hissed.

Red Cheeks lifted her voice. "You will be paying for . . ."

"I'll call you *ugly* if you like," I said, giving in to a powerful ugly rising inside me. "Ugly!" I said. "Ugly, ugly, ugly." Mama's face helpless, imploring, fueled me. Red Cheeks's open mouth and the titillated silence of the young women fueled me. I felt capable of hurting Mama, wanted to hurt her, to blacken her expressionless beauty, to be too loud, too large to ignore. *"Ugly, Ugly, Ugly!"* I said, mangling every piece of lace I could get my hands on.

"Madelyn, stop!" said Mama.

"John!" Red Cheeks squawked.

I smelled onion breath and the thick hands of a stocky little tailor grabbed my arm. "Yyyou!" Red Cheeks railed. "You tell me you're going to pay for . . ."

But Mama was busy landing her elbow in the tailor's gut, then yanked my other arm so hard we stumbled back against the thin leg of the support pole. Cloth walls shuddered and crumbled into the street. For a moment, we sat in a heap beneath the canvas. When we emerged—with Red Cheeks, the tailor, and the young women—to face an audience pointing and chewing on smiles, Mama slapped me. Hard. So hard I heard a high, raspy ringing.

I didn't look back at her, didn't think. Closed my mind and ran as fast as I could past the butcher and the warehouses, past the levy pier, the hulking gray glass factory and the Negro shantytown huddled near the inlet of Jones Creek. And because I was running with the river, it seemed as though I was running very fast and far and half expected—climbing exhausted up a steep rise in the bluff—to find an open landscape, empty as I felt, stretching into the distance.

Instead, I looked back to find that I had been running along a bend; the river curved to a crescent, and there, still on my heels, gaping like misshapen teeth in a wrinkled half-smile, were the town's mottled rooftops.

Frankly, I nearly cried with relief. Self-righteous anger, just now so delicious, soured. Only seeing how easy it would be to return allowed me to imagine myself bold enough to continue.

Not even this confidence lasted, for though she had not followed on foot, Mama's voice trailed behind, muddying my resolve. Practical inconveniences began poking their heads into the sun: Where was I going? What would I do when I got there? I peeled off my shoes, and with a shriek that sent a broom of blackbirds from the thicket, hurled them off the bluff, only to become aware of how sharply the jagged shale cut my feet. The dull sweetness of the dogwoods, once so pleasant, now reminded me how hungry I was, and would be, and this last thought finally made a sniveling fool of me.

In that moment, I became supremely conscious of how responsible Mama was for my each and every woe—and for the woes of the
world beyond, I was sure. A litany of sins marched across my mind's
eye and attached themselves to Mama's skirt in an eager, growing
chain: Dot's death? Obviously Mama's fault. My angry red markings,
the mosquito bites bubbling from exposed skin, the thicket scratches
on my arms, my throbbing temple . . . she was to blame for the
newsprint staining my face and hands, for the dull, horrid food. And
yes, I saw now, for the war, and all wars hence!

Cross-legged on shale, I sat for what seemed like a long time,
holding desperately to my indignation, glaring across the wide,
indifferent river. That morning the thought of William out here too,
somewhere, alone with his bedroll and camera, might have been
a comfort to me. "What do you say, Maddy?" he might have said.
"Shall I take you away with me? Shall we travel the world together?
London? Paris? Rome?"

Now the romance of this fantasy was marred by Adam's tale and
by my own deepening gloom. I was hungry. The sun was sinking;
I was getting cold. A circle of vultures overhead tightened, broke
ranks, and circled again. Around the bend came a man poling a skiff.
I listened, but the river's pungent breath soon squelched all but the
low gasping hum of his song. Then he disappeared, song and all,
beyond the island, and confronted with nothing but the immensity
of the far horizon, my courage withered. Defeated, I roused myself
and made my way from the rocky bluff trail I'd been following down
a switchback path to softer ground, and turned upriver, walking
slowly back to Mama, back to Reliance.

Before long, I reached a shoal wide as two men lying head to
toe. The trail stopped here and picked up on the other side. I'd have
to climb the bank to get around, but rested a moment, watching

steam snake from the warm shallows where current eddied. Tree roots reaching from the bank-caught driftwood, a dented tin bucket, a molding leather boot. Milkweed rimmed each in white. And there, in the shadows on the far side of the shoal, two hulking vultures jockeyed for position over some other thing tangled in the roots.

It was big. A goat? A calf? Shrugging their shoulders, the vultures heaved toward the sun. A dog, maybe. But before I'd taken two steps closer, a chill shivered through me.

A young woman bobbed there in the water. Scum greened her black hair. A tattered yellow dress bunched between her legs. Leaves masked all but one blue staring eye. Her left arm wedged in the root stems; her toes bobbed like knobs of birch in the dark water.

She might have been sleeping there. She might kick and splash. She might sit up to scare me.

I can't say it occurred to me that she might be the young woman who'd gone missing weeks ago. Instead, I remembered a bloated milk cow I'd found stinking up Dot's corn patch a few years before. The young woman did not look as dead as the cow had looked, especially with that one open eye. As dead as Dot, ash faced, in her bed. I remembered wondering who might be missing that cow, but don't think I wondered the same about the young woman—until I bent closer.

A thin gold chain hung around her neck. I reached down to grab it, jerked away again at the cold, catfish feel of her skin, then using a stick to pull the chain clear, unclasped the latch and held it in my hand. On the end was a charm made of two interlocking circles. A figure eight.

I stuffed it, quick, into my pocket.

"Don't look at me like that," I whispered to that terrible eye. "You not gonna need it. Don't be looking at me like that because—"

"Madelyn."

I nearly pissed myself. She spoke! And she knew my name. But, no, the voice had come from behind me. I turned to find his silhouette, black against the sun.

"William," I said, stupidly.

8

William sent me back to Reliance ahead of him, but I remember nothing more until the path opened and the town appeared, lamplit, glowering above me. "I'll take care of this," he had said, easing the great bulk of the camera on his back to the ground. Was there tension on his face? Grief? Any sign he knew her? I don't remember. I remember thinking, *Good. William will take care of this,* having little idea at the time what *this* meant. "Don't say anything," he'd said, so gently. "Do you understand, Maddy? I'll inform the constable. Don't say anything to anyone. Can do you that, and be a good girl?"

Not until I stood barefoot by the pier did the charm deep in my pocket and the image of the dead girl with her blue staring eye and her body laced in milkweed come back as shivers all through me, and I began to run. Past the dock and the last of the market vendors, gathering their carts; past the Patch, up Main Street to Union, and the only word on my lips was "Mama!"

Hanley, not Mama, grabbed hold of me in the print-shop alleyway.

"Hey, easy! Easy, Maddy. Goddammit."

"Let go, Hanley!"

"Are you okay?"

The question briefly crippled me with gratitude. He glanced over his shoulder. The kitchen lamp stamped a square of light in the yard. "He's not happy. Did you get lost? Say you got lost, and be sorry. Be sorry as you can, and maybe you can stay."

We found Mama in the kitchen, standing against the wall near the larder, hands white around a broom, like some kind of cornered haunt. My heart nearly kicked a hole through my ribs. The sight of her so pale and motionless must have spooked Hanley too, because he took his hat in hand but found nothing to say to her. Any words in my mouth dried up, for no sooner did she see me, than she seemed to look through me; I felt this numb remove settle over my shoulders the way sleep does. Whatever urgency ran me up that hill vanished. I turned away and walked past her, straight down the hall to Mr. Dryfus's study, hardly caring what he'd say. He was sitting behind his desk, face grim, meerschaum pipe poised like a gavel.

"Leave us, Hanley," he said.

Even if I'd tried, I don't think I could have heeded Hanley's advice to be sorry. I didn't feel sorry. Didn't feel much of anything, hardly noticed my torn skirts, my skinned knees, my bloody feet. I'd lost my bonnet, too, but in the stuffy air of the study, a kind of giddy belligerence overwhelmed what remained of my reason.

"Your sister has been worried," he said.

I mumbled a response.

"What? What did you say?"

"I said, 'I doubt it.' Sir."

"Young lady. The constable has been searching for you, and the deputies."

"I don't care."

"She's not herself, Mr. Dryfus. Lyman."

Mama. It was Mama in the hallway. She took one step toward me through the door, just one step, and then, as if restrained by some invisible wall between us, came no closer. "She's not been herself."

What did I want of her? To rush and hold me? To slap me again? To cry?

Too much. I always wanted too much.

Hanley returned, this time with Clara. All three watched Mama as if poised to catch an infant falling from the ceiling. I don't think I meant to say it, but I was so appalled by the frightened uncertainty in her face, and by my own rising anger, that the word slipped from my mouth almost without thinking.

"Mama," I said. Then louder, punctuating the word like prayer, like a curse. "Mama, Mama, Mama."

Then my breath caught, for the color had gone out of her. She stood staring at a spot on the floor, her hand to her belly, breathing slow as if she would be sick. I thought *I* would be sick. *This is not my fault!* I wanted to tell her, if only to convince myself. *We would have been exposed sooner or later, right? We would go. I want to go. We should go away now, Mama.*

She filled her lungs and looked at me, and I felt a relief so strong my legs were strings.

"Mr. Dryfus. I got something to say," she said, still looking at me. "Mr. Dryfus, you going to be a daddy."

IN THE ATTIC ROOM, MAMA stripped my clothes and bathed my bramble cuts; a single candle flicked our shadows against the wall. Hanley had gone home to his sister's house. William had returned with the constable and left again with Mr. Dryfus. The house was silent and cold. I wrapped Mama's arms around me but felt in her hipbone, her collarbone, her chin on my shoulder, the great distance between us and pulled away again.

"Maddy?" she said.

"You did it," I said. "Gone and made yourself *indispensable*."

"Maddy, please."

"Don't call me Maddy. Dot called me Maddy. You call me Madelyn."

"Madelyn, please."

"Please?" But something in her voice, something that had been there for weeks, poked me now as revelation. I turned to face her. "Mama, whose is it?"

"I tried to tell you before."

"You tried."

"I did, Maddy, but you've been so moody, so quiet, I was afraid . . ."

"Whose is it? Mama—"

"John's," she whispered.

That shut me up. Dot's boy? Dot's boy, John? The breath went out of me. Of course it was! Of course, I must have known, but most of us have a talent for seeing no more than we wish to see.

"He came upon me, Maddy."

"No more, I reckon, than any of the others came upon you."

The blue vein on her temple pulsed; I could see desperation rising with her anger and relented. "You tried . . ."

"Everything," she said.

"Ergot?"

"Everything. Tried and tried. It held on." She smoothed my hair. "I thought maybe it'd loose itself, but—" She paused. "Maddy. You won't run away?" Outside a dog barked, then stillness. "You won't leave me, will you?"

Hate, that simple, stubbed toe of an emotion, which colors everything an explicable black and white, would have been so much easier
than love. I loved her. Certainly not in the grateful, dependent manner I imagined girls were meant to love their mamas, but grudgingly,
irrationally. For a moment, I found myself suspended between love
and hate, or swinging between those poles so quickly I couldn't tell
the difference, and I was overcome by a glorious, though brief, indifference. I didn't think about the dead young woman in the river, or
William, or the baby, or the dumbstruck expression on Mr. Dryfus's
face when Mama told him. And in the clarifying absence of these
thoughts, I knew:

Mama had not fallen in love with any letters. Her acceptance
of Mr. Dryfus's proposal had had nothing to do with love or its
promise. It had not been a hopeful or even an impulsive act, merely
a desperate one. He had been, I realized, the first *Matrimonial Times*
man to offer.

"Maddy?" Mama said.

But I had sunk heavy and warm into my own body. Had I the
words to express what I felt then, I would not have had the will. *You
won't leave me, will you? You won't leave me?* The question stank up my
head, stank up the room, stank up my heart, soured the light squeez-
ing from the moon, and left other questions piling in its place.

Where did she think I could go without her? And what right did
she have to need me?

9

A dead woman in the river. Mama pregnant. I'd had shock enough for one week, surely. Yet, one more revelation waited when Hanley, bursting with excitement, joined Mama, Clara, and me in the kitchen the next morning.

"Her arms, they were so tangled in tree roots they had to cut her out," he said. "Not even the vultures could get at her."

I pushed my plate away. Mama, toying with her cup, fixed her eyes on me. We'd circled all morning but said nothing to each other, and the silence was a clock ticking between my ears. The way her hand hovered above her belly. That watchful tension in her face. A baby. Why didn't she tell me?

"Adam thinks the Papists did it." Hanley eyed my plate. He'd already wolfed down the portion Clara gave him. "But she was a Papist."

"Did what?" I asked.

"Killed her."

I choked on the small bite in my mouth. Mama looked up. Hanley, pleased to gain our full attention, grinned.

"I thought you knew. Her throat was cut. Ear to ear." He drew a finger with a certain relish across his neck, before his eyes strayed back to my plate. "You going to eat that?"

It was evening before William returned from the courthouse with Mr. Dryfus, and the next morning before I could steal away to the photography shop. In the night, rain had come, the air tart with cold even as the potbellied stove in the shop chuffed comfortably. From behind the black felt curtain of the darkroom, I could see movement.

"Closed!" he called, and when he emerged, blinking into the light, his face beneath his beard was ghostly pale. He wiped his hands on his trousers. His shirt was open at the collar, his feet bare. River mud flaked from his boots, discarded to my right. I took an involuntary step away from them.

"My apparition?" William said, a question in his voice.

I'd picked up, without thinking, a picture book lying by the door and now stared at it, the mouthful of words I'd walked in with gone to mush.

"Flip through," he said. "Faster." I did and the stout little woman pictured spun a wobbly pirouette. "There's a man who's going to show me how he makes them in the city. It's a flip book, a moving picture."

I put the book down.

"What, Madelyn?"

"It wasn't true about her throat being cut. I saw ..."

William didn't move, didn't say anything.

"You know I saw her. I ..." But for some reason, I held my tongue about the charm I'd found. I didn't know why.

"Her throat *was* cut," he said after a moment.

"It wasn't."

"I did it."

I wasn't sure what I'd heard. He pulled a glass plate from the camera, examined it as if he'd merely been explaining the workings of the emulsion process.

"You? You cut her?"

"Catholics consider suicide a mortal sin. They would not have buried her next to her brother. I knew she would have wanted—"

"So you cut her?"

"Madelyn!" His tone froze me. He held the glass plate in both hands as if he might crush or throw it. Instead, with great deliberateness, he placed it atop the camera, and his shoulders folded in upon themselves. "Her name was Aileen, Aileen, Aileen."

"William?"

"I'm fine." He did not look fine, but I said nothing, for he had come close, an arm's length away, the taut, ready heat of him, overwhelming.

"I know it's hard for you to understand. But what I did, it was—it was an act of kindness. A necessary kindness. I gave her family a truth they could live with. Do you understand?"

"No."

"Murder, Madelyn. Random, senseless murder. Do you understand?"

I stared at his long bare toes, trying to separate the word *murder* from Madelyn.

"She killed herself. Madelyn?"

I looked up at him. "But why, William? And how do you know?"

"Shhh." And the fact of him so warm, so close, left no room for questions.

"Look at me." He tipped my chin. All fear and reason left me. "Don't you see, Madelyn?" he whispered. "It's better this way."

Yes.

"You trust me, don't you?"

Yes.

"This will pass. You will see. She will remain a beautiful mystery, our Lady of Shalott."

And then he took my hand, not the clear but the stained one.

"I can depend on you? On your," he paused, searching for the word, "discretion?" And didn't I agree that we need never speak of this again, to anyone?

Then slowly, ever so slowly, he brought my hand—not my clear but my marked hand—to his lips, and kissed it.

I RETURNED TO THE PRINT shop. Linen snapped wet on the line. A chicken squawked at some indignity, and I knew I would keep William's secret. I tugged a sheet from the line, balled it in my arms, pranced like a fool around the yard. Yes, I would keep his secret. I would keep his secret, and he would be grateful. And every time he looked at me, I would feel the touch of his lips upon my hand. *An act of kindness.* Yes. *An act of kindness,* even as the notion scratched like hens through the back of my mind. Did I suspect him then? Was I capable? Had he tried to kill himself? His Mama? No matter. *No matter, no matter,* for hadn't it been the darkness pressing the seams of his charm that most appealed to me?

FOR AN HOUR THE FOLLOWING day, a wailing procession disturbed the town's discomfited silence. I waited, listening hard to the talk, but no one, not even Hanley, suspected what William had done. It seemed everyone preferred to believe the girl's death had been a murder, and lacking a suspect, blame was cast wherever blame was convenient. Mr. Stockwell's Sin Society blamed suggestive artwork, novels, dancing, liquor. Liquor implicated the Germans, who blamed the Irish, who blamed the Negroes. I waited. The truth—as much as I knew of it—heavy on my shoulders. But William said nothing, so I said nothing. I held my tongue when shop windows in the German district were smashed, and later when three Irish boys were beaten bloody behind the warehouses. I said nothing when hooded men with rifles set fire to Negro Town. I don't know what else happened there—I suspect, now, far more than was ever reported—but by the time flames turned to ash, only a few shacks were left and no one seemed to remember, much less care, that a dead girl had been the cause. Mr. Dryfus squeezed only a few lines about her between a column on the Lady's Auxiliary Luncheon and another about potato bugs ravaging farms east of the bluffs. This, too, weighed on me.

A girl. A servant. A Catholic. A nobody, like me. No sooner dead than forgotten. Except maybe by her blind old father and an aunt, who were Catholic and poor and nobodies, too. I thought maybe I should say something to them—maybe give them the charm I'd found. I did neither. I wore the charm, instead, hidden under my blouse. I tried to remember if I'd recognized the dead woman from the cigar box of naked ladies in William's room, but I couldn't remember her face beyond that staring eye, and when I looked again, the cigar box was gone. Twice I dragged Hanley with me to visit the white painted cross marking her grave in the Catholic cemetery. But what could I do? Nothing.

Then William closed his shop for the winter, and there was nothing I could do about that either. Some kind of business in Saint Louis, he said, but couldn't tell me when or if he'd be back. He said little to me after the kiss. I reasoned he had no choice but to ignore me. Otherwise what would Mama think? He left Clara a pie, left me only his secret—more, at least, than he left Mama.

I hadn't heard the last of him, or the dead girl, Aileen, of course. Dot used to say the dead don't always shuffle off into heaven or hell. Sometimes they hang around to make use or nuisance of themselves. And Aileen did haunt me. Does, I should say. For months her image, tangled in roots in the river, one blue staring eye, visited my dreams. And she would haunt me in a more substantive manner a year later when William finally returned and I left the print shop for Miss Rose's house.

Even now, more than thirty years later, when I close my eyes and feel the weight of the charm on my chest, there she is again in the river, clear as a photograph.

AT THE PRINT SHOP AT the time, however, two more pressing excitements all but overwhelmed the death and William's departure. The first, of course, was the baby. The second was an unexpected invitation to dine, in the New Year, at Oak Hollow, Melborn Stockwell's house on Millionaire's Row.

PART II
1875

10

Oak Hollow, a stern, federal-style house of yellow Roman brick, stood like a gatekeeper on the corner of Tenth and Hazel, beyond the courthouse. Here shop fronts and terraced homes, still decked in wreaths and holly, gave way to the grand houses of Millionaire's Row, each secure behind its own moat of grass and garden.

Really, it was only seven blocks from the print shop. We'd walked. But as my eyes tracked from paving stones to columned porch to blue-painted door, the distance seemed much farther. I could feel how tense Mama was beside me, how nervous and proud to be invited into that house wearing a new gown. There had been little enough money for cloth after Dryfus paid for the ribbons I'd ruined at the market, but even without gloves, pelisse, or corset, it was the most exquisite garment Mama had ever sewn. Puffed sleeves fell to a low, lacy neckline. Beneath the blue muslin, lilac flounces gave life to her every movement and hopefulness to the smiles she'd tried on all afternoon in the attic mirror. She piled her dark hair atop her head in curls that framed her face, and though I didn't say so, I thought her as beautiful as I'd ever seen her.

You'd never have guessed she was carrying. She wanted to keep it that way for a while, at least, and Mr. Dryfus? Well, he'd become ever more obliging.

I was wearing Mama's Sunday dress, too large in the bosom, which hardly mattered. My inclusion in the night's events, from what I could tell, demanded no finery. I was there to keep company the resident invalid, Mr. Stockwell's youngest, a girl about my age whose name I didn't know or had forgotten. Dinner. Mr. Dryfus had promised me dinner, and while the smell of roasted meat wafting out of the Stockwell's front door could not have pleased him, I was nearly giddy for a taste.

No other guests were arriving. I thought maybe we were the first, but when the housekeeper, a squinting, thin-lipped woman, showed us into the sitting room, a collection of jackets already hung. The floorboards moaned overhead and men's laughter rumbled in the room adjacent. Were we late? Mr. Dryfus was never late, and I could tell from the way he gripped his cane that the possibility troubled him. The housekeeper taking our jackets looked twice at Mama. "Would you like a wrap?" she asked.

Mama, pausing, shook her head. I marked this but thought nothing of the offer until, shepherded into the foyer, I saw, stepping down the staircase, another woman, trailed with graceless urgency by what could have been her younger twin, still a girl, but barely. Mama grabbed my arm, held tight. Both of them, the woman and the girl, wore embroidered gray satin, fancy, drab, and buttoned up tight to the chin.

"But Mother," the girl exclaimed, "I am *not* overexcited!"

"Later, Georgiana," warned the woman. She turned to welcome us, her manner apologetic—until her eyes fell to Mama's bare chest. Her breath caught. She looked quickly away.

"Mr. Dryfus," said the woman, then, tightly, "Mrs. Dryfus."

The girl, tense, seemed to notice us for the first time, when the oak door to her right groaned open to a cloud of smoke and male voices. Mr. Stockwell and two other men emerged laughing; the girl's posture softened and with it all outward defiance. "Little bird!" said Mr. Stockwell and pecked her on the cheek.

On his visits to the print shop, I hadn't paid Melborn Stockwell much notice. Later I learned he'd come by his money the old-fashioned way, by marrying into it, and was engaged in some manner of gentlemanly business that required little of his effort or attention. He was also a deacon of Reliance First Presbyterian, but was best known in the town for what Hanley and most everybody else called the Sin Society. Its full name was something like The Reliance Society for the Suppression of Vice or The Committee for the Suppression of Vice. He also paid for the privilege of contributing to the *Register* a weekly column on "the general and widespread deterioration of society." He called it *Oracular Axioms*.

Mr. Stockwell was not a handsome man; he wore fine clothes poorly but was not, as a woman would be, conscious of this fact. Hanley could mimic exactly his habit of rocking heel to toe, back and forth, when he spoke. Now the motion emphasized his odd shape: more back than leg to him, big chest, no discernible neck. Yet he walked on the balls of his feet, with an almost feminine grace. Twin islands of facial hair curtained a surprisingly petite mouth but left his chin, like the top of his head, bare as an empty stage.

"Mr. Dryfus," he said, rocking forward. "Have you ever seen such virtue in a face?"

He meant, I realized, the girl, Georgiana. Virtue, maybe, for neither Georgiana nor her mother was pretty. Still, there was a fierceness about the girl. A despair. I could not take my eyes off her. Her eyes, a little too wide, were gray like her mother's, but lively; her nose

hooked toward a strong, cleft chin, and after Stockwell corralled Mr.
Dryfus into the parlor with the men, she turned that chin away from
us and back to her purpose.

"You must. You simply must speak with him, Mama!"

Mrs. Stockwell, leaving Mama and me standing there, gave an
order to the maid, who bobbed away.

"Aunty will care for me, Mama," Georgiana persisted. "You know
she will care for me. And Paris! And to study painting! You did.
Aunty said you were exquisitely talented, and you know she does
not give compliments." She adopted the tone and affectation of the
phantom aunt. "'May Ann was divine, exquisite!'"

In spite of herself, Mrs. Stockwell smiled and Georgiana kissed
her on the cheek. "Oh, Mama. Thank you, Mama!" and disappeared
up the staircase as the maid returned with a ghastly gray shawl.

Mrs. Stockwell turned back to Mama. "Would you like a wrap?"
she asked, though this time it was not a question.

She led us up the stairs to the first door on the right, and as she
opened the door, voices inside softened. Directly, Mama and I faced
four women conspiring around a vanity mirror, each of them, like
Mrs. Stockwell and her daughter, trussed to the neck in cloth. Gas
lamps threw yellow light on their expectant faces and dark shadows
on the brown Brussels carpet. There were two other vanity mirrors,
three armchairs, and a green horsehair couch monopolized by gray,
tasseled pillows and five lady's hats exclusively and evenly placed.

Mama had no hat. The wrap hung loose around her shoulders. A
door slammed below; skirts jostled.

Really, I had no idea what Mama would do—she was stronger
than she looked, and ferocious. She'd once cut a backroom man
deep with a knife she kept under the bed; never did say why. I
wanted her to do something now. Say something. From the shadows

of the doorway, I could see faces amused, some pitying, all pinning her with that vicious civility against which girls and women are so vulnerable. After all, there was no clear grievance to redress, nothing so obvious as a gauntlet thrown, nothing against which to retaliate. Still, I felt like ripping the curtains off the wall and jumping on the chintz armchairs; but both of us stood, accepting each introduction with the grateful humiliation of beggars accepting alms. Mrs. Harvey Morrison, Mrs. Joshua Bennett, Mrs. Nicolas Walsh, Mrs. Ashfield Bender.

"And Mrs. Smith, of course," said Mrs. Stockwell of another woman who stood apart from the rest, next to a long sash window. "My cousin."

Mrs. Smith's nose perked at its tip, and her eyes, beneath feather-thin brows, were vaguely Oriental. She grasped Mama's large hands between her own tiny fingers, and the intimacy of the gesture sent a ripple through the room.

"My dear Mrs. Dryfus. I am ashamed to admit that we have not yet met. Susana Mobile Smith. We are neighbors, nearly. I own the dress shop on Seventh Street—Elegant Attire." With her little hands, she framed the words in midair. "I've customers all the way from Saint Louis and am proficient in all the latest French styles. Sadly," she said with more judgment than sadness, "one finds little use for these skills outside the cities. But my, your lacework is exquisite. Really, May Ann, have you ever seen the like?"

Mrs. Stockwell had not.

Mrs. Smith gave Mama a moment to become grateful or impressed, then leaned in close, winked. "I embarrass my cousin. I believe we have been invited to keep each other company."

"MIND, SHE IS NOT TO be overexcited, and you must guide her to happy thoughts," said Mrs. Stockwell as she led me to her invalid. "Since her nurse left us, I'm afraid she has been especially susceptible to morbid fascinations."

"Where'd the nurse go?" I asked to be polite, though I can't say I much cared and I did not, then, think of the dead woman in the river. I was thinking of Mama alone with those women. Mrs. Stockwell ignored or maybe didn't hear me. Some great sadness or frustration, like the oily tail of heat spouting from the gas lamps, quivered across the pale center of her eyes.

"And you mustn't let her speak of Saint Catherine," she said. "You will not allow it."

She opened a door next to a claw-foot table below a calotype of a thin, staring Quaker woman. Below, voices rose and fell. Inside, a stale, sweet talc-and-sour-milk scent peculiar to infants draped itself over me. It was dark. Only a thin line of light seeped between a crack in the window curtains. When Mrs. Stockwell retreated, closing me into the darkness, I could see nothing beyond the hulking shape of a canopy bed. Then I heard a high, breathless voice.

"I have been waiting."

I might have believed the bedclothes had spoken, but as my eyes adjusted I saw a slight presence tugging herself upright. Huge eyes blinked from a narrow, ghostly face.

"No, please don't go." I had not moved. "Close the door." The door was closed. The voice, barely a whisper, carried a barbed authority that made me bristle.

"I have been waiting. Are you an angel? Were you sent for me? Thank you, Saint Catherine, for sending me an angel to strengthen and beautify my will."

I said nothing. Her Mama did not wish her to speak of this Saint

Catherine person, but had said nothing about speaking to her. Plus, Hanley had told me that Mr. Stockwell could hear the voice of God, so such things might be normal in this house. The sash window seemed large enough to conceal a whole choir of veiled saints, and already the room felt crowded from the presence of two girlish bodies.

"Come closer. Closer." I approached and the girl's cold hand gripped my wrist with far more strength than I imagined possible. I sprang away, and she draped herself moaning over the side of the bed.

"Why would you do that? You are *not* my angel. And, oh! I have been waiting. Waiting . . ."

"Your Mama brought me." I remained out of reach of all but those wide, woeful eyes, staring with the hardness her grip had revealed before.

"Never mind." She patted the bedclothes smooth. "Then we shall be special bosom friends, shall we? And you shall mourn me at my death."

She appeared inordinately pleased at the prospect.

At first the stagnant air and darkness made the room close as a cave. Now objects began to fix themselves in place. A curio cabinet filled with wooden figurines and bric-a-brac took shape. From three descending shelves, an audience of porcelain dolls looked on. A coal fire smoldered in the hearth. From the rocking horse and the infant's cradle, this must have been the nursery, though I suspected, in spite of the diminished voice and frame, she was only a year my junior, if that. Above the bed was a framed photograph of an infant in a coffin, dressed in white with white flowers in his hair.

"My brother, Melborn Abernathy Stockwell III. This is my new friend, Mel," she said to the photograph. "My name is Abigail. Abigail Jane. A plain, plain name. Don't you think?"

My name, apparently, was of no consequence to her.

"Yes." I said. "Terribly boring."

"Oh! You don't *really* think so? Well!" Healthy color seized her cheeks. "Then I think you're ugly. I wasn't going to say anything, but you've been so rude about my name, I feel you have given me no choice. And your dress is rags, and that atrocious bonnet. It only makes you"—she paused—"conspicuous. Well?"

"Well what?"

"Aren't you going to apologize?"

I would as soon have pounded her as apologized, but held back for the baffled injury welling in her eyes. She was the first to look away. I was the first to speak.

"Are you hungry?" I asked. "You want to eat?"

"I'm fasting for purity," she replied, "but I'll watch you."

"I ALWAYS FEEL I'M WATCHING a play, or maybe a puppet show," said Abigail. We returned from the kitchen by way of the servants' staircase and sat spying on the dining room through the balusters, reconciled as well as we would ever be and full to the point of delirium. For someone who was fasting, Abigail had eaten an impressive amount of lamb.

"If I squint my eyes like this," she said, "I can see the strings. Try it."

I *could* see them. Strings of light trailing from the gas chandelier tugged the cuffs and sleeves of diners, governing their movements. Mama's puppeteer was clumsy, untrained. She kept shrugging the wrap back into place; her hands hovered unsure over the baffling assortment of utensils. Mr. Dryfus's puppeteer was not much better; he could not, without building potato levies, prevent his meat from bleeding into his greens—an effort that annoyed Mrs. Stockwell but clearly entertained Mrs. Smith, the only lady at the table, besides Georgiana, without a spouse. A woman in pearls complained of poor attendance at the Auxiliary luncheon. They went on about taxes and flooding and Ulysses S. Grant. Talk which mostly bored me, but I had no wish to return to the nursery. Abigail slipped her head between the baluster slats and propped her chin on the step. I did the same. Mr. Stockwell, leaning in the direction of Mr. Dryfus, said, "Sorry?"

I hadn't heard his question or Mr. Dryfus's reply, but Stockwell blinked as if poked, and a hush fell over the table.

"Of course I forgot, Mr. Dryfus," said Stockwell, "that you do have a certain *stake* in maintaining Miss Rose's approval, am I right? Which in my mind is no excuse, no moral excuse for allowing her to continue these sordid extravaganzas, these . . ."

"Soirees." The word slipped from Georgiana's lips. Her mother gave her a look. All other conversations were cleared to the side with the dinner plates.

"Last month," said Mr. Stockwell, "She hosted a troop of singing gypsies from New Orleans."

Mr. Dryfus made no comment.

"They danced upon the table!"

"Had the meal first been cleared?" asked Mr. Dryfus.

Mrs. Smith laughed out loud, but neither Dryfus's tone nor posture had changed, and the rest seemed unsure if the statement was a joke. I wouldn't have thought him capable.

"Am I to understand, then . . ." said Mr. Stockwell, co-opting the whole party in his next sweeping gesture. "Are *we* to understand that you condone even her most recent charade at the voting booth? Philanthropy does not give one license to mock the—"

"Perhaps," Mrs. Smith interjected. Forks clinked on small dishes of cream cake. "Perhaps she was making a point. A political statement."

"I would like some coffee," said Mrs. Stockwell. "Susana," she said pointedly. "Will you take coffee?"

"Political statement?" Stockwell's chuckle carried no trace of amusement. He raised his chin and voice. "She wishes to . . . to agitate. The prodigal daughter returned, throwing money around to win favors—and whose money, I'd like to know—influencing weaker minds in the name of some foreign," he said, wiping each word from the air, "radical, free-loving, European . . ."

Mrs. Stockwell called for the coffee.

"Mr. Stockwell," said Mr. Dryfus. "You speak as though I condoned Miss Rose's *extravagances*, about which, I must say, I have little opinion at all. I'll grant you, her sense of moderation leaves something to be desired."

Stockwell made to speak.

"But," said Mr. Dryfus, "she pays for the flyers and the ads she takes in the *Register*, just as you pay for yours. Surely you do not believe I have the luxury of turning away paid advertisements." He hesitated, staring at the bloody meat on his plate. "That is the hidden object of your *hospitality*, is it not?" The accusation stopped every mouth, and still Mr. Dryfus continued. "That I might pull her ads because they might offend a few readers who were never obligated to read what so offended them, or to attend any gathering they determine damaging to the moral character? As I have said before, I should hope a moral person would be able to discern what is and is not damaging to the character. With training, even the depraved can improve his natural propensities and overcome, to an extent, his shortcom—"

"It's the extent which concerns me, Mr. Dryfus!"

"Who is to judge *for* them then?" And then Mr. Dryfus did another extraordinary thing. He stood. Eyes followed him, and by sheer elevation—he was quite a tall man—his voice gained an edge I'd never heard before. "You, Melborn? The courts?" He looked about. "The committee?"

"If the Church cannot!"

Maybe it was embarrassment or holy fear that moved her, but at her husband's statement, Mrs. Stockwell raised her eyes from the table and found us watching from above. Her exclamation pulled all faces upward. Abigail plucked her head through the balusters and slipped away.

I was stuck.

My ears, having slipped so easily through the wooden slats, got stuck in the rungs, leaving my poor head exposed to the shocked and fascinated gazes below. The puppet strings had snapped! I had become the show. I struggled like a trapped animal. Mama stood. Mr. Dryfus, already standing, turned my direction. My cheeks blazed, my eyes blurred with tears. After what seemed like an hour, I felt a small hand soft between my shoulder blades.

"Oh dear, now, easy now. Shhh. I don't know, Rebecca. We may have to cut her out."

"Be still, Madelyn!" hissed Mama.

"Unless . . . Tilt your head, dear." Mrs. Smith, easing a satin handkerchief around my forehead and over my ears, slipped me through the slats, explaining as she did that I should not be embarrassed, which, of course, made the embarrassment worse. Probably I was not long on their minds. My shame merely shattered conflict into laughter, but as the party dispersed, ladies to the drawing room, men to the parlor, I imagined they were laughing at me and felt a rage so exhausting that by the time I was free, it had burnt itself into sour paste in my mouth.

Mrs. Stockwell ushered me back to her youngest daughter's side before we departed. "My darling little invalid," she said and kissed Abigail's cheek. The transformation was remarkable. Abigail's every muscle had relinquished vitality and strength. "Make her come back, Mummy," she said, but I slipped out the door and down the stairs in time to hear Mr. Stockwell's final words to Mr. Dryfus in the foyer.

"... you may be hard pressed, Mr. Dryfus, if the good members of the committee were forced to withdraw their patronage from your shop."

Of course, at the time, my humiliation was still too raw to comprehend this threat, much less to pity Mama her failure with the ladies. But now I know. I know that wars are fought over the control of words and fashions and manners, and that Mr. Dryfus, and Mama too, whether she understood it or not, had chosen a side.

"Mrs. Dryfus?" said Mr. Dryfus, limping behind Mama up the walk. "Please. You mustn't worry yourself. Stockwell depends upon the German vote. He would not take his business to the *Democrat*. Rebecca."

Mama stopped. Mr. Dryfus lingered a step behind her, his breath bridging the space between them. Freezing fog had crept from the river; every small sound crackled through the cold. When they walked on, they walked together.

"Well," came a voice behind me. I turned to find Mrs. Smith picking her way down the frozen pavement. She threw her arm and shawl around my shoulders. "That was very nearly an enjoyable evening."

1 1

Mr. Dryfus was not wrong, exactly. After the disastrous dinner party, Mr. Stockwell and the Sin Society did not take their business to the *Democrat*. Instead, they bought the other paper in town, the *Sentinel*, and hired their own editor. So when Mrs. Smith offered to pay Mama on commission for her fancy work and to teach her dressmaking besides, Mr. Dryfus had little choice but to agree.

"As long," he said, "as your labors do not threaten your condition," which was becoming rapidly, a little too rapidly, apparent—a fact that if Dryfus noticed, he ignored.

Only Clara's response, on the night Mama told Mr. Dryfus about the baby, had been suspect. The incessant shake of her head stilled; she placed her hand firmly on Mama's belly and from the look on her face, must have known. Still she said nothing, because Mr. Dryfus, he had been stricken at the news with a helpless, hope-filled smile, which ever after seemed to come upon him like a yawn or sneezing fit, tipping his mustache to reveal a set of crooked teeth, white as I'd ever seen.

I couldn't help it, I liked him better for it.

For the baby's benefit, Mr. Dryfus imposed upon Mama mandates and prohibitions against anything that might *over-excite the child's animal organs*. "A mother alone——" said Mr. Dryfus, who had been reading a great deal on the subject, "her thoughts, her diet, her habits and experiences—endows or burdens the unborn child with each of its defining characteristics."

Once, he reported, a pregnant woman had unwisely visited a menagerie, where a monkey leaped upon her shoulders. As a result, the child had been born with a small prehensile tail and a predilection for climbing. Another woman, craving the last cherries of the season, reached in vain for fruit beyond her grasp, and the unfulfilled longing caused cherry blotches to appear above her child's elbow.

"Can you recall?" Mr. Dryfus asked Mama. "Did your mother subject herself to any shocks or immoderate longings before your sister's birth? Did she desire tomatoes, apples, radishes?"

"Mama hates radishes," I chimed.

"Hated." Mama kicked me under the table. "She hated radishes. So do I."

Undermining Mr. Dryfus's efforts was a cohort of German women from Clara's church, who provided Mama a daily ration of foods guaranteed to excite the animal organs: sausages, meat pies, sweetbreads, which I happily sampled. This offering also entitled them, it seemed, to lay their hands on Mama's belly and subject her to their own onslaught of judgment and advice. Each night, while Mama busied herself with fancy work, Mr. Dryfus read Goethe, Kant, and Spinoza aloud in German, asking no more than Mama's presence, and by her presence, his child's. If he posed philosophical questions, he posed them generally, demanding no response from either of us, as if anticipating conversations he would one day have with his child.

He wasn't talking to Mama any more than the German ladies

were feeding her. He was talking to his baby, and though I could tell he was trying to remain scientific and serious about the whole development, some nights when the window frosted white and the lamp burned low, I could see in his eyes fearsome emotions clear as the telegraph man's dots and dashes, if you knew what to look for.

He never managed to show Mama anything more than a growing regard. But I suppose he felt it safe to love the baby inside her; he thought he was loving part of himself.

What Mama thought about all these attentions, I can't say. She had more practice guarding herself than Mr. Dryfus. I have more pity now, but no more understanding than I did at thirteen, watching her bent over her tatting, hiding all she thought and felt behind that shield of industry. As her belly grew, her silence took on a new authority, which frightened and pulled me closer. I found myself touching her shoulders, her skirt, her forearm, whenever I could. Never her belly, though that was what enthralled me. The belly, the baby between us. I'd never felt so drawn to her or so trapped and lonely in my life.

That is, until the baby came.

Karl Johan Dryfus, born on the twenty-fourth of May, by most accounts two months early, was big, unblemished, orange as a pumpkin. "You're a lucky woman," Mrs. Smith told Mama after it was over. "The first one is usually much harder." From the noises coming out of Mama, it sounded hard enough to me. Banished to the kitchen, I kept the water boiling, the rags fresh, and worked up a good frothing hate for Mr. Dryfus, who sat at the table, pale as a cabbage; wasn't even his doing, after all. I called the baby Little John, out of spite, I guess, but the name stuck. Only Mama called him Karl. He would look nothing like her. Any resemblance to Mr. Dryfus was declared only with great imagination, but no one, least of all Clara, seemed inclined to point this out. Within a month, Mr. Dryfus changed the sign on his shop door to read LYMAN DRYFUS AND SON. That fearful joy on his face? That was, I knew, what love looked like.

And I could see, clear as anything, Mama loved the baby too.

It was the way she held him as he suckled, aware of nothing else in the room, the way she watched him sleeping. And God help me, I imagined terrible things: Little John falling on his head. Little John, blue faced, floating in the river. Other times, holding him soft against me, I wished . . . Well, I wished Mr. Dryfus *was* Little John's daddy. Or that Mama had not told me any different. Then I could believe there was such a thing as a family. Could imagine my father, Landis Wilcox, in a gray peacoat, carrying me around in the crook of *his* arm, loving me unreasonably. What if Mr. Dryfus had been my father? Clara my grandmother? William my beloved? This is what I did each night in the attic, imagine for myself some other past. Wasn't this what Mama had done, after all? Tie the loose scraps of her life into an acceptable reality?

It didn't help that we'd had no word from William. This fact weighed heaviest on Clara, I think, but I missed him too, and especially the refuge of the photo shop. Each night in my scrapbook, I composed him letters. "Dearest W——, How long and harshly my days pass in your absence!" Inane, flowery nonsense, and imagined his Dear Miss Branch letters to be his response. Sometimes, as William used to, I'd pick interesting faces passing on the street and hold them in my mind as long as I could before the picture blurred away. And if ever the memory of the dead girl, or of William standing above her on the river bank, snuck into my mind, I'd think instead about his lips on my stained hand. "You trust me, don't you?"

✦❦✦

JUNE AND JULY PASSED, A busy, humid blur. August finally raised its sweaty haunches off the town and lumbered away around the river bend; the floodwaters settled; there was a bite to the air again. Hanley and I sat as we had all summer, in the composition room with the window wide, sorting type from the week's printing into cabinets.

That is, I sorted type. Hanley, long legs propped on the Washington Press, was reading aloud week-old news about Indian wars and going on about colonel this and general that, when the shop bell jangled. A handsome young gentleman—a real dandy from the look of him: fob watch, a fancy gray vest, and matching top hat—peered through the doorway. He blinked in the window glare. I could smell the Macassar oil that slicked his hair, sure as I could see his wedge nose jutting over his wide, clean-shaven jaw.

"You get any bigger, Hanley," he said, "the calvary have to put a saddle on you. What, Maddy?" He took his hat in hand. "Have I changed so much?"

"Wilhelm?" Clara's voice, crackling down the hallway, saved me from a response, but not from the shock at the sight of him. At the sight of him so transformed. Clara charged in, shuffled him into a hug, thrust him away again, ran a palsied hand down his cheek. "*Mein Gott,*Wilhelm!" Then she pulled him with her into the kitchen.

"Maddy," said Hanley. "Maddy, come on," and bounded after them. Little John's cries announced Mama's return from the dress shop, and when finally my legs moved me to the kitchen, I saw that Mrs. Smith, the dressmaker, had accompanied her.

"Why, Mr. Stark," she said. Hanley fetched beer from the larder. Clara checked her stew. "Wait until the young ladies get a look at you."

The prospect did not please me.

Mrs. Smith, fashionable but oddly proportioned, had a wide

bottom and short legs that in any other woman would have looked
out of agreement with such a slender neck and arms; instead they
seemed to anchor her and give weight to her observations and opinions, of which she had a great many. There was no longer a Mr.
Smith, but that didn't mean she was a war widow, as I first thought.
Two months after the war ended, her husband, a lieutenant in the
Missouri regulars, got himself shot dead in a duel on Smallpox
Island, over another man's wife. So she sold his tailoring business
in Saint Louis, cashed in his investments, and bought the dress
shop in Reliance. Hanley told me this, but it was no secret, having been in all the papers, much to the dismay of her cousin, Mrs.
Stockwell. She would have had to go much farther than Reliance
if she wanted to be shed of the gossip, and really I'm not sure she
did, for it lent her a kind of immunity from the usual standards and
judgments. Mama, I knew, in her own guarded way, appreciated her
frank outspoken generosity. Most of the time, I did, too.

Mrs. Smith looked back at me, a question on her face, and
motioned to an open chair as they all sat down. I stayed put
against the wall, staring a hole in the back of William's combed
head as he flattered Clara, admired Mama and Little John, teased
Hanley. I'm not sure if, for all my romantic imaginings, I ever
really expected him to come back. Now here he was: no beard,
no scars on his face. No blemishes of any kind. His clothing and
manner all wrong, too tidy; perfectly trimmed to please. He'd
been to Saint Louis and New Orleans and back again and went
on about the photos he'd taken, the flip books he'd made, and the
galleries he'd seen, while I pressed the hand he'd kissed against
the charm hidden beneath my blouse and burrowed like a little
blind beetle into my despondency.

The shop bell rang; I hardly heard it, and was surprised to look up and find him looking at me. "What do you think about that, Maddy?" William asked.

But by the time his acknowledgment registered, William's smile dried up. His eyes skirted mine. They fell on Mr. Dryfus, who had emerged stiffly from the darkened hallway. Mrs. Smith, sitting up, looked with intrigued confusion between the two men.

"You're not staying," said Mr. Dryfus.

"Hello, Lyman," said William.

"You do not write or send word of yourself. Have you any idea how worried Mutti has been?"

"Lyman," Clara pleaded, stepping forward.

"No," said William. He stood, but when he did, his manner cracked; stained black fingers raked his face, and in that brief action, I saw him again. My William, broken and struggling with himself. What a selfish relief I felt!

"I mean yes," he said, recovering. "You're right. You're right, Lyman. I was . . . I had to . . ." Then, giving up on an explanation, "I'm sorry."

This was not the response any of us, least of all Mr. Dryfus, expected. His mouth opened, closed.

"I'm sorry, Mutti." William took Clara's hands in his own. "I won't be staying here, but I will be returning to Reliance, to my shop, for a while at least. I have taken a room at Madrigel's on Fifth Street and established a kind of, well, an agreement with Miss Rose that may in time prove"—here, oddly, he looked at Mrs. Smith—"fertile?"

Mrs. Smith did not respond. Little John, lurching in Mama's arms toward Mr. Dryfus, gave a frustrated squall.

"Agreement?" asked Mr. Dryfus.

"A patronage, of sorts," William said vaguely. "After she comes into her inheritance. Fitting, don't you think?" Then, to the question on

Mrs. Smith's face. "Old Man Werner was a great patron of my mother's work," he said.

"You think he plans to leave her something?" asked Mr. Dryfus.

"I don't know," William, shrugged. "But it won't hurt to be of use."

"Whose money is she spending now?" asked Mrs. Smith.

Hanley grinned. "Probably the dead husbands'."

"Is that what they're saying?" asked William.

"What aren't they saying?" said Hanley. "If it isn't the weather, it's Miss Rose."

"Ever since she tried to vote," said Mrs. Smith.

"Well, that was her purpose, was it not?" said Mr. Dryfus.

"And why can't the vote have been her purpose?" Mrs. Smith demanded. "Anyway, I think she encourages rumors. The more people believe about her, the less they will know."

"What do you know about her, William?" asked Hanley.

"Not much. As much as she wants. But one of us might know more soon." William, then all of them, looked at me.

"Maddy?" Hanley laughed. William was not joking.

"Miss Rose is looking for a girl. I recommended Maddy."

"Me?"

Mama, watching, listening to all this, stood up. "A girl for what?" She handed Little John to Mr. Dryfus. "A girl for what?" she repeated.

William pulled his eyes from the spectacle of Mr. Dryfus and the baby. "Well, I don't know exactly." He turned, considered me, a muted conspiratorial smile on his lips. "She will have to go and see."

I followed him to the shop front, the gravity of this last development not nearly so affecting as the knowledge that he had been thinking of me. Even far away in the city. Even with his gentleman's manners and costume, he'd been thinking of me. I didn't care if anything came out of meeting Miss Rose, suspected nothing would. William had been thinking of me.

"William. William, I've never said anything about . . . I'll never—"

"I know, my apparition." He reached over my head for his jacket on the rack. "I was right about you, what I told Miss Rose. You are . . ."

"What?"

Hanley lumbered down the hallway toward the composition room, watching us. William leaned close, his bare face full of sharp and unfamiliar angles. "Discreet," he whispered.

12

Two days later, face scrubbed, hands clean, Mama's best dress sagging in all the wrong places, I set out to meet Miss Rose at the Werner Manor. William would not, as I had hoped, accompany me, the only advantage I could see in this venture, for I was sure the interview would end with a quick and final dismissal.

Even so, it was a welcome novelty to leave the shop at that hour and step out into the new-washed morning. The glassworks whistle blew at ten minutes to the hour; shop boys scooted to their posts. Men in top hats met in twos and threes like a gathering choir on the courthouse steps. Still, everything was hushed; the fog over the river held even bird calls close as secrets until the church bells clanged nine, and all at once men and birds seemed to fully rouse themselves to the day.

Only after the pavement ended and houses thinned beyond Millionaire's Row did I become appropriately nervous about where I was going. By the time Tenth Street branched east to Godfrey and I stood on the cusp of a plunging drive attended by a trim regiment of cypress, mice were doing flips in my stomach.

Miss Rose had come to Reliance from New York City, a place so far away and foreign to my experience, it might as well have been another country. That she had been an actress and then a theater manager no one disputed—if rumors were true, she was planning a theater in town by the docks, in her father's abandoned warehouse—but no one seemed to agree just what this implied about her character or her proper regard. I'd seen her about town plenty that year. That is, I'd seen her plumed hats and gaudy dresses from a distance, her profile behind the crepe curtains of her hansom. Her presence lingered like a scent; her name lingered, certainly. Shop owners happily cataloged whatever she bought. On the strength of one such report, Mrs. Smith sold her entire stock of dyed hat plumes. She was a radical, a nuisance, a countess, a blessing, a madam, a suffragette. All of these things, and none of them. Hanley told me she'd been married three times. "Rich men all," he said.

"Then why is she still Miss Rose?"

Hanley shrugged. "Just what she calls herself. The last man was as old as her father, kicked the bucket a month after the wedding. Another is in with the loonies on Blackwell's Island."

"And the other one?"

Hanley didn't know, but whatever evil pleasure he took in frightening me soon fell away. "Oh, Maddy. It's all talk, you know. I'm sure you'll probably be fine."

But this reassurance and every other thought swept from my head when the cypress drive opened to a tangle of roses and browning topiary. On the ridge below sat an eight-sided manor, three stories tall, ringed with porches and topped with what looked like a little glass house. From up there, it reminded me of a jewelry box I'd seen once on the shelf of Dixon White's Dry Goods back in Susanville. Gave myself shivers imagining Dixon White's grubby hands reaching over the sycamore grove, and lifting its roof straight from its walls.

As I approached, I heard voices, laughter, someone chopping wood. In the courtyard, the most extravagant turkey I'd ever seen thrust its cobalt chest around the porch, and with a bob of its tonsure dismissed the universe with the same impressive indifference with which the butler greeted me at the door.

"Never mind, Robert."

The butler stepped aside and a finely dressed young lady, about my age, framed herself in the doorway. Curls and thick, dark braids wound about her head, but it was her contemptuous expression, not to mention her perfect complexion, that rendered me inferior.

Without a word, she led me through a marble foyer that opened to a vaulted gallery cored like an apple by a spiral staircase and drenched in light spilling from the glassed cupola. Servants bustled about, sweeping floors and dusting statues—little ones on ledges and big ones so lifelike and numerous, I mistook them at first for a still and silent crowd.

"That's a samurai helmet," the young lady said, for I had stopped, to regain my bearings, before a curious black hat with winglike flaps, displayed at the base of the staircase. "Ah. Don't touch!"

"I wasn't—"

"It's Japanese," the young lady said.

"Oh."

"From Tokyo. That's in Japan. Women there paint their faces white and their lips red and they act out fabulous dramas without saying a word. *You* don't know where Japan is, *do* you?"

I ignored the question, and her tone. "Well, what's it do?" I asked instead, then wished I hadn't.

"Do? It doesn't *do* anything. Miss Rose loves to collect beautiful things," she said, lips pinching into a smirk. "And oddities."

I might have pounded that smirk right off her face, except she was climbing again, casting behind her a long list of shalts and shalt nots. I was to say, "Yes, Miss Rose," never "No." No one said *no* to Miss Rose.

As we reached the second floor, a sound, much like a labored human moan, tumbled down from the third, but neither the young lady, her white hand gripping the bronze handle of a heavy wooden door, nor the servant, dusting the baluster, paid any notice. The young lady opened the door and ushered me inside. Then, telling me to stay put, she crossed the great carpeted room and stepped out onto a balcony.

Even if she hadn't ordered me to wait there, I'm not sure I could have moved, for that room was a wonder of curiosities: paintings, sculptures, trinkets. A little statue of a hugely pregnant woman with a trunk, legs, but no head sat on the mantle to my right. What froze my legs in place, however, were the mirrors.

Mirrors everywhere, of every shape and size. Mirrors framed on the wall, balanced on stands, propped behind a broad, polished desk. Mirrors winking across the room at one another. I could not look anywhere without seeing myself and might have fled, except that with a breeze through the open balcony door, came the enormous figure of a woman in a blue-gray checkered gown, along with a sharp, sweet scent. Rosewater. Lavender.

I watched, mesmerized, as she ducked beneath the door frame, easing those caged skirts and layered flounces over the threshold. The young lady followed, then a slouching man in a very nice suit.

"But this scheme of yours," the man was saying, wiping his bald head with a handkerchief. "Are you in earnest, or making a point?"

"Does it matter?" Miss Rose replied. The girl eyed me, but remained a shadow behind Miss Rose.

"Yes," said the man. "Yes, I'd say it does."

"Fine. In earnest and making a point. Mrs. French says a woman would be perfectly within her rights to run, even if she was not allowed to vote."

"She was making a point, I think, Rose, about the absurdity of—" he paused. "I really do not think she intended anyone to act upon her words."

Miss Rose laughed. "Well, that is where Mrs. French and I differ. I have never believed words alone possess the power to change anything."

The man tucked his handkerchief in his breast pocket.

"Aldus," said Miss Rose. "You cannot doubt that I came here to care for my father. And I would have come even if my fortunes had not—"

"Of course," said Aldus.

"But one cannot bear complacency. One cannot, after the life I have lived, retire into obscurity and abandon causes to which I have been so long conscripted. And this town needs . . ."

"What?" asked the man, smiling.

"Me." She took him by the arm. "Dear, dear Aldus. Don't think I don't adore your advice."

"Huh." He kissed her cheek in a baffled, brotherly way. "Even if you never heed it."

"Yes," she said and, looking up, spotted me. They said their goodbyes. Miss Rose asked him to remember her in New York to a very long list of people. And then he was gone, and for the first time I felt the full weight of Miss Rose's attention.

"Violet?" Without taking her eyes from me, she rested a hand on the pretty girl's shoulder. "My little ornament," she said into the girl's ear, "go fetch Mrs. French from her studies."

The girl left. Twin clocks on the fireplace mantle struck the

quarter hour. "Come here," Miss Rose commanded in the thin ringing that followed, but I felt rooted in place by a strange, stone weight
of anticipation, or dread, or both.

"Closer, girl. Come closer!" she said.

Rosewater and lavender. I tried to close my senses to all but the
smell, yet I could feel Miss Rose's eyes like a touch; and then a touch,
kid gloves across my stained left cheek. I jerked away and might have
run, except that her voice and manner abruptly changed. She turned
from me to scrutinize herself in a three-paned vanity mirror behind
the desk. "My dear, my dear," she said.

Not just the woman, but that great abundance of cloth—all those
flounces, pleats, and gathers—reflected, reflected, and reflected again
to dizzying effect in that three-paned mirror. I took hold of an armchair to steady myself; she placed a hand to her curls much as a man
might adjust his hat. She was older than I thought a Miss should be
(how old, I couldn't say) and more striking than beautiful, with light,
widely spaced eyes, knobby cheekbones, and a long, narrow nose. It's
hard to describe the disorienting effect she had on me, but there, in
her presence, all the rumors I had heard became flat as paper dolls
and I felt an overwhelming urge to please her.

"Your sister"—she caught my eye in the leftmost mirror—"is a
beautiful woman."

I had nothing to say to this and looked away.

"I have always liked the shape of my nose. How would you . . . ?
Look at me. How would you document such a feature? I once paid
a girl to draw my nose to size. The result I framed and placed by
my bedside." Again she caught my eye in the mirror. "One must
remind oneself of one's small perfections." She turned to face me.
"Can you draw?"

"No."

"Have you tried?"

"No."

"Then your answer is premature, is it not?" She circled me, wrapping me in her scent and the rustle of cloth. My knees were shaking. I stared straight ahead at the window curtains. "Our Mr. Dryfus believes that character is foretold in the features. Do you agree this is the case?"

"He's writing a book about it." He had been, too, every day since May. A big book with a very long title.

"And that makes him right?"

"Don't know."

"*I* don't know," she corrected me. "I have a higher opinion of Mr. Dryfus than he might think. He is a man who understands but refuses to become a slave to popular opinion. *Men* gain respect for such resolve."

A thump above our heads and what sounded again like a high human moan; I know Miss Rose heard it too. Her head angled to the ceiling, but her eyes remained on me. "You *can* read?"

"Yes."

She handed me a thick leather volume from her desk; the hastily cut pages, serrated and torn, made the strict columns of verse inside all the more intimidating. "Well? Read."

I did, but with no thought to meaning or inflection, intent only on touching each word correctly.

"No! No. No!" She revised the line in a trembling alto that seemed to rise with great force from somewhere near her liver. "'Of bodies chang'd to various forms, I sing: Ye Gods, from whom these miracles did spring!'"

My second attempt deteriorated into stutters and stammers.

"Enough. Good enough. Viii-oh-let!"

Violet composed herself in the doorway. Behind Violet stood a wiry, gray-headed woman, wearing the first pair of bloomers I'd ever seen.

"Mrs. French! I have discovered a girl who may suit our needs," said Miss Rose as if she'd found me wandering the wilds. Holding me by the shoulders, she pushed me toward the other woman, who fixed oculars to her nose only to stare over the wire rims.

"Introduce yourself," said Miss Rose.

"Madelyn."

"Speak, my dear, as though you mean to be heard. You are not meek, are you Madelyn? You must not be meek for the designs we have for you."

Violet chortled behind her hand and I all but snarled at her.

"Good! Good girl!" said Miss Rose. "I knew I had seen boldness behind that mask of yours. Janus-faced little fiend, are you not?" And then turning from me. "What do you think, Mrs. French? William spoke well of her"—she paused—"intelligence."

The housekeeper appeared behind Violet in the doorway. "Miss? Sorry to bother, Miss, but the Master—" Miss Rose silenced her with one raised finger. Mrs. French considered me.

I glared down at the carpet, could feel my heartbeat in my temple, and when finally I dared to look up again, found Mrs. French's eyes behind those oculars, pinched to a discriminating half smile. "She may do," said Mrs. French.

WHEN DOT DIED, I HAD no idea how completely the circumstances of my life would change. For weeks I wallowed in grief and ignored, as best I could, the dread that descends when the unknown imposes upon the familiar. That afternoon, as I stood with Mama in the print shop study, listening to Mr. Dryfus read the terms of my engagement, I was still only vaguely aware that another such crisis was upon me.

"What's it mean?" Mama said. "'Exchange for services rendered.'"

"It means," said Mr. Dryfus. "To receive one thing for doing another. Miss Rose wishes Madelyn to sit with Old Man Werner and read to him and, *assist the nurse as need arises.*" He looked skeptically at me. "In exchange, she will receive an education."

Mama distrusted that word. To Mama, education was a fancy house she'd never been invited into. Mr. Dryfus bit his pipe, looked back and forth between us, but kept his thoughts to himself.

"No," said Mama finally. She turned to Mr. Dryfus. "No. I say I need her here, with me. With the baby. No. I say they can't have her."

"Well, I'm afraid," said Mr. Dryfus, "I'm afraid this is not your decision. Or mine." He folded the letter and slid it over the desk to me. "Madelyn?"

13

The truth is, if Mama had not been so quick to say no, I would not have been so quick to say yes. I answered as much against her as for myself, and we both knew it.

She followed me from the study to the base of the stairs, sparing not a backward glance for Mr. Dryfus calling her name. "You leaving me is what you're doing. Leaving me to be a servant in a rich lady's house."

I had not expected a quaver in her voice. It stopped my breath. "Not a servant. You're just. You're jealous," I said, regaining myself. "You're jealous because Miss Rose is going to make me educated."

And then for spite, I guess, because we both knew this promise had not been made. "She's going to make a *lady* out of me."

Mama said nothing. I looked up, half-expecting a cuff, but found instead a look of thoughtful disgust on her face. "This about William. That it?" she said.

Hanley, holding a grinning Little John under one arm like a sack of potatoes, stepped through the kitchen doorway. Mama didn't care who heard her. "You're doing this to impress William?" And then bending close, grabbing hold of my arm. "Don't be a goddamn fool, Madelyn."

"Doing what, Maddy?" asked Hanley. "What is she doing?"

"Let go of me, Rebecca." I said, yanked my arm free and ran up the stairs.

After that I had no choice but to appear eager and confident when I was anything but, and when the anger burned off, well, I felt like a fool. What had I said yes to, exactly? I hadn't even met Old Man Werner. And what if—What if I did not "do?" Nothing of Mrs. French's examination, carried out in the manor library the hour before I returned to the print shop, suggested I would; that she had not rescinded her qualified sanction seemed, as I tossed sleepless in my attic room, an even greater mystery than it had at the moment.

Apparently, I didn't know how to hold a pen, to sit in a chair, to pronounce vowels; I had not known what a verb or a noun, much less what a participle was (though it sounded like someone religious in the Bible). I had been unable to pick out Illinois on a map, much less Reliance or Chicago or London or Rome. Dot had taught me to figure some, but I had never painted and never read a score; the only music I knew were bawdy songs backroom men taught me. I had seethed with humiliation, of course; my deficiencies had never been paraded before me so incisively. It bothered me, but not as much as it might have, because by the time Mrs. French finally declared the examination over (thank Jesus and all his many participles), I had had little intention of returning to the manor, William or no.

I still didn't quite believe it when late the next morning Miss Rose's shiny hansom rattled to a stop before the print shop to collect me. What Mama thought of it? I don't know.

Clara kissed me on the forehead, Hanley said good luck, even Mr. Dryfus said goodbye. Mama didn't say a word to me all morning, just stood there with Little John, watching through the print-shop window, her face unreadable and drawn. I tried to make a show of it, but was unsure how to conduct myself. An old Negro driver in fancy livery asked for my trunk, but I had no trunk. Besides the clothes on my back and the charm around my neck, all I had, inside Mama's old carpetbag, was a dress, extra drawers and underthings, rags for my monthlies, and my scrapbook. I'd had the forethought to hide William's "Dear Miss Branch" letters behind a crate in Dryfus's attic, but I couldn't bear to leave my scrapbook and didn't fancy handing the carpetbag over to him. He thought better of taking my hands in his white gloves to help me up, so I climbed up myself and made a point not to look back until the print shop was out of sight. I stared down at my offending hands, instead.

To pass time and to keep my mind dull, I'd been sorting type in the print shop with Hanley, and though I scrubbed them bloody, my fingertips were still ink black; my dress collar too, I discovered, for the first thing Violet said, when again I stood in the marble foyer of the manor was, "Well. Don't you look the little char girl!"

I felt like cutting off my hands, or slapping her face, or running away to the river; better than crying, which I fought the whole way there. From the glare of the gallery, Mrs. Hardrow, the housekeeper, appeared, stepping smartly, a small pale servant in tow.

"There you are, Madelyn. Susan, her bag," she said to the servant already reaching.

"No!" I said, clutching it close, then seeing their faces. "No, thank you. I'll be keeping it."

Miss Hardrow, a stern woman of middle age, had a handsome pockmarked face and large, colorless eyes that gave away—but also, it was clear, missed—nothing. She considered me, then my carpetbag, then she nodded to the servant. "Never mind, Susan. I think, after all,

I should like to show Madelyn where she is to stay. You won't mind, Madelyn, waiting until after luncheon."

I didn't answer. It wasn't a question.

Although the day was overcast, shafts of light through the cupola gleamed on scrubbed marble floors and statues, looming tall above me as I followed Mrs. Hardrow. She walked me through the gallery, past the sweating glass doors of the conservatory, to the library. What, if anything, she knew of the inauspicious hour I'd spent there with Mrs. French the day before, I didn't know. "Wait here," was all she said, not for what or how long, then closed the oak doors behind her, shutting me into relative darkness.

Blood beat in my temple. I must have stood a full minute, tense and listening, for the door to open, I suppose. Instead I heard footsteps in the room above, wind rattling six ceiling-tall windows. Cut-glass lamps danced rainbows over tabletops on which they rested and on the polished wood floor. Yet it was the smell that recalled with unsettling clarity the wonder that arrested me at first sight of this room the day before: pipe smoke, leather, dust.

The smell of books. So many books. More than I'd ever seen, lined up, leather bound, covering two whole walls, floor to ceiling. After Mrs. French began her examination, I became dulled to all but my wounded pride. But my first glimpse of those books then, as now, awakened in me a kind of wonder, a kind of cautious awe.

A movable ladder rested against the far wall. I looked at the closed door behind me, then starting at the ladder, walked the length, thumping my fingers along book spines, and back again. Mr. Dryfus's office shelf (not to mention Hiram Cassidy's satchel) were a pauper's offering next to this. Had that woman, Mrs. French, read each one? Was that why her eyes were poor? My hand came to rest on a title. Just easing it from its place, breaking that rank and file and holding it in my hands, felt so thrillingly reckless, I didn't even open it; instead, I slipped it back and nosed over to a thick volume already open on the table.

It was weighted by something round and silver and shiny. A fob watch, but without a chain, the letters H. F. worn smooth to the touch on the back. I picked it up, and looked at the book, which was heavy with words, but of quite a different character than the one Miss Rose had read aloud. *After the event of marriage, the property of a married woman shall . . .*

"What. Are. You. Doing?" Each word a sentence. I spun to find Violet poised in the doorway. I hadn't heard the door. "What is that?" she said, striding in. "Did you take something?"

"I didn't. I wasn't." The watch was still in my hand. I didn't know what else to do so I put it back on the book. "I was just—"

"If you take anything that is not yours, I will tell Miss Rose and you will go back to where you came from."

She looked at me then as if estimating the level from which I'd come, eyes settling briefly on my carpetbag. Then, with a thin, false smile, she turned and walked out into the brightness. "Come along."

The sweating glass doors of the conservatory were open now. My stomach growled. I could smell cooked meat and see three or four people at luncheon through the glass. Violet went the other way, left at the spiral staircase, before the dining room, and stopped in front of a door made to look like a panel in the wall. The door opened to a narrow service staircase. I climbed down after Violet to a stuffy, dimly lit corridor so contrary in character to the vaulted rooms above, it took me a second to orient myself. Two servants, arms full of linen, hardly glanced at me as they rushed past and didn't say boo to Violet. She greeted no one in the scullery or servants' hall. She spent a sharp word on a young man in a footman's vest, leaning against the kitchen door frame. He looked over his shoulder at her, finished whatever he was saying before moving. Inside, the cook, a short, florid woman with a beaklike nose and wattle chin, looked up from a list she was making at the prep table.

"Whot's this, then?" she squawked. Light seeped through a narrow window, eye level with the ground outside, but the savory smell raised my spirits considerably. A carcass simmered over a shiny black range; three loaves of bread and an apple pie cooled on the sideboard. I'd have pie for supper, thank you, or apples. I'd eat my weight in apples.

The cook stood up. "No, now. Got no time for no mo' of this *help.*" A freckled girl with frizzed red hair, paring apples at the far end of the table, gave the cook a disgusted look. "I'm supposed to be running a kitchen not some kind of wayward home for . . ." She peered closer. "What's the matter with this one? She dumb?"

"I'm not dumb!" The assumption stung more than usual. "And I'm no servant, either."

"Good thing, by the look of you," said the redhead. Violet smirked.

"Alby," said Cook, but was staring hard at me as if expecting I was hiding something under the ugliness that would volunteer itself to her alone. I squared myself, but managed only to glare at her feet. Cook shook her head, gave a little laughing grunt.

"But you're hungry, I guess, and you'll say yes ma'am, no ma'am to the hand that feeds and clothes you. Just like this one." She angled her wattle at Violet. "Huh, but you ain't a servant."

She spun to the oven, pulled out another pie. "Out the way." I stepped aside and she placed the pie on the sideboard next to the other one. It smelled so good, I was ready to call myself a servant or a toad for a bite. Cook shut the oven door with her boot heel, stirred the pot, and turned around shaking her finger at the room at large. "Not a help then you're a hindrance, what I was taught. Be of use in the world, my ma tells me, and play the part the good lord writ for you to play, and I don't complain, do I?"

The redhead looked up, down, bit her lip.

"I carry on. I carry on saying not a word about it, though if I was to say, I would tell that woman, that it'd be kind. It'd be Christian to tell me when I got another mouth I got to feed. Missus got no idea how hard it is to—"

"She's *not* for Miss Rose, Mrs. Nettle," said Violet curtly. "She's to attend the master."

The cook's little mouth closed over whatever it was she was going to say. The redhead's eyes widened with alarm. I glanced between them, then back at Violet whose satisfied expression did nothing to comfort me.

"What's wrong with the master?"

"Well, now," said Mrs. Nettle, with some hesitance.

"It's haunts," said the redhead, leaning forward as though haunts might now be listening. "It's the haunts what visit him."

A bell in a row of bells rang in the hallway. "Violet!" I heard dimly through the floorboards. Violet jerked at the sound and hurried away, more than happy, I'm sure, to leave me in the clutches of this revelation.

"Not a servant, huh," said Mrs. Nettle, watching Violet go, then bade me sit. The redhead scooted closer. Cook frowned but didn't stop her.

"Spirits what told Old Master how to build, where to build this place." She looked about her.

Dot was for spirits, but I was never sure what I believed for myself and what I believed for Dot. Contemplating it at all brought unwelcome thoughts of the dead girl in the river. "I'm not sure I believe in . . ."

"Don't matter, do it?" said Mrs. Nettle. She set a plate of stew before me. "What is, is, whether you believe or not. You, get back to it," she told Alby.

"Well, who are they then?" I asked, my mouth full, "the spirits?"

In my experience, spirits weren't meant to haunt any old stranger for no reason. The redhead sat rigid straight. I stopped chewing, half expected to turn and find a spirit hovering there behind me. But it was only the housekeeper, Mrs. Hardrow, arms crossed, in the door-way. Alby bent to her task with new industry.

"Alby," said Mrs. Hardrow.

"Missus?"

"Alby, I know you have been smoking. If I catch you, you will be dismissed without a reference."

"Yes, Missus."

14

"Call yourself what you wish," said Mrs. Hardrow leading me up the narrow servants' staircase, past the first landing, the keys and bangles she wore on a chain around her waist jangling softly. "So long as you do what you are told and keep your own business. I will not tolerate a wastrel." She paused, glancing back in the darkness, her voice clipped and flat. "Or a thief."

Violet, I thought.

Miss Rose and Mrs. French, she said, carrying on, occupied adjacent rooms on the second floor. Violet kept quarters next to Miss Rose. Most of the servants slept in the carriage house, except for the driver, Cyrus, and his boy, who slept in a loft over the barn and cared for the horses and the garden. Mrs. Nettle, the cook, and Mr. Roberts, the butler, kept rooms a respectable distance apart in the basement. Mrs. Hardrow's quarters were on the third floor, where the old master was kept under the care of Nurse Lipman, with whom I would share the room adjacent the Master's. My days would be divided, though not equally, Hardrow said, between the sickroom and my studies, with reasonable time set aside for exercise and leisure. The balance would be determined by the old man's health and disposition, did I understand?

She pushed through a service door to the third landing. White
light poured through the glassed cupola. It took a moment for my
eyes to adjust, and when they did, I saw a grim and shabby sister of the
other two floors. Three rugs, blanched pea-soup green, overlapped
the scuffed wood floor. No sculptures. No portraits or draperies. All
manner of sounds rippled up the spiral staircase, which when I ventured to look, seemed to coil forever down, down and down again.

Still, it was not the great distance to the gallery below but a
labored moan from the door opposite that stopped my feet. To this
door Mrs. Hardrow strode and stood waiting for me. "Go on," she
said. "Open it."

I opened that door to the stink of piss, and shit, the sharp scent
of liniment—but no haunts that I could see, though I couldn't see
much. One sputtering lamp on the last of its wick was the only
light. Felt curtains shrouded the windows, and a number of paintings slumbered darkly on the walls. In the center of the room, a great
canopy bed was moored like a ship, and in its center, I saw the turtlehead of a skeletal old man asleep on the pillow. A powerfully built
woman with a broad, sweaty face snored by his side in an armchair.
Mrs. Hardrow motioned me to close the door, and without having
said a word, she closed the door on talk of spirits.

The room I was to share with Nurse Lipman had but one rumpled bed, one dresser, no window. It was oddly shaped to fit the space
with five walls and three doors—one to the hall, one to the closet,
one to the master's chamber, which squeaked open. The nurse's head
poked through the door.

"Missus?" Upholstery-patterned sleep lines crisscrossed her cheeks.

"The door, Nurse Lipman," said Hardrow. Lipman stepped in,
closed the door, but the sickroom stink lingered, as did her anxious
expression. Hardrow acknowledged neither.

"Missus," said Lipman, "I was up all last night with him, or I swear I never would have fallen asleep."

"Very well," said Hardrow, turning to go.

"Missus, I wonder if I might . . ." Lipman motioned that she wished to speak to Hardrow in private, on the landing. Hardrow wouldn't have it.

"What, Nancy?"

"It's just that . . ." Lipman looked over at me, back to Hardrow. "I'm sorry, Missus. I know you said, but can you say it again?"

This time Hardrow yielded. Not only yielded but placed both hands on the nurse's broad shoulders, waited until Lipman met her eyes. "You are not being replaced, Nancy. You have done a fine job." Her sharp nod was the period at the end of her sentence.

MINUTES LATER, MRS. HARDROW LEFT me to wait outside the parlor where Miss Rose and company were concluding their visit over coffee. Nerves made a fine jumble of my guts, but at least I'd meet her here. Better than in that dreadful office full of mirrors. When I had managed to sleep the night before, I'd dreamed I'd been trapped inside that room—bad enough until the walls began to shrink close. Then there'd been nowhere I could turn without seeing myself.

The door swung open.

Miss Rose, in purple taffeta, walked out arm in arm with a compact little man, eyes darting, birdlike behind wire spectacles. Mrs. French, in a shapeless worsted dress, followed.

"There will be little risk, I assure you, Captain," said Miss Rose, her voice as deep and embracing as the smile she gave him. "You need only deliver the articles to the city. Mr. Limb has agreed to handle the orders abroad. William Stark will convey the articles from the city. You remember his famous mother, I'm sure. And I will see to the rest. Fitting, don't you think, that the methods my father employed in the cause of freedom will now also be employed in this case?"

The man paused at this, peered at her through his spectacles. "Surely you do not equate—"

Mrs. French opened her mouth as if to intercede, but was too late.

"Oh, but we do, Captain!" said Miss Rose. "What else but a slave would you call a man with no right to represent his own wishes, to develop his God-given abilities, or to support himself by his own merit? What do you call a man with no right to govern the functions of his own body? I have described, Captain, the American Woman. We are pursuing reasonable goals by reasonable means. And when a government makes reasonable acts criminal . . ."

"'Then reasonable people commit criminal acts.' Herbert French, yes, yes." He pulled on his gloves. "I have read the work."

Miss Rose looked at Mrs. French, who shook her head to the silent communication between them. "And?" said Miss Rose.

"This case differs," he said. "Surely you can see that. Your father had much to lose by endeavoring to free his fellow man from the bonds of slavery. Much to lose and very little but moral capital to gain. Surely you see that in this case, unlike the first, profit might easily be"—the captain paused and chose his next word carefully—"*misconstrued* to be the motivating factor. Someone might say you wish to make a mockery of his sacrifice for your own profit."

Miss Rose put one gloved hand to her mouth as if suppressing a sneeze, pulled it away to a burst of laughter.

"Oh, Captain!" she said. "I did not know you for a humorous man."

The Captain wasn't laughing and did not look the humorous sort.

Their talk turned to pleasantries. I paid no more attention and might not have paid attention to anything they said, except for the mention of William. I couldn't imagine that Miss Rose's larger affairs would ever have anything to do with me.

Mrs. Hardrow showed me into the parlor. Violet sat with her back to me at the piano playing three notes up, three notes down, again and again, until we heard the shake of a halter and wheels on gravel as the carriage pulled away. Miss Rose returned, laughter gone, her face much altered from the pleasant expression it had held. "A *humorous* man, Captain Latimer. The nerve to suggest . . ."

"Rose," said Mrs. French trailing her back into the room.

"To suggest that I . . . And what if I do profit? Why should profit nullify the intent? I tell you, if it were profitable to fight injustice, then injustice would become as scarce as gold."

"But he did not say—"

"I'm talking about what he implied, Lorena. Why are you defending him? This venture was your idea in the first place."

"The idea, yes, but the venture—"

"And just how many women do you think an *idea* would benefit? Mrs. French?"

Miss Rose lowered herself into one of three green divans arranged in a semicircle but didn't appear any more comfortable. Whalebone kept her straight as an exclamation point, taffeta rustled around her legs, and as the feathers in her hair settled, her face changed again, this time to a despair that seemed to overtake her only after a moment's consideration.

"Does your Mrs. Livermore make a profit from her endeavors, Lorena? Quite a profit, I think. And yet, because my convictions, though they are widely held in secret, are publicly disfavored, they are . . ."

"Suspected, overlooked," Mrs. French supplied, staring out the window, her back to the room. "Disregarded, trivialized."

"Tri-vi-al-ized!" Miss Rose declared, as if she'd pulled the word from the air. "I will not be trivialized. Violet!"

Violet, poised at the piano, rushed to Miss Rose's side. "Play," said Miss Rose. Violet rushed back to the piano to play the song that accompanied those three notes she had been repeating. All the time, I had been standing near the entryway beside a fluted vase as tall as I, transfixed and more than a little embarrassed by the performance. I was not used to such displays of emotion by a grown woman. She spotted me by the vase.

"You. Girl. Come here."

I had been the only unacknowledged member of Miss Rose's audience and would have preferred to keep it that way. Now the novelty of my presence in that house swept fresh upon me; she raised her hand sharply to her head, and my attention to her curls, her feather, her lavender scent, and I could not look away.

"You are what, again? How old?

"Thirteen. But small, Miss."

"Thirteen but small," she repeated as if what I'd said was of great and lasting import. "And you have no other dresses? Mrs. Hardrow?"

Hardrow made a note of it in a little book that hung from her key chain. She also, no doubt, noted my carpetbag, which I still held behind me. I'd seen the way Nurse Lipman looked at me even after Hardrow's reassurance, and I wasn't about to leave it just anywhere for her thick fingers to pick through.

"And you have met my father?" said Miss Rose.

"Seen him," I said.

"Have seen. *I* have seen him."

"What I said."

"You have not," Miss Rose said. "You have not seen him. You will never see him. What you saw was the aged shell of a man. My father founded this town. Did you know that? Founded and named," Miss Rose said, giving me no chance to answer. "He will be remembered for this, and that memory, too, will be a shined up shell of who he was."

She held my gaze, a terse half smile on her lips. Violet left the piano to stand by Miss Rose's side but was paid no notice.

"Do you know why he called this town Reliance? Do you?"

I looked at Violet, at Hardrow. No help. "The spirits told him to?"

"The spirits!" Amusement lifted her face. She might have held me on a platter. "She's been here a day, not even a day, and already she—Who has filled your head with *spirits*?"

Hardrow caught my eye, gave a short shake of the head. Violet said nothing. I gulped.

"No one, Miss." Miss Rose adjusted her hat. The blue vein on her temple pulsed.

"The spirits told you then! Fabulous. And what"—she sat back, crossed both arms before her—"What have the *spirits* told you about me?"

I had heard nothing in particular, but sensed "nothing" might not be the right answer.

"Don't." I caught myself. "*I* don't know."

"You don't know, or won't say?"

"Don't know, Miss." I stood, squirming, as she watched me, one finger tapping the side of her exquisite nose. William spoke about different kinds of seeing, different kinds of looks, but I couldn't place this one. I couldn't imagine what it was she was seeing in me. A Janus face, whatever that was?

The butler, at the door, cleared his throat. "Mrs. Milfred Drabney, Miss Rose. Of the Wayward Home."

But Miss Rose's countenance again altered, quickly this time, with no apparent deliberation. The color left her face, her eyes glazed, she folded or rather fell onto the settee, one hand to her temple. "Miss!" said Violet. Miss Rose batted Violet's hand away. Mrs. French crossed the room and sat close without touching her.

"Rose," she said. "Maybe you should . . ."

"Nonsense. Richard." She motioned to the butler, and with him, a moment later, a frowsy little woman in Quaker gray waddled through the door. Miss Rose put her hand on my shoulder and helped herself up, weighing much less than I imagined, as if she, too, were made of cloth and ribbon. Her skirt sprang into shape around her. She reached for Violet, who hovered behind, then linked our hands, and pushed the two of us—her ornament and her oddity— out of the parlor.

"Mrs. Drabney!" Miss Rose's voice rang out in greeting. "A delight to see you. How can I help?"

15

The instant we were out the door, Violet wrenched herself free and swiped her hands down her pinafore. "I don't know what you think you are doing. Miss Rose has a girl. Me."

"I'm not," I said, "I wasn't *doing* anything." And then out of bafflement as much as ire, I gave her what I considered the teeny-tiniest of shoves.

Violet collapsed across the polished marble, flailing and crying as if I'd slugged her. It was such a wrought performance, I just stood there, watching.

"Madelyn!" said Mrs. Hardrow stepping out of the parlor.

I looked down at gasping, sobbing Violet and back to Mrs. Hardrow, all but helpless in the face of such a display. I wished I had slugged her. "But I didn't! I wasn't *doing* anything. She's just . . . She's not even bleeding!"

If I'm not mistaken, Mrs. Hardrow came close to a smile, then righted herself, and me, with one word. "Enough! We do not lay hands on one another in this house."

Miss Rose called. Violet simpered triumphantly back to the parlor. Mrs. Hardrow held my gaze. "Do you understand, Madelyn?"

A servant, sweeping nearby, swallowed a giggle; my hands made fists.

"Madelyn?" said Hardrow.

I mumbled some response, and Hardrow sent me outside to "acquaint myself with the grounds," which if meant as a punishment, felt an honest relief.

The sun was bright; the air tart. A pair of pompous, blue-breasted turkeys (peacocks, Mrs. French had called them) were strutting back and forth in front of the carriage house. Beyond the carriage house, I found a hen yard and a stable, busy with voices. I turned the other way, toward the gardens overlooking the river. Wind jostled the trees down the bluff. A skiff, small as a child's toy from this distance, drifted downstream, and though perhaps the urge was there, the sight of that tiny vessel alone on the wide river arrested immediate thoughts of flight. Where would I go? Even if Mr. Dryfus would have me back, no way my pride would allow me to face Mama. I wandered instead into the gardens.

There were two gardens. Three if you counted the kitchen garden in the clearing beyond the carriage house. Four if you counted the conservatory. The two I mean were the maze of trimmed shrubbery beyond the gravel drive, and the rose garden in a raised clearing at the center. A garden within a garden. I'd never seen anything like it. I wandered through trellised archways of climbing vines, past hip-high walls of trimmed shrubs out of which, at intervals, figures grew—a perfect sphere, tiered saucers like stacked plates on a stalk, an elephant. A dancing bear and a dancing woman stood across from each other where the path opened to the rose garden.

I looked again. A thin trail of blue smoke wafted from the bear's mouth. "Hello?" I said. The frantic rustling I heard turned my stomach. I'd thought I was alone, but when I stepped around I saw the redhead, Alby, from the kitchen, sitting on a ledge of rock, blushing as if caught doing her business.

"You're smoking," I said.

"Am not."

But she was. The pocket of her pinafore was smoking. A small yellow flame leaped from the fabric. Alby sprang from the bench, bringing forth a whole dictionary of curse words, and revealing the culprit, a cob pipe she'd hidden in her pocket at my approach, now snapped in two. After she got done with her little fire dance, she faced me like a boy, feet wide apart, hands on hips, head cocked to a challenge.

"You rat on me, I'll pound you," she said.

She wasn't fooling me. I could smell fear beneath that bravado as sure as I smelled smoke.

"Not gonna rat," I said, grinning at her in spite of myself.

"You laugh, I'll pound you too. Hear me?"

I heard, but once I started laughing, the urge twisted into an impotent fury—directed at Violet or Mama or myself, hard to say, but for a full minute I raged around that clearing with a branch I'd picked up, thrashing shrubs as though they had faces until I had no breath left in me. Felt a little better for it.

Alby watched all this, eyes wide at first, and when it was clear the fit had blown over, stepped closer.

"Look at you," she said. "You missing someone somewhere, ain't you? Huh? Someone missing you? Mama? Daddy? First time in service, I reckon."

I'd turned away from her, still breathing hard, but she came around to meet my eyes. "Hey." There was a gap between her front teeth. The freckles bridging her broad, flat nose were the same color as her eyes.

Not a servant, I almost said, but this left open the question of what I was, and I still wasn't sure. "Mama's dead," I said instead, the quaver in my voice lending validity. "Cholera. After the war. Lots of folks died. I never knew my daddy," which was true.

"Yeah. Well." She kicked at the gravel, and the little brown birds scratching through the shrubs jostled and settled. "I woulda given you mine if you'd asked for 'em." She made space for me on the rock ledge under the bear and examined the charred hole in her pinafore. "Sumbitch owned my mamma, God rest her, but never owned me, and I ran off and left him to his stumps and sermon-izing, and I'll run from here too if'n old Nettle don't leave off me. And Hardrow."

Her talk calmed me some. She was fourteen, maybe older, but small like me. Probably she could pass for white if she wanted, and it was my impression she knew a great deal about the world. She glanced sideways at me; I looked away.

"I want you to know I didn't mean nothing by what I said in the kitchen, about you not having looks enough to be a servant. You don't and that's the truth, not an outright meanness." I was willing to concede this. "Who done it to you anyway?" she said.

"Nobody done it to me."

"Mightn't be a curse."

"Nobody done it," I said. "And I don't believe in curses. Or spirits."

She shrugged as if to say I could believe what I wanted at my own risk. "My daddy, he might call a face like yours a blessed misfortune. Know what that is?" I didn't. "It's when the bad things, accidents and such, things you'd best avoid if you could, turn out alright in the end. Good, even. Might be the confoundingest type of grace, but grace just the same. You think of Job suffering so that he could get back tenfold what he lost. Or Mary Magdalene. If she ain't been a whore, might never 'a' met the lord our savior Jesus Christ by the well, am I right? That's blessed misfortune.

"I think, maybe"—she looked close at me and I let her—"maybe a mark like yours is worth something. Money, I'm saying. Cash. Ever heard of Dog Woman? Born furry head to toe. I paid my penny, waited near an hour to see her in Saint Louis. All she got to do is sit there all day and let people look."

A fate worse than death to me, but I didn't say this.

"But now I look at you awhile though, you ain't nearly so beastly as I thought, not nearly so much as Dog Woman. Where's it travel?"

"Head to . . ." I pointed to my thigh.

"Even so," she said.

I was very nearly flattered by this, but had no desire to stay on this vein. "Run where?" I asked. "I mean, if you was going to run, where would you go?"

"Easy. West." She turned her face to the sun. "Arizona. Maybe California," saying the word with such relish I couldn't help remember the flavor of John's letters home to Dot. Mango. Pineapple. Banana. In my imagination, the whole of California was edible. My stomach growled. Alby stood.

"Lordy," she stuck a finger through the burn hole in her pocket. "Nettle and Hardrow both going to skin me. I better get back."

I didn't want to go back. Didn't want her to go either, already felt for her an outcast's kinship—not the same as trust, mind you. "Alby?" I said and nodded to the third floor of the manor, thinking talk of haunts might hold her. "Why'd the spirits tell him to build a town here?"

"I don't know. Something about how the rivers join up here.

Meeting-up place of bodies and souls, or some such. Have to ask
Nettle."

She took a long look at my carpet bag. "You coming? Come on."

AFTER MRS. DRABNEY OF THE Wayward Home departed, Miss
Rose took to bed with a headache. Violet retreated to her room,
Mrs. French to her studies. I ate two helpings of fatback for supper in
the kitchen with Alby while Mrs. Nettle sifted weevils from a measure of oats and a hugely fat cat purred under the table. Next door, in
the servants' hall, we could hear companionable laughter. Word had
spread that I'd slugged Violet and there was no use trying to deny it.

"Probably deserved it," Alby said. "Vile Violet. Goes around acting
like royalty when, from what I hear, Miss Rose found her rotting in
the tombs for thieving and promised to make her an actress."

"Thieving?" I asked.

"Miss Rose, now, she was something on the stage," said Nettle.
In the mud-yellow lamplight, she hadn't noticed the hole in Alby's
pinafore. At least she hadn't said anything, and I could tell she was
not the kind of woman to miss a chance to criticize.

"Not that I ever saw her," said Nettle. "Me? Now I am not the
kind of woman to patronize a theater." I looked at Alby, not sure
what kind of woman was supposed to patronize a theater. "But my
brother, he saw her at the Park in New York the week before Lin-
coln . . ." She let the sentence fall. I heard voices and footsteps up the
little staircase to the basement's outer door. Servants jostled into the
courtyard toward the carriage house.

"Anyway, I reckon the stage was what come between them, old
master and Miss Rose."

"Thought it was a young man, what got between them," said
Alby.

"A young man on the stage. An *actor*," she said, shooing the cat and throwing the contents of the sifter into the fire. "Carried off her heart, then carried her away when she was not much older than you. When he died, only the stage was left to her. Old master wouldn't hear her name aloud." She damped the coals, spread her heavy hands down her apron. "Never again spoke it."

"Why?"

Nettle, looking at me as if I were daft, picked up the bread bowl.

"Why? Couldn't conscience a daughter on the stage, that's why. Though, you ask me . . . You ask me, he's to blame as much as anyone. Everyone's born to their own lot, and you ask me, it's a base cruelty to educate a girl beyond her station and sex, if you don't expect her to act on it. Now, course, Old Man can't say anything either way. But you ask me . . ." She leaned in.

"Mrs. Nettle."

It was Mrs. Hardrow in the darkened doorway; a gust of air accompanied the voice and damped coals seethed red. Nettle raised her wattle chin.

"To bed, Madelyn," said Hardrow. "You too, Alby."

Alby slipped out to the carriage house between the two women now sizing each other up like duelists, and I think that's when it hit me—not my brain, which knew, but my gut—how out of place and out of sorts I was.

Nurse Lipman would not be happy to see me. The memory of the old man's turtlehead and the sound of the wind moaning through the eaves of the cupola punctured Hardrow's silent assurance against the existence of haunts. Not even pride offered comfort. As the women had words, I stood fidgeting, close to tears in the hallway, yearning as I never supposed I would for my cot in the little attic room in the print shop. Nettle, agitated, brushed by me down the hall, but Mrs. Hardrow, turning and finding me still there, paused. She lit her candle, and leaning close, blew out the lamp above my head. "Come along, then," she said.

One by one she blew out each lamp on our way up the stairs. By the time we pushed through the service door to the third-floor landing, her little flame was the only light beyond starlight through the cupola. She handed me the candle, put her strong hand softly on my shoulder, pointed me the way, and bade me good night.

16

I'd found Nurse Lipman splayed across the bed we were to share, leaving me only slivers of mattress, which together might have been enough to curl into. Her breathing wasn't right. I knew she was awake but lay down with my carpetbag by the closet without saying anything, because even if I'd been up for a tussle, I could tell she was more than my match. I must have slept because I woke to her toe in my side. "If Hardrow asks, you wanted to sleep on the floor," she'd said. Now in the sickroom, with equal force: "Tell him who you are."

"Madelyn."

"Louder."

A gray film fogged the old man's eyes; his pale bald head was a patchwork of green, purple, and blue, and the whole room stank of waste and mold. Why the windows were still shuttered and the curtains drawn, I didn't know. The only light was a flickering oil lamp that cast unsettling shadows across the walls and over the portraits staring down.

"I'm Madelyn Branch, Mr. Werner. Maddy. Nice to meet you?"

He reached with one bony hand. I jerked back. Nurse Lipman laughed and something between a grimace and smile scarred Old

Man's face. He craned his neck and opened his toothless mouth. "Wiaaa!" A mournful moan, and again. "Wiaaa!"

"Now, now, Mr. Werner," said Nurse Lipman and gave his cock, making a tent of the sheet, a fond little tap. Then with the broad, flat heel of her hand, she pressed his head back into the pillow and in the space of five minutes heaved him on his side, cleaned him front and back, changed the soiled square of material, and laid his dangling bones down again, as if to illustrate how little my assistance would be needed.

I didn't need convincing. I had passed a long, vexing morning in the library with Violet, who, I discovered, also took lessons with Mrs. French. Violet, who could recite in French and German and who, until Miss Rose called her away to sing, sat at the table smirking at my every mistake. Meat pie with gravy for lunch had brightened my spirits considerably, but I had no desire to spend the afternoon cooped up in the sickroom.

Old Man groaned again.

"What's he saying?" I asked, watching her. Nettle was sure Lipman must have stuttered as child, or been what she called "compromised." I suppose this was meant to explain how Lipman at twenty-nine (that is, still young enough to marry, barely) could be content alone with Old Man every day, with little to no diversion beyond Sunday service and choir every Tuesday at the Lutheran church.

"Sounds close to a word," I said.

Lipman shook her head. "Just a sound he makes. He's been, well, agitated."

A knock turned our heads. The landing door opened to a shock of light and air and my stomach did a flip. Miss Rose's dark silhouette filled the doorway. She'd been abed all morning with a headache but was dressed fine now, her skirts too wide for the threshold, her hair an elaborate pattern of braids and curls. She stood, handkerchief to her nose, as if waiting for the stink to leave or some cue to enter. I could not take my eyes from her.

"How is he today, Nurse Lipman?"

Old Man's neck craned again, toward the light or Miss Rose's voice; I couldn't tell. His mouth opened to nothing but a wheezing breath.

"Fine. Fine as ever, Miss. I was just about to fetch his lunch."

Miss Rose entered, easing through the doorway, then stood over the bed staring at Old Man, the handkerchief obscuring her expression and muffling her voice, which, when she spoke again, sounded oddly wooden. "Bonjour, Papa," she said, and bending with great care, holding her head still as if to hold a crown in place, kissed him on the cheek.

She didn't appear to notice me until Lipman, with a jerk of her head, motioned me out of the room.

"You are not to worry my father with news of any kind. Do you understand?"

I stepped back into the room. Miss Rose looked at me in the darkness.

"No romance or maritime stories." As if she suspected I knew a great many by heart. "He was a merchant marine in his early manhood; his memories of the life he led then—before my mother died—they must still haunt him. If there are spirits in this room," she glanced about. "If there are spirits, they are given life by regret."

She handed me the odd book of verse I'd struggled with two days before. "This will do for reading. Keep it with you. Read it over first so that when you read aloud, the words do not resist your tongue. 'Of bodies chang'd to various forms, I sing . . .'" Her smile fading with her voice as her eyes came to rest on her father.

"Right. Well. I'll just fetch his lunch then." Lipman left. Miss Rose remained silent. The book felt heavy in my hands, and I wasn't sure what to do. Stay? I wanted to slip away, but by and by Miss Rose spoke again.

"Why is it?" she asked—me or the old man; I wasn't sure. "Why is it that one must always be reminded of one's own mortality?" She looked at me.

"I don't know, Miss."

"There will be a record of my father, in Mr. Dryfus's book?" I said I guessed so. "How much of a record? How many words, how many pages for a life such as his?"

I hadn't read any of Mr. Dryfus's book. "Two pages, I guess."

"And what, I wonder, will be written of me?"

I didn't recognize the question to be rhetorical. "Depends," I said.

"Oh? On what?"

"On who writes it, I guess."

I thanked my stars for the knock on the door, because from the look her face, I was afraid I'd said something truly daft.

Lipman set Old Man's mush on the bedside table. Miss Rose, turning with care, left us—she seemed relieved to do so—and I had no more contact with her for three days, until after morning lessons and lunch, a servant came to fetch me.

It had become clear by this time that I was to be more Mrs. French's than Miss Rose's project, and thus far I had proven neither an apt nor an eager student. That's not true. I was eager, but hated to be wrong, especially in front of Violet. Even after Violet left me alone with Mrs. French, as she did each day an hour before lunch to practice her scales and attend Miss Rose, frustration all but overwhelmed me.

Really, I wasn't at all sure Mrs. French knew how to teach. There was not a McGuffey Reader in the house, for one thing, and we spent a great deal less time spelling, drawing, learning sums, and reciting than I expected. Whatever my struggles at the Susanville School, I had been adept at parroting facts that the teacher, Mr. Lynd, had written on the board to memorize. Mrs. French had the terrible habit of responding to my answers with questions and of posing questions that did not seem to have answers—at least not answers she saw fit to give me.

On the second day, for example, after Violet left, we read aloud a story in which a man, who'd been compelled to leave a cave of shadows he'd called home, returned to share all the difficult and wonderful discoveries he'd made beyond, only to find that no one believed him. They called him crazy. I found it a very strange story indeed, not just in the way it was told (two men talking), but also in what happened. Mrs. French did not seem inclined to offer clarity.

"What makes no sense?" She asked in response to my complaint. Rather than taking a place across the table, she had seated herself by my side, and her closeness, as much as my confusion, flustered me. She wore the same shapeless, worsted housedress. Her thick gray hair was braided down her back, and her forearms, tanned like her face, were thin, vein-tracked, muscled.

"Well, why'd he leave in the first place?" I asked.

"What does the story say?" She tapped her pencil on the thick book before us.

"That he was compelled. Forced, right?" She nodded. "But who forced him?"

Mrs. French said nothing.

"Why'd he go back?"

"What does it say?"

"You know what it says!" I blurted. "I'm not asking what it says. I'm asking why."

"A shrewd distinction," said Mrs. French.

"Maybe he was crazy!" I said, done with this nonsense. "Or feverish, the white light and such. Maybe he should have stayed put in the first place and saved everyone a lot of grief."

"Maybe," she said, equable as usual, except this time I looked her in the eye and found there a smile and a restrained but obvious amusement, which I decided to resent, though that was not easy either. She had one of those faces with lines and ridges so stern that any smile broke it into another face altogether, youthful, almost—almost, but not quite, handsome. And though it is true her voice—pinched and reed thin—was a poor vehicle for passion, something in those eyes, or maybe in that lithe little body, so vital and young compared to her face, made demands of me.

When she did speak openly, she spoke in declarative riddles—effusive riddles at that. "Woman must not be content to become a temple, beautifully adorned, admired, empty. *Woman*," she said again, this time slowly and with great emphasis, "must build within herself a full and independent city of abilities. Only then can she stand alone, a citizen in the kingdom of man to which she has so long been subject. Woman is not born dependent, girls. She is bred that way."

I'm not sure what Violet, who hadn't yet been called away, thought of such a statement, but it was not what anyone else I knew said about women. And I imagined real prophecies were meant for larger, more imposing voices. Voices like Miss Rose's.

In the face of these contrary methods of instruction, I became increasingly contrary. On the third day, after Violet left, Mrs. French placed before me paper and pen and asked me to write. I all but revolted.

"Write what?" I asked.

"Whatever you wish." Then she returned to her own seat at the other end of the oak table and opened her book.

It's hard to describe the anxiety that overcame me as I stared at the blank page. I had with no provocation written letters and poems and a great many other things in my scrapbook over the years, but I didn't know what to write for Mrs. French. Even if I had known, I was sure whatever I wrote would turn out trite or silly, or just plain wrong. I was mad at her, mad at myself, and when finally she left her own studies to observe my progress, I braced myself, fearing, half hoping, for some kind of clear and unequivocal response.

She merely considered me through, then over, the rim of her oculars. "Look at you, Madelyn." She said this with firmness but no malice. "Look at you. You cannot afford not to try. Do you understand that? You will have no choice but to make something of yourself. To be self-reliant. To discover a vocation. To make money, Madelyn. Do you understand?"

She took off her oculars, rubbed the purple imprint bridging her nose, stared down at me for a response I hadn't made. Then she tapped the blank page before me. "I want you to compose one statement, one clear statement, before we're done today. I want you to tell me what it is you want."

"What I want?" I asked, incredulous.

"What you want."

At this she took herself again to her place across the table and resumed reading. Outside, the wind rose; tree limbs scraped the library's leaded windows; the blank page, fluttering softly, mocked me. I sat glowering at the top of Mrs. French's gray head. Then, in a vigorous rush of defiance, I wrote:

To start, I don't think I want a city inside me. I looked up. Mrs.

French turned her page. *Or a temple. I want love!* I added another
exclamation point for good measure. *I want to be loved. And I want to
be beautiful. Beauty is the key that opens hearts.*

Nearly overwhelmed with my own profundity, feeling, indeed,
as though I had shouted those words aloud, I shoved the paper
beneath her nose, stopping whatever thought cut jagged lines into
her brow and gaining for my boldness a stare that just might, as Hanley claimed, freeze men in their tracks. It was not that stare, however,
but the way she read my words, pen in hand, judging every phrase,
that froze me. An eternity passed. My courage, too.

"Ma'am?" The housekeeper, Mrs. Hardrow, from the doorway.
"Sorry to intrude, but Miss Rose would have a word about . . ."

Mrs. French looked up at this. Both women looked at me.

"She would have a word."

Mrs. French nodded with some annoyance, then with a breath
stood and left me in the library, staring from across the table at my
paper. Even before nosing my way to her chair, I could see that Mrs.
French had written more in the margins than I had in my whole
statement.

I do not want, she had written. *I do not want a temple inside of me.
If your convictions are to be taken seriously, you must state them with
conviction."*

She had underlined *Beauty is the key that opens hearts.*

Good, she wrote. *This is a much stronger statement than the first—
elegant, in fact. Do you hear the difference between them? I do suggest
replacing the fallacious absolute, "the key," with "a key." Beauty is a key
that opens hearts.*

*As for love, my dear, it is my opinion that we are better off desiring
only . . ."*

Here the housekeeper had interrupted the response. Desiring

only what? She did not return to finish her sentence, and I was still distracted and ruminating after lunch, as I followed the servant sent to fetch me—for what purpose she didn't say—to the guest room on the second floor.

Cream curtains danced in open windows; the canopy bed anchoring the green Turkish carpet was so imposing and my thoughts so oppressive that I didn't at first notice the copper tub. Nor did I connect the steaming water buckets and the presence of a servant, a stout, young, red-faced woman, with her intention. It was the second servant, bumping through the door with an armful of dresses, who sent me leaping onto that bed to wrap myself, arms and legs, around a bedpost, shocking both of them, and me too. Foolish to strand myself like a treed raccoon when I might have made for the door, but there I was.

When asking didn't work, they tried prying me off, one at a time, then one on either side, until I was screaming, biting, mad as a cat and just as heedless. This went on for some time before the stout one, growing weary, bloodied my lip with the back of her hand and was about to lay it on again, I'm sure, when both stood quick off me.

In the doorway, Miss Rose glistened in purple silk and taffeta. The third eye of a peacock feather rose high above her hat. "What on Earth!"

Mrs. French appeared behind her, then Violet, but the other curious faces dispersed with the arrival of Mrs. Hardrow. Said the servant who'd bloodied me, "She won't budge, Miss. We—"

Miss Rose held up a hand for silence. Mrs. French's eyes tracked from tub to servants to me and back again.

"What have you to say?" Miss Rose asked, and so I told her.

"I'm not going to strip to my skivvies in front of that cow. Not for you or God himself!"

The cow caught her breath. No one said anything. Everyone was watching Miss Rose, who looked as if someone had snuck around and pinched her hard on the behind.

"You little fiend," she said, giving each word the attention of a sentence. Violet smiled. I was in for it, sure, but beyond caring. No one but Dot, Mama, and the great Almighty had ever seen me in my glory. Banishment would be superior to the humiliation expected of me. Even so, when the clock on the mantle struck the quarter hour, regret as much as defiance rang through me. I tightened my grip, staring so hard at the Turkish carpet to keep tears from falling that the pattern began to melt before my eyes.

"You *glorious* fiend," said Rose.

I looked up. Violet stopped smiling. Between Miss Rose and Mrs. French passed a silent communication I couldn't read. Miss Rose sent Violet and Mrs. Hardrow from the room, but her presence seemed to expand and fill the empty space, leaving little real estate for Mrs. French, staring down at me.

"I am going to make some assumptions," said Miss Rose, picking up one of the dresses abandoned in a pile by the bed. "I am going to assume that it was the assistance, rather than good hygiene or my generosity, that you objected to with such . . ." She paused.

"Decisiveness," Mrs. French supplied.

"There is soap by the tub, and towels," said Miss Rose. "I expect you washed and dressed in half an hour."

I looked at Mrs. French, back to Miss Rose. What if I was not washed and dressed in half an hour? What then? But I didn't ask this. And after another silent communication, the women walked out. The door clicked shut. Steam serpents whisted from the copper tub;

the mantle clock tick-tick-ticked. I counted twenty ticks, then with difficulty, my limbs tense and bruised, I unwound from the bedpost and tried the door.

Open.

Well, a locked door would have decided me, but an open door? I swung it wide and stood with one foot across the brightly lit threshold. The landing was deserted except for a chambermaid crossing the landing with an armload of linen.

"I'm leaving," I told her. "I'm leaving and you can't stop me."

"Suit ye'self, miss," she said and carried on out of sight.

I stepped back into the room. I closed the door, stood alert and for a moment, undecided.

By the time I was done, as much water wetted the carpet as browned in the tub. I felt like I'd left more of me inside than came out again: half expected my mark to have washed away with the summer grime. But, of course, there it was, clear as a line on a map and bright as strawberries, especially in those tender regions that never saw the light.

The difference I felt more than saw. The difference was the gravel beneath the skin of my chest, twin nipples alert in the cold. The difference was the wisps of dark hair coarse under my arms and in the cleft between my legs. My fingers, I let them travel there and linger—and what came to mind, along with the odd warmth coiling in my belly, was William.

The clock struck the quarter hour. I crouched, dripping and naked under the towel, and listened. No movement outside the door. I counted another minute, two, then retrieved the charm from the end table, exchanged the towel for a blue dress, a donation from the Wayward Home box, maybe, but the nicest I'd ever worn. Still no one came for me, and after a while, I realized no one would. I left Mama's dress balled with the towel on the floor and took myself upstairs to read to Old Mr. Werner.

That's what I meant to do, at least. Somewhere between the landing and the servants' staircase, I changed my mind.

MRS. FRENCH WAS NOT IN the library, or the parlor, or the gallery. I found her resting in a wicker chair in the conservatory, with a sketch pad. If surprised at the sight of me, she didn't show it. Another woman, most any other woman, would probably have made some blithely encouraging comment about my appearance or the dress, would have felt obliged to do so. Mrs. French said nothing.

"Desiring only what?" I asked, pleading as much as demanding. "On my paper, you said I'm better off desiring only . . . Only what, Mrs. French?"

I could not have endured one of her questions in return. She must have seen that.

"Desiring only," she said after a moment's indecision, "that which you might by will and effort attain."

I stared at her. I don't know what I expected, but I didn't feel anything, satisfied or otherwise. Just spent and a trifle disappointed. "Oh," was the only response I could muster. I turned to go.

"Madelyn," said Mrs. French. I stopped but didn't turn. "Nothing. I—" She took a weary breath. "See you tomorrow, my dear."

17

It was only looking back on them that made the next three weeks pass quickly. Nurse Lipman, having accepted my presence, conceded one drawer in the wardrobe and part of the bed—so long as I kept my feet clean and off her side, courtesies she did not feel compelled to reciprocate. We woke before dawn to wash, change, and feed Old Man. Lessons with Mrs. French and Violet began at eight in the library. I had an hour of idle time after lunch, then three hours in the sickroom reading to Old Man in the yellow, kerosene lamplight, then back to the library, then dinner, then bed, then do it again. And haunting me all the time weren't spirits so much as Mama.

Live people can haunt, you see, as well or better than the dead, and in those first weeks, I measured everything I saw or did against what Mama might say or think about it—silly, given that Mama was never one to share what she thought or felt. To keep her out of my thoughts, I occupied myself, even at idle times. Which is not to say I was useful. Servants accomplished all labors I used to. Mrs. French, who was never idle, encouraged me to wander the gardens and write about plants that most attracted or disturbed me, to improve my descriptive skills (because heaven forbid if even idle time did not pass in service to self-improvement).

Mostly I read in a crook in the sculpture-gallery wall nearest the conservatory. A lighter fare than Plato—Collins, Cummins, Dickens, Radcliffe—populated the library shelves, and Mrs. French censored nothing. Or I'd sit back and, listening to the strange and constant movements of that house, imagine those marble statues breaking from their pedestals, to resume those scenes of love and terror in which they were frozen.

One statue in particular, nearest the conservatory, enthralled me.

It was of a young woman, a garland in her hair. She was running, but looking back, her mouth open, a cry on her lips. One of her hands, reaching up, became five branches with leaves. One foot, planted hard against the earth, became a root; her belly was bark. To be honest, I nearly jumped out of my skin when first I saw her. She appeared so lifelike, so fearful, so soft to the touch, it was an honest relief when I summoned the nerve to tap her thigh and found it stone.

One day midweek, as I sat reading beside her, Miss Rose burst through the great double doors of the manor and into the foyer, shedding wrap, hat, and gloves in furious haste. Robert, the butler, trailed after.

"The good women of the Ladies' Auxiliary," she said, "have no need for the vote! No need, they say. And that Mrs. Morrison. *The women of Reliance do not wish to have the vote thrust upon them.* Thrust upon them? Had you any idea just how boorishly arrogant that woman was?" The butler had not. "The presumption! And she would not be allowed past the lobby of the New York Hotel wearing that dress. Except to clean it. Violet!"

She looked about. It was quiet, the servants occupied elsewhere. She spotted me and I felt my guts sink.

"You. Where is Violet?" I rather made a point of avoiding Violet.

I'd also been quite happy to avoid Miss Rose. Since the bath, I'd been a brainless, forgetful, stuttering fool around her. The unaccustomed impulse to please did this to me. I had no practice in flattery or self-aggrandizement, and in a frenzy to say something, anything of value, I blurted half-formed thoughts I then felt foolish about and later drove myself silly wondering what she thought about me, when it was obvious Miss Rose thought little about me.

Hardly an afternoon passed when Miss Rose was not visiting some relief foundation or orphans' home or entertaining this or that charitable concern. She woke late each day, at nine, and labored for an hour over her toilette with Mrs. Hardrow. Breakfast at ten, Mrs. Nettle told me, was a pastry or a sweet bun and a poached egg in a silver cup. At eleven she called Violet from the library to play piano and practice vocal scales and elocution exercises such as "nine hundred ninety-nine nuns interned in an Indiana nunnery." While she liked to complain that she was ab-so-*lute*-ly exiled from society in that river town, she still managed to secure dinner plans three days a week, and visitors, mostly men, always seemed to be coming and going. And of course, there were the soirees, every third Wednesday of the month (the next one in a week) to which Mr. Stockwell so objected.

Every third Wednesday, society arrived in the shape of local musicians, artists, and singers—Reliance had its own small bohemian set, William primary among them. With them came a host of uninvited guests—shopgirls and clerks in their Sunday best—who all became, by the end of such evenings, Rose's "brilliant, brilliant darlings" and she their "Heavenly Rose," the name that emblazoned broadsheets when she graced the New York stage. Now and again this core was enlivened by a troupe of acrobats, a famous actor, or a writer en route to or from the West. All came to eat and drink, to perform and luxuriate in Miss Rose's lavish praise, and to repay praise with the flattery Miss Rose demanded. Sometimes the young men stayed for days, wandering the gardens with note and sketchbooks and pensive expressions, entertaining what could only be divine revelations. Most often they stumbled away the next morning, bound for fame or obscurity or worse. I didn't know. There was to be some sort of benefit gala that night in town. But since I arrived at the manor, there had only been one soiree, which I'd watched from the second-floor balcony, hoping for glimpses of William (who hadn't come to visit me, as I'd expected).

Now I could feel Miss Rose's gaze upon me. "I'm speaking to you," she said. "What are you doing there?"

"Nothing," I said, but nonetheless felt guilty. "Only looking."

Miss Rose considered the statue. I considered Miss Rose. She wore a fitted bodice, a high monkish collar, a white bustled skirt splayed like the tail of a swan. I was aware I was staring. Aware, too, that she expected this of me.

"You like this?"

At first I thought she meant her dress, but she was speaking of the statue.

"Yes," I said. "No. I mean, it's beautiful. And terrible."

Violet rushed through the conservatory entrance. Miss Rose ignored her. I was sure I had said something foolish.

"You are right. Quite beautiful. Quite terrible." She turned as if to make a formal introduction. "This is Daphne. She was a beautiful nymph, desired by Apollo. She ran away and when she appealed to the Gods to save her, the Gods, in their great wisdom, transformed her from a girl into a laurel tree. And left Apollo untouched."

She raised one arm in much the same pose as the marble orator to her left.

"A beautiful woman's face is not her own. It is"—with a sweep of her hand she acknowledged her stone and marble audience—"like a statue or a portrait on the wall, destined for public consumption. Women gaze with envy upon another woman's beauty and find the tiniest imperfection the greatest of comforts. And men? Men admire, in a woman's face, the reflection of their own hopes and fantasies. They find themselves under a spell of their own making and call it love. They write poetry and make war, not for the woman, but for her face. And then blame the woman when her face feels nothing in return."

Miss Rose's arm remained aloft. Violet began to clap, and Miss Rose, dropping her arm, looked hard at me.

"Well?" She placed a cautious hand to her curls. "I thought it quite good. Mrs. French is not the only wordsmith in this house. Yes, I shall recite it for tonight's gala. Enough, Violet!"

Violet stopped clapping.

"Mrs. French has been rather impressed by your progress."

This was news to me.

"But you." With one finger, she tapped the side of her nose, then with the same finger, pointed at me. "You are often underestimated, I think. You will come see me, tomorrow, after your lessons."

I glanced at Violet, knowing the comment was too close to a compliment for her taste, and after Miss Rose, gathering her skirts, left us there, I braced for wrath.

"It will be lovely, divine, exquisite," Violet said sweetly.

"Violet!" Miss Rose called.

"Christine Willison is going to sing *Faust*. I may recite *Lear* or *Macbeth*. I have not decided. William will be there. Too bad," she said—"too bad you are not invited"—and rushed after Miss Rose.

I glared after her. I had mentioned William only a few times in Violet's presence, but like all royal witches, she was monstrously perceptive.

She also had, to my untrained ear at any rate, a full and lovely singing voice she was not bashful about showing off, and a good eye for drawing. Her trim waist and pale complexion were points of pride, as were her nails, blunt and perfectly clean, and she walked very prettily, like a dancer, on the balls of her feet. While she was not nearly so advanced in her studies as she first led me to believe, her memory was remarkable—she needed only to read a poem to know it. What I hated most about her, I think, was that I would have liked to like her, and whether I admitted it or not, I wanted her to like me; I think she knew this, too, because for weeks she'd dangled the possibility before me with the odd kind word, only to yank it away with subtle and calculated meanness. I was used to being feared, sometimes pitied out of hand, but these were cursory reactions to my appearance. No one had ever taken the time and effort to abuse me so artfully.

After three weeks in the manor, I could guess, from the tone of her voice alone, with whom she might be speaking. Her "Miss Rose tone"—deferential, soft, quick to agree, withholding all contrary opinion—must have been a great effort to maintain, because the moment she was beyond Miss Rose's hearing, she sought some servant to abuse. Really she must have been quite lonely, but I had no pity. Her "Madelyn voice" promised to be a work of expertly understated nastiness.

I could only imagine the voice she might use on William.

The thought worked on me all afternoon and was still festering when I escaped Old Man for the rose garden before dinner. It was late October, a metal taste of snow in the air and the gray sky loud with geese heading south. Upriver, the Missouri spilling into the Mississippi looked like a coffee stain on a piece of brown worsted. Mist hushed from warm eddies near the riverbank, and the oaks and maples were brilliantly dressed.

They reminded me of fancy ladies. Of Violet. Of William.

Of William in a vest and top hat. William with his freshly shaved face and new manners, shiny as a pocket watch. Would Mama be there at the gala as well? Feeling the solid weight of the charm beneath my blouse, I took it off to admire—my habit when alone and thinking—when Alby, pipe in hand, emerged from the topiary. I closed my fist quick around the charm.

"Dear Lord, if I peel another potato, gonna turn into one! How am I meant to learn a kitchen if all she ever got me doing is peeling this and scrubbing that?" She slumped beside me. "Huh. What's the matter with you, then? Look like someone shot your dog. Smoke?"

"Nothing's wrong."

"No? And you got nothing in your hand either, huh? What is it?"

"Nothing."

Alby searched her pocket for a match, found only a broken half. "You take something, huh? I always say Miss Rose got so many treasures, not likely to miss a little, but Cyrus says don't go pissing on the hand that feeds you."

Cyrus was the driver and the gardener, a Creole. Alby, whose mama had been Creole, was about the only one who could understand what he said. She flicked the broken match away, nudged closer. "Lemme see."

"I didn't take anything from Miss Rose." But there was no way around showing her. Even in the waning light, the little eight-sided charm sparkled richer than anything I had a right to own. Her shrewd eyes pinched.

"Found it," I said.

Alby said nothing.

"Someone gave it to me."

"Yeah? Who?"

"William."

The name, out of my mouth before I knew it, gave a sharp little thrill.

"William Stark gave it to me," I said. "But he told me . . . he told me not to tell anyone." The developing fib raised my spirits considerably. After all, who's to say William wouldn't have given me such a charm, if he'd had one to give? Soon the statement felt more like an embellishment than a lie. And if a lie, then a harmless one, surely.

A different picture had formed in Alby's head. "Well, I'll be!"

"What?"

"Well, I just wouldn't-a guessed a girl—town girl, what I mean—like you would be giving for favors. Lizzette maybe." We'd caught Lizzette, the cow of a chambermaid who'd slapped me, and the houseboy, Tom, rutting behind the garden shed the day before. "I'm not judging, mind, but you got to be careful."

"Not like that. It's not! I'm not giving anything for anything." And here, I gathered myself. "I. I love him. And"—I was standing now—"he loves me. We're in love!"

The laughing call of geese pierced the sky above. Alby, wisely, said nothing; she didn't need to, for those last words rang hollow even to me, and made me tense all night, and defensive when Violet, with more than her usual sweetness, greeted me the next day. She spent all morning giving me self-satisfied smirks across the table without saying anything about William or the gala, and damned if I'd ask. So I was in no good mood when, at the appointed time, I knocked on Miss Rose's office door.

From the sound of her voice within, Miss Rose was in no good mood either.

I followed Mrs. Hardrow into the room, staring at my feet, and still those mirrors caught pieces of me like blackberry thorns. Miss Rose hunched over the desk, muttering to herself, her gloved hand stained black from the frustrated scratch of her pen. Dozens of discarded pages lay scattered about the carpet. Dozens of pages, and not even foolscap! Miss Rose lifted her head carefully, as if it carried a great weight. Then she balled the page she'd been writing and tossed it in disgust on the floor at my feet.

"Pick it up," she said. I did. "Read." I did. "Aloud," she said.

When I was conceived, the Mississippi flowed backward.

I handed the crumpled page back, and she threw it again into the air and watched it plummet lifeless to the carpet among its fellows.

"There it is, Madelyn. My life. The blank pages of my life!" Her eyes rested upon me as I stood one awkward moment, two, feeling as I often would with Miss Rose, that I was little more than another mirror before which to practice phrases and faces for some anticipated performance. She sat back as much as her dress would allow, then recast her gaze upon me.

"You know Mrs. Smith the dressmaker, do you not? Your sister works for her, I believe? Stand up straight. Look at me." I did both. Her smile, replicated in so many angles, pinned me in place. "What does Mr. Dryfus think of such"—she thought for a minute—"such industry? A great many men believe themselves more progressive in principle than they are comfortable being in practice."

I didn't know what Mr. Dryfus thought.

"And you. You have not been back to visit your sister since arriving, is that right? Mrs. Hardrow tells me you haven't even asked. I hope there is no rift between you?" I said nothing. "It is often said

that family bonds are the hardest to break. This may be true. Maybe."
Her eyes darted to the ceiling, to Old Man. "But once broken, they
are very, very hard to mend.

"I want you to do something for me, yes? Look at me. Yes?"
Digging into her desk drawer she produced a paper-wrapped box—
roughly the size and shape of the cigar box of naked ladies I'd found
the year before in William's desk—and a note. "I want you to take
these to Mrs. Smith. Will you do that? Straight to Mrs. Smith. Wait
to see that she reads the note, and don't leave without a reply." She
stared down her long, beautiful nose at me. "Then, my dear, go home
to your sister. My father can do without story time this afternoon."

IT'S HARD TO EXPLAIN THE effect Miss Rose had on me. She
was not particularly tall, and her girth was an illusion of cloth, but
she wore height and girth to the greatest possible effect, her posture
and gestures so grand as to seem part of a script only she had read.
It can't be said that I was afraid of her exactly (though I was afraid
of displeasing her) or that I admired or trusted her. Not then. Not
yet. I merely succumbed to her dazzling presence as you might to a
sudden fever, helplessly, without forethought or will.

Nevertheless, by the time I reached the town green, I had all but
recovered myself.

"Go home," she had said. "To your sister."

A church bell, then another, chimed two o'clock, and boys and girls
spilling from Main Street School scattered like birds in all directions.
Fine. Fine, I would deliver Miss Rose's box and note. But beyond that
I wasn't sure. Because. Because technically I had no sister, did I? No
home, either. The thought a dry scouring rush on the back of my
throat. Technically, I wouldn't be disobeying if I didn't visit.

After all, Mama had not seen fit to visit me.

18

Elegant Attire, the only establishment owned by a woman on Union Street's terraced block of brick shops, smelled of paraffin and herb sachets. A bustled gown dressed the window; a little cast-iron stove, shined up nice, crouched beside bins of buttons and beads. Inviting displays of fabrics, collars, and cuffs arranged by color and texture brightened the long wall. Ribbons dangled from spools behind the counter, where I couldn't see but heard Henry, Mrs. Smith's deaf old dog, whining in his sleep. There were no customers. To my relief, no Mama, either. I thought Mrs. Smith might be on an errand until, behind the felt curtain partitioning the shop front from the cutting room, I heard two or three voices—distinctly male voices—garbled and rough. "There in a minute!" Mrs. Smith called out from among them.

I peeked around the curtain and found two men seated to tea with her at the cutting table—Emil Le Duc, the cobbler, and Simon Hershal, the druggist, whose businesses stood shoulder to shoulder with the dress shop.

"Shouldn't be allowed," Hershal was saying. Le Duc, holding his china cup with nervous care, nodded agreement. "As much a crime,

I say, to threaten a man's livelihood as his life. Take him to court if he won't listen to reason."

The "he" I guessed was the same "he" who had kept shopkeepers on that street complaining all summer: Sonny Schwartz, whose sin, apart from being a Jew, was opening a general store that carried factory-made shoes and dresses and a whole cabinet full of patent medicines (guaranteed to cure all but man's final complaint), all for a fraction of the usual cost.

"I'm afraid the law is on his side, Simon," Mrs. Smith replied.

"Well, change the law then. Isn't Stockwell running for mayor? Where does Stockwell fall on this?"

But Mrs. Smith had risen, and to my delight and embarrassment, beamed at me. "Why Madelyn! What a nice surprise. Welcome!"

I tell you, no one else on earth has ever said that word with such sincerity. A good thing for Mrs. Smith's business, too. By choice or necessity, most women in town made their own dresses or altered ready-mades to fit. Mrs. Smith was not the only one with skill and a sewing machine. Even so, a great many women stopping in only to browse the fabrics or trimmings stayed for tea in the back room where the men now hulked. Most of the time they left the shop with the peace of mind they'd been looking for, or the promise of such, and patterns, lace, and yards of cloth they had not.

Probably it was the transparency of her own calamitous past that compelled even those who didn't share her political leanings to share their own troubles and embarrassments, not to mention their hopes and fears. They forgot, I guess, that Mrs. Smith did have secrets. She had all of their secrets, varied and numerous as button blanks. Indeed there was little about the town's constellation of household concerns that Mrs. Smith did not know by insight, rumor, or confession— though she never *seemed* to know.

"You're looking well," she said, stepping through the curtain. The men gathered their hats. "Still shouldn't be allowed," said Hershal on his way out. Le Duc lingered conspicuously by the display of lace collars. Mama's collars. "I rather expected to see you last night at the gala," Mrs. Smith continued. "Miss Violet made quite a showing. That girl thinks a great deal more of herself than she ought."

"Violet," I said. "She's nothing much. Miss Rose bailed her out of the tombs after she got caught thieving."

"Miss Maddy, where'd you hear that?"

I faltered at her tone. "I just heard it."

"Well, it's not the case," she said, but made no effort to revise the story. "Do you think it kind, spreading that on hearsay?"

I was chastised, maybe, but not at all penitent, and Mrs. Smith wasn't the kind to brood over other people's sins. Soon she was talking about how pretty they'd made the Turner Building, with the banners, and little round tables, each set with candles and a cornucopia, oh, and the dessert table! "Can't for the life of me understand why your sister wouldn't come along. I told her it was for a good cause but she"—Mrs. Smith held a ribbon to my gingham hand-me-down, her tone offhand—"she hasn't got any help, has she? With the baby since you left?"

I don't think she meant this as a judgment, but it felt like one. Probably she was just curious. Mama was, I suspect, one of the few souls in town whose secrets remained secret to Mrs. Smith.

"What about William? William was there, wasn't he?" I asked, trying to sound nonchalant. Mrs. Smith obliged the change in direction.

"What about William? All the young ladies want to know, don't they? Walked once around like he was looking for something, put his nickel in the box, and left without a dance."

My heart leaped at this. No wonder! No wonder Violet had said nothing about him!

"That man . . ."

"That man what?"

"Oh," she rolled the question away with the ribbon. "Never mind. What was it you said you needed?"

I'd nearly forgotten the box in my hand.

"What's this?"

"From Miss Rose."

"Miss Rose? Well." Opening the box, she held in her palm a curious rubber cap, like a thimble made for a very large finger. Then in one motion, she snapped her mouth and the box lid closed and glanced over her shoulder at Le Duc, who was still pretending interest in those collars. Then she read the note, looking all the while a bit feverish, though I couldn't think why. I'd read the note on the way to town, naturally. There'd been no seal. Miss Rose had not said not to. And to my mind, there had been nothing of any interest. Nothing to be feverish about, at any rate.

> Dear Mrs. Smith,
> Enclosed, please find samples of the aforementioned French fashions. If you come to believe, as I have done, that more articles after this nature might be secretly in demand, then we might, together, see to it that this demand is met.

"You okay?" I asked. She tucked the box and the note deep in her apron pocket. "I'm meant to wait for your response."

"Of course."

She rummaged in a drawer, scrawled "Agreed" on a half sheet of paper, and placed it with a button blank in the palm of my hand.

"For your scrapbook." Then turned back to Le Duc, still worrying his hat.

"Emil? Is there something more?"

Beyond thinking a rubber thimble a daft idea, I didn't give the contents of the box or Mrs. Smith's reaction much thought at all. I was going to visit William. Mama, well, Mama could wait. Of course, I had no idea, as I hurried away from the dress shop, the state in which I would find him.

STREAKS OF SUNLIGHT BROKE THE slate sky into pieces and lit the hat brims of ladies strolling the shops; old men, gossiping by the post office, tipped their wrinkled faces to it. He walked around like he was looking for something, Mrs. Smith had said. Or someone? Someone, maybe me? Or Mama, I conceded, but buried the thought, and rushed down the alley to William's studio only to crash headlong into a young lady hurrying away.

We sat stunned on the ground across from each other. Sketchbook pages, obscured in the alley gloom, littered the ground between us; I did not at first recognize her for Mr. Stockwell's oldest daughter, Georgiana, until she jumped up to gather the pages.

"Wasn't my fault," I said, but watching her I felt bad. I had not seen her since the night at the Stockwell house and so couldn't say why I thought her changed. Her face thinner, maybe? Or maybe it was her hands, which were shaking. "I'm sorry, Georgiana. Are they ruined? They're not ruined, are they?"

The sun slipped behind a cloud. The darkness deepened.

"It's closed," she said, hugging the sketchbook close, giving no indication she knew me. "The photo shop. I looked and—it's closed." Then she ran from the alley.

A buggy clattered down Union Street. A dog barked, and another answered one block over. Somewhere a man called out. "The other way, Jack!" But the alley was still and silent. I climbed the staircase and found the studio door *was* closed; not unusual, especially when William was at work in the darkroom, but . . .

I put my ear to the door, heard nothing at first. Then a scuffing, fast and rhythmic.

The latch was open. I pushed through. The scuffing stopped. It was dark and cold. The ceiling shades were drawn. The fire was out. The stove door lolled open. When my eyes adjusted, I could see the flower stand languishing on its side upon the stage.

And there facing the stage, his breath a vanishing fog, sat William in the rocking chair, arrested in a frightening stillness.

"William?" He wore the white jacket with many pockets, but his boots crouched on either side of the chair. His blouse lay rumpled upon the stage, his trousers were draped over the camera to my right.

I ventured closer. "William?" This time his head jerked. He stank of spirits. "William, what are you doing?"

"Oh. Oh, it's you. Of course it's you, my apparition," he said, but did not turn to look at me. "Do you know what day it is?"

"William?"

"Do you?"

"Thursday, I think."

"Thursday," William scoffed, shook his head. "Thursday."

"I'm going for Clara." I took an indecisive step for the door.

"Madelyn, don't!" I hesitated. His face was stubbled and drawn. His eyes had no light in them. Had Georgiana Stockwell seen him in this state? "This will pass," he said. "The day will pass. If you would just hand me my trousers?"

"I'm going to go get Clara."

"Then I shall get them myself." He stood and wavered closer, his thin torso writing with black hair, his cock so shriveled and vulnerable. If he expected to startle me, he was disappointed. I'd seen my share of cocks through the hole in the backroom wall in Susanville, and really, what impressed me then was never the size and shape of that changeable appendage so much as the fearful pride men took in it. No, it wasn't his nakedness—not only his nakedness—but his closeness that made my breath catch. I studied the yellowed crust of his toenails, the veins coursing blue over raised, white tendons.

"Madelyn?"

Footsteps on the stairwell. Then a jangle of voices breached the space between us. I ran to the door and called: "The shop is closed!"

"What are you doing up there?" It was big Nora, her little friend Angela in tow.

"Be nice, Nora. Remember, she's slow," said Angela.

"He is ill today. He can't . . ."

They looked past me, for William, dressed but barefoot and untucked, now braced himself in the doorway. I hoped they couldn't smell him from where they stood.

"Ladies. Very sorry to disappoint you. Malaria, you know. Maddy has sent for the doctor."

This seemed to satisfy them—the disease afflicted so many men since the war—but their trust made me nervous in a way I couldn't explain. I closed the door, helped him back into the chair. I covered him with the white jacket, lit the stove, and sat watching his eyes flutter, counting breaths until the church bells rang five. I was due back at the manor, but couldn't leave him alone like this, could I? There was only one person I could think to help, and when I snuck into the print shop to find him, Hanley came without question.

"How long he been like this?" he asked.

I didn't know. Long enough for Georgiana Stockwell to get an eyeful, I reckoned, but didn't tell Hanley that. "He kept asking if I knew what day it was."

"What, you mean Thursday?"

I shrugged.

"We should get Clara," he said.

"No, Hanley." I grabbed his sleeve, quickly let it go. "He said. He doesn't want her to know. He said it will pass."

William lolled in the rocking chair, legs splayed, drool down his chin.

"*Scheisse,*" Hanley said.

"I have to get back," I said. "Hanley?"

"Okay." Hanley, hulking and gentle, pulled the visor off his head and crouched next to William. "It's okay. I'll take care of him."

A confused upwelling of fear and warmth and gratitude stole my voice. I didn't doubt him at all—quite the contrary—though that must have been what he thought.

"Don't worry, Maddy," Hanley said. "Go."

19

A week later in the kitchen, the cook, Mrs. Nettle, stood puffed up, hand on hips, mouth pursed.

"What I tell you to fetch?" she asked Alby, cracking her on the thigh with a towel. "Don't even remember, do you? And don't think I can't smell what you been up to."

Pies, tarts, and cakes for the night's soiree lined the sideboard. The teapot screamed. I heaved it off the heat, scooped myself a bowl of stew simmering on the stovetop, then sat to my lunch, listening to the fluster of preparations, excited for the festivities, though I expected only to haunt the occasion from the second-floor balcony. I didn't care, so much. Lessons had been short that morning. There would be music and good food, and the trample of feet above told me guests had begun to arrive.

Nettle, cussing, turned back to the stove, and Alby scurried over. "What was it she wanted?" I told her. She slipped out past Susan, the chambermaid, who rushed in.

"Miss Maddy," said Susan. She was waifish and tall with brown eyes too big for her skinny face; she was also the only one in the house to call me Miss, one of the reasons I liked her. The drawing-room bell rang in a line of bells.

"Quick, Miss Maddy, leave that. Miss Rose is asking for you."

"Well, ain't you just the fair-haired child," said Nettle.

I was not so optimistic; it was all I could do to swallow the bite in my mouth. Miss Rose had been nursing a headache when I'd returned the week before. Mrs. Hardrow had taken Mrs. Smith's response from me and had asked nothing about my sister or the print shop—a relief, because I knew the technicalities I'd conceived to justify my defiance would not hold up under scrutiny. I was still, a week later, suffering a mild guilt and a not so mild fear of discovery, which eased when I found Miss Rose in the parlor.

She perched on a settee, addressing a diminutive redheaded man in a white suit.

"Of course you may, but I fear he will be of no help to you on your book, Mr. Clemens. Mr. Bixby paid a visit a month—over a month ago?" Hardrow, in the corner, confirmed this with a nod. "And if father did not know *him*, well . . ."

William—combed, shaven, tucked into a gentleman's vest—stood up from behind a high-backed armchair.

"Ah, Madelyn," said Miss Rose. "The Reverend's wife has just sent her regrets, and Mr. Stark, here, suggested you might be willing to fill her place at dinner tonight. Would that be agreeable to you?"

William, the gentleman again, in a gray vest, his oiled hair gleaming. I could see no crazy in his eyes. "Maddy?" he said.

I made some kind of affirmative response.

"Now," said Miss Rose, "run upstairs and see that father is not indisposed."

I managed to remain composed until I reached the gallery, then scampered up the servants' staircase and slammed into the sickroom. Old Man snorted. Lipman jolted from a sweaty sleep. "Jesus and Joseph!" she said. "Better be a fire!"

We stripped Old Man's shirt, wiped gruel from his face and chest, and as Lipman hiked her skirts and climbed onto the bed to brace her sore back against the headboard, we could hear Miss Rose's laughter, controlled as a song, wafting up the spiral stairs.

"I'm meant to go to dinner," I said. "Tonight. At the dining table." And at this clarification found the thrill polluted by a stronger surge of anxiety.

"Well. La."—Lipman grabbed Old Man under the armpits and heaved him upright—"Di. Da! Pot." She pointed at the chamber pot, then hopped down. Miss Rose, knocking twice, swung wide the door as I slid the pot beneath the bed.

I felt a twinge of guilt treating the turtlehead (I'd begun to think of him as *my* turtlehead) this way, like a living, shitting sack of potatoes. I felt for him trapped there on that bed, in this room, inside himself, but Lipman got her knickers in a twist if I ever said anything about it. "Nothing poor about him. Poor is starving on the street, not living to be old as God and pampered like I pamper him."

You pamper a baby you do more than clean and feed it, I thought. *You hug it, kiss it. Love it.* Of course, it's easy to do with babies, which are little and cute, even if they're ugly. Not even Miss Rose visited Old Man every day or stayed long. She'd sit stiff and quiet as a skeptic in church, looking like she had something meaningful to say, but never saying a word. No wonder Old Man raged sometimes. He was love-starved. I did my best to be gentle. I even hung rosemary sprigs from the garden on the bedposts as I had for Dot the winter she nursed

Mama back from scarlet fever, then nearly died of it herself. But it
did little for the stink.

Drawn by the light, Old Man's head craned toward the door. I
brushed a hair from his forehead and pulled Miss Rose's chair into
place by the bedside. William and Mr. Clemens remained outside
until Lipman, never fond of company, shoved past them to fetch the
linen.

"Mr. Werner, sir," said Mr. Clemens, coming in, hat in hand. "Sam
Clemens here."

"Don't have to yell," I snapped at him. People were always doing
the same with me.

"Madelyn," said Miss Rose. William smiled.

"I see his lips moving sometimes when I read to him, is what I
mean. I reckon he can hear okay, even if he can't say so."

Clemens's tempered voice thickened into a drawl. "You said. Well,
you said I'd be back to the river one day." Clemens clutched his pipe,
but this and his unruly mustache made him look like a boy trying
to dress as a man. "You were right. I hoped. I hoped to speak about
what it was like, back in the early days."

Old Man's mouth opened, closed, opened again like a beached
fish.

"I am sorry, Mr. Clemens," said Miss Rose. "You knew him on
the river?"

"Everyone knew him. Knew *of* him at least. Your father was the
first man to send packet boats north of Natchez."

Clemens was doing the other thing I hated, talking as if Old Man
was already dead and gone, but I kept my mouth shut, my eyes on
William.

"Swore a vision from heaven revealed to him a town, no Shaker
city, but a metropolis rising out of the bluffs. Imagined the levee

churning with steamboats and goods heading all ways of the com-
pass. He was still talking that way when I met him—in '57? '58?
Listening to him, you could almost believe the age wasn't dying out
from under us."

"He didn't count on the war, I guess," said William.

"Or the panic," said Miss Rose.

"Or the railroad," said Clemens.

The war, the railroad, the panic. It was odd to hear talk of a time
before these things, like hearing of a time before the moon and the
sun and the stars.

"Not every visionary is a prophet, Mr. Clemens," said Miss Rose.
"This country's full of visionaries believing themselves prophets and
demanding of others a great deal of misplaced faith."

"He was right about Chicago," said Clemens.

Miss Rose offered to show Clemens her father's river journals.
William stayed behind. We were alone. William and I—and Old
Man, who moaned, "Wiaa!" his eyes milky white, searching.

William's expression changed. "What is that?" he asked.

"What's what? Oh, just a sound he makes. Nurse says it's nothing.
You think he's saying something?"

"No." William sat, elbows to knees, chin to hands in Miss Rose's
chair. "I don't know. God, look at him."

I looked at William.

"He must be near a hundred years old. He seemed about that old
to me when I was a boy."

"You knew him as a boy?"

"He brought me things. To please my mother." He paused.
"Everyone loved my mother."

He so rarely spoke of his mother, I was afraid he'd say no more.
To be honest, it strained my mind to imagine him a boy, with a

mama. Much less a daddy. In the photo shop, I'd told him about Landis Wilcox, my father—as much as I knew without giving Mama up—but this had inspired only a sneering retort that made me drop the subject for good. "So you're a bastard," he'd said. "Just like me."

"She was beautiful?" I asked watching him.

"No," he said. "Not beautiful. Alluring, I would say, like Miss Rose, except not so conscious of the fact. And talented. That's one of her paintings there." He pointed to the portrait over Old Man's bed—a red-faced graybeard, with Miss Rose's nose over a broad chin. "That's him. How I remember him.

"Maddy," he said after a pause. "You're okay here, with him. You're not miserable?"

"Oh no, William!" But his face had become serious and dark and my guts tightened.

"Maddy," he said. "About last week—"

"Dearest William!" It was Violet in the doorway. William shut his mouth. "Won't you take a turn in the garden?" she said.

Dearest William? A turn in the garden? I scowled at Violet.

"Join us, Maddy?" said William.

"Oh, she must stay here with Old Master," she said as Lipman labored through the door with fresh linen.

"Go on, then." Lipman heaved her basket to the foot of the bed. "No, now, don't think a thing of me up here night and day while you . . ." She waved her hand and included in the gesture all I might do outside that room. I could have kissed her sweaty head, though I knew I'd hear about her sacrifice for the next three days. "Off with you!" she said.

20

To be honest, I'd come to enjoy reading aloud to my turtlehead; it made no difference to him how often I stopped and reread for meaning or for the fine sound of a line. The *Metamorphoses* reminded me of the Old Testament, which I preferred to the New because it was full of bizarre occurrences. Floods, parting seas, and men living in the bellies of whales didn't seem all that different in scale from races of men growing out of serpents' teeth or people transforming into trees or birds or cows. It reminded me, too, of newspaper stories Hanley and I read that summer—about scandals and murders and wars and young people dying horribly for love. Once in the *Times*, I read about a girl (rich) and boy (poor) who ran away to swallow arsenic and die (horribly, of course) in each other's arms. And, well, there was no doubt in my mind, no doubt at all, that Thisbe would eat arsenic for Pyramus.

I wanted to tell William this, to reassure him. I didn't need him to explain last week. It was enough that he thought an explanation necessary. In the glow of his presence, all aspects of my life at the manor brightened considerably. I wanted to tell him about Alby and

Mrs. Nettle and Hardrow, and Miss Rose's gowns, about my lessons with Mrs. French . . .

But not, of course, with Violet listening. She hooked one arm under his elbow, steering him toward the gardens and would have left me behind if William hadn't offered me his other arm. I could feel bone and muscle through his jacket. No more booze. He smelled of shoe leather and Macassar oil and spoke with great and worried affection about Clara, who would not give up cooking, though her lungs were not healthy and her shakes worse. "Rebecca does what she can, but with the baby, she's running herself ragged," he said.

The complex tangle of longing and guilt I felt at this was bearable because he was talking to me alone when he said these things.

"Hanley sure misses you," he said after a pause.

"Hanley?" said Violet breaking in. "That great big ugly devil. What do you think? He asked me to dance at the gala!"

"Hanley? Asked *you*?" I asked. Hanley *went* to the gala? A peacock strolling with regal sloth unfurled the blue eyes of its preposterous tail.

"And?" said William.

"Well, I told him no, of course." Violet brushed her curls behind her ear as if brushing Hanley aside.

William should say something, I thought, especially after Hanley cared for him. I should have said something, but kept quiet. William excused himself to sit on the grass by Mr. Clemens, who lounged, pipe in hand, in a lawn chair in the clearing between the manor and the kitchen garden, overlooking the river. Miss Rose had settled beneath her parasol on the stone bench next to him. There was a cold breeze, clouds to the south.

"The right way to do autobiography," Mr. Clemens was saying, "is to start at no particular time in your life, wander at your free will all over your life, talk only about what interests you at the moment, drop it the moment it threatens to pale. I have been thinking about the subject for some time, and I cannot conceive why anyone would write an autobiography that marches with him to his grave!"

"For some time, Mr. Clemens?" Miss Rose scoffed. "A man of your young age?"

"Oh, I don't mean to publish," said Clemens. I sat down on the grass a few feet from William. "Not for a hundred years, at least, after my death. At least a century, so I may be honest as I can manage, and whatever meanness, ignorance, or bias I reveal will be forgiven as a product of the age."

"And are you not honest?"

"I am a humorist, Miss Rose. Outside of that box, I am not allowed an opinion."

"Such is the plight of woman, Mr. Clemens, though we do not have the privilege of choosing our box or profiting from it."

He did not reply. She did not, as I expected, press the issue, which meant he must be more important than I'd imagined.

"Come, Mr. Clemens," she said instead. "What opinions can you possibly have that merit censure?"

"Well. Well," he said again. "Democracy, for instance"—but paused.

I followed his smiling eyes down the garden path to find Mrs. French stepping briskly in bloomers and a man's boots; a broad straw hat covered her shoulders. She carried a net and a collection basket, her face bright from her exertions.

"Samuel Clemens," said Mrs. French, and Clemens stood up to meet her. "We expected you a week ago, at the gala."

"Lorena," he said, and grasping her free hand, peered with boyish enthusiasm into her basket. "What conquest today?"

"Mr. Clemens suffered an unavoidable delay," said Miss Rose.

"And a profitable one I'm sure, Sam," said Mrs. French. "How is your sister?"

"Contentious, overbearing, fit only for a city of angels. She sends her regards, of course."

"Mr. Clemens was just about to tell us his remedy for democracy," said Miss Rose.

"Oh?"

Mr. Clemens offered his seat, but Mrs. French waved him down, put her net aside, and sprawled cross-legged on the grass beside me. Only Violet remained standing.

"And what about democracy?"

"Mr. Clemens thinks democracy a failure and universal suffrage the surest way to crush the nation," said William leaning back.

"Sam!" said Mrs. French.

"Now I don't mean restrict the vote. I don't mean that. Here's what I would do," said Clemens. "Give men of education, merit, and property—give such men five, maybe ten votes to every one of your ignorant Joes. As of now, Joe can be made to vote for any cause by anyone who can persuade him through fear or profit to make his mark on the line, even if that cause does damage to him and his family."

"And women?" said Mrs. French. "Do you include women in the class of educated worthies?"

"Well, now, that's another issue."

"It is the same issue, Sam!" said Mrs. French.

He was wise enough to let the statement pass unchallenged. After a respectful pause, he said:

"There's an election coming next spring. Is that what I hear?"

Mrs. French had not yet forgiven him for his last comment. Miss Rose answered. "The mayoral elections, in April."

"Well, I bet—I bet you half the ignorant bastards in this town would make their mark for R. S. Werner if they saw the name on a ballot. Never mind that he ..." Clemens stopped himself. "Well, that he is not in the best of health. He was mayor two times?"

"Three," said Miss Rose, looking sharply at Mrs. French, as if a thought had passed between them.

"Three times, in bygone days, when the grass was always green and prosperity grew on trees. And that alone—his name and that alone—would be enough for our dear voting public. Enough of this." He stood, angled his hat just so. "Lorena, don't be mad. Come see what I have brought."

Soon the six of us and a good number of servants, as well, gathered in the courtyard around a bizarre two-wheeled contraption of wood and welded iron fitted with a handle, a small saddle, and pedals. Mr. Clemens patted the saddle.

"A velocipede boneshaker," he said with pride. "A bicycle. The newest fashionable conveyance."

Mrs. French, who had been circling the contraption with rising interest, allowed Mr. Clemens to demonstrate its faculties. He made a trip around the fountain to great applause.

If I've led you to believe Mrs. French a mirthless prisoner of her own intellectual pursuits, it is only because this was my first impression. She possessed a tinker's fascination with gadgets like this one (she owned two of William's flip books) and a love of vigorous exercises (she considered taxonomy and botanical painting light amusements). When she was not in the library, she could be found with a collection basket by the river searching out insects and plants, or in the conservatory behind an easel, where her efforts to "capture the transcendent life of the putty root orchid" always left her disappointed. I thought she might count as heathen, for she talked of nature—that is, Nature with a capital N—but never about God in the Bible terms I was used to. Plus, she seemed overly fond of making up proverbs for my benefit. "Only a fool insists on revealing what she knows the moment she learns it, Madelyn. She might as well expel a meal as soon as she consumes it. Let it nourish you first. Digest, Madelyn!"

She certainly didn't dress like a Christian lady. Often she wore bloomers, but was as likely to ramble in men's trousers; even on formal occasions, she wore a man's tapered jacket over worsted brown or black skirts and white silk ascots. She never wore a corset. (She and Miss Rose had long debates over the facility and purpose of this female fashion, in particular.) So focused was she on each present task, that until about a week before, I'd never wondered about her past or even imagined she might possess one, like other people.

I don't know how the subject came up, but Mrs. Nettle told me that Mrs. French had been disappointed in love, then refused to say more about it—a sign of ignorance, I knew by now, rather than courtesy, as Nettle pretended. So the next day, while I was meant to be figuring sums, I worked up a roundabout way of asking her about it.

"Mrs. French, I been wondering." Mrs. French bent over her notes, lips moving over phrases with care, did not immediately respond. Violet looked up at me from her primer. "You said we're better off wanting things we can get by will and effort, right?"

Mrs. French finished her thought, then cleaning her oculars, considered my question with a respectful attention I was not yet accustomed to. In four short weeks, such attention had forged in me the inconvenient habit of considering my own thoughts with more care as well. Previously I imagined one thought as good as any other, simply because it had arisen out of the same mysterious well inside me.

"Why *can't* you get love that way?" I persisted. "That's what you"—I searched for the word—"implied, right? That you can't." And looking briefly at Violet, I came to it. "Have you ever been in love, Mrs. French?"

I watched her (Violet and I both watched her) with fascination and not a little horror, for I was sure that, before she recovered herself, emotion flashed across her eyes. "My dears," she said, "you are young and ridiculous. The first is forgivable; the second . . ." she waved away the possibility of forgiveness with a swipe of her hand and didn't answer the question.

For some reason—maybe it was William standing there or the curious energy with which she examined the wooden struts of the boneshaker—my question and her evasion came back to me. "Sam, may I?" asked Mrs. French, but she had already shed her net and basket.

"Really, Lorena, you will surely break yourself," said Miss Rose.

"It is sometimes easier to start on a hill," said Mr. Clemens.

"Lorena," said Miss Rose, holding her hat against the rising breeze. "Madelyn, go with her."

Off we went, one of us on either side of the handlebar, pushing the hefty machine with such energy that when we stopped and turned, I found the manor a disconcerting distance below. High above, geese tracked shadows over the roof, the gardens, the fountain, but Mrs. French didn't notice, much less speculate about their species. She ran her hands over the bicycle frame, her face beneath her gray hair so eager and young, I felt obliged to provide the voice of reason.

"Mrs. French. Mrs. French are you sure you want to . . . ?"

She flung one leg over the iron bar, and was now straddling the contraption with both hands firmly on the handle and one foot on the pedals. Mr. Clemens had begun to walk and wave his arms. "Not so far!"

"Madelyn." Mrs. French took a tremendous breath. "Let go."

I did as I was told. The wheels began to turn, the machine to wobble, then steady as it picked up more and more speed, hurtling Mrs. French, whose legs, too slow for pedals, flared out on either side, then clamped over the frame. I was running now, down the hill after her, as Mr. Clemens ran up.

"Brake," yelled Clemens as the contraption whooshed past him. Now we were running together down the hill.

"Brake!" yelled Clemens.

"Whoa!" yelled Mrs. French, pulling back with all her might on the handlebar to no effect. "Whoa!" as she hurtled toward the fountain. Onlookers scattered. Violet screamed. Mrs. French swerved left, gave a short, clipped yelp, and plunged into the topiary. A plume of birds flew up as one body, then scattered. For a moment no one else moved, until Miss Rose, hiking her skirts, began to run as best she could.

"Lorena!" she cried. Soon Mr. Clemens and I were kneeling with her, breathless at Mrs. French's side. "Lorena!" said Miss Rose, her hands hovering above Mrs. French's supine body, as if afraid, after such a spill, a touch would break her.

"Back up now," I heard Hardrow say and the pearl necklace of faces staring down upon us dispersed.

"Lorena," said Miss Rose. "Are you terribly hurt? Dear Lorena. Say something!"

Mrs. French, eyes wide, struggling for breath, raised herself to her elbows, as the crowd moved another collective step back. "I think," said Mrs. French as if she had been lying there considering it, "I think next time, a smaller hill."

OF COURSE, THERE WOULD BE no next time for the splintered remains of the velocipede boneshaker, but apart from a sprained ankle, a few scratches, and one admirable bruise on her knee, Mrs. French survived undamaged, suffering far more from the attention paid her. She had not performed for the sake of the audience, as Rose might have, but to satisfy her own impulsive curiosity. Nevertheless, by the time I was sent to dress for dinner, her calamity had become, in Miss Rose's dramatic retelling, an event of great allegorical weight: a death-defying plunge of Woman strapped on the back of modern invention and surviving, bruised but victorious.

21

In a nasty show of magnanimity, Violet declared that of course we would dress for dinner in her room. Goodbye now, William, come along, Madelyn, poor dear.

So there I sat at Violet's dressing table as the chambermaid, Susan, considered my tangled rope of hair. She had finished with Violet, who was now posing before her vanity in an ankle length lilac gown with a hint of a bustle and a gently plunging neckline. The dress she so generously lent me was green tulle, calf length, with puffed shoulders: a girl's dress.

"Oh!" Violet cried. "It is dreadful to be both vain and ugly." She glanced over her shoulder. "Be grateful you are not vain, Madelyn."

"I'm not going," I whispered to Susan. It wasn't only William's presence making me anxious. I could hear carriage wheels on gravel and imagined a house full of strangers with eyes sharp as needles. You could comb and curl and braid my hair all you wanted, there was no way to prepare my face to meet them.

"Of course you're going," Susan whispered back. "Miss Rose says. And when Miss Rose says—Oh, what is that, miss?"

For I had, in nervousness, begun to toy with the charm around my neck.

"It is very pretty," said Susan.

Violet, tugging herself from her reflection, peered over my shoulder. "Where did *you* get that?"

"William," I said, and this time the lie, so quick from my mouth, tasted much like the truth. "Mr. Stark gave it to me."

"Well, I think it's very pretty," said Susan. Violet's nose flared. Her silence as much as her expression should have been fair warning to me.

But voices and music, not to mention savory smells, had begun to waft from the gallery floor. I let Violet go on ahead. One thing was sure, I wasn't about to stay in her pocket all night, playing the ugly dressed-up doll to her benevolent angel. Instead I lingered at the balcony overlooking the gallery, an anxious lump thickening my throat. Violet, light as a dancer, began to distribute charming comments among the dinner guests, young men mostly, whose voices at first tempered, now tested the wide and vaulted space. The houseboy, Tom, smartly dressed and looking fine, walked among them with a silver tray of drinks.

A door, then another, closed behind me. Miss Rose, then Mrs. French, who was limping but trying not to, emerged from their separate rooms. Mrs. French dressed in her usual public costume: worsted black skirt, white blouse and cravat, with a black fitted vest. Miss Rose wore blue velvet with a bustle of textured black lace; three giant ostrich feathers quivered atop her head. Such a mismatched pair would never have been hitched to a dray.

"Madelyn," said Mrs. French. "You look"—she gave me a quick up and down—"tidy."

"Thanks," I said, miserably. "You too."

If Miss Rose noticed me at all, I couldn't tell. She stood with the flat of one hand to her chest, the other over her stomach, breathing. "Miss Rose, are you . . ." To Mrs. French, I said, "Is she . . ."

Mrs. French, raising a finger to her lips, joined me at the balcony rail as Miss Rose, released from some kind of trance, squared her shoulders and descended the spiral staircase. "She must make her entrance," said Mrs. French. "Watch."

One by one, heads turned, voices hushed; even the gathering storm outside seemed to hold its breath as Miss Rose's shadow, appearing before the woman, extended a hand to receive the applause they gave her. "Charles Lock, you darling boy!" she said linking arms with a blond, balding young man. Her ostrich feather towered over him, and though tinged with intimacy, her voice could be heard above everyone. "Sigmund tells me you have been to Rome to see our Harriet. She has promised me a Persephone. Have you met . . . ?" She introduced him elsewhere, then traveling guest to guest, engulfed each in the limelight of her exclusive attention before moving on to bestow her presence elsewhere, the feathers of her hat visible from anywhere in the room.

"Well." Mrs. French straightening her cravat, placed a hand on my shoulder. "Once more unto the breach?"

A misty rain fogged the gallery windows and erased the world outside the manor. Miss Rose laughed. Others joined. But where was William?

"Senator, Mrs. Biggs," said Mrs. French to a very tall man beside a very round woman who greeted us in the gallery, "I'd like you to meet my promising new student, Madelyn."

Senator Biggs barely acknowledged, much less questioned, Mrs. French's description; his wife looked on me with pity. "What?" I bristled. Mrs. French's blunt nails dug into my arm, then let go.

Someone very good was playing the piano. Not Violet. There was Violet, hovering behind Miss Rose near the conservatory. Then bodies parted and I spotted William, near the parlor, his back to my Daphne statue, shaking his head in response to something a thin, bending reed of a woman in a gray gown had said. Another man joined them, as did a Negro—Reverend something, very well dressed, which was nearly as much a shock to me as the pink letters AK branded across his left cheek.

"Mrs. French," I said. "Mrs. French, that lady with William, who is she?"

"Well, Richard! Look!" The senator's wife tugged her husband's ear. "It's Madame Molineaux. You didn't tell me she would be here."

"It's all of it heretical nonsense," said the senator. "Of course you agree, Mrs. French. Communicating with spirits in tips and taps? Imagine that woman profiting from the grief of others."

"I wonder," said Mrs. French, "what your grandfather would have thought, Senator, if someone had told him his grandson would one day send messages, by *tips and taps*, through wires across continents and oceans? Absurd, he would say. Heretical?"

Mrs. Biggs beamed. "See now, Richard, if Lorena French . . ."

The dinner bell rang. Senator Biggs caught the eye and then the arm of Mr. Clemens as he passed. "About that book I've got in mind, sir. It's only the writing that's left to do."

"His father won't even send a telegram," the senator's wife confided to Mrs. French. "Says if everyone starts sending such correspondences, well, it will be the death of language. Really!"

"Mrs. French," I said, beset with anxiety. Hungry as I was, I had been dreading dinner. I still remembered Mama's performance at the Stockwells', and wished to God for a puppeteer of my own, strings to guide my hands and manners. "I don't feel good. I think—"

"You do not feel well. Of course you don't. You'll be fine. I will be sitting there," she pointed to a spot across the table, next to the balding Charles. "Watch me."

But a silver tureen blocked a clear view of Mrs. French's plate, and she was soon too engrossed in conversation with Charles to remember her responsibility. The cutlery, the crystal, the white glazed china plates might as well have been Violet's mocking smile, which I *could* see clearly. She sat four chairs down, across the table—next to William, of course. The thin lady in gray, Madame Molineaux, sat on his other side, so that I couldn't watch him without catching the eye of one or both of the other two.

Miss Rose placed me to the right of Mr. Clemens, who sat next to Miss Rose at the head. In hindsight, I recognize that many of the incredulous looks I received might not have been on account of my appearance but because of my position next to Clemens, whose nom de plume and growing fame must have been known to everyone but me. I also see the purpose the arrangement served, for it defused any envy that might have arisen if, say, Reverend Reynolds rather than Senator Biggs had enjoyed the position. And, of course, with only me to his right, Mr. Clemens's attentions would be directed first and foremost to Miss Rose, herself.

To my right, a musician of some kind—Mr. Girard by his tag—sat straight as a railroad tie, as the senator's wife, on his other side, bombarded him with an unchallenged onslaught of her thoughts and opinions. Mrs. French waved Tom away with the wine. "I'll have what she don't," Mr. Clemens declared. Tom filled my glass. William laughed at something Violet said. Madame Molineaux caught me staring.

No, her gaze rested, or seemed to rest, over my shoulder, but when I looked I found only the moon winking between clouds

through the window. Molineaux swirled her glass and took a sip.
I took a sip, almost spat the sour taste, and looked around to see if
anyone noticed. No one seemed to, all caught in a giddy waiting
stillness that had settled over the table, until Miss Rose stood up into
it. She welcomed everyone, toasted the upcoming centennial, then
made a funny speech about a preacher who'd denounced free love
only to be caught with another man's wife. To which Mr. Clemens responded, "I would rather go down in history as the claimant
than as Mr. Beecher." He elaborated to a chorus of laughter, which
splintered into private conversation, linked and splintered again. The
woman question, the greenback, the whiskey tax, the season at the
Park, the superiority of Racine's heroines to Corneille's, back to the
woman question.

"If sainthood is required to run a household, Senator," said Miss
Rose. "Then no less should be demanded of those who run the
country."

Tom fills my glass, which isn't quite empty. Mrs. French again
says no, as does the Negro reverend. Oysters, then two kinds of
soup, arrive from the butlery. Mr. Girard chooses the broth; Clemens, the cream, so I choose cream. Spoons sing on bone china.
The chandelier sprinkles light. Voices. The chatter of rain. Moaning
wind through the cupola. Goodbye, soup bowls. Tom fills my glass,
and I have decided that the other faces at the table look like living
portraits framed against the red velvet cushions of their tall chairs. I
drink. Mrs. French throws me a strange look, and William, William,
William catches Tom by the sleeve, shakes his head, and they both
look at me. Clemens casts his fork aside and picks up his lamb chop,
so I do the same, resolving to tell Mrs. Nettle now. No, later. Tonight.
That she must be the best cook in Reliance County, in the United
States, in . . .

The senator's wife. Mrs. Biggs, the senator's wife, is asking me something. "Mozart or Beethoven?"

The musician, too, crosses his arms, waiting.

"She won't know," says Violet. I feel eyes. I feel wine and oysters and soup sloshing in my tummy.

"Neither?" I manage, and Mrs. Biggs claps her hands.

"Oh, quite right, my dear! How is it that the history of great composition has been reduced to only two composers? What about Bach, Mendelssohn, Schumann? What about Chopin? True brilliance dies young, you know," she informs the quiet musician, Mr. Girard. William smiles and I am smiling.

"I have heard it said"—Senator Biggs's wife continues as if the speaker might be lurking in shadows above the chandelier; she has a thick brow that spans both eyes, and she pronounces each word as if she means to taste it—"that Chopin is too energetic and disruptive to the gentler sex's sensibilities. But surely one cannot lift one's soul too high above the ground."

"Disruptive to the sensibilities!" says Miss Rose who has, with the rest of the table, joined the conversation. "Who on earth makes these ridiculous declarations? What is the purpose of art but to disrupt, to heighten, to excite the sensibilities?"

"Within reason," says the Negro reverend. Reynolds. Reynolds is his name. A breeze moans through the cupola.

"Whose reason, Reverend? Yours? Mine? Mr. Stockwell's? Did you know his Sin Society has drawn up a petition against my theater? A den of obscenity, he called it, without once inquiring what we plan to produce."

Miss Rose describes a few of what she considers Stockwell's most notable physical attributes, and pretty soon everyone except Senator Biggs and the reverend is laughing. It takes me a long time to stop laughing. Then a lemon torte in the shape of a smile sets me giggling, and not even a look of warning from Mrs. French sobers me.

"I wouldn't underestimate Stockwell's power in this town," says Reverend Reynolds.

"There is a Mr. Stockwell in every town these days, zealots all," says Clemens, finishing his drink. "Myself,"—he points to himself— "I believe it a far more strenuous exercise to remain a skeptic. There is never a time when the skeptic can lay down discernment and rest on the assumption that a position, which is neither logical nor reasonable, must nonetheless be true."

"I have heard his daughter, Georgiana, is quite an artist," says the senator's wife.

"A painter," says William, quickly. I look over at him. "That is, I have *heard* she wishes to be a painter."

DINNER IS OVER. MY FACE won't stop smiling. I don't remember what's funny, but it's okay, because suddenly the manor is full of people smiling: shopgirls and young men from town, doused in cologne, oiled hair damp and steaming. They are talking in clumps in the parlor and reciting poems on the gallery stage and playing cards in the conservatory and dancing to the music of the string quartet that seems to have blown in with the wind. I find William pinned beside the spiral staircase by Big Nora and Little Angela.

"Easy, Maddy," says William. "Are you okay?"

"Oh, William," says Nora. "You are such a dear."

Miss Rose calls everyone to the parlor for a recital. I stumble along after Nora, clinging to William's arm. And when I sink down beside him, cross-legged on the parlor carpet, I feel as though I've left part of myself, maybe the ugly part, behind. Nora and Angela whisper. Mr. Girard sits at the piano. And oh my, my! If this is

Chopin, the senator's wife is right. She is right about how the music lifts the soul!

"No, Maddy, sit down." William's hand on my shoulder. People clap. People talk and laugh. Miss Rose recites a poem, then stands until applause rises enough to permit a bow. Tom at my side with coffee, but I don't want coffee and say so.

"I should ask the same of you, sir," says Madame Molineaux to Reverend Reynolds. Everyone who has not returned to the gallery, quiets to listen. "You who prays to a god who once assumed corporeal form and then ascended." Madame Molineaux glances around at her audience. "To where did he ascend, Reverend? Where lies the realm into which you send your prayers?"

Her eyes circle not just the faces, but also the shadowed walls behind us. I think it very funny.

"Shhh, now Maddy. Hush," said William handing me his coffee, which I don't want, but drink because it is William's.

"Who's here? Is someone here?" whispers the reverend's wife. "My dear baby? Harold!"

The woman's face gapes with grief, and the giddy joy I'd been feeling sinks.

"I don't know," says Madame Molineaux, her eyebrows arched. "Shall we find out?"

"What fun! A séance!" says Nora.

A hand on my shoulder sets my hair on end. "Madelyn." It's only Mrs. Hardrow. Solid, indelible Mrs. Hardrow. "Mr. Stark, pardon. Miss Rose would like a word with both of you."

I do not, not believe in spirits. I used to hover in the doorway as Isaiah's wife, Ruth, conjured Dot's husband back in Susanville. But I'd never spoken with him, nor did I expect a reply when I addressed my worries to Dot after she had passed. Should I have attended Dot's soul more carefully? Maybe, I think, wobbling up the stair after William, maybe Dot is angry with me for neglecting her, and if Dot is angry, what about the dead girl, Aileen?

One lamp lights the office. I see first a great looming shadow on the adjacent wall, and then its maker, Miss Rose, by the settee, arms crossed, foot tapping. Even so, I remain insensible to the peril of the situation until I see the smirk on Violet's pretty face.

Says Miss Rose, "I demand so little for my hospitality. A bit of gratitude!" She stomps, no doubt making manifest some disgruntled spirit conjured below in the parlor. "A bit of loyalty for my generosity and *you, you* repay me by . . ."

She takes a great breath; the ostrich feather bobs with indignation. Still I remain more fascinated than afraid until her next words. "Let me see it."

"Miss Rose," says William. "What's this about?"

"Thief," Violet pipes. "I knew she was a thief. She wears it around her neck."

"Now, Madelyn!" says Miss Rose. "Let me see it."

What can I do but bring my precious charm from beneath my blouse?

"You see!" says Violet. "You see, I told you. She's a liar and a thief. She says William gave it to her."

"But I. I didn't . . ." I take a wobbly step toward the door, but there again is Mrs. Hardrow, turning me back toward my accusers. William's pale skin looks sickly blue.

"Oh," Miss Rose says. In the dim light, the mirrors are dark moving pictures and my tummy is a jostle with them. I close my eyes. "Well. That is not mine."

I open my eyes.

"It was mine," says William softly. "Madelyn is telling the truth."

The truth? "I gave it to her." He what? "It was my mother's. Old Mr. Werner gave it to her when she was new to this country and all alone in the world. And I . . . I gave it to Madelyn for the same reason."

He gives me a look and I stay silent, even as a baffled triumph flaps in my belly.

"But she wasn't!" declares Violet, a desperate edge to her voice. "She wasn't all alone. She came here with her—"

"Violet!" said Miss Rose. "I think you have said quite enough for one night."

On the strength of these revelations and the wine, the room begins to gyrate. The charm had been Willa Stark's? Had been William's. And William lied. William lied for me!

But my belly must know there is more behind William's lie than loyalty to me. At any rate, the rush of triumph I feel reveals itself in a curious way. I turn to Violet, intending only to give her my most belligerent smile, and vomit down the embroidered front of her lilac dress.

And so we both make our exits from the festivities that night: Violet, weeping into the care of the chambermaid, Susan, while I, groggy and limp, am cleaned up, bullied out of my dress and into bed by loud-suffering Nurse Lipman.

OH, BUT NIGHT WAS NOT yet over. Another shock awaited me. Just past midnight, by the look of the moon, I woke to voices and a low, wailing moan rattling the shards of stained glass I saw when I opened my eyes. When the colors fell away to darkness, I knew I was alone in the bed. No offended spirits. No Lipman, either. A trickle of yellow light seeped beneath the sickroom door. A moan, more like the bleating of a lamb than a human sound, grabbed my heart

and squeezed. It took me several minutes to find courage enough
to push through.

Old Man, mouth wide open, thrashed on the bed. Mrs. Hardrow
in her nightdress, dark hair wild, had managed to wrap both arms
around his legs. She held on while Nurse Lipman flattened herself across his chest, and still my poor turtlehead fought. "Wiaa!" he
moaned.

"Stop!" I heard myself cry. "Stop! What are you doing to him?"

Lipman motioned with her head to the bottle and the rag on the
nightstand. "Now, Maddy, before he hurts himself." I did as I was
told, doused the rag with ether, held it over Old Man's nose and
mouth until those terrible blind eyes rolled in his head; the hand
holding my arm slackened; his body became a limp wire, and we
three, still tense and battle worn, backed away from him, into an
overarching silence much louder than his voice.

Only then did I notice another presence in the room: an old
woman in a nightdress, standing with her hand over her mouth as if
to suppress a cry. A bald old woman with a fringe of gray hair on her
white scalp. She slipped away through the hallway door.

Said Lipman to Hardrow, "He's been agitated all afternoon, and
worse tonight, Missus; I was going to. I mean I should have doused
him before bed, but . . ." Lipman gestured at me with her head.

I hardly noticed. I was staring out the door after Miss Rose.

22

"Met the demon liquor last night, did you, Cinderella? Head hurt?"

One gray incisor winked from a mouthful of strong yellow teeth. It took me a moment and a blast of stale breath to confirm it was Nurse Lipman smiling down, rather than one of the haunting dreams that had passed for sleep that night. She dumped my bedpan into the wide-mouthed receptacle, wiped the pan with a towel, clanged it down. "Get up. It's late." Then she handed me a drink much the color of what she'd just discarded.

"Ugh. Pickle juice?"

"You'll feel better. My da used to swear by it, and I got enough to do"—she nodded to Old Man's door—"without playing nursemaid to the likes o' you."

A thorn of guilt gouged me through the relief I felt. "He's okay, then?"

"Still kicking." I liked to think she cared for Old Man (that someone did), but wasn't sure and wasn't sure I could blame her either way. There wasn't much left to love. Indispensable—so long as Old Man lived, we were both indispensable. She stared into the wardrobe mirror, pulled at the sagging skin around her eyes.

"I tell you, though. Never seen him rage so bad as that. Drink, now. All of it."

I took a sip. She poured fresh water into the basin.

"Nurse Lipman?"

"Huh?" She scrubbed her face as if to take the top layer off, swished water through her teeth, spat.

"That *was* her. Miss Rose, last night in the sickroom. Wasn't it? That was Miss Rose?"

"No." She dried her face.

"No?"

"Nope. Didn't see nothing but a raging old man last night."

"But . . ."

"And neither did you. Nothing worth gabbing about to your loudmouthed friends in the kitchen. Understand?"

I chewed on this. "Well, what happened to her, then?"

"Happened, she says. Nothing happened. She's old, that's all." She turned to the mirror. "Happens to everyone."

I confess I hadn't been much aware of Miss Rose's age. Her splendid dresses, her hats—her wigs too, apparently—and the regal way she wore them, deflected such impressions. I had known she was *older*, but bald? I'd sooner believe I'd seen a spirit, and wasn't sure what I felt about it, except that the confirmation allowed me to separate another fact from the haze of wine and dreams.

William had lied about the charm. William had lied for me. Which meant he cared for me. Mama had taught me this equation. To lie for me is to love me. *I gave it to her when she was far from home and all alone in the world.*

But wait. The *her* must have been Aileen. He must have given Aileen the necklace. Then something else occurred to me. He lied for Aileen, too.

Not just lied. Cut her throat, then lied. The thought was a cold finger down my spine. Cut her throat to give her family a truth they could live with. So that she could be buried next to her brother.

Lipman was staring down at me as if looking for leak holes in a boat. "Swear it. Not a word."

"Who else knows besides Hardrow?"

Nurse Lipman could not keep the pride from her voice. "Nobody."

"Not even Mrs. French? Violet?"

"Nobody. And you gonna tell nobody. Right? Or it's both our asses."

The sickroom door closed behind her. The great clock in the entrance hall, then a chorus of mantle clocks, chimed six times into the silence. Late? Early enough. But there was little sense in crawling back into bed only to be roused again. Anything past five was late to Lipman, and if she couldn't sleep, then by God neither would I (never mind that she napped most of her day with Old Man). I dressed, tended my matted hair, and followed the smell of baking bread to the kitchen where Nettle and Alby sat with cups of coffee between them, for once companionable.

"Go on, then, what happened next?" asked Nettle. I picked up the cat and slumped into a chair. They were talking about the séance. Lizzette and Susan, uniforms crisp and faces weary, joined us with cups of coffee. "I didn't think Miss Rose believed in haunts," said Susan.

"Believes in celebrity, don't she?" said Nettle. "Go on, then."

Apparently Alby had sneaked upstairs to watch the séance, at great peril to her job, and had seen Madame Molineaux summon not only Mrs. Biggs's baby son and the musician's late mother, but also Benjamin Franklin, Joan of Arc, and several other departed luminaries. The performance, a great success. "Can't believe you missed it," she said to me.

Susan pulled her shawl tight around sturdy, narrow shoulders. "She didn't miss Violet."

"Vile Violet," said Alby.

"Best stay clear of her for a time," Nettle said. "Imagine she got naught but misery in mind for you."

"But why?"

"You really don't know? It's territorial. You're encroaching on Violet's territory."

"I'm not . . ."

"Course you are, deary. Can't say as I pity her over much, but it's the truth, God's own. Miss Rose is the only thing in the world between that girl and the Wayward Home. Now me, now I never did understand people what treat their own misfortunes as license for nastiness, but—"

Lizzette, quietly scowling all this time, pushed her coffee cup away. "Let's see it, then. Let's see this charm of yours."

All four huddled close and I couldn't very well say no. Lizzette's lips pursed. She sat back, arms crossed over her broad chest.

"Listen, sweetheart," she said with no sweetness. "One little necklace don't make you his girl."

"Anyone ever give you a necklace, Lizzette?" asked Nettle.

"No need, is there?" said Alby. "Spread your legs for a—"

"I'm saying," said Lizzette, "that man a gentleman to ladies, maybe, but you wouldn't be the first candle he dipped his wick into, believe you me. Only one reason a grown man gives a girl like you something like that."

"And I'm saying better keep your own knickers on, deary, or—"

"You go to hell, Alby!"

"Just pissy, you are," said Alby. "Caught her Tom with another kitten last night. That's right, idn't it?"

"Alby!"

Everyone, even Nettle, stood up to find Mrs. Hardrow in the doorway, arms crossed like Saint Peter at the gate, her one-word admonishment so strong, Lizzette didn't even think to gloat. All business, bearing no trace of the night's trials, Mrs. Hardrow gave the breakfast order and many more besides. The reverend would be leaving at nine, the senator and his wife would stay for lunch with Madame Molineaux. Mr. Clemens would depart for Saint Louis on Sunday with Mr. Stark.

My ears pricked up. I'd thought William left the night before. I didn't care what Lizzette said about him. What did she know? Anyway, my affection had nothing, or at least much less, to do with his wick than she thought. The love I coveted? Well, it was made of chaste kisses, of secrets and gestures and declarations. Besides, I'd seen Lizzette with Tom; I'd watched what Mama did with backroom men, and it wasn't love. Not by my account. That was rutting, pure and simple.

Lizzette and Susan bobbed with the precision Hardrow's tone demanded and hurried away. Alby excused herself to the scullery. Even the big gray cat scuttled off my lap into the hall, leaving me alone under Hardrow's scrutiny. Miss Rose's secret, cool as an unspent penny in my pocket, felt heavy now under her wooden stare. I waited for her to say something, and when she didn't, I said, "Mrs. Hardrow," with as much gravity as I could muster. "Mrs. Hardrow. I just want you to know. I want you to know I can keep a secret."

I admit I didn't expect much, but did expect *some* response to what I felt to be a noble declaration. Instead, Mrs. Hardrow turned and left without a word.

Miss Rose was occupied all morning with her visitors. Mrs.

French's ankle had swelled enough in the night to confine her to her quarters. Violet begged ill. So I took my headache to the library, collapsed into Mrs. French's favorite armchair with a book but merely stared at the pages. Only my legs, propped on a little leather stool, were visible from the door; nonetheless, Susan found me there.

"Oh, here she is, Mr. Stark." My feet thumped to the floor. Peering around the upholstered back, I found Susan beaming over William's shoulder.

"Maddy," said William. He glanced at Susan, who had found the bookshelves in urgent need of a dusting. "Walk with me," he said.

He looked more himself in rumpled clothes. Stubble darkened his cheeks, and as he stepped from the conservatory's loamy warmth to the frosted grass, he caught his breath. The cold air felt rough as new linen. Here and there branches littered the ground, but patches of blue sky showing through the clouds looked scoured clean.

"I thought you went back last night," I said trying to sound light. I'd be lying if I said I didn't know what he wanted to talk about. I just didn't think we'd talk so soon, and was not at all sure the turn it would take. I hadn't known he'd given the dead woman the necklace when I took it. Knowing wouldn't have stopped me, but still, this is what I would tell him. Anyway, what was he doing, giving an Irish girl a necklace in the first place? His mother's necklace.

Unless he cared for her more, maybe much more, than he admitted?

Unless he loved her.

"Mrs. Madrigal locks the boardinghouse at ten," said William. "I slept, tried to sleep, in the parlor."

"Guess you heard Old Man, then. He's not like that all the time.

Mrs. Nettle says it's no wonder he had a fright last night with all the spirits loosed in the house. She says with one leg in the grave, he's more likely to see spirits gone before him."

"Mrs. Nettle?"

"The cook."

William nodded. I wished he'd come out with it, but he seemed nervous, not the cracked but the cautious kind, and didn't say anything more until we'd wound through the topiary and were sitting close, thrillingly close, shoulder to shoulder on a stone bench among the roses.

"You gave it to her, didn't you?" I said finally. "To Aileen."

"And you stole it."

"I didn't." My hand found the charm beneath my blouse. "I mean, I did. But I—"

"I gave it to her," said William; a jealous flutter lit my gut.

"But. But William, it wasn't like you said last night. She wasn't all alone. Her family, her daddy at least, lived in the Patch. I've seen where he . . ."

"Family or no, Maddy, she was alone. I've said too much. I can't say more except that I did what I could for her. Tried to do what I could, but she . . . God!" he said, wrenching himself upright, blocking the sun. I couldn't breathe. Those were tears in his voice; he raked his hands through his hair. "God, what a fool I was!"

He *had* loved her! I knew he loved her. And all at once I knew the answer to the question he'd asked me on his crazy day last week in the photo shop. Thursday wasn't the answer. Not the answer he'd been looking for. Last Thursday had been a year to the day since we'd found Aileen dead in the river. Oh, William!

He was pacing, upsetting birds flitting through the undergrowth, and then just stood there, looking at me, thinking what, I didn't know, for now he bent to his knees beside me, taking my hands into his own.

"Maddy. Listen." He blew warm air into my palms, closed them as you would a book. "I can't say more," he said softly. "I would if I could. I can't. And Maddy?"

He raised my chin, his pleading eyes so hard and dark. His thumb caressed the back of my stained hand, then moved from my hand to my cheek, his lips inches from my own, and I felt a heavy warmth, not altogether pleasant, deep in my belly.

"I need to know I can trust you to be silent about this. You said I gave you the charm. Fine, okay. I gave it to you. That's the end of it. Yes?" he said. "Maddy?"

"Yes," I whispered.

"Oh, Maddy. Maddy, that's my girl. My dear apparition."

Then he bent, kissed me flat on the forehead, and walked away.

He kissed me, I thought doggedly, watching him go. He loves me. If he loved Aileen, who was Irish and Catholic—which might even be worse than ugly—if he loved her, then why couldn't William love me? Maybe already loves me, I thought, clutching that necklace tight as a noose around my neck.

So distracted was I by these ruminations, I had all but forgotten Miss Rose's bald head until Susan fetched me to her office later that afternoon. Susan left and closed the door; the curtains gaped, then settled and the room, even with those mirrors reflecting each small movement, felt so uncommonly still, I hardly dared to breathe. My eyes locked on Miss Rose, who remained consumed with some object, a book of some sort, open on her desk.

Gone was the old bald woman, helpless in the shadows of the sickroom. In her place stood Miss Rose in a royal blue frock, white bustle, white lace dressing the seams. Luxurious brown curls, pulled into a loose chignon, framed her high cheekbones and stately nose.

Of course, I knew my mark to be an order of ugly beyond a bald head, but the revelation of her appearance or, more to the point, of her daily transformation, struck me giddy with curiosity—and hope. Even from where I stood across the room, I could see what I had not seen before, that the color of her cheeks had been painted on, the half-moon shadows beneath her eyes, powdered over. How many wigs did she have? Would she show them to me?

Entranced as I was, I did not consider what so enthralled her until she looked up, and my eyes fell to the desktop. Yes, it was a book.

No. A scrapbook. *My* scrapbook. A high voiceless sound squeezed from my throat.

"Oh, Madelyn," said Miss Rose, a vision of nonchalance.

How did she? *Violet.* But when? Last night sometime? This morning. This morning while Lipman was with Old Man. Pleaded illness and snuck upstairs and picked through my things and stole my . . . !

"It seems," said Miss Rose. "That I have some business with Mr. Dryfus this morning." She tucked my scrapbook into her handbag. "Why don't you accompany me?"

23

After William's kiss, I'd felt as tall as an oak, but this turn had shrunk me to a spiny shrub beside Miss Rose in the hansom. It was dark inside, the curtains drawn against the cold, and her scent, lavender and rosewater, no less than her layered skirts, filled the cabin. With each bump in the road, I thought I might be sick again. Thought maybe I *should* be sick again.

How much of my scrapbook had she picked through? How much had Violet seen? How much could they know? Each trinket in that collection of odds and ends had a story to tell me, but I wouldn't have thought they'd mean much to anyone else. Besides some silly poems and those letters to William, I had written down very little. Even so, a quick survey of the pages would reveal two glaring secrets: my infatuation with William, of course, but worse, Mama's and my true relation to each other.

What was Miss Rose going to do? Expose us? Why? Because I'd seen her without her wig? Mama would blame me. Would Mr. Dryfus cast her out? And what about Little John? And how could Violet—!

Doing poorly was she? Snuck upstairs, is what she did, picked through my things and stole my scrapbook. Vile, vile Vi-oh-let. Sat-isfying fantasies of violence bolstered me only until the hansom jerked to a halt before the print shop.

"Miss Rose, I won't. I'm not going to say anything about your . . . about . . ."

"About what?" The muscular authority of her voice shaking the curtain.

Your lumpy bald head! I almost said. Your old, ugly, lumpy, bald head! But said nothing, for she was, with Cyrus's help, climbing down. I sat there in the hansom, unsure. While it's true that part of me wanted nothing more than for Mama to stand accountable for our lies, another, larger part was frantically concocting some expla-nation.

I climbed down after Miss Rose. Inside, no one was minding the counter. The high, pained bleat of Little John's cries, surging from the kitchen, was our only greeting apart from the scent of coffee and sauerkraut permeating the place. The Washington Press was thump, thump, thumping, which meant Hanley was in the composition room. Maybe, I thought, maybe Mr. Dryfus was out? But Miss Rose, knocking and opening his office door in the same motion, proved this hope false.

"I may be some time," she said, cool as you please, and, stepping into the other room, closed the door on me.

My heart beat a dozen times for every shuddering thump of the press. Then I heard the kitchen door open, Mama's voice and Little John's cries soften, and the thin thread holding me back snapped. I burst into the office to find Miss Rose staring down on Mr. Dryfus, behind his desk.

"Mr. Dryfus," I blurted, having little notion what I would say until I heard myself saying: "It's my fault, Mr. Dryfus. My—"

"Madelyn!" said Miss Rose.

"Fault?" said Mr. Dryfus.

"It was Madelyn's idea," Miss Rose cut in, which left Dryfus and me both fairly baffled. "To approach you first about the printed matter for our Nativity play. Wasn't it, Madelyn?" Her painted eyebrows arched and flattened. "You were right," she said. "Mr. Dryfus is not one to be deterred by Mr. Stockwell's silly petition against my theater, are you, Mr. Dryfus? Not with the profit he shall make." She paused. "And the service which we shall render the community, of course. A glorious beginning to a glorious new season in the arts!"

Mr. Dryfus, looking resigned and weary, made no sign of having endured any greater revelation than this.

"Now," said Miss Rose, turning forcefully my direction. "Go visit your *sister*, Madelyn. While Mr. Dryfus and I discuss terms."

As I closed the office door, the numb relief I felt passed to confusion and then to a kind of impotent and resentful gratitude, which marks so many of my memories of Miss Rose. Why would she bring me, if not to tell? Why make me think she would tell? I was all tangled up, and Mama coming down the hall with a gnashing, crying Little John didn't straighten me any. Her eyes found mine. She stopped short, holding Little John so close that my heart became an empty open hand within me. A kind word, Mama. Please. Any tenderness at all would do. I gladly would have rushed over, laid claim, and hugged tight the both of them, but the invitation flickering across her face vanished.

"Well," she said instead, "if it ain't the educated lady." The hurt in her voice as much as the venom stung me.

"What's wrong with him?" I didn't know what else to say. In the dim hallway light, Mama looked haggard and disheveled in a way

I'd never seen. Her face bony, her eyes weary, her hair unkempt. The shop was a mess, too, I realized, dust and paper everywhere, the coal scuttle empty. Little John whimpered, hushed.

"You care?" Mama scoffed. "Don't care a lick about us when you're up there in the manor, do you? Don't visit. Don't even think of me and all the work you left behind, do you? No sense pretending you care now."

She might have said more, but the study door opened to the swish of Miss Rose's skirts. I stood for a long, harrowing moment, caught between them, until Miss Rose broke the rasping silence.

"Good day to you, Mrs. Dryfus."

Without a word, Mama turned and walked back into the kitchen, taking with her a part of my heart, not to mention any sacrificial impulse I suffered on her behalf. Not knowing what else to do, I followed Miss Rose out the door and into the hansom. I turned my back to her, stared hard at the bright fragments of town passing through cracks in the curtain, determined to think nothing, to feel nothing, to rise out of myself and look down until I appeared from above as small as I felt. And I would not cry, I would not.

"Madelyn."

"It wasn't my fault," I said. "It wasn't my idea to come here, or to lie or—"

"It wasn't her fault, either. Madelyn, listen."

"No!"

No one said "no" to Miss Rose. She sat upright, straight and still. *Be sorry*, I thought, but I wasn't and couldn't bring myself to say so.

"Why'd you bring me with you if you weren't going to tell?"

"What options did your mother have, Madelyn? What?" And then she paused as if choosing a word from a shelf. "Assets?"

"Assets?"

"Skills, Madelyn. Skills rendered for a price. What assets beyond her beauty, her sexual labor. Her maternal labor?"

"Don't talk about Mama like that."

"Like . . . ?"

"Like that! Like you know. What do you know? You don't know anything! Rich lady like you with your big house and your dresses and your"—I took a mighty breath—"your wigs! You don't know!"

And before I knew it, I was telling her everything: about Landis Wilcox and the big white house, about the day I was born, and the day Mama returned. About Dot, the garden, the goats, and the backroom men. About John and his wife and the ad in the *Matrimonial Times*. By the time I was done, we'd crested the manor drive and jostled to halt beside the fountain; I was gutted, breathless, horrified. The horse, a piebald gelding, whinnied hello to the barn; blackbirds trilled from the hedges. The carriage gave as Cyrus jumped down. He opened the door and Miss Rose, silent for the longest stretch I'd known, pulled it closed again.

"And the baby?" she said. "He looks nothing like his father."

"Yes he does," I said, though I'm pretty sure she suspected this.

Briefly, ever so briefly, I felt the weight of my past lift as far as the low cabin ceiling, only to settle again heavier. What was I thinking, telling her all this? Now, in the aftermath of this traitorous lapse, I saw all of us—me, Mama, Little John, even Mr. Dryfus, who loved Little John as his own son—huddled small as mice in the palm of Miss Rose's hand. And the secret I held in exchange (one old, bald head) seemed awfully wet powder by comparison.

After an agonizing silence, she spoke again, low, almost a whisper.

"And do you think, do you really think, your mother would have chosen that life for herself? For you? You think she had a choice? Oh, that poor brave girl."

Through a crack in the curtain, I could see Robert, the butler, standing nervously by the carriage to see what the matter could be.

"Miss Rose. You can't—"

"Oh, I could, Madelyn." She stood ablaze in the glare of the open door looking down at me. "We've already established how easily I could. But would I? Why would I tell? Think, Madelyn." She tapped her temple. "What purpose would that serve?"

"Miss?" said the butler. "Mrs. Wiltshire from the Lady's Auxiliary is waiting. She says . . ."

"Fine, yes." She waved him away. "It seems to me, Madelyn." Digging in her satchel, she handed me my scrapbook. "It seems to me we both hold secrets the other would rather keep secret."

I was shattered, shaking, though I didn't know it until Miss Rose disappeared into the manor and I climbed from the hansom to find my knees wobbling. Cyrus hovered close, but I have never been the fainting kind. Instead, the day's emotions chattered like a room full of people, louder and louder, making no sense at all.

Until one sound rose over the mangle. Laughter.

My eyes adjusted to the winter glare. Violet, feeling ever so much better, stood on the porch, near the conservatory, next to William and Mr. Clemens, laughing. At me? At something Clemens had said? I didn't much care. Vile Violet was laughing, turning this way and that before the men, so that her skirt billowed prettily.

Make no mistake. I knew exactly what I was doing as I placed my scrapbook beside the fountain, dried my eyes, and marched around the porch steps. Without so much as acknowledging William or Clemens, I grabbed a great chunk of Violet's pretty hair and yanked, tumbling us off the porch, into the flowerbed. Oh, we rolled and kicked and scratched and bit, shredding Cyrus's winter bulbs and crushing the latticework, until icy water stole the breath from me and left us both heaving on hands and knees at Mrs. Hardrow's feet.

Miss Rose stared down at us from the porch with an open-mouthed William and flabbergasted senator, who had postponed his departure until Sunday. Only Mr. Clemens and perhaps Lizzette, whose head poked over the second-floor balcony, seemed amused. Miss Rose, furious, stomped down the steps but kept a distance from our bloody, mud-stained persons.

"Explain yourselves!"

"She!" We levied our accusations in the same overlapping breath. "Attacked—stole—me—my scrapbook!"

"No, she did not," said Miss Rose.

Violet and I, unsure who had been exonerated, glanced at each other.

"Mrs. Hardrow took your scrapbook. At my request. Now . . ." she said, but looked back and forth between us, clearly at a loss. "Out of my sight. Both of you."

24

Mrs. Hardrow interpreted "out of my sight," to mean "confined to your rooms." Her betrayal stunned me, though no more than the day's other revelations. I hadn't minded Hardrow, liked her even, thought she might even like me, but such casual affinity was nothing compared to the loyalty Miss Rose commanded. Didn't matter, anyway. I wasn't about to apologize to Violet, who, after fighting with such unexpected vigor was now shrieking and carrying on like a child. Hardrow called Lipman to attend her while I, scrapbook in hand, trod upstairs, terribly sorry for myself, to await Lipman's return. She stopped short at the sight of me, chuckling.

"Well, my Lord and savior. Here I was thinking she must have had the worst of it. Let me see."

The cut above my left eye had bled down my front, but would not need stitches, she said. She cleaned my scrapes, assessed my bruises, splinted my sprained ring finger to its neighbor, all the while telling me what a fool I was, putting at risk a position like this, and for what? I hardly listened. That day had pummeled me

from every imaginable angle, and only self-righteous pride prevented me from crumbling. Surely my days at the manor were
numbered. I told myself I didn't care—*they* couldn't make me go
because *I* had already decided to leave. When Miss Rose finally
called, on Monday, after two nights and a day of seclusion, I was
ready with my carpetbag packed.

Miss Rose lounged on a settee in her bedroom in a cream silk
dressing gown, powdered, and perfumed. Locks of hair gathered at
her crown and coiled down her back. Her attention rested on six
bolts of thick fabric displayed on the opposite settee.

"For the winter curtains, Madelyn," she said lightly. "Heavens, not
that one. Or that." Hardrow gathered the offending samples.

I had never been inside Miss Rose's bedroom. Though it faced
her office on the other side of the spiral staircase, it was a mirror
only in shape and size. What struck me most was the clutter. I had
expected a room as carefully arranged as Miss Rose when she left it,
but hats, collars, scarves, shoes, and underthings were strewn on the
floor or draped over armchairs. Dresses hung from the bedposts and
off the vanity mirror. Portraits and paintings of every size and subject
fought for space on the wall; artifacts and filigreed trinkets—carved
porcelain eggs, a jeweled elephant, a headless stone woman with a
belly full of baby—jumbled every flat surface.

But it was the japanned tallboy, black embossed with gold and
closed with a bronze lock, on which my eyes lingered. I felt, in spite
of myself, a shiver of wonder, for it must have contained the only
articles of her costume not displayed in the disorder: her wigs. I
assumed she had more than one.

"What do you think, Madelyn?" said Miss Rose. She was speaking of the curtains.

I recovered my scowl.

"I don't think you need new curtains."

"Oh? And if you did?"

Among the remaining samples was an olive green fabric, the same shade as the wallpaper. "Fine," I said. "That one."

"No," she said quickly. "No, this one I think."

"The other one matches the wallpaper."

Hardrow clearly thought I'd lost my mind, but what else could I say? Why were we talking about curtains, anyway? If she knew the one she wanted, why did she . . . ?

I lost my thought in Miss Rose's smile. "But she is right, is she not, Mrs. Hardrow?" Mrs. Hardrow said nothing. Miss Rose fixed her eyes on me. "And we are not afraid to say—or to act on—what we think is right, are we? This one, please, Mrs. Hardrow."

Hardrow left us. I would have given my left toe to make her remain a buffer between me and Miss Rose, shimmering in her dressing gown. Even stripped of her usual layers, her presence filled the space between us, threatening my visions of brave insurrection. I held my carpetbag tight as she circled me, walking slowly as she had the first day in her office, her scent, lavender and rosewater, and her voice holding me in place.

"I see you plan to leave us."

I nodded, for all my defiant words deserted me.

"I see," she said thoughtfully. "And where will you go?"

"New York," I said. "Or Paris. Or Rome."

"Oh yes, beautiful cities, particularly Rome."

"Or maybe West."

"I see," she said reasonably.

"Don't!" I said, turning to face her.

"What?"

"I'm not dumb!" Her laughter cut my declaration short.

"Oh, but you are a *fool*! A young fool who knows nothing of desperation. How will you get to New York or Paris or Rome? Or haven't you considered that? What will you eat? Where will you sleep, Madelyn? Your mother has protected you well enough to make these indignities you believe you have suffered seem large. They are mere scrapes, Madelyn, to those you would suffer as a friendless, ignorant girl, alone in the world."

"I'm not—"

"Do not oppose me, Madelyn!" Her cavalier tone vanished. "You will lose! To think of you embarrassing me with that display before the senator and Mr. Clemens. Unacceptable! Unacceptable in one so obviously intelligent. You have no manners, no tact, no self-control, and your temper! Passion is an asset, Madelyn, but temper—" She spoke from experience, I think. "If Mr. Stark had not argued on your behalf, I might have dismissed you out of hand."

I glanced up to find her anger, if that's what it had been, lifted like a curtain. Her eyes narrowed; a smile teased her lips.

"Do you know what it is he sees in you, Madelyn? I think I do. I think I did from the first. Now," she said in a tone that suggested we had come to some definitive agreement. "I have discussed the matter with Mrs. French, and she refuses to relinquish her mornings with you or hear of any disruptions in your lessons. She is an obstinate woman, my dear Lorena. Did you know that until I met her, and put her straight, she'd published only under her husband's name? And why is that, do you think?" she asked, then answered. "She is not meek, our Mrs. French, but rather a pessimist for all her courageous ideals." She leaned back ever so slightly in her chair. "But I shall have you. You will come to me three days a week, after you are through with my father."

Believing the conversation over, she turned back to examine three gowns draped across the canopy bed. I was not sure I'd conceded. Not sure I hadn't, either. She held to the light a blue satin dress with canary yellow flouncing.

"Why?" I asked. Miss Rose turned and my courage faltered. "I mean, to do what?"

"Why, Madelyn," she said, as if this should have been obvious, "to make a record. A record of an extraordinary life." She draped the dress over one arm. "My life, Madelyn."

"You mean I got no choice?"

"Oh dear," she said. "Have I chained you to the grounds against your wishes? If you were so eager to depart for those great cities, I should think you would have left yesterday, or this morning, and saved us both the labor of this encounter.

"Or do you wish something else in exchange? Very well, Madelyn. What is it you want out of this arrangement? Remember, I have already agreed to keep you, feed you, educate you. But if you feel compensation is yet required, tell me what you want. Stand up straight, Madelyn, and tell me what you want."

What did I want? A peacock screamed outside. A tumult of rain dashed the window. The demanding weight of Miss Rose's silence pressed upon me, yet I could not say the word. However many times I'd dreamed, even written the desire down, I couldn't say it, and I flinched when she did, though she spoke the word quietly.

"*Beauty*, Madelyn, is but the perishing bloom of youth. 'Every fair from fair sometime declines.' Look at me."

Through my tears, I could see fine lines webbing her eyes, grooves framing her mouth, her cheekbones so sheer and fragile that for a moment the ghostly image of the old woman overwhelmed me. And for all of this, I still thought her beautiful, maybe more beautiful than I had before. Self-righteous anger left me, and having no other source of resistance, I found myself drawn to her, inexorably drawn, by a wretched, needy hope.

"I will give you more. What, you ask? What will you give me, Miss Rose, though I remain ever so ungrateful?"

She turned to one of the vanity mirrors standing at attention by the bed, raised her head, lowered her shoulders and filled the room. "Comportment, Madelyn. I will teach you how to carry yourself, how to talk and walk, what to wear and how. Come."

She pulled me close and turned me around until we were framed together in the mirror.

"I know what you want, Madelyn," she said, holding my face between her kid gloves so I could not look away. "But you are mistaken. A woman's power comes not from her beauty, but her allure." The word stopped me cold. "It will be your carriage and your manner, not your face, that tells the man in the first and the farthest corners of the audience what to think of you."

She swept my hair from my face while I stood, clutching that carpetbag, tears in my eyes.

"Look. Look, Madelyn," she whispered and stepped away, leaving me alone in the frame. "What do you see?"

A scowling, ratty-haired girl in a hand-me-down dress. A girl with a black eye, nail gouges scoring one cheek, a birthmark on the other.

"Look," she said. "Do you see what I see?"

So BEGAN THE NEXT STAGE of my education in the manor.

The following afternoon, I arrived in Miss Rose's office to find a little writing desk beside the settee. On top was an inlaid pen inscribed with the initials R. S. W., an inkwell, and watermarked stationery doomed to suffer the indignity of my penmanship, barely passable even when I wasn't rushing to keep up with the

great flourish of words with which Miss Rose described any simple thing. She never sat long, but paced, gesticulating with such
animation that I sometimes forgot to write anything, losing myself
in her . . . well, her memories, I guess. I wasn't sure. For how could
she have been born on a frigate in the Atlantic, on a sugar plan-
tation in New Orleans, and in Maine in midwinter? And how
could her mama have been a French heiress, a Creole princess,
and a dance hall girl? She tried on versions of her beginnings like
dresses, twirled them before me, altering them as the mood suited
her, or discarding them entirely. And as if these variations weren't
enough to baffle me, she also embraced Mr. Clemens's suggestion
of beginning her recollections at no particular time in her life,
wandering freely all over, and dropping a topic the moment it
threatened to pale.

"When I was conceived," she said, "the Mississippi flowed backward . . ."

"Once, when playing Iphigenia at the Adelphi in London, a
woman in the balcony was so moved by my performance that she
leaped to her death in the pit . . ."

"I was for a time mistress of the King of Bavaria . . ."

"In California, before the war, I loved a man who died twice in
one day . . ."

And off she'd go as long as the thread lasted.

On the second day, she laid open before me three vellum scrapbooks bulging with articles, playbills, pictures and reviews. "You
are not the only one with the documentary impulse, my dear," she
said fondly touring the pages, her richly layered voice enveloping
me. "A girl of my standing was not supposed to take the stage,
Madelyn. But the stage, you see,"—she turned a page—"it was
my siren call, my saving grace. It made an independent woman

out of me, beholden to no one, except, of course"—and here she laughed—"the audience."

Tarnished gray tintypes and lithographs of Miss Rose as Cleopatra, noble head adorned with a diadem; as the sprightly Puck, grinning over the shoulder of a bearded Oberon; as Saint Joan in armor, tied to a pyre, ecstatic supplication on her face. Miss Rose as the tormented Hamlet. "No female character allows for the full exploration of human sorrows as does that of Hamlet, Madelyn. I have never thought him mad. He arranges the details of the play, represents the assassination of his father. Such," she said, "is the conduct of a sensible person."

What a thrill it was to write *I* did this, went there, saw that, when I had done nothing of note in my life! I fled with Miss Rose and a young actor, Pierre De La Croix, from New Orleans to New York; followed her from chorus to leading lady to actor-manager. I floated with Miss Rose down the Thames in a flatboat and high over the Seine in a hot-air balloon, staring down on slate-shingled roofs and towering cathedrals. Theaters and cities came and went. And then the war.

In Chicago, performing during the war at the Soldiers' Fair, she met Mrs. French, one of the organizers, along with Mrs. Livermore, "who never much liked me, though I made her three thousand dollars on eight performances alone."

"You will discover, Madelyn," said Miss Rose, closing the scrapbook for the day, "that I have been unjustly persecuted, no matter my endeavor. For I am original without trying to be so, my voice, my profile distinct, and I have never been able to lend myself to any hypocrisy. And that is a high crime against society." She looked down at me.

"We are creatures quite apart, my dear."

Vulnerable as I was, it didn't take her long to win me with such gestures and statements of sorority. My presence, she said, loosed the words inside of her. And I gained a great deal of cruel satisfaction knowing how much this intimacy distressed Violet.

If intimacy is what it was; we never again met in her bedroom. After that first day, I found her in her office, her wardrobe and wig in place. I never once saw her without her gloves. If she felt a headache coming, she would not see me. (She saw no one on these occasions but Mrs. Hardrow.) At the end of every session, she gathered my scribblings and her scrapbooks and locked both in the bottom drawer of her desk with a little brass key she wore on a chain around her neck. And although she addressed me, Madelyn, when she spoke it was as if the walls of the office fell away and a curtain opened to a distant audience, greater in number even than the myriad reflections attending her.

The only part of our time I dreaded took place the moment I walked in, before lessons in elocution and recitation, before sitting down at my desk. Each day, you see, Miss Rose made me stand before her vanity mirror, and look at myself.

"Lift your chin, Madelyn, and your dignity will follow. Smile. My dear, are you in pain? Relax your shoulders. Your shoulders, Madelyn. You must learn to see yourself as you wish to be seen."

She could not fathom that maybe I did not wish to be seen. Except, perhaps, by William.

25

The rope broke, and the red curtain, sagging morosely over the newly erected stage, crumpled to the ground.

"Not good enough, Mr. Brisson," Miss Rose sang. She stood, arms akimbo, in the middle of her father's warehouse, her dress and hat a splash of color in the otherwise drab expanse. Nearly a month had passed. There were three days until Christmas, one until the Nativity play, and Miss Rose's grand vision of a theater had yet to overwhelm the dilapidated reality of that drafty brick building.

R. S. Werner had built his warehouse, a grain silo, and a gristmill along the waterfront, years before the war—maybe because the spirits told him to, Miss Rose allowed, but also to steal a share of trade floating south from the confluence of three rivers into the Mississippi. The spirits should have told him to put his faith, or at least his money, in the railroad. Had he done so, other investors might well have shunned Alton for a slightly northern route from Springfield to Saint Louis. Reliance, not Alton, would have flourished.

By the time I arrived, ugly, cumbersome barges transported most of the dwindling river cargo. Only two steamboats a day stopped in Reliance, weather permitting. The town was living off the brewery and the glassworks and the farmers, mostly Bohemians, tilling the inland prairie. The gristmill had closed, and Old Man's warehouse, emptied of goods, was suffering clear signs of its unsanctioned uses, namely cockfights and Saturday night boxing matches. Patches of dried blood stained the splintered floorboards; I'd found more than a half dozen human teeth in the sweepings. And, after four days of airing, there remained a mangy, wet-dog smell to the place. Really, I was beginning to worry that Miss Rose's plans for it might be, as Mrs. French feared (and Stockwell surely hoped) too ambitious.

"What part *she* playing?" a young man laboring by with a broad bench asked his partner. "God?"

"The angel Gabriel," said the other. "God didn't have enough lines."

"Madelyn, there you are," called Miss Rose brightly. "Come. Look at that stage. Does it look straight to you?"

The day was gray. Dreary light through six great windows on the north wall seemed to sweep the darkness into corners, but even this illusion couldn't account for the strange angle of that stage.

"And opening night a day away. Well! I once produced *A Midsummer Night's Dream* in a tent in Hangtown with a skunk-drunk Oberon. The fairy queen ran off with a gambler the day before opening, and still we made a success of it! Of course," she said, beaming down at me, "my audience was less than discerning."

Really, I'd never seen anyone throw herself with such joyful and aggressive conviction into a project. Mr. Stockwell had been forced to withdraw his petition against the theater. He'd found arguing the immorality of a Nativity play awkward, as Miss Rose expected. I'm not sure, however, she expected how quickly interest in the venture would grow. Within a week of its announcement in the *Register*, Miss Rose's play had blossomed into a pageant, which would feature the Firemen's Brass Band, the German Choir, Mrs. Alvin Soto singing "Ave Maria," and others—performances meant to "unite the town in this most hallowed of seasons," but as easily might become what Mrs. French dreaded, a pissing contest of Christmas cheer (although she would not have phrased it that way). I doubted Miss Rose would consider the latter a failure so long as there was good attendance, but I could tell Mrs. French was worried, and this worried me.

Needless to say, work on Miss Rose's memoirs had come to a halt. Today, even Susan and Lizzette had been drafted to sew costumes and decorate. For the last three days, after reading to Old Man, I raced to the waterfront to play gopher, wearing the title of assistant stage manager, which suited me fine, because it meant I would not be expected to step onstage, much less share it with Violet, who, as the Virgin Mary, had spent the last two weeks cradling an overgrown squash and practicing tragic expressions. At Mrs. Smith's suggestion, Emil Le Duc, the cobbler with whom she shared a shop wall, had volunteered to play Joseph. Main Street School's first-grade boys and girls had been hee-hawing, lowing, and clucking their parts all over town for a week. The role of the Messiah was to be played by Little John.

Finally, in a stroke of inspiration, Miss Rose flattered Judge Bennett, Mr. Wallace Mack, the assessor, and Mr. Alfred Kroft, the clerk, into playing Wise Men. This meant that as the Angel Gabriel, she had spent these two days of rehearsal telling them just where to go and what to bring.

"Perhaps an iron rod, Mr. Brisson, instead of a rope?" suggested Miss Rose, then turned back to me. "The playbills and broadsheets?"

"Hanley's bringing . . ."

"I said iron, Mr. Brisson! An iron rod to stretch the length of the stage. Surely you have such a thing at the docks?"

He surely did not, but I knew who did and shuffled off, happy for any excuse to barge into William's studio.

I FOUND WILLIAM ALONE, HOLDING before his eyes a peculiar little device, much like binoculars but with twin photos joined side-by-side by a vertical seam and attached where the front lenses should have been. Never sure of his mood, I waited to be acknowledged.

"Well," he said, taking the device down. His eyes were clear, his hands steady. "Is it soup yet?"

"The stage is crooked, and the curtain won't hang right. But other than that . . ."

"Other than that." He smiled and I relaxed some, though I wasn't pleased.

I expected him in public to act as if we shared no secrets. Yet even on those rare occasions I caught him alone, he held me at a distance with the same teasing banter that had governed our time *before*. That is, before we'd found the dead young woman, Aileen. Before he'd kissed me and then lied for me. He acted as if nothing had changed, when I, for one, was changed. I didn't imagine I was alluring yet, but I knew hundreds of new things I hadn't known before: I could recite a dozen poems from memory, knew what fork to use when, and walked without clomping when I remembered to think about it. I wore new clothes—new to me, that is—and today a corset, which frankly was making raw meat of my vitals.

Mrs. French had opposed the garment for reasons she'd cited by author and page, but the choice had been mine, and I was not ready to admit my regret. And I wasn't going to let Mrs. French's distrust of William worry me, either. She had told Miss Rose that William must want something to be making himself so useful.

"Of course he does," Miss Rose had laughed. "He wants to go to Europe to take his pictures. He thinks I will send him. I might."

She meant after Old Man died and left her the estate, a certainty not even Mrs. French questioned. I didn't wish death on Old Man but maybe wouldn't have minded so much if Miss Rose sent me abroad with William.

He fussed with his device, looking at me sideways as I fidgeted in my stays. Whalebone made turning in any direction a whole-body endeavor.

"What's wrong with you?" he asked. "Why are you standing like that?"

"Miss Rose says that if I wear it day and night for two years, I might achieve an admirable waist." I said this with an enthusiasm I no longer felt.

"Oh, Maddy," William said.

"What?" I asked, for he looked truly dismayed.

"Don't let her make a Violet out of you."

Which pleased me very much, as you might imagine, but not nearly so much as the device he handed over. The photographs were identical images of my Daphne statue at the manor. But when I looked at them through the eyepiece as William had done, the images became one full, lifelike whole; the girl and the room beyond sprang into life. I found myself reaching out to touch her plump marble thigh, then jerked the device away to look again at the flat photographs from which she'd risen.

"William!" I said.

"It's called a stereopticon."

"It's wonderful."

"Well, don't tell Miss Rose. It's a surprise."

"I am discreet, remember." His face darkened. Not the right thing to say.

"What did you say Miss Rose wanted?" he asked. I hadn't said but told him now, and together we considered the long iron bars that held the cloth in place over the studio's glass ceiling.

"And I'm guessing no is out of the question." Indeed the workmen were already on their way to William's shop.

H ANLEY, WITH AN ARMLOAD OF playbills and broadsheets, caught up to me as I passed the print shop.

"Hey," he said. "Why are you walking like that?"

"Me?" I said, annoyed. I had been trying for elegance. "Look at you, Hanley." He was limping, too, after all. Beaver hat too high on his head, sleeves and trouser cuffs too short, a fresh bruise on his brow, he looked every bit the brute Violet thought he was.

"Fighting again," I said.

He said nothing, continuing down the street; in the corset, I struggled to keep up.

"I'd as soon fight for a snake as for that Adam Harrison," I said. "That boy walks around like he's king of this place, and can't even fight the fights his mouth runs him into."

We passed the dress shop, and still he said nothing.

"Well?" I asked, breathless, frustrated. "What does your sister think about you fighting so much?"

With a swiftness that shocked the both of us, Hanley turned on me. "Shut up about it," he said, fists clenched, his great bulk pressing down on me. "You hear me? You don't know anything about anything!" He slammed the box of broadsheets to the ground and strode away, leaving me too startled to say boo.

"Madelyn?" said Mrs. Smith stepping out of the dress shop with

Mama. "Was that Hanley?" she asked and then, putting her arm around me, figured out why I was heaving so. "Come in here. Let me loosen that thing."

HANLEY STILL HADN'T COME BACK by the time the four of us—Mrs. Smith and Mama, with Little John sleeping in his basket, and I, carrying the broadsheets—reached the theater. I tried not to think about it. The two o'clock steamer had arrived with a serviceable upright piano, which the workmen manhandled into place. The broad benches sat in orderly rows. The choirmaster, the bandleader, and Mrs. Alvin Soto, having received their marching orders from Mrs. French, abandoned the crooked stage, which left Miss Rose and the Nativity cast to admire their little silent star.

Silent, that is, until it came time for Mama to hand Little John over to Violet.

Lord, the way he shrieked startled all of us, Violet most of all (the squash had never objected). He bucked and screamed and would have nothing of Emil Le Duc, either, or Mrs. Smith, who offered herself as understudy Mary. The workmen hushed. First graders, scattered around the theater, paused their mooing and cooing in shocked respect until, at Mama's pleading look, I snatched Little John and didn't think anything more until together we'd shushed and loved him quiet.

"Well," said Mrs. Smith. "Well," she said again.

This time I looked up to find every eye upon me.

"No. Uh-uh," I said, standing up. Little John burbled happily. "No."

"Maddy," said Mrs. French in her "be reasonable" voice. "You have only to hold him."

"We'll find another baby, that's all," I said, looking at Mrs. Smith for support. "There must be another baby, boy or girl, it can't matter."

"No lines at all," Mrs. Smith offered.

Only Violet appeared as horrified at the prospect of bequeathing her starring role to the likes of me. Everyone else had turned to Miss Rose to ratify the alternative, when Mama's voice piped into the silence. "I'll do it."

I could not have heard right. I was sure I hadn't heard right, until Mama, taking Little John from my arms and holding him tight, said it again. "I'll do it. He wants me. I'll do it."

"Good. Settled," said Miss Rose and, before some other crisis could hamstring her production, spurred the company to action.

PRAY FOR BLIZZARD, OR FLOOD, or quake. Until this new wrinkle, I had been looking forward, with some concern but mostly excitement, to the Christmas pageant. Especially since the closest I'd come to a theater had been the buckboard stage of a traveling minstrel show with a lardy confidence man spouting Shakespeare, or close enough, and three blackfaced white boys acting fools. What was Mama thinking? She had never been the hallelujah type, but what, barring a strong nudge from the Holy Spirit, could have possessed her? The more I thought about it, the less conscionable the thought became. Mama standing before the town on that stage—or on any stage.

It took me all night, but by the next morning, I'd summoned courage enough to confront Miss Rose.

"Madelyn," she said. Her tone nearly undid me. She was sitting behind her desk, in her office, Mrs. Hardrow attending her. "Did I call for you?"

I shook my head.

"But I can see by the way you are standing that you have something of great urgency to divest. Your body speaks, Madelyn. Be aware of what it is saying."

"I don't think it's a good idea," I said in a rush, then glancing at Mrs. Hardrow. "About my *sister*. People will talk."

"People *are* talking, Madelyn. Always talking. You are mistaken if you think she does not already suffer the perdition of public judgment. Anyway. It is too late now to change. The show must go on, and so it will. Leave us."

THE NIGHT CAME. NO RAIN, no snow, no flood or quake. Through the high windows behind the stage, I could even see a few stars peeking through a silver ragbag of clouds.

"Madelyn," Violet hissed as I placed the last luminary candles. "Ma-da-lyn," said Violet. "Where is Hanley? He's supposed to hand out programs."

"How should I know? Can't you do it?"

That's all I said, but what she must have heard was, "Now that you've got nothing better to do."

The slight was not intentional. I'd much, much rather Violet act the Blessed Virgin than Mama, already in the outbuilding we were using as a backstage with Little John. Mama's part was simple, to be sure. All she had to do was stand onstage and look beautiful and fragile. Next to great big Emil Le Duc, everyone I knew, except maybe Hanley, would look fragile. That wasn't the point. The point was . . . what? Why did I feel this sense of dread?

Violet shoved the programs to Susan, who handed them to the houseboy, Tom, who took his position at the door happily enough. The broad benches filled. William and Mr. Dryfus, walking slowly with Clara, settled in the second row on the left. Lutherans, Baptists, Unitarians, and Presbyterians mingled cautiously, their voices rising with the heat and stink of bodies; but no matter how many handshakes and smiles and shows of fellow feeling they shared, the night still bristled with a kind of competitive elation that formed a second ceiling with the pipe smoke, halfway up the window frames.

Mrs. French could feel it too. I could tell from the set of her shoulders.

Together we lit the stage lamps. Tom snuffed the houselights. I took position behind the curtain on the other side of the stage with Miss Rose, who stood, radiant in cream silk, breathing. One hand on her chest, the other on her abdomen, breathing. I thought again of Mama backstage, but couldn't imagine what she might be thinking or feeling. The brass band tested its lungs, as Mrs. Alvin Soto trilled her scales. Mr. Heinrick shepherded his choir from wings, and a cough-filled silence teased through the audience.

"Geist!" mouthed Mrs. French from the other side of the stage. "Maddy."

"Mr. Geist," I hissed. "Mr. Geist. Now!"

The ancient barnacle of a man, slouching before the piano, jolted upright. Music erupted. People clapped. Miss Rose took the stage. People clapped again, then laughed at something she said. Mrs. French waved from the other wing, and after a struggle with the rope, I tugged the curtain open, and the pageant began.

I mean no disrespect to the German Choir, whose robust harmonies hovered in the rafters long after they left the stage, or to the brass band, or to Heidi Leggatte, who recited "a humorous poem of deep sentiment," or to Mrs. Alvin Soto, whose brave attempt to nail the "Ave Maria" was matched only by the audience's equally brave effort to withstand it. But I remember little of the performances leading up to the Nativity scene.

I opened the curtain. I closed the curtain. The luminary candles waved streaks of light up the brick walls, and as the play approached, my belly began a nervous wave of its own.

Enter from the back, walking the center aisle, the wandering Wise Men.

Behold, Miss Rose, the Angel Gabriel on high, upon a stool, stage left.

See, the North Star bull's-eye lamp, suspended from a rope above the curtain.

Ignore the first-grade farm animals fidgeting in the wings.

Lo, Joseph, staff in hand, and by his side, the Virgin Mother with child.

Mama, that is. Mama with Little John slung close to her chest under her robe. Mama, draped in gray homespun, her lovely face pale and tragic in the lamplight. Mama wide-eyed, stricken at the terrible pressure of eyes upon her. I could hear my heartbeat. My fists clenched. Just one snigger, one whisper, denigrating or not . . .

But there was no sound from the audience. No sound at all, apart from one collective breath at first sight of her so vulnerable and lovely.

"No room," said Mr. Heinwerken, as the innkeeper. "No room," said Mrs. Smith. "No," said Mr. Leonard.

"No room for *you*" is what I heard, remembering the seething looks Mama endured on the Susanville street and in the Stockwell home. "No room for *you*" is what Mama must have heard as well, for to my horror, she began to cry. Soundlessly, her eyes gleaming, the set of her jaw defiant. Next to Emil Le Duc's girth, she stood out like a small glittering figure of cut glass. Mrs. French, across the stage in the wings, looked unsure, and Miss Rose, beside me, wore the same distressed expression she wore the day Mrs. French threw her leg over the bicycle seat. Wind, gentle all night, hissed through the eaves, the only sound.

Until an exasperated little voice crackled from the wings. "The main-ger!"

Mama blinked. The crowd turned. A blond boy wearing donkey ears broke from the wings to the stage. He stared, hands on hips, at Mama, paying no mind to the audience or to the tears in Mama's eyes.

"Mrs. Dryfus, look," he said, pointing with the bossy impatience of one much older at the basket of straw behind him. "*There's* the main-ger! You're supposed to put the baby in the main-ger."

Mama, grief arrested, looked at Emil Le Duc, who, a moment ago helpless as the rest of us in the face of real emotion, improvised.

"Praise God!" he said. "The ass is right!"

This might have offended the more pious audience members had they been able to hear him. As it was, laughter pummeled all but a squinting and aged few who had heard nothing and seen less to laugh about. Across the stage, Mrs. French, gripping the curtain pole as if holding herself back or preparing to charge from the wings, heard him, as did Miss Rose, in very much the same posture by my side. She saw, as I did, that Mama was having a time freeing Little John from his wraps.

Mama rushed to me offstage; the farm animals tumbled on. "Help," she whispered, and when we'd freed Little John, she walked back onstage and laid him red faced and walleyed in the manger amid a medley of lusty barnyard impressions. Order might have been restored if the Wise Men hadn't missed their entrances, forcing the little donkey back offstage to herd the Wise Men into place. After which Little John, patient all night, opened his lungs and let the Lord know exactly what he thought of all this foolery.

Eventually bows were taken. Eventually the German Choir came back for closing hymns. And while the mood of solemn consecration Miss Rose wanted was never achieved, a new warmth rippled through the crowd of smiling faces. I'd seen fainting women and flailing men wild with the Holy Spirit. This was different: gentle and binding, like a major chord through a piano's wooden body.

"Well, of course," said Miss Rose after bows were taken, cookies passed, and mulled wine poured. "I thought why not use a mother and child?" Violet and I exchanged looks. "Nothing like real emotion, a mother's love, to capture the drama of the scene. Rebecca was wonderful, was she not?" And continued to cast commentary like chocolate coins to the knot of people surrounding her.

I was watching Mama—Little John, too, and Mr. Dryfus, puffed up, shocked, and proud as I'd ever seen him (William had left with Clara)—but mostly Mama, whose dark eyes found mine across the benches. Pride and bafflement and love, all of these ached through me; yet I was afraid to approach her, knowing I'd never find words to tell her all I felt, or I'd say the wrong thing. So I blew out the luminary candles, folded the tablecloths, made myself nominally useful until, with a backward glance, Mama left with Little John and Mr. Dryfus.

It was only then I remembered Hanley'd missed it all.

26

The next morning, Christmas Eve, Miss Rose ordered me to the print shop for the holiday. I made a token resistance, but really, I didn't mind going. Wanted to go, in truth. Watching Mama cry in front of all those people had been the shock of my life, and not only because I knew her tears had risen from that vault of memories she kept locked. I'd supposed I understood Mama well enough to guess, one day to the next, what she'd do, how she'd behave. Even keeping Little John a secret made sense, given what I knew. Now I wasn't sure.

What I did know was that I wanted to be as close as I could to her, if only for a few days. And after six weeks transcribing Miss Rose's recollections, I knew, maybe for the first time, what I *needed* from Mama—an account of herself. Some explanation of her life and mine and the way things were between us. Walking through town, down Union Street to the print-shop alley, I became determined to do what I hadn't had the courage for: I would ask her. The very thought filled me with hope, with fear and an offended sense of entitlement, which bolstered me until Mama answered my knock on the backdoor and my resolve scattered.

I couldn't say anything. Not even hello. She held a broom. She wore a frown and an apron over a pretty muslin housedress, and her lovely face, no longer pale and fragile as it had been onstage, was flushed and damp with heat. I can't tell you the expression in her eyes, because I could not meet them.

"Well," she said finally. "Come in, if you're coming," and I followed her inside.

Christmas that year was not nearly so sparse as the last. This is not to say Mr. Dryfus developed a religious bone, but that year, for Little John's benefit, Dryfus invited the season into his home. No goose graced the table, of course, but there were sweet breads, stollen, marzipan fruits. William came to string popcorn around a pitiful little fir tree. I sat between him and Clara at the Lutheran church for Christmas Eve carols, and on Christmas Day I was proud to give the few things I'd made: a scarf each for Clara and Mr. Dryfus, a rag doll for Little John. I brought for Mama a piece of paper from Miss Rose—Mama's first commission for a dress. For William, I'd cross-stitched with great care (I usually had little patience for such things) the first four stanzas of "The Lady of Shalott," which he promised to frame on his studio wall. I even brought Hanley, who'd oddly not been around, a little cob pipe, to prove how graciously I'd forgiven his behavior the day before the pageant. Indeed the day passed so well, I'd all but given up my intention of asking Mama anything.

That is, until the night of Saint Stephen's, the night before I would return to the manor. Mr. Dryfus was in his study, Clara in bed. I sat with Mama beside Little John's cot in William's old room, watching her snuggle him to sleep in a lacy smock she'd made him. The sash was open, the moon bright and cold, the street so quiet the only sounds were a dog far away and Mama singing a song Dot used to favor when picking slugs off tomatoes.

The way she held him, as much as the song, got to me. If I'd thought about it, I would have recognized this as the wrong time to confront her, but hearing that song and watching her rock Little John opened a wound of spite and longing inside. I knew, sure as I knew anything, Mama would never leave Little John as she had left me. And as she laid him in his cot and closed his door, the questions I'd been swallowing for two days fell clumsy from my mouth.

"Why'd you leave me with Dot? During the war. Did you go looking for him, Landis Wilcox?"

Mama didn't seem to have heard what I'd said. She remained still, her hand on the latch, staring down the hallway.

"I think I deserve to know!"

She heard that. "That's what you think, huh?" she said. "You think . . ."

She didn't finish, for below, outside the shop, we heard a frantic voice calling, "Mr. Dryfus! Mr. Dryfus!"

Mama and I reached the staircase in time to see Dryfus open the door to a breathless deputy. William, my first thought, and from the look on her face as she shuffled in, Clara must have thought the same.

"All of them in bad shape, Mr. Dryfus," the deputy was saying. "The woman worst of all, and now the baby's coming, and she won't let the doctor near. She's asking for Clara, and Constable Shultz thought . . . well, he thought you'd be able to calm the boy, talk some sense."

"Hanley?" I said.

Mama, in the shadows beside me, stepped forward.

"He's murder mad if I ever seen it," said the deputy. "Nobody gonna get close without shooting him first, or shooting Robey, who climbed under the house with the pigs and won't come out, neither. I'd shoot Robey myself, give me leave, honest."

"He's talking about Hanley?" I asked.

"Madelyn," Mama said, but I had decided.

"I'm going," I told Mr. Dryfus. "I'm going too."

I threw on my overcoat, telling myself, even as fear clamped my chest, that Hanley was alright. Everything would be alright. Mama sent me to fetch Mrs. Smith to watch Little John, and when I returned, the three of them, Mama and Mr. Dryfus on either side of Clara, were ready to go.

We shuffled along as fast as Clara was able until we reached the butchers' block, south of Stuttgart, where streetlamps ended, as did any streets of mention. The houses beyond were scrap-wood shacks owned by the glass factory, though dockworkers lived there too, and men working the lime pit. And something in the beat-down state of those hovels, or maybe in those dark windows, made me remember the look in Hanley's eyes before the pageant. The violence in them. The helplessness. I kept trying to remember what he'd told me about his sister (not much), or her husband, Robey (nothing at all). I kept thinking about all those bruises . . .

Two blocks over, I saw lanterns, and then men holding them. Fifteen or twenty men huddled close, their breath a heaving white fog. They smelled of liquor and smoke, and I stayed as close to Mama as I could until we passed through to find the deputy and the constable, a barrel-chested man, hunched beside the falling-down porch of Hanley's sister's place.

"Not that it'd be much a loss, Robey," the constable called under the porch. "But you stay there bleeding like that, them pigs bound to tear you up, and this place stinks enough without you rotting in pieces."

A bent figure in the shadows beside the porch staggered into the lantern glow. "He comes out," the figure growled. "I'll kill him."

It was Hanley. He was swaying side to side, his left arm hanging loose from his shoulder, his nose smashed to one side, blood dripping down his mouth and chin; yet none of this scared me so much as his eyes, fierce as his voice.

"Hanley?" I said, but Mama held me fast, and I let her. Robey, under the porch, began yelling, "Muriel! Muriel! *Spatzi! Ich liebe dich!* Muriel!" and crawling out, sat on his haunches, hands in the air.

Not Hanley, not the Hanley I knew, but a beast with the same voice, same build, raged through the two men holding him back and kicked Robey in the head once, then again, before Mr. Dryfus, brave or crazy, I didn't know which, stepped between them. He reached out to touch Hanley, then didn't because Hanley began to sway again, and the two men trying to hold him back, now held him up.

"Late. You warned me, Mr. Dryfus, but, oh God, my sister."

He slipped to his knees between the men. No sound but wind hissing through trees, until inside the shack a low wail spiked into a scream. I felt nothing. I felt cold. I felt nothing but a sharp, shivery cold through my whole body, and still would rather have stayed with the men, in the yard, than follow Mama and Clara inside.

The shack was two rooms divided by a curtain, now torn from its mounting. A splintered chair was heaped in the corner by an upturned table. Beside the stove, an iron pot vomited stew over bloody floorboards. I heard, above the moaning in the other room, a catlike hiss, and looked to find a small boy in the loft, thin arms locked around two baby sisters. A sallow-faced woman, hair wet with sweat, emerged from the back to speak with Clara. Then, with a few stiff, kind words she coaxed the boy and his sisters from the loft and took them away. Clara, masked in the same indomitable calm she wore the night we went for William, ushered Mama and me with her into the back room.

No windows. No air. The stink of blood and waste went straight to my head. I could see nothing. Then a frame bed. Then an insensible mound in the middle, all flesh and tendon straining. Clara relit a lamp by the bed, and I could see the mound's swollen-shut eyes beaten the color of bark. It was not Hanley's sister, Muriel, lying there. It was no one at all, only open legs, a bruised belly tracked with fist marks the brownish-blue color of root stems—and then arching like one possessed, she screamed.

My legs went limp beneath me. Clara crouched in the mess between the mound's legs.

"Maddy." Mama's hand on my arm. "Maddy, we need water, rags. Lot of them. Go."

It didn't take long. Two neighbor women had boiled water and gathered a pile of their own sheets. Mama beckoned me to Muriel's side while she balled up the soiled bedclothes and gave Clara the new. Muriel grabbed my hand so tight I thought she'd break it.

"Is he? Tell me, is he?"

"Hanley's okay," I managed to say, though I wasn't sure. "I think he's going to be okay."

Muriel's head shook wildly. "*Robey*," she hissed. "Is Robey . . ." The pain again.

This time I didn't, I couldn't answer but tore myself away and out to the porch to find Hanley in his shirtsleeves sitting on the stairs.

I stood watching, as wary of his great stillness as I had been of his rage, yet felt an overwhelming tenderness. He jerked but didn't budge when I called his name. Someone had cleaned him up, but blood still oozed from a cut above his swollen-shut eye; his nose looked as if it had been forgotten, then been tacked crooked on his head at the last minute. His left arm hung useless by his side. I found a filthy old quilt bunched behind a crate. Laying it over his shoulders, I eased down as close as I dared on the step beside him, then closer as a tremor escaped him. I, too, was shaking.

"I was late, Maddy." His voice was flat, his eyes straight ahead. I was not afraid of him. "Mr. Dryfus is always telling me not to be late, and I meant to be back before he was, but I was late and that bastard. He was already laying into her."

I didn't know what to say. I didn't say anything. Images of the dead woman in the river kept forming in the back of my mind, and a shivering cold rose so slowly on every side of me, I didn't even fight it, just sat for a long time watching our breath cloud and vanish. I don't know how long. Until the spectacle lost its appeal, and only Mr. Dryfus and a few drunken onlookers remained, until the black sky began to soften, until the cries inside stopped, and no others rose up to take their place.

Clara called for Mr. Dryfus. He emerged again with Clara heavy on his arm, her shakes oddly still, her breath a rusty gate. She laid a hand on Hanley's head as Mama, drawn up tight within herself, passed a wrapped package the size of a loaf of bread to the neighbor woman.

"Hanley," said Dryfus. "She's okay. She lost the baby, but . . . Come back with us, son. Mrs. Markell is going to stay. There's no use you . . ."

But Hanley shrugged off the quilt and walked into the shack without another word to me, to anyone. I felt nothing then, couldn't even manage angry. I wasn't angry, not at Muriel. Or even, though I wished to be, at Robey. I wasn't mad at Hanley for lying about Robey beating him. He hadn't lied, after all. He'd simply said nothing. Even so, I couldn't shake the feeling that I must have known. At least, I must have known there was more to those bruises than war play and fisticuffs. Or if I didn't, then Mr. Dryfus—lots of people must have known and done nothing to stop it.

I remembered, later, what Alby had said about "blessed misfortune." Dot used to say something similar. She used to say, "Maddy, God reveals his grace in our misfortunes." Meaning what? That all misfortune was a good thing? That God wanted bad things to happen so we remembered to need him? That God wanted Robey to beat his wife, to beat Hanley who, for so long, offered himself in his sister's place? I wasn't sure what I thought about God, but I didn't believe that. I don't think Alby or Dot did, either. What kind of God would do that? It was one of those things you say to make yourself feel better for being so helpless. I never have been ready to feel better about that night.

Mr. Dryfus took hold of one of Clara's arms; Mama, the other. I waited until Mama looked back for me, and when she did, I followed at a distance, my feet numb and heavy, conscious of cook fires and voices rough with sleep falling from windows. I remember standing at the top of the green, open like a hand beneath the courthouse. I remember how small and far away the three of them, Mr. Dryfus and Clara and Mama, looked in the palm of that hand, how ghastly the great oak appeared with its naked arms upstretched in the morning light. But that's all. I don't remember turning north, away from them, up the frozen pavement, past Millionaire's Row. I don't remember the split in the road or the sight of the manor huddled on the ridge. I don't remember curling into a ball in the seam of warmth beneath the kitchen door, where Mrs. Nettle must have found me.

27

Gray winter light slanted though the curtains. It took me a moment to figure where I was—in the manor, one of the guest rooms from the look of it, with no idea how I'd gotten there, or that New Year's Eve had passed without me. My throat burned. My tongue was thick and useless. I felt a strange dead weight upon my chest, cotton between my ears. Through the cotton, a voice:

"Well, now, look who decided to join the living? No, now. Stay down." Lipman pressed me back into the pillow. "You been days in delirium, gabbing all sorts o' nonsense—women turning to trees and such. Stands to reason, with that book you read old man filling your head with no good." She roughed her hand across my forehead. "I tell you, hon. Thought we'd lost you. Thought it was scarlet fever, thank merciful God. No. Stay down, I said. Your sister's due in a minute, and no sense overtaxing."

Even more shocking than waking up in that fancy room was seeing Mama walking through the door with Mrs. Smith. She'd been there every day for four days since the danger passed, Lipman told me. Today she and Mrs. Smith wore walking dresses;

Mama a pretty lace fichu, her hair in a chignon. She sat tracing the fleur-de-lis pattern on the arm of her chair, glancing up at me now and again in a way that made me nervous. Mrs. Smith did the talking for both of them.

Hanley was okay, she told me. No saving his eye, and his arm might not be good for much. "But he's okay. His sister will be." She paused. "Robey, too." She looked at Mama, back at me. "They let him go, Maddy. Kept him two nights, and then they let him go."

"They . . . But why?" I managed, my voice unsteady.

It was Miss Rose, resplendent in the doorway, who answered.

"Didn't you know, Madelyn?" She wore a forest-green gown, ermine cuffs, braids and curls atop her head, each movement a hush of fabric. "A man," she said walking in, "might be arrested for cruelty to a horse, but he has every right, under the *law*, to beat his wife—even at the cost of his unborn child. Such an outrage would never, never be allowed if women had the vote. Don't you agree, Mrs. Dryfus? No, don't get up. I came only to witness our young scholar back from the dead. Work on my book is useless without you, Madelyn."

Mama, dwarfed by Miss Rose, sat awkwardly down.

"Well," said Mrs. Smith, "he ran off, at any rate. But that means there'll be no money coming in. Other than what Hanley brings. Muriel might take in laundry. Mr. Mason, at the glassworks, will take her boy. But the house . . ."

Miss Rose roused herself. "She *will not* lose the house." Then looking from Mama to me: "Mrs. Smith, may I have a word?"

We stared after them, Mama longer than I. She fiddled with her handbag, then stood, heading for the door, I thought, but closed it instead and sat again, this time on the very edge of the chair, gripping that handbag. Her dark eyes, for a moment so far away, came to rest on me. And what I felt was fear. Weak as I was I felt a fear deep inside that overwhelmed all spite and longing.

"Mama?" I said.

"I wasn't looking for him, Landis," she said. "When I left Dot's, I wasn't—"

"Mama, don't."

"Let me!" She put her hand up, closed her eyes. "Things in this world, they aren't like they are in your books. It's not so . . ." She stopped, sat there, fishing for words and not finding them, started over, telling about the promises Landis made, how he said it was nothing wrong, what they were doing, though she knew it was and always felt wrong after. "But he talked so fine, about so many things," she said. "I didn't disbelieve him.

"A few months after he went off warring, I figured what was ailing me. I seen my mama grow big enough times to know, but kept it close until Mama guessed what was what. She mighta kept me, sin or no, but sent me begging a place at the big house, else daddy come home and kill me."

Landis's mama, Mrs. Wilcox, wouldn't even see her through the door. So Mama set off, already big, and not knowing anything but the name of the man Landis had gone to fight for: Zollicoffer.

I'd known most of this, a sketch of it anyway, and maybe, maybe I should have been content to let wondering die years ago. To let it be. To assume the rest. That Mama didn't find him. This would have made it possible to believe—to go on believing—that after she stumbled on Dot's house, after I was born, she went looking again for him, my father. That she did love him and went looking and that was why she left me. If I'd been writing the story, as I had been for most of my life, that's what I would have written. What I wanted to believe. Maybe I should have been content with that and never asked for the truth.

Because the truth was, Mama did find Landis, three months after she started searching. She found him on the north bank of the Cumberland River. It was November, the river swelling over its banks. She'd come upon the regiment and a ragtag band of camp followers days before. Since then she'd been begging soldier to soldier and might not have recognized Landis at all, filthy and bearded like the rest, except for the second look he gave her. The last look he gave her.

"He stood there," Mama said, her voice cracking, staring into that room like the memory was onstage before her. "He stood there acting like he never in his life had seen me. Never even laid eyes on me. Wasn't nothing I could say to prove it."

There were men everywhere, she said, all around, gathered close. They started up teasing Landis and poking at Mama's belly, touching her all over, ripping her dress, until one of the men broke it up. She didn't remember much after that. Somebody—same man, maybe— gave her coffee and hardtack to eat, wrapped her in his peacoat. Sent her away. Next day the pains came.

Mama told the end sitting straight as a nail in that chair. Like someone reciting a Bible story of people long dead and gone, all but the moral remaining, and that's what got to me. What it all was building to. That's what made the tears come, and the anger, in spite of hearing all she'd suffered.

"You weren't looking for him? When you run off and left me at Dot's, you weren't looking."

Mama shook her head.

"Then why'd you run off, Mama? Because of me. You left because of me."

Her silence, the hard shard of grief on her face held the truth of it, and I—ruthless, broken girl—still pressed.

"Well then," I asked, "why'd you come back?"

Her answer, a whisper: "Same reason."

PART III
1876

28

That January, shades of gray erased the line between sky and horizon. By the time the eagles came, the river between the Illinois and Missouri shores had frozen into colored panes of jagged ice, driven one atop the other by the current, cracking and moaning at all hours. No skiffs or steamers braved the bend for weeks, and when they did, they found the river beneath reshaped, banks shifted, sandbars lurking where none had been, to catch a wheel or snap a rudder.

Even so, that winter felt neither as long nor as bleak as the last. With Mama's admission, something essential inside of me had shifted as well. Inside Mama too, I think, though of course, after that day, we didn't talk about it. "Same reason," was all she'd said, thin fingers gripping her handbag and I, stunned and desperate for anything more to say, said nothing. She opened the door to leave. The curtains swelled. White light, like a thousand knotted threads of lace, dazzling in their complication, filled the room, and when she shut the door, settled back into gray. Sick with grief and gratitude, I cried myself to sleep.

Really, I'm not sure if I can say what I felt for her in the days of convalescence that followed—not forgiveness, exactly, and anyway

Mama hadn't been asking. I can say that in my dreams, alongside
Aileen dead in the river and Muriel bruised in that frame bed, there
now lived a girl, a pretty girl, a girl cursed with beauty, marching
alone through a war. Oh, Mama! Poor brave Mama. As far as all the
things that might have happened between the time she left me at
Dot's and her return, well, I've learned enough by now about the
lives of camp followers to imagine the burdens she must still bear.

For a while after this I found myself, for lack of a better word,
unmoored. But also freed. With Mama's admission, the jagged line
between us sharpened into focus. I felt, maybe for the first time,
free to love her as she was—and to grow apart from her, to grow
up. Into what, into whom, I didn't know. In my uncertainty, I clung
to that promise of transformation Miss Rose and Mrs. French each
had made in her own way. And, of course, to my infatuation with
William.

WHEREAS, BEFORE, I'D LINGERED WITH Nettle and Alby until
the last minute before lessons, now I arrived at the library early
enough to sharpen my pencils and arrange my books before the
clocks chimed eight; when they chimed noon, I'd stay to finish a
page or rewrite a thought. I poured over my French and German
grammars, muddled devoutly through whatever Mrs. French gave
me to read, be it Euclid, Plato, Wollstonecraft, or Emerson. It felt like
a fever, this new determination, and might well have passed, except
that Mrs. French treated it as a permanent condition, going so far
as to invite me to ramble the riverside with her several days a week
thereafter.

"Self-reliance is all well and good, Madelyn," she confided on
one of our walks. We'd stopped, huddled in the cold, to watch eagles
plummet toward the ice and circle again. "So long as one is given the

opportunity to develop one's individual talents and character. What if the eagle were told her realm was the nest and, although she possessed wings, must never be allowed to fly?"

As the pages of her manuscript accumulated, Miss Rose, too, began asking me to accompany her—to the Wayward Home, for example—and trusting me on more errands about town. Now, when Mama or anyone else saw me coming, they knew I came in Miss Rose's name. When I confronted my image in Miss Rose's mirror, I saw my mark, yes, but also felt a new, tissue-thin dignity, extending from that bony region where my head met my neck, deep into some vital part I hadn't known existed.

I figured it was only a matter of time before William noticed, too. You see, I'd quite effortlessly ignored any comparisons, intended or not, Mama had made between her experience and my own life.

That William was so often in Saint Louis on business for Miss Rose didn't bother me. I knew from books that true affection between lovers required hardship and separation; each absence allowed me to repair my idea of William, to trim away any incongruity in the character I'd made for him. By the time he returned, he fit nicely into the role of my secret admirer, too bereaved over the loss of another to acknowledge, much less express, his affection.

But, of course, this hopeful self-deception would not be long in the world. It would be one casualty in the turmoil of the coming months. I was lucky, by comparison. Miss Rose would lose much more than hope; she had much more than hope to lose.

AFTER THE FIRST THAW, in February, Miss Rose resumed her soirees. By the end of the month, the newly christened Reliance Theater boasted a new stage, footlights, and a working curtain. She hired Hanley to distribute flyers and manage the house on the weekends and hired his sister, Muriel, to take tickets. Three members of the Lyceum Circuit, Mr. Alcott among them, and a traveling company from Albany had been slated for the summer season. In the meantime, Miss Rose hosted a magician and hypnotist (a husband-and-wife team), and Lydia Lemarch, a nervous, bird-thin soprano with the brownest teeth you ever saw. Once, unexpectedly, a troupe of Chinese contortionists rolled down Grafton Road in a Conestoga wagon and sold out six shows in three days before continuing south to Alton.

And after every show, there appeared in Mr. Stockwell's rival paper, the *Sentinel*, anonymous condemnations, which Miss Rose read aloud with relish.

"Listen to this, Madelyn. Listen."

One unfortunate young lady, subjected by an irresponsible aunt to the display of a contortionist, suffered, for two days following, wide-staring eyes and a protruding chin. I laughed as she parodied the description. *Even the most benign of the dramatic arts,* she read on, *excite the passions, encouraging immoral and unclean thoughts to proliferate.*

She tossed the paper on her desktop, serious again. "To some men, Madelyn, all thought is unclean. They are better off not doing it."

Of course, I could tell she was not entirely displeased. Ticket sales at the theater were never as swift as after one of Mr. Stockwell's condemnations. "I should write them myself, perhaps."

She didn't need to. Stockwell was nothing if not persistent, and before long, he broadened the scope of his crusade. Claiming a postmaster's authority, he and four men from the Sin Society raided William's shop, looking for images of a "lewd and lascivious nature." I'd seen William angry before, with Mr. Dryfus, but I'd never seen him as livid as he was when recounting to Miss Rose how they charged in, confiscating plates, ruining prints, rummaging props.

"And they found?" asked Miss Rose. I watched him close, thinking about that cigar box of naked ladies.

"Nothing," he said, caught me staring, and looked away. "Of course."

A week later, Stockwell raided Lloyd Herman's Bookshop, demanding every copy of Baudelaire. When Mr. Herman, a stout Frenchman with a sickly wife, refused, Stockwell demanded Whitman as well. To this action, Miss Rose responded in the *Register: The sphere of individual liberty has shrunk, indeed, if it cannot protect all that lies upon one's bookshelves. If the Lily White sold books, perhaps Mr. Stockwell would consider that establishment, and its patrons, worthy of reform as well?*

The last sentence originally read: *If the Lily White sold books, instead of bodies . . .* I know because I wrote it down that way. Mrs. French convinced her that she'd enjoy a more favorable response if this explicit reference were implied—but there was little response at all. Such commentary sold papers, maybe, but roused little more than amusement from most people in Reliance. And Miss Rose? Well, I honestly think she was beginning to find Mr. Stockwell and his Sin Society a bit of a bore.

That is, until one day in the second week of February, as we were finishing in her office, Miss Rose received a letter that raised the stakes of that feud and, it is clear to me now, propelled into motion both the glorious and the bitter events to come.

The letter, you see, was from her nephews, Willard and James, brewery owners in Saint Louis. They wrote to say they had received a letter of their own from a "Concerned Citizen," kind enough to warn them of the damage their aunt might be doing the family name—not to mention the family coffers. And to say that "any alteration to Grandfather's will would be viewed with extreme suspicion."

"Concerned citizen!" I trailed after as Miss Rose, marching from her office to the library, thrust the letter at Mrs. French. "What a meddling ass Stockwell is!"

Mrs. French, after reading the letter, peered over her oculars. "And perhaps more resourceful than we had thought?" But her voice tapered. She'd noticed, as I had, the expression on Miss Rose's face. Anger, yes, but more as well: the unguarded and mesmerizing glow of inspiration.

"Rose?" said Mrs. French.

"The name of Stockwell's oldest girl, the painter." I felt a little jolting tingle in my gut at this. "What is it? Georgia?"

"Georgiana," I said, though she wasn't asking me.

"Rose?" said Mrs. French.

"Lorena, you cannot expect a budding artist to reach her potential without study of masterful works. Well"—she took the letter back, folded it twice—"it happens that I own several such works."

29

So it was that two days later, Georgiana Stockwell, oldest daughter of the town's self-proclaimed moral paragon, arrived in the courtyard on horseback with Mrs. Smith, bundled against the cold. She leaped to the ground, taking in the fountain, the topiary, shaggy with winter growth, and the clipped rosebushes.

"Mother thinks we are out for a ride on the bluffs," she said.

"And so you are, my dear!" said Miss Rose. "Welcome."

At tea in the conservatory, Miss Rose spoke of nothing but artists and galleries and salons abroad, how in Europe a young lady with potential might develop her talents—if she were to find a patron, of course. Did she know William Stark's mother had been a painter? Mrs. French choked a little on her biscuit. Neither she nor Mrs. Smith said much of anything during the barrage. Beneath Violet's pasted smile, I saw a steeper grade of the jealous malice I felt at the attention Miss Rose lavished upon her; Georgiana remained oblivious to everything except Miss Rose's words. When tea was over, Miss Rose sent her alone with her sketchpad to explore the gallery, insisting that we five stay right here to consider our spring wardrobes.

"Actually, Miss Rose . . ." said Mrs. Smith. The hesitancy in her voice, so unlike her, wrested my attention from Georgiana's wandering form. "There is another . . . a rather delicate matter I hoped to broach." She glanced between Violet and me. "The matter of French fashions?"

She had Violet's full attention, too, now.

"Demand is waning?" said Miss Rose.

"No. Well, not exactly. Perhaps I might demonstrate?"

From her pocket Mrs. Smith produced one of the giant rubber thimbles I delivered, on occasion, to the dress shop. She turned to look at me.

"Madelyn. Will you tell us what you think this is?"

Her reaction did not please me.

"There, see!" she said brightly. "She doesn't know. The ladies in my cousin's circle particularly, they don't know, either. Nor do most of the merchant's wives. Much less what to *do* with it. The shopgirls, and the Lily White girls, some know, and they talk about such things. But the ladies, they don't know."

"Know what? What is it?" I said. Violet stretched the rubber between two fingers and must not have known either, or she would have delighted in showing me up.

"Mrs. Biggs confessed that she keeps the article under her bed, like a talisman," Mrs. Smith continued, "as if that will protect her. And, well, I did not feel qualified to explain, adequately, that is, the physiology. My cousin May Ann was the only one to ask and, frankly, I didn't know what to say."

Mrs. French looked at Miss Rose. Miss Rose put her teacup down.

"Mrs. Stockwell bought one?" asked Miss Rose.

"She . . . No. I gave her one. If you only knew what that poor woman has suffered. Of course, how could you?"

"Oh," said Mrs. French, taking a breath. "Oh dear. How many?"

"She's lost three, I think, since the baby died," said Mrs. Smith. "The last one this summer. Such sadness I have never known, thank the Lord. Such pain."

Miss Rose pushed her plate away, and the look in her eye, well, it scared me. Mrs. French saw it. Violet, too.

"And Melborn, he—" said Mrs. Smith. "Well, he is a man. He cannot restrain himself."

"Huh," said Mrs. French.

"And he fears for his soul, lest he stray."

"He has strayed before," said Miss Rose. It was not a question. Her tone, definitive. This time Mrs. Smith noticed, too.

"I don't. I really don't think . . ."

"What are you suggesting, Mrs. Smith?" asked Mrs. French.

"Well. Well, a class, I suppose. A seminar, of sorts."

"Here?" said Mrs. French. "You are suggesting we have them here? But they would not come, would they? Especially if our purpose was clear."

"Not if our purpose was clear. Not if they believed they would be discovered, no." Mrs. Smith's attention swayed from her cup to Georgiana, sitting now in front of Daphne, her drawing pad open on her lap. "But yes. I do believe they would come."

"They will come." Miss Rose folded her napkin. A chill wind rattled the conservatory's glass wall.

"Mrs. French," I whispered in her ear, when finally we stood up from the table. "Come for what?"

"THE FEMALE ORGANS," MRS. FRENCH said, "might be visualized as a lily or a fleur-de-lis." She stood in the fractured light of the library armed with a pointer and four crudely enlarged diagrams, hand-drawn in chalk from Mr. Knowlton's text. Pamphlets, complete with diagrams, lay open on a library table, around which sat Georgiana, Mrs. Smith, and three women carefully chosen from Mrs. Smith's client list: Mrs. Biggs, the senator's wife, Mrs. Shultz, and Mrs. Hershal.

And Mama, *my* Mama, filled the sixth chair.

Except for Mama—who initially had come to fit Miss Rose to the dress she'd commissioned—each woman arrived that day by special invitation to pursue a confidential benevolent venture, and for truffles and tea, which was growing cold as Mrs. French, pointing to various regions of her diagram, enunciated with the same precision with which she recited Latin roots for our morning lessons: labia, lips, clitoris.

"The shape is repeated and much more defined," she explained, "in the internal sex organs: ovaries, womb, birth canal."

Mrs. Biggs gasped. Mrs. Shultz's mouth, poised for the last several minutes above her cup, shut. Mama looked back toward the door where Violet and I sat out of the way, riveted, silent as ghosts.

"One sees the same orientation in certain medieval French sculptures, called *vierges ouvrantes*, or opening virgins," Mrs. French added as an aside, then went on to describe, in detail and in the same tone of academic disinterest, the erogenous zones. "Which, you will notice, are distinct and separate in form and function from organs of purely reproductive purposes."

She ended with an explanation of the proper fit and application of the device.

This assemblage of women did not normally associate. They might know one another through their children or various town functions or, in the case of Mrs. Hershal and Mrs. Shultz, through the singing club. Until that day, none had known that each had purchased a device in common; and after recovering from the shock, a carefully understated curiosity dampened the outrage they expected of one another. The next week, three more women joined them, including Mrs. Joshua Bennett and Mrs. Nicolas Walsh, who had attended Mr. Stockwell's dinner party. That week, Mrs. French sent each woman home with a directive: "to explore for themselves those regions of their bodies from which life grows."

"I am not a doctor or a moralist," said Mrs. French, "but I reject the assumption that ignorance preserves morality. Ignorance merely ensures woman's subjugation. She is given directives when she might be given choices. I will therefore speak clearly, without flourish, and please, if you possess knowledge that would benefit the room, I invite you to share it. We speak about our health, ladies, and the health of our daughters, and one must not sacrifice one's health to propriety."

Mrs. French wore worsted skirts rather than bloomers on these occasions, so that only her words might incite scandal. Her authoritative manner of speech, which not even Mama seemed to distrust, necessitated no response. For several weeks, in fact, the women— nine, then eleven, then fifteen in number—crowded around the library tables, sweets and teacups in hand, listening in silence as if they believed their voices, not their bodies, would place them definitively in that room. Until one day during a pause, Mrs. Biggs said in barely a whisper: "I touched it." Red eyes blinked over her teacup. "The clitoris."

That admission first deepened, then cracked the silence into gasps. "Well," said Mrs. Walsh. Mrs. Hobbs giggled. Nods of reluctant acknowledgment gave rise to more admissions (from everyone but Mama, who rarely said a word to anyone) and questions to which even Mrs. French hadn't all the answers.

Ovary. Fallopian tubes. Vagina. Womb veil. Pessary. Condom. French envelope. Woman's companion. Such startling and detailed descriptions of parts and items I had not known existed, or had existed nameless or endured vaguely under veil of euphemism. Every so often, I'd catch Violet's eye. Had Violet, like me, touched the fabled clitoris? Had Mama? The prospect enthralled as much as horrified me. Fat Mrs. Biggs, thin Mrs. Wells, Mrs. Smith with her long back and short little legs—all of us shared hidden parts! Parts that should, Mrs. French argued, bring us closer in strength and purpose, rather than "tearing us asunder by baseless conflicts grounded in nothing so concrete as physiology."

All told, there were six meetings of the Benevolent Society. They met at eleven every Tuesday and agreed, first tacitly, then by motion, that husbands need know nothing of the society's true purpose. That husbands need not know was for many, I think, the prime advantage of the womb veil, which could in an emergency be explained, Mrs. French reminded them, bringing the last meeting to a close, as a method of correcting a prolapsed uterus. Feet shuffled. No one seemed eager to stand. A despondency fell, until Mrs. Biggs, glancing about, raised her voice.

"Wait a minute," she said. "Wait! That's it? That's all there is on the subject?"

A roomful of heads turned to Mrs. French, but it was Miss Rose, lingering in the doorway behind who answered.

"Well," she said. "Well, there are *other* subjects."

MY OWN AWAKENING MIGHT WELL have colored that spring all by itself, and who am I to speculate about the intimate lives of senator, shopkeeper, and merchant wives? But I'm sure I witnessed discreet smiles on the lips of women as they passed on the street, a bounce, maybe even joy in their steps not present before. I do know, because it was my job to deliver them, that demand for French fashions increased dramatically.

Still, of the fifteen Benevolent Society members who crowded around Mr. Knowlton's text, only five returned the next week for the first meeting of the Reliance Suffrage Society: Mrs. Smith, Georgiana Stockwell, Mrs. Hershal, Mrs. Biggs. And again, to my surprise, Mama.

The exodus outraged Miss Rose.

"Perhaps they were not properly grateful for her hospitality," Mrs. French admitted. We were walking the river side by side, a windless, overcast day. She wore trousers. I wore a pair of her old bloomers, rolled at the waist, and carried her collection basket like a squire. "Even if they were, I'm not sure how she expects them to show it. Four of those women are wives of men in Stockwell's Sin Society, Madelyn. Their very attendance at an event in which the body is so plainly discussed, with texts their husbands would sooner burn, was a bravely subversive act." She said this with admiration and held back a tree branch as I stepped under. Her explanations were more candid and generous outdoors. "They are not reformers. They are wives and mothers who desire some measure of control over their lives. But they mostly love their husbands, I imagine. They love their children and have little wish to change a world they have a reasonably privileged place within."

Her voice trailed off, but I thought nothing of it until, walking on a few steps, I looked back to find her still at the water's edge, staring west over the river, her sturdy frame dark against the silver sky.

The great sadness I felt in her, even at that distance, scared me. She appeared so self-contained, so confident, especially these last several weeks lecturing with her diagrams and pointers. I'd come to expect nothing else, though I knew little about her. She never spoke about herself. It was Miss Rose who told me how the two of them met, during the war in Chicago, working together on the Sanitary Fair with Mrs. Livermore. From Miss Rose I'd learned how alone Mrs. French was in the world: her boys, twins, killed in the war; her husband, Herbert, dead in the Chicago fire.

I can't say if it was their memory arresting her there by the river. I only know that, as if I were looking through a stereopticon, the rather fixed and flat picture I'd had of her rounded into life, and I felt a devotion so unexpected and acute, the memory brings tears to my eyes.

"Mrs. French?" I called when I found my voice. But she had roused herself, reaching me in two strides.

"They are not like you and me, Madelyn." She laid her hand on my shoulder, and we walked on. "They think they have too much to lose."

Of course, I didn't understand what she meant. Neither did Miss Rose, I guess. Didn't or wouldn't or couldn't. At any rate, it was just after this, with the election, that real trouble began.

30

"*Concerned Citizens*—sign it *Concerned Citizens of Reliance.* Now read it again."

Miss Rose, pointing over my shoulder, stood back to listen. It was an afternoon in March, three weeks before the municipal election, and though cold still held nights tight as a collar, days were warmer, longer, the air ripe and green. I ached to be outside with Mrs. French, breathing in the season, but Miss Rose was still unsatisfied with her editorial.

"Again, Madelyn."

> *To the voters of Reliance County:*
>
> *As concerned citizens of Reliance, we have not discovered, among current candidates, one man with the character necessary to lead us out of the economic upheaval and corruption that has plagued this city, indeed this country, for more than a decade. We therefore call upon a proven leader to enter the fray, a leader dedicated to the defense of the rights and freedoms of all citizens, a visionary capable of steering us away from the treacherous sandbanks of corruption into the clear deep water of prosperity. A leader . . .*

I sensed Miss Rose's attention waver and looked up to find Mrs. French, arms crossed, in the doorway.

They had had a row the night before. Not unusual. Argument was a kind of rough play to them, a contest of wits and wills they could draw out for hours, sometimes days. Mostly the arguments ended well, but for several weeks, really since the Suffrage Society formed, the women's voices had held jagged edges I was unused to. Nettle blamed their mood on springtime, when everything bursts forth, spirits and plants and passions alike; but I knew those edges had everything to do with the election and probably with Mrs. Livermore's visit, as well.

I'm afraid any description I might offer of the woman who had extracted herself from the carriage two days before would seem an exaggeration, as would any description of Mrs. French's exuberance. She all but bounded like a girl from the manor to meet her.

"Oh, you dear Big Livermore!" she cried and threw her arms around the tallest woman I'd ever seen, with broad shoulders she didn't care to hide beneath a shawl. From what little Miss Rose had said of Mrs. Livermore, I'd imagined a trumpeting tyrant, short and fat, with a witch's scowl and a stubby and perpetually wagging finger. Instead, an inviting smile lit the woman's long oval face. Her red-blonde hair, parted in the middle, swirled in cheerful disarray.

"Darling, Mrs. French," she said. "Where on earth have you been stowing yourself?"

Her eyes, glancing critically about, darkened at the sight of Miss Rose, who greeted her in kind; and there was nothing pleasant about the pleasantries exchanged in the parlor. Oh no, she could not stay for dinner, had to rush to make the two-o'clock steamer—a lecture in Saint Louis. She was in such great demand in the West, you know. "But I had hoped for a word with Lorena," she said. "A private word."

For the next half hour, the two walked the grounds arm in arm, and even before I heard what Mrs. Livermore said upon departure, a nugget of quiet dread planted itself in my heart.

"Don't say no, my dear Lorena," she said, folding her great frame back into her carriage. "Consider my offer." And then, a comment I'm sure was aimed as much at Miss Rose on the porch as at Mrs. French: "Your talents are wasted here, I think."

Miss Rose remained until the carriage was a dust trail up the drive before she stomped into the manor. I, pretending to read in one of the woven deck chairs, sidled up to Mrs. French.

"Mrs. French?"

"Hmm?" she said, staring after the carriage.

"What did she want? What offer?"

Mrs. French put her hand flat on my head. "My dear, do not make yourself miserable about what is to come or not to come," which told me, as clearly as her embattled posture now, that I had reason to worry.

"I thought we discussed this," said Mrs. French, striding past me in mud-streaked trousers. "I thought we agreed."

"Well, I changed my mind, didn't I?"

Should I leave them alone? They seemed to have forgotten me, and I wasn't sure it wise to remind them.

"Run for mayor," said Mrs. French. "By all means run. But do so honestly. Under your own name. No subterfuge, no trickery. We have scoured the municipal code. You are within your rights to run, even if you may not vote, so why would you—"

Mrs. French's nose scrunched as if a sharp smell had passed. Miss Rose smiled.

"Because, Mrs. French," she said. "Because I plan to win. I have managed theater companies on both coasts, organized tours, handled budgets, hired and fired men more substantial—and godly—than Mr. Stockwell will ever be. I can manage a town of this size."

"That is not the issue, Rose. You know it's not. This cannot end well. It might even damage the cause."

Miss Rose's smile fell, then her words, like stones. "*Your* cause."

"*Our* cause, Rose—yours and mine. And yes it may." Mrs. French gathered herself. "It is fraud, Rose. Election fraud."

"How? My name is R. S. Werner. Rose. Sharon. Werner."

"Was—" said Mrs. French, but Miss Rose spoke over her.

"And who else is there to challenge Stockwell? Tell me that. Who is to show that man he does not own a mandate over this town? Doolittle is a fool to run on prohibition; the Irish vote won't amount to a majority for a hard-money democrat like Donovan. And we're left with Melborn Stockwell, the best of three bad options. Thinks he can gain, through fear and condemnation, the same respect true leaders gain by strength and substance. You think he inspires from his moral high ground? Bah! He simply makes anyone who opposes him ashamed to disagree. Anyone who opposes him is not just wrong, but immoral.

"Well." Miss Rose crossed her arms, raised her chin. "I don't for a second imagine Melborn Stockwell to be as pristine as he likes to pretend. A moral man's virtue is not so easily threatened that he must impose his views on others. Thank the stars you are not his wife. Or his daughter."

Mrs. French looked up at this, but said nothing. Miss Rose spoke as if she had.

"He will not stifle that girl, Lorena. He will not."

I'd assumed Miss Rose's interest in Georgiana was just a way to get back at Mr. Stockwell for writing to her nephews. I wasn't sure anymore. They lunched and walked the gardens arm in arm every Thursday, after suffrage meetings (when Georgiana was supposedly attending a sewing circle with Mrs. Smith). Twice Miss Rose had posed for a portrait, which would have been fine, except after praising the work to William, she'd asked him to pose the next week.

I'd wished to God I could draw then!

As often as not, he—always groomed and dressed as the gentleman—came for lunch on Thursdays with Georgiana and saw her off again. I'd watched him enough to know he wasn't really interested. He was too stiff and polite, not himself at all. I, on the other hand, felt drawn to Georgiana in that awkward, heart-fluttering way younger girls are drawn to older girls. Maybe William's presence attracted me, or maybe I recognized in her desire to become a painter my own as yet unconscious desire to become, not someone new, someone else, but whoever I was, and to be loved for that.

Whatever the case, the attention Miss Rose and William paid Georgiana did not please me.

Evening was falling, light through the window turning gray.

"And as for the election," Miss Rose continued, "you can't tell me Stockwell hasn't already bought Mr. Haxby's votes at the brewery and Mr. Mason's at the glassworks and thus the votes of every man who works for them. Fraud, indeed!"

"That's not the point, Rose."

"Good. Why don't you come to the point, Mrs. French? On second thought, never mind. I don't believe I need your opinion on the matter. And if you feel," she searched for the word in the crown molding, "*wasted* here, maybe you should—"

"Rose, stop. I've made no decisions about that."

"Fine."

Miss Rose turned her back; Mrs. French, poised to speak, thought better of it, and when she left the room, I felt as though half of me left with her. Violet was troubled, too, or she would not have stuck her head from the music room after Miss Rose dismissed me.

"Well?" she said, concern tempering the contemptuous expression I was used to. "What's wrong with them? What happened?"

That she had to ask *me* this question might have been as distressing to her as the situation itself, but I didn't have the heart, now, to lord this over her, nor did I entirely understand what was going on. "It's this election," I said. "I wouldn't worry about it."

But I was, and Violet's concern left me more worried. When the light had faded and swallows were thrilling the eaves, I sought Mrs. French in the conservatory. I didn't want her to leave me.

Pearls of condensation fattened and dripped down the glass walls. Mrs. French's collection basket lay abandoned by the door with her net; she slumped before her easel, paintbrush in hand, staring at a half-finished painting of blue phlox. Her hair gleamed silver in the evening light. Worry scored her forehead. I wasn't sure I should disturb her until, looking up, she patted the wicker chair next to her.

"It's bad?" I asked. "What Miss Rose is doing? Running for mayor, I mean?"

"No. Well," she said, a great weariness in her eyes, "it is not, strictly speaking, against the law."

But, Mrs. French had expected her to campaign *as a woman*, to argue her position publicly. Mrs. French had been preparing these arguments for weeks. Now that Miss Rose decided, without consulting her, to run under initials she shared with her father, Russell Stone Werner, she wasn't even going to announce her candidacy. Instead William, Hanley and his buddies, and the bookshop owner's sons would paper outlying precincts the week before the election, and the green on the day of, with ballots. (Mrs. French explained that it was the candidates' responsibility to print and distribute their own.) Miss Rose would make arguments after.

Mrs. French did not say, "after she won."

The advantage, from Miss Rose's perspective, was that if no one knew she was running, no one would try to stop her.

"That's a good thing, right?" I said.

"Not to my mind, no, Madelyn. You see, to many a nostalgia-glossed memory, the name R. S. Werner will call to mind a younger incarnation of the man upstairs, the man who founded this town and served three terms as mayor—back when the pig was fat and times were good."

I was not used to sarcasm from Mrs. French.

"A good number of people who vote for R. S. Werner, you see, will be voting in ignorance for a memory, not deliberately for a woman. Rose Sharon. Miss Rose."

"And . . ." I said, still unsure. "That's bad?"

"Well, it's certainly not honest." But here a smile lit her direct, serious eyes. "Of course, we are speaking of politics, are we not?" She nudged me in the shoulder. "What do you think Mr. Clemens would say if he knew his remark about the witless voting public would be tested with such purpose?"

"Are you mad at her?"

Mrs. French considered me over her oculars. My shoes scuffed the flagstones.

"Madelyn," she said after a pause, "if I go with Mrs. Livermore, it will not be on account of Miss Rose."

I don't know how she did that. No one else I'd ever met could hear in what I said whatever it was I could not bring myself to say.

Maybe she had a touch of Madame Molineaux's second sight? I wasn't much comforted. She still might leave me.

"But, yes, I am angry," she said. "And I am . . . concerned." She placed her paintbrush on the tray. "Concerned she may take things too far again."

Again? I thought.

"And sometimes I do wonder . . ."

"What, Mrs. French?"

"If perhaps her own glory means more to her than any cause." She said this in a rush, then abruptly faced me.

"I'm sorry. I should not have said that to you, Madelyn. You are right to admire Miss Rose. Her life has been a triumph. A triumph after so much sorrow—such loss."

I nodded, though Miss Rose had told me little to nothing about her sorrows or losses. She'd told me so much else, it had never seemed an omission before.

"I had no right to—"

"Mrs. French?" I asked. "Mrs. French, what happens if she wins?"

For a moment her face mirrored the curiosity and fear prompting my question. "I really don't know, Madelyn. I suppose we will have to wait and see."

31

I'll be honest, at the time, suffrage was still an idea out of Mrs. French's books: ponderous and abstract, with little bearing, I thought, on my own life. I cared about the election because Miss Rose and Mrs. French cared, though I still didn't fully comprehend why the two were so at odds over it. What I wanted was reconciliation between them—my sun and moon. If Miss Rose and Mrs. French were out of sorts, so, too, was the new order of my universe.

They weren't arguing at all. That was the worrisome thing. In the last several weeks, they had become too polite, vehemently polite. Mrs. French, watchful, quiet, retreated into the library, working on what, I don't know. But her wariness made me wary, even in the face of Miss Rose's certitude.

Not since the Nativity play had I seen Miss Rose so decisive, so radiant, filling every room she entered with an enchanting (if somewhat frantic) confidence, which demanded my confidence as well. For three solid weeks, she ate well, slept well, suffered no headaches; if she suffered from anything, it was from fits of generosity—she'd promised a new roof for the Wayward Home and a library next to the Lutheran school. After printing her "Concerned

Citizen" editorials, Mr. Dryfus agreed to print her ballots—in secret, of course, and at a generous profit. If Mr. Stockwell suspected she was up to something, well, Miss Rose reasoned, he would have suspected regardless, wouldn't he? None of the handful of people who knew of Miss Rose's scheme had anything to gain by squealing. No one who knew was able to resist the swift current of Miss Rose's optimism.

No one except Mrs. French.

So I guess I should not have been surprised to find myself, the morning of the election, trapped with Mrs. French and Violet in the library, as usual.

Violet made eyes at me across the table. Whatever we thought (or didn't think) about suffrage, we agreed the occasion warranted a break from studies. But such a suggestion from Violet would have been heard as an attempt to shirk mathematics, of which she was not fond.

"Mrs. French?" I ventured.

"Hmm?" She did not look up.

Really, I couldn't believe she could sit scribbling notes as if the day was like any other. Outside, a few clouds clumped like sheep in a powder-blue sky; light chimed through the cut-glass lamps. We could hear Miss Rose's voice above the bustle of servants preparing for a dinner party planned for the next day. A celebratory dinner, though no one was yet calling it this.

Violet nodded at me to go on.

"Don't you think it would be important—educational—to attend the election? I mean . . ." Mrs. French finally looked up, and I continued bravely. "I mean if we are to vote one day, wouldn't it be good to see how it's done?"

She took off her oculars, rubbed the bridge of her nose, and I knew I'd won. Noes came quick and irreversibly from Mrs. French's lips. "Perhaps. Perhaps it wouldn't hurt to observe the machine."

Miss Rose would not join us. Simply too much to do before the dinner party, and besides, she couldn't show herself until after the vote. But we should by all means go and report all we saw. Nettle packed us a lunch. We three changed—Mrs. French into a brown muslin dress that would raise no eyebrows, I into a blue calico and a straw bonnet big enough to spy behind while avoiding eyes of strangers. Violet, wishing to distance herself, if only in taste, from the two of us, insisted on her pink walking dress and then complained about dust when she discovered we would not be using the carriage. I made sure to skip along, kicking as much dust as I could, and when Violet told me I was being unladylike, Mrs. French said, "If a lady is capable of doing something, then it must ladylike."

Oh yes, it would be a glorious day!

Tiny indigo buntings blinked through the underbrush. Farmers from outlying precincts were still crowding the road, all of them stiff in their Sunday best. Beyond Millionaire's Row, the portico of the courthouse rose above a bower of new-growth oak, and with it, a riot of voices, the clap of hands, the tinny melody of an organ grinder. And on the green: men, men everywhere. In paupers' rags and city-going finery. Sitting, standing, smoking, munching peanuts and pawpaws, cursing back and forth, thrusting hellos and handshakes to other men with the correct allegiances, and forming small, exclusive conclaves of banter and ballyhoo to exclude men with the wrong ones.

William was supposed to be canvasing the green with Hanley, but I couldn't see either of them. The organ grinder wound a new tune. Across the street, a knot of people, men and women, swayed together. "Bible thumpers?" I asked Mrs. French. *"Bible thumpers?"* I said, shouting this time to be heard.

"Socialists," she said, but offered no further explanation, for out of the wash of bodies Mr. Stockwell himself emerged.

I took a halting step back into Violet, who gave me a shove.

"Well, well, well. Missus *French,*" he said biting down hard on her name. He'd dressed in a tailed black jacket and top hat, but if the combination was meant to make him look taller, it failed; his neck disappeared beneath the starched collar and his burnsides stuck out like a pair of clipped walrus tusks on either side of his fat face.

Cocksure. That's what Dot would say of him. That man is cocksure, but ready as any chicken for the pot. I felt my hackles rise—saw, too, a change come over Mrs. French.

"I trust," he continued. "there will be no . . . *display* like the last election."

Oh, yes! Maybe it was his tone or the way his watch chain stretched like a grin across his belly, but Mrs. French's demeanor had changed. She raised her head, lowered her shoulders, and when she looked back at Violet and me, her eyes gleamed with competitive vigor. "Like the last election?" she said as if considering. "No. Now, if you'll excuse us."

Mr. Stockwell did not, and when he stepped in front of her, even Violet bristled.

"Where is *our* Miss Rose today?"

Our Miss Rose! I thought. Mrs. French laid a restraining hand on my shoulder. Her voice remained even.

"Attending business at the manor," she said. "Of course,"

"Of course."

This time, Mrs. French veered around him, took two steps. Then she stopped and turned so abruptly, Violet and I nearly fell into her.

"Mr. Stockwell?" she said. "May the best man win."

Really, it's too bad Mrs. French's voice was so thin; Stockwell had no idea she'd thrown a gauntlet. Whereas I? Well, I could barely contain my fighting pride. Any lingering ambivalence about the election vanished. Miss Rose was going to win. I was now quite sure and all but marched through the throng behind Mrs. French to a flat stretch of grass beyond the great oak, where other women lunched and children fussed and tumbled. There we spread our blanket, a conquering flag. Which didn't make a lot of sense to me. I couldn't see anything of the courthouse or the election from there.

A black man selling pawpaws from a cart, rickety as his voice, clattered by. Girls sold foxgloves. Grimy, hungry-eyed boys begged food until a deputy scattered them like so many blackbirds. Violet, sitting straight as a doll, arranged her skirts on the blanket so not one inch would touch the grass.

"You might as well have stayed at the manor," I said.

"Mind your own, Madelyn."

Even standing, all I could see of the courthouse was the portico, nosing into the air. Across the green, I could see Mrs. Smith with Mama, Little John on her hip (he was becoming too much for Clara alone), and a few other Suffrage Society ladies gathered like bees around the water pump in their yellow sashes. In a few minutes, Mrs. Smith and Mama joined us.

Without Little John clinging like a monkey, I'm not sure I would have known Mama from a distance. For moments at a time, now, I hardly recognized her, and when I did, I felt a kind of distant pride. It wasn't her dress, which she had made, or her sash or hat, which she'd bought with money she'd earned making Miss Rose a dress. Not only these things. It was the upright way she was carrying herself as she walked this way. The way she looked other women in the eye; the way they looked at her, a wife, a mother, a lady of business. Two

weeks ago, I'd found her alone at the dress-shop cutting table, bent
in furious concentration over what I assumed to be a bit of fancy
work—until she swiped it beneath the table.

A book. Mama reading a book.

Neither of us had mentioned it, of course. She didn't mention
William's charm around my neck, either. So things had remained
between us: watchful, cautious.

"Any idea how we're doing?" Mrs. French asked Mrs. Smith.

Mama took Little John back to the shop to nurse. Hanley, emerg-
ing from the crowd, waved a ballot in his good hand and called out:

"Tired of hard-money men getting rich off the debt they created? Tired of government poking its nose into your mail and into
your homes? Tired of hypocrisy and corruption and greed? Then R.
S. Werner's the mayor for me!"

Mrs. Smith clapped. "Bravo, Hanley!"

"Last one," he said. "For your scrapbook, Maddy?" Along the top
of the ballot, in fancy script, I read, NATIONAL GREEN PARTY. Below,
in smaller print, selections for assessor, clerk, sheriff, ward counselors.
And for mayor: R. S. Werner.

Violet sat up, batting her eyes as if hurt. "What about me, Hanley?
Where's mine?"

Sun lit red highlights in her hair. Really, she was exceptionally
pretty. Hanley blushed. I grabbed his good arm. "Let's get a closer
look at the courthouse."

Mrs. French, frowning at the growing chaos of bodies, didn't
seem sure about this, so I didn't ask permission. "Stay with Hanley!"
Mrs. Smith shouted after us.

The polls had opened hours before, but it was lunchtime now,
and soon I found myself pressed on every side by a rank hubbub of
shoulders, boots, and trousers. If I lost Hanley, it occurred to me, I

might get crushed, so I stuck as close as I could, inching forward in fits and starts, until finally we found a channel, crossed the street, and climbed the steps to the porch of the Turner Building. From there we had a much better view of the polling window, open on the south side of the courthouse.

Even then I was a little disappointed. Except for the men, bunched like ants around a morsel, nothing distinguished this window from the four others gaping from the first floor. Behind us, a rough swill of voices, then several dozen glass-factory and brewery workers, singing and stumbling over one another, trooped around the corner from the Third Street grog shops. A ruckus of shoving rose up, out of nothing it seemed, on the far side of the green. I'll be honest. I expected election day would be more, I don't know, somber? The beer and sour apple stink of bodies, the party agents shouting slogans and promising violence and favors, even the two toughs flanking the polling window, reminded me of nothing so much as a gambling hall. I was not at all sure I wanted to vote if this is what it would be like.

Two men yanked another dressed in funny clothes from the polling window and shoved him to the ground.

"Foreigner, I guess," said Hanley.

"How do you know?"

"Looks like one."

But he wasn't looking at the man anymore. He was looking at me, a queer expression on his face I wasn't sure how to read.

After the night of Saint Stephen's, I didn't see Hanley again for two weeks; when I did, on my way to deliver one of Miss Rose's editorials to Mr. Dryfus, I found him in the composition room, apron strings dangling dangerously close to the iron jaws of the press, trying with one arm to do the job of two. I knew better than to offer help but didn't want him to know I'd seen him struggling, either. So I went back to the shop front, slammed the door, and stomped in like I'd just arrived.

I couldn't help but stare. The bruises, the eye patched over, the arm in a sling, the nose left of center. He would have scared me if I didn't know him. Scared me a little anyway, even after he showed me the articles he'd saved for my scrapbook—crimes of passion, loves lost, that sort of thing. He talked the news as usual: Indian wars, a railroad strike in Chicago, a steamboat accident near Cairo that killed some foreign dignitary's son. But between us sat this snorting bull of awkwardness that rose up whenever we were alone together.

It was there now as we stood side by side.

"What, Hanley? What's wrong with you?"

The ruckus grew louder.

"Nothing. It's just . . ." He wasn't looking at me anymore but staring, jaw set, at the courthouse. "I wanted to tell you. I decided. I'm not going into the army. I know I always talk of it, but I can't. I mean, I can't leave my sister with him out there somewhere."

He didn't have to say who *him* was.

"Alright," I said, watching him close. I never wanted him to go away in the army, but I knew how much it meant to him. I knew I should say more, but didn't know what.

"You saw me that night," Hanley said, nodding his head. "I could have killed him," then looked at me like he wasn't so sure anymore. "You think I could have killed him?"

The thing was, I wasn't entirely sure what Hanley wanted me to say. I wanted to say no, but it wasn't true, and I knew he would know. I'd seen his face that night. The constable had been right. Murder mad.

"Yeah, I do. Maybe rightly so," I told him.

"He comes back," he nodded. "I'll kill him."

The silence that fell across the green alarmed us. Well, not fell exactly, but rippled from the direction of Fourth Street, like a stone thrown into a pond. Hanley and I climbed up the rail of the porch for a better look and saw Reverend Reynolds of the First African Baptist Church, smiling big in the face of a lot of frowns and walking slow toward the courthouse with six well-dressed Negro men. He stopped and shook hands with eight or ten white men, guns conspicuously holstered, who closed ranks and formed a kind of ballast around the reverend. If not for those guns, it might have been funny looking—all those heads turning—but no one was laughing. I felt my guts seize, looked to Hanley, who was watching that crowd like he was watching a thunderstorm, not sure yet of the threat. "We better go," he said.

Most women on the lower green had bundled their blankets and herded their children home. Mrs. French, waiting there with our blanket, pointed us to the print shop, and I was glad to go.

Glad, that is, until, walking in, I saw William leaning on the shop counter next to a giggling Violet.

"Well, there she is," said William, "We were just talking about you, Maddy. Hello there, Hanley."

Hanley excused himself back to the Turner Building with notepad in case anything did happen. Mrs. Smith, standing in the hall, shouted up the stairwell. "She's here. She's back, Rebecca." Mrs. French handed me the blanket, then asked for a word with William and Mr. Dryfus in the study, leaving me alone in the shop front with Violet.

She knew I wanted to know what William had said about me, what had been so funny. So I bit my tongue.

"I think," she said, watching me, "William looks just like Lord Byron. Don't you? He says he's off to Europe as soon as he can. I'm sure Miss Rose will send him. Reliance is no place for talent."

I could tell she considered herself among the misplaced.

"But that Hanley," she said. "He looked a brute before. Now, well! William says"—she leaned in—"he says they'll never take a *cripple* like him in the army."

I couldn't help it, I started at this. My heart clenched because I heard the truth in what she said. It hadn't been his choice after all. Hanley hadn't decided anything. Violet gave a shrug of mock surprise. "Well, why would they?"

"The moment the result is known, William, come to us," said Mrs. French striding from the study. She beckoned us to follow and did not slow until we reached the cusp of the cypress drive. There, wind gusting through the leaves, she stopped, cocked her ear as if she could hear in the wind the thrum of voices.

"What, Mrs. French?" I said. "What is it?"

"I don't know." She shook her head. "A feeling."

Violet and I looked at each other. If we knew anything about Mrs. French, it was that she was not governed by feelings. At the manor, she took silent leave and went straight to Miss Rose. Violet turned to follow.

"Violet, wait."

I still wanted to know what she and William had been saying about me, but damned if I'd ask her that. "Reckon Mrs. French got a premonition? Reckon she thinks we're going to win?"

"Do I *reckon*?" said Violet. "Dear Madelyn, why do you persist in speaking like a heathen?"

"Fine. Do you think—"

"I don't know," said Violet.

"Well, what happened in New York, then? Mrs. French said she's afraid Miss Rose might go too far again. What's she mean, *again*?"

To my surprise, Violet's blue eyes glistened. Her pretty nose flared. "You horrid heartless beast! Don't ever ask me that again, Madelyn. Never again."

THAT EVENING, IN THE ROSE garden, Alby lit her pipe and leaned back to blow smoke. "People in this house got more secrets than is good for 'em," she said. "Bet it's different out West. Out there you arrive and say, 'This is who I am and to hell with anyone who don't like it.'"

"I'm not sure that's how it is anywhere."

"Some kind of an expert in everything now, that it?"

I reached for the pipe and she gave it.

"I told you I'd teach you to read," I said.

"Bah," said Alby. "Lots of good Latin do me, anyway. Lots of good it do you. Fancy words, fancy dresses, fancy dinners. Just makes you expect more of the same. You think I'm jealous, but I say you'd of been better off learning a kitchen with me, instead of playing poet lady. Might've had options, Maddy, and now you'll be thinking you got to live fancy to have any life at all."

"Options like your dog woman?"

"Nettle won't say it, Maddy. But I'm gonna. You listening? Now I don't mean to hurt you, but here it is: All those big words and big ideas they're stuffing in your head don't change the ways of the world. And you just better get your head around the fact people always gonna look at you like they look at old Cyrus. At me, too. They gonna look at you and see a color first. Fancy walk and talk and clothes or no, they gonna see a color. What's more?" She took the pipe back. "You're a damned fool if you think Miss Rose will give you anything more'n a boot out the door when she's through with you. As big a fool as Violet. Bigger, since she never had nobody to tell her straight."

"That's not true!"

"She's playing with you, Maddy. Don't get how you can't see that. She's rich. It's what rich people do. You think you mean anything to her? Well then, all that learning's making you blind. She ain't nothing but a selfish, vain woman who does good things so that people will think good of her. Impressive on the outside."

"That's not true. It's what some people think."

"It's what everybody thinks, everybody she ain't witched blind to it. But hey, maybe Lizzette's right? You mighty easy to witch, ain't you? Give you a fancy dress, or a charm, and you loyal as a—"

"You take that back!" I demanded, standing now, my fists clenched, but Alby, reaching up, pulled me down again.

"Just be careful, okay? That's all I'm saying."

32

The next morning everyone in the household was quiet and tense. Everyone except Miss Rose, who was not quiet.

Up before dawn, Miss Rose now paced the dining room assigning places for the dinner party, her voice gaining volume with every chime of the manor's many clocks. "Reverend Reynolds will sit there." She reconsidered. "No, there. Across from Judge Bennett and Senator Biggs . . . Hmm, what do you think, Mrs. Hardrow?"

Mrs. Hardrow waited until she told her what to think. All morning, Miss Rose had been running the servants ragged with indecision, first ordered the white and gold Copeland China and Francis I Sterling, and after it had been polished, changed her mind in favor of the Wedgwood Service and Strasbourg Sterling. I was almost glad to retreat with Violet into the library but found Mrs. French no more calming. By midmorning, I hardly cared what the election news might be, if only William would come and put us out of our misery.

Now I know I should not have been so eager, because when finally William arrived, just before noon, he was not alone.

By his side was a rumpled, bleary-eyed Mr. Dryfus and Reverend Reynolds, holding himself so stiffly I thought he must be having trouble with his bowels. Mr. Dryfus looked without seeing me, and when I caught William's eye, he shook his head, so I knew. I knew before I'd followed them to the door of Miss Rose's office and heard Miss Rose say:

"Stockwell then? Well, shit."

To be sure, I didn't expect to join them, would have rather nursed my considerable disappointment in the garden, but with a gesture from Mrs. French, Mrs. Hardrow beckoned me inside with her. "Not a word," Hardrow said. We stood in the back, by the wall of mirrors, the windows to our left brimming with light.

No one was sitting. Miss Rose and Mrs. French stood in the middle of the room, their backs to the windows, across from Mr. Dryfus, William, and the reverend. At first I thought Miss Rose's curse had turned the pale scar on the reverend's cheek red. He cleared his throat, but Miss Rose spoke over him.

"And I suppose it takes all three of you to tell me this?" She was looking at Reynolds as she said this. "By how much? Well, what was the margin?"

"Not Stockwell, either, Miss Rose," said William.

"Not—"

"Donovan," said William. Mrs. French's eyes widened. Miss Rose, about to laugh, stopped.

"Not Donovan," said Miss Rose. "Donovan? Donovan won?"

"Not by much," said Mr. Dryfus, pipe in one hand, cane in the other, though neither seemed to steady him. "Because the ballots under dispute were printed on my press, and because your name— or your *father's* name, as the case may be—appears on the ballots, we are both now at the center of this *scandal*. I thought it expedient to consult you as to a plan of action."

The word "scandal" deepened Mrs. French's frown. But Miss

Rose—Miss Rose merely folded gloved hands before her. "No plan," she said lightly.

The reverend balked. "Excuse me?"

"No plan. I have done nothing wrong. You, Mr. Dryfus," she said, "have done nothing wrong. We have all acted within our rights, as the law now stands." She ran a hand down her bodice, an attitude of victory upon her. "The people have spoken. The people have spoken, and they do not want Stockwell."

"They do not want a Democrat either, Miss Rose," said the reverend forcefully. "Your actions split the party vote and all but handed the election to Donovan. And the fact of the matter? The fact is that if those who voted your ticket knew this would be the result, they would have voted Stockwell. Even if he is overbearing."

"My father was overbearing. Stockwell is a tyrant who would use the position to further his own limited agenda."

"And what have you done?"

"What have I done?"

"Rose," said Mrs. French.

"What have I done, indeed, but fight for years for the freedoms and rights of half of this country's population? For your wife, Mr. Reynolds. For your daughter."

But the reverend only shook his head, a sad, patient, patronizing movement that echoed in his voice and rankled Miss Rose. "No, you betray us. After the gains the Negro has made. Are you not grateful? Did we not work for this progress side by side?"

"Oh, I remember. The grand statements. The promises of progress."

"Yes!" said Reynolds, though he must have heard the sarcasm in her voice.

"And yet that promise has been broken, has it not? Tell me, how many men from your congregation voted yesterday, Reverend. Five? Six? Under the protection of how many white men with guns? How many hundreds and thousands of Negroes were turned from the polls by force? By fear? Women might remain politically enslaved, Reverend Reynolds, but the Negro remains practically so. And why? I'll tell you why. Because seven years ago you—and Douglas and Garrison, all of you—allowed yourselves to be duped by that ridiculous argument. How absurd! How absurd to believe your rights could be won only so long as the chains remained around the necks of your strongest allies."

"Rose," said Mrs. French.

"Reverend Reynolds, *sir*." She did not use the word with deference. "We agreed to postpone, not to cede indefinitely, the battle for women's suffrage. We combined our energies in one direction, not to fight one particular injustice, but to fight injustice in its ugliest and most obvious form. But let me assure you, Reverend, that had we thought the rights of the Negro would be won at the cost of our own, we would have thought better of our effort, and you, sir, would remain a fugitive."

"Rose!" said Mrs. French, but it was no use; all vestiges of restraint left her. Her forehead was mottled. Tears in her voice. For a horrifying moment, she appeared as fragile as the old woman I'd encountered the night after the soiree; and though I did not understand half of what had been said, I felt tears and a surge of helpless loyalty.

"No," she said quietly now. "No, I am not *grateful*. I am quite justly ungrateful, and so should you be."

Then she turned to stare through the curtains. Reverend Reynolds opened his mouth, closed it. He straightened his lapel, walked to the door. "This conversation is not over," he said.

"Yes, it is, Reverend."

Mrs. French followed him into the hall. I didn't hear what she said, or his reply, but she returned alone. William and Mr. Dryfus worried their hats. Miss Rose, staring out the window, quivering with rage, ignored them. "Thank you for coming," offered Mrs. French. "Both of you." And then they, too, were gone, down the staircase, out the double doors, which closed definitively behind them.

Miss Rose stood with her back to the room, framed in window light and reflection, but trailing, also, a singular shadow, long and dark across the carpet. I could hear servants below, still preparing for the dinner party; birdsong surged, softened again. Mrs. French approached; they stood side by side in a brittle silence Mrs. French finally broke.

"You should not have said that to him. You are right, but you should not have said it." Miss Rose said nothing. "About Donovan, Rose, I didn't think. I never thought . . ."

"Did you read Mrs. Livermore's comments in the *Post* yesterday?" But gave Mrs. French no time to respond. "'All of these ladies,'" she recited. "'All of these ladies traipsing into voting booths, flaunting themselves in halls of congress, they are nothing but plumed peacocks as damaging to our cause as a parade of wastrels down Main Street, with no other hope, or purpose, than to bolster their own fragile legends.'"

"Oh, Rose. Rose, she did not mean you."

"Of course she did. And Mrs. Woodhull, maybe even Mrs. Anthony. Of course she did."

"She only means . . . We must be patient, Rose. Take the long view."

"Huh."

"The world does not change quickly. The people are too many, the needs too many."

Miss Rose wasn't listening. Her head had tipped as though a

thought had landed; she turned abruptly and her eyes locked with mine.

"Did you know, Lorena," she said, still looking at me. "Did you know that poor girl they found dead in the river last year worked for the Stockwells before the Lily White? Did you know she was pregnant?"

She turned to catch Mrs. French's reaction, which was just as well, for that last word was a door slamming in my chest; the breath went out of me. Just like that, all their high language crumbled to the floor.

"What are you suggesting?" Mrs. French, gathering herself, started again. "Are you suggesting the baby was . . . ?"

"Stockwell's," said Miss Rose.

"How do you know? It's important, Rose. How do you know?"

"Georgiana."

"How does she know?"

"Servants talk, Lorena. You know that as well as—"

"And she told you? She said Stockwell was the father?"

"As much as said."

"As much as?"

"Oh please, Lorena!"

"What did she say?" Mrs. French insisted, following Miss Rose to the door. "It's important, Rose. What exactly did she say?"

"He did it, Mrs. French. I know the type. He got that girl pregnant. And then . . ." The half-smile on her face sent a chill through me. "And then isn't it curious? That girl wound up murdered."

She left us then. Mrs. Hardrow followed. Mrs. French, shaken, for once unsure, looked across the room at me.

"Madelyn?"

Murder, Madelyn.

"I won't say anything," I said.

"There's nothing to say."

I wasn't so sure. I wasn't so sure I shouldn't say something to William. Pregnant. Had William known? Did he suspect Stockwell? If he had, why hadn't he said so?

"Madelyn," said Mrs. French. "Look at me. We don't know he did anything. We don't know anything for sure. Madelyn, do you hear me?"

What I heard, what we both heard would relegate even this horrid intrigue to the periphery for a time: A thump. A short piercing cry. A drum of feet above our heads. Old Man, who had languished one foot in the grave for as long as I'd known him, had chosen that day, of all days, to jump in with two.

33

Only shreds of light slipped beneath black crepe curtains, but I could see, as I lay on my side, the outline of Nurse Lipman's packed suitcase by the wardrobe. Lipman rolled over, nudged me in the back with a knee.

"Hey. Maddy," she said. "Ah, now, you'll be okay. Though you'll miss me, won't you? No need worrying about me, Miss Maddy. I got a head on my shoulders, good references. Modern woman of the world, I am." More sadness than pride in her voice. She sat up, stretched. I watched her, ashamed to admit I was neither grieving over Old Man, nor properly mourning the loss of Nurse Lipmann, who, after all, had shown me as much care and kindness as anyone in that house. Other, selfish concerns were souring my gut.

"What if Miss Rose doesn't keep me now?"

"That what's bothering you?" One of the things. "Well, she hasn't said anything about it, right? Hardrow not said anything? And you made yourself useful in other ways. What's the word?"

"Indispensable," I mumbled.

"That's it. Indispensable in other ways. Okay then."

She planted a rough kiss on the side of my head, lit the lamp, pulled her nightgown off and her chemise over her droopy breasts, giving each a good rub before attacking the buttons of her traveling dress.

It was not what Miss Rose said that worried me. In the three days since Old Man died, she'd stepped from her bedroom only to haggle over funeral arrangements with her nephews and the lawyer, Mr. Schneider, who'd arrived (though not together) two days before. She allowed no one inside except Hardrow to dress her and Violet to sing and hadn't said boo to me. Without Old Man to tend, I was feeling awfully dispensable. Not to mention vulnerable to bad dreams and thoughts I had been trying to avoid—about Stockwell and the dead woman, Aileen. About William.

Had he known about Stockwell? Had he known she was pregnant? Haunted by these questions though I was, I had discovered a reluctance to ask him, not that the last few days had afforded an opportunity. Lipman dropped to her knees for a hatpin, and I forced my thoughts back to the matter at hand.

"If Miss Rose doesn't keep me?"

"If she don't?" Lipman swiped a scrap of paper from the dresser and scrawled, as best she could, *Illinois Central Hospital for the Insane.* "Got a cousin works there gonna try to get me on. You need to, you come find me. Right? Now, don't see me off or you'll make me cry, too, and I ain't cried leaving a house since I left my mama."

So I curled small in that suddenly big bed until I heard her trap pull away, then put on the mourning dress Mrs. Smith loaned me and did the best I could with my hair without lifting the black crepe covering the mirror. Nettle warned me doing so before the funeral was as good as inviting Old Man's spirit to take up residence in the reflection, and while I wasn't sure I believed this, decided it best to err on the side of caution. Miss Rose must have decided the same.

She'd ordered all the clocks stopped at twelve twenty-seven, the time Lipman found Old Man, and over Hardrow's quiet objections, had postponed the funeral three days in order to find enough crepe to shroud every mirror, portrait, blind-eyed bust, and statue. Every window, too. Even the glassed cupola. Living with Old Man's shade might have been preferable; now any time a door opened and a breeze jostled the shrouds, it seemed a whole houseful of haunts had taken residence.

The effect was worse, though not much, on my nerves than the stink of Old Man's corpse, fast overgrowing the wagonload of flowers and herb sachets Hardrow had ordered to mask it. I guess it was lucky there'd been so little of him left to rot.

I slipped down the spiral stair to the dining room and found Miss Rose's nephews, strident, beardless fellows with boxy nutcracker mouths, stuffing their faces and casting appraising glances over the buffet silver, the cut-glass chandelier, the cutlery, even at Tom, who stood at attention by the dumbwaiter. I felt like walking up and kicking them in the shins, but they looked at me as if half-expecting this. So I grabbed a pastry and, abandoning them to their speculations, retreated to the kitchen. Nettle, face red, hair as damp as her blouse, hustled a tray of tarts out of the oven and another in. Two Negro hired girls were paring apples at the table. Alby, slop bucket in hand, bumped past me through the door.

"Can I help?" I asked.

"Yeah," said Nettle. "Stay out of the way."

Outside I watched the stableboy brush down the gelding and Cyrus stuff topiary trimmings into scrap bags. Bees hummed in the cherry blooms and flowering plums; for a while I meandered the rose garden, bursting into bud, and when none of this eased me, slipped back inside and slumped into an armchair in the library. To find Mrs. French hunched over a book was a comfort even though she didn't seem to notice me.

"Miss Rose's nephews look like they're ready to eat up the cutlery with their breakfast," I said.

Mrs. French turned the page. I tapped my foot, watching subtle shifts of thought cross her face. Pretty soon I wandered over.

"Do you need something to do, Madelyn?" I was standing in her light.

"What are you reading?"

She leaned back, cleaned her oculars, her mourning dress little departure from her usual attire.

"Probate law."

"Oh," I said, but didn't pretend to know what this meant; Mrs. French had a nose for false confidence.

"In case they do try to eat the cutlery with their breakfast," she said.

At ten, guests finally began to arrive: Mrs. Drabney from the Wayward Home, Judge and Mrs. Bennett, and towheaded Mr. Sims, a young lawyer from Springfield who boarded with them. Mrs. Smith followed with the cobbler, Emil Le Duc, often in her presence of late. Then came Mama and Mr. Dryfus and Hanley, too. No William, yet. They gave their jackets to Roberts and their condolences to Miss Rose, who though frighteningly gaunt, wore a reassuringly extravagant dress, a fitted sheath of blue-black lace and silk, flaring into a bustle of layered crepe. A black mesh veil obscured her face.

Was it sadness I read there? A headache? I hoped sadness, because I hadn't managed more than a distracted and selfish remorse for Old Man. I found myself watching her closely; everyone was watching her, even as they shook hands with the nephews standing like blocks of wood to Miss Rose's right. One by one, guests blinked into the candlelit entryway, their voices spiriting away in the cavernous space. Only then did I recognize the larger effect Miss Rose had created with all those shrouds and candles and darkness, even with the flowers and Old Man's stink. The manor a stage! A funeral scene in one of Miss Rose's plays.

Except it wasn't a play.

"Well, you look very nice, Madelyn," said Mrs. Smith. Mama, every bit the lady, wore gray with black lace. Half the ladies in attendance were wearing her lace. "Very put together," said Mrs. Smith. "Doesn't she look nice, Hanley?"

Someone, Mrs. Smith from the way she was smiling, had put Hanley together; his shirt and trousers pressed, his eyepatch clean, his hair oiled. Embarrassed, neither of us mustered a response. Emil Le Duc and Mr. Dryfus joined us. Then a hush.

Melborn Stockwell emerged from the porch glare, and even breeze-blown shrouds seemed to still.

I knew enough to expect Stockwell. Donovan and Doolittle, too, were expected, especially, Mrs. French told me, because the election results were still in doubt and each would be eager to claim Old Man's memory for his own use. The whole town was expected, if not at the viewing, then later at the cemetery. Shops and factories closed; pubs opened early, and all day church bells would ring the half hour. They were ringing now.

Still, the shock remained, because, well, I'd never actually seen Mr. Stockwell and Miss Rose in the same room; from the watchful expressions around the room, no one else had, either. Behind him came a little convoy: his wife, the invalid Abigail, and Georgiana, who kept her eyes trained away from Miss Rose and on the hem of her mother's skirt, then Reverend Reynolds, who seemed to balance his dignity on the tip of his chin, and then the Morrisons and the Walshes. Outside, a horse jangled its tack. An oriole called, but for an awkward moment both of them—Miss Rose and Mr. Stockwell—stood before each other entirely at a loss. They reminded me (forgive me, Miss Rose) of a bulldog and a poodle, who after months of barking insults from opposite yards, discover the gate between them open.

Miss Rose squared her shoulders. A caustic smile lifted Stockwell's thin lips. If her veil unsettled him, he didn't show it.

"My condolences, Miss Rose," he said too loudly. "For your loss."

Behind the veil, Miss Rose's eyes shone, her nose angled like a dagger.

"Thank you, Mr. Stockwell."

"He was a remarkable man, your father. We all owe him a debt of gratitude—a great deal of *respect*." He rocked forward into the word, thumbs in vest pockets, chest thrust out as if he thought even birds outside should stop their chatter to listen. Most people did.

"Yes," Miss Rose replied.

"For his faith," Stockwell continued. "Yes," someone echoed behind him. "His founding vision. His moral fortitude."

"I am glad you think so, Mr. Stockwell," said Miss Rose.

"Melborn," his wife entreated, glancing at faces in the room.

"But you see, we *all* think so, Miss Rose," he said, including the room with a broad gesture. A good many heads nodded agreement—with what, I wasn't sure. The exaltation of Old Man? The criticisms of Miss Rose embedded in those exaltations? Both? I felt a strong urge to walk right over there and . . . what? Accuse him? Defend her? How? No direct attack had been made. He hadn't even mentioned the election. I knew there must be a good reason Miss Rose withheld her own accusations but I couldn't think of what it might be. Mrs. French, by the parlor door, cast me a warning, her hands palms down as if to say, "Easy, Maddy."

"Melborn, dear." Stockwell's wife tried again. "There are people waiting to . . . We should really . . ."

Stockwell, cheeks red with triumph, led his disciples toward the refreshments.

"Oh! What a beast he is," Mrs. Smith whispered as they passed. I wondered how much Mrs. Smith knew about it. Wondered again where William was. "I think she handled herself very well."

"A beast, maybe," said Mr. Dryfus. "But no fool."

"Mr. Dryfus, don't tell me you side with that man!" demanded Mrs. Smith.

"I did not say that. But we must acknowledge the strength in his *design*. Even those who did not support Stockwell, who might even have applauded Miss Rose's election scheme, might now feel *reasonably* obliged to be offended on Old Mr. Werner's behalf."

"Reasonably?"

"And with what happened last night . . ."

The party followed the flow of traffic to the dining room. Hanley stayed put.

"Bunch of glassworks boys fought the Paddies by the docks last night," he said. "Rumor's going around if there's a strike like they say, the Paddies will step in with Donovan's blessing. I guess they're getting a head start fighting. Nobody died yet, though."

"That's good, I guess." I said.

Together, we picked our way past gossiping, well-fed mourners, teeth and faces jaundiced in the lamplight. Mr. Donovan arrived, right after Mr. Doolittle and Mr. Baynard, the outgoing mayor, a gout-ridden man with a spinster niece who fluttered about him like a colorless moth. "Yoo-hoo, Mr. Sims!" Big Nora, arm in arm with

Angela, breezed by, chasing the lawyer. "Oh, don't you just *love* a
good funeral? For an old man especially. Then it's not such a shame,
is it? Then it's rather a party. Oh look, Nora!"

All those pushy people! In the gardens, the gallery, the music
room, the dining room. I was in no fine mood by the time Hanley
and I edged our way into the parlor. There Old Man lay helpless
against all those gawking eyes. It's true I didn't know Old Man much
better than I had eight months before, but I'd felt his presence, and
now his absence, as they had not. Made me mad, the way everyone
seemed to hold him on their plates with their tarts, taking bites
as they talked of other things—the whiskey trials, the election, the
potato blight.

Hanley spotted William on one side of the casket, speaking quietly with Georgiana Stockwell. She looked at him, leaned in to say
something, and when he smiled, my heart twisted.

"I'll be back, Hanley. I've got to . . ." and leaving him midsentence,
I picked my way through the throng to William, tapped him on the
shoulder and when he leaned down, whispered in his ear.

"I know she was pregnant." He blinked down at me. "Aileen."

This had rather more effect than I expected.

"Come with me," he said, and leaving Georgiana to gape, seized
my arm and pulled me with him out the door. Finding the porch
occupied, he continued to the garden. Behind the garden shed, he
turned me to face him, all frivolity in his manner gone.

"Where did you hear that?"

"Miss Rose," I said.

"Where did she?"

"Stockwell did it."

"Stop playing games, Madelyn!"

"Miss Rose *said* Mr. Stockwell did it! She said Georgiana told her."

William, breathless, paused. "Georgiana?"

"As much as told her." I yanked free, close to tears, wishing I hadn't said anything. William leaned against the garden shed, hands to his face, tugging that phantom beard and staring west across the river.

"It's true, then? William?"

Beneath shouts of boys playing tag in the topiary, I heard the insect hum of human voices from the manor beyond. First, only William's eyes met mine. Then, after a moment's consideration, his attitude changed. He turned.

"She came to me," he said. "For help, Maddy. Look at me." I looked at his chest, at his lapel. "I gave her the address of a place to go in the city and my mother's charm to pay for it. I did what I could for her. I told you that."

"You didn't tell me she was pregnant," I said. "If Stockwell did it, if you knew, why didn't you—"

"This is not some romantic fancy, Maddy! Who would believe such an accusation? Only her memory would suffer." He held me by my shoulders at arm's length, and still I could not meet his eyes. "Do you understand that? Her memory would suffer, Maddy. I would suffer. Do you want that?"

"No, William."

"It doesn't matter what happened. It doesn't matter now. Say it." His breath hot in my face.

"Maddy?" Hanley called, then appeared with Mama down the path. "You okay?"

"Say it, Maddy," said William.

I looked at him then, right in the eye, and found there an anguish that made me all the more uncertain. "Doesn't matter," I said with no conviction, and pushed past Hanley and Mama, toward the manor.

34

"Madelyn, darling girl! Tell me what they are saying about me."

We had laid Old Man to rest in the Twelfth Street Cemetery, four acres of Union dead, on a west-sloping hill overlooking the river bend. Now, the morning after, Miss Rose had stripped black crepe from her office mirrors and windows, and a tense April sun peeked in. She'd discarded her deep mourning, too, for a royal blue tea dress of linen and lace; and while at first it was a relief to find her brimming with energy and vanity, I could sense the sharp edge beneath and see from Mrs. French's posture that I'd interrupted something. I didn't want to rub them wrong.

The fact was, I'd paid little mind to what anyone was saying about Miss Rose. I'd spent the funeral ruminating on what William had not said. He had not, as I expected, or rather as I wanted, confirmed Miss Rose's accusation against Stockwell. Not in so many words.

"Well?" she said. "They cannot say I neglected my duty. You heard how they spoke of him, I suppose? More god than man, I should think. Now don't think me insensitive, Madelyn, I cried my share of tears for my father. Yes, Mrs. Hardrow?"

Mrs. Hardrow, pushing through the door handed Miss Rose a

note. Mrs. French spoke up: "If that is another request for charity, Rose, I say again it would be wise to wait until we have—"

"Oh, as you wish, Lorena! *Nothing* was being said about me, Madelyn? Mrs. Hardrow, before you go . . ."

The lawyer, Mr. Schneider, a gaunt, unassuming man, well dressed but badly groomed, popped through the door as if sprung from a clock. And to my surprise, to everyone's surprise, William followed him. William, clear-eyed, clean-shaven, barely looked at me.

"Mr. Stark?" said Miss Rose. "Can I help you?"

"I have asked Mr. Stark to join us today, Miss Rose," said the lawyer. From Mrs. French's expression, she had no prior notion of the invitation, nor did the nephews who charged through the door as Mrs. Hardrow shooed me out.

I ventured no farther than the balcony, sliding down cross-legged, my head pressed to the balusters, hearing little beyond the laughter of two hired girls collecting mountains of crepe in the gallery, for what purpose I couldn't guess and didn't care. A shadow draped itself over me. Violet glared down. She carried a script under one arm as though she'd been working with great industry.

"Don't you have anything to do?" she asked, as the office door bashed open. We jumped. The taller nephew, face red as a plum, stood in the doorway, one finger raised as if he'd burned it.

"We warned you. If something like this happened, we would not, *we will not* stand for—"

Miss Rose's voice was a hammer striking an anvil. "Out!"

Downstairs, the hired girls hushed. Violet and I edged close enough to see Miss Rose, head raised, eyes flashing, crumble into the settee. Violet ran to her side. Mrs. Hardrow called for salts. For a moment I stayed where I was, watching William, rigid and pale, holding himself upright on the back of an armchair. Mrs. French, squinting at a document in her hand as if it might catch fire, now fixed her eyes on the lawyer.

"Please remember." The lawyer folded his hands neatly before him. "That I am merely the messenger." He looked across the room at Miss Rose, then William. "If all parties are amenable, I would suggest coming to reasonable terms outside of probate."

I stepped back to let him pass. William followed as far as the stairwell. "There's been no mistake, Mr. Schneider?"

"No mistake, Mr. Stark."

"What's wrong?" I asked, carefully. "William?"

Staring up, dazed, in the direction of Old Man's room, he glanced blindly at me, then followed Schneider down the stairs and out the door. Bees knocked dumbly against the window glass; the glare from the cupola suddenly blinding. Susan came running with salts. Violet fanned Miss Rose with her manuscript. Mrs. French, document still in hand, the only steady soul in that raging sea, stepped beside me.

"Mrs. French?" I took a breath. "What happened?"

"YOU KNEW, DIDN'T YOU? YOU knew Old Man was William's father."

Having run all the way from the manor, I barged breathless into Mr. Dryfus's office. Mama from the kitchen and Hanley from the composition room, poked their heads into the hall. Mr. Dryfus, shocked from his labors, stood up, and then, grasping his pipe, sat purposefully down again.

"Come in, Madelyn. Close the door." I did. Pages he'd been marking flurried across the desk and, I swear, those portraits of important men on the wall leaned closer. "How do you know about that?" Dryfus's eyes met mine. "Does William?"

"He does now."

I told him about the will, how Old Man left William everything in something called a trust: the manor, the brewery titles, the railroad bonds—everything but a strip of swampland in New Orleans that had belonged to Miss Rose's mother. This would go to Miss Rose. The nephews would get nothing.

"And you knew all along, didn't you?"

Dryfus tapped ash into a pile on his desk, pointed to a chair, but I remained standing.

"Not about the will," he said finally. "But about William's parentage. I knew, yes. Mutti found Mr. Werner's letters to Willa Stark in her studio after she died. Creditors were pressing," he explained. "We didn't know how to reach William, or if he was still alive. Mutti had been William's nurse, the closest thing to family Willa had, so we took what we could."

Hanley had been right. Cholera had killed Willa Stark, though William later blamed himself for running away to war against her wishes. He had been only fifteen at the time. Willa and Clara begged Mr. Dryfus, then a typesetter at the *Westliche Post*, to follow William to Camp Jackson and talk sense into him. "You are too young," Dryfus told him. It was just after the siege. Riots had left behind burn-scarred walls and hot tempers. Volunteers in homemade uniforms shouted abuse at Dryfus through the gates. "Think of your mother," he persisted. "Think of Clara."

William wouldn't listen. "Only women and cripples are staying home," he had said, and Dryfus left him to his fate.

While the war lasted, they had no word from William. Willa Stark refused to speak of him. She worked constantly, slept in the studio, rising to paint with first light, moving from one canvas to the next throughout the day as the light changed. Then the war ended. A month passed. Two, and still no word of William. She stopped

painting. She would not eat or sleep. She began making little lac-
erations on her thighs—Clara found the rust red stains on the bed
sheets. She was already half mad when the scourge came.

"Her physiognomy alone should have warned a wise man away
from her, much less her profession," said Mr. Dryfus. "Yet every man
I knew loved her. She was . . ."

"Alluring," I said in spite of myself.

"And unattainable. Yes, and talented. Saint Louis was full of artists
capable of a likeness. Willa Stark was different. She had a remarkable smile, which she never used in flattery, and hands." He looked
at his own with a trace of embarrassment. "Hands that spoke when
she spoke, and a bearing so composed, so utterly indifferent. Until she
painted you."

"And then?"

Mr. Dryfus came as close to blush as I'd ever see.

"Then she *looked*," he said. "She filled you up with looking. I
don't think people came so much for their likenesses. They came to
be seen by Willa Stark, to see themselves as she saw them, to take a
piece of her away with them."

The very romance of this idea, coming from a man I'd thought
incapable of such perceptions, was enough to enchant me. "Did she
paint you?"

"She offered as a favor to Mutti when I was still a very young
man. But I never felt . . ."

He looked at the chair where his cane lay. He didn't have to say
anything more. I knew how he felt.

Old Man Werner was smitten with Willa. Everyone could see
that, though no one suspected him to be William's father. He was
very old (more than twice her age) for one thing, and too much the
moralist. As a young man, he'd been a merchant mariner, a lecherous

fool. He told this to anyone who would listen. Testified, he called it. Yes, he'd whored. Yes, he'd cheated and gambled. Then God took his wife to punish him and sent cries of slaves he'd transported to torture his sleep. One day, one of those voices told him to sell his share of the ship, go north on the river to found a town and atone for his sins. No one knew he'd left children behind until much later when his son came north to join him in business. No one knew until the war began that his daughter was the scandalous Miss Rose.

Mr. Dryfus wasn't sure when or how Werner met Willa Stark. But for all his testifying and moralizing, Werner's devotion to her never waivered.

"Just an old man's fancy, we thought. But when Willa died eight, nine years ago, about the same time I bought the shop, a year I guess, before William returned, he locked himself in the manor and he never came out again."

Mr. Dryfus rubbed his hands over his face, looked over at me. The day outside had clouded over. Wind tapped at the shutters.

Clara was going to tell William about Old Man Werner when he returned, if he returned. Yet when he did, Clara gave him Willa's jewelry—a few bracelets, necklaces, and charms—but not the letters.

"Why not?" I had forgotten myself and taken a seat.

"I don't know. He wasn't the same anymore. Still every bit as spoiled and belligerent, but not the same. Not quite right."

We sat silent for a moment, but I could feel, building since the second mention of those letters, a foreboding I was helpless to ignore.

"Mr. Dryfus. Mr. Dryfus, you still have them, don't you? The letters?"

He said nothing, but stood, circled the desk and limped through the door. I understood this to mean he was through with me, and I was about to retreat, should have maybe, when he returned with a bundle of envelopes tied with a string and a spooked expression on his face. He closed the door again. He put the bundle on the desk before me and stepped back.

"Go on." He remained standing, clutching his meerschaum pipe hard enough to make dust. Little John cried out. He closed his eyes to the sound. "Go on," he said again.

The first letter had been much read, the envelope tattered and smudged, the handwriting, styled, precise, reassuringly unfamiliar.

My Dear Willa, I read: *After the first snow in Reliance, but few leaves stop the eye short of the horizon . . .*

I stopped. I put the letter face down, for of course I knew the words by heart, and felt my heart tighten. I might have dropped to my knees and hidden under the desk if doing so could have prevented that dreadful understanding from settling upon me.

Old Man had written the letters I so cherished. Not William.

Oh my beautiful letters! I should not have asked to see them. Why had I asked? And why was Mr. Dryfus still watching me like that, rigid as a man on a witness stand?

"For some time"—he spoke to the wall behind me—"I have felt contrition for this *treachery*, which I did not orchestrate, but did nothing to expose, and . . ."

"Mr. Dryfus."

". . . and for *pretending* a greater capacity for romantic expression than I possess."

It had been Hanley, he explained. Hanley had copied those letters, and Hanley had posted them, at Clara's bidding. Dear Clara. She'd been afraid her son would end his days alone. By the time Mr. Dryfus learned he'd asked Mama to marry him, we were on our way.

"At first I kept silent, for spite, I suppose. I didn't expect she'd stay. I didn't expect . . ." Somewhere near the kitchen, Little John squealed. Mr. Dryfus went white. He took a breath. "I have tried. I have tried, but I find I cannot bring myself to tell your sister the truth, to *disappoint* her, in case . . ."

Stop talking. Why didn't he just stop? "Mr. Dryfus."

"No, hear me out, please. I am asking," he continued. "I ask you to be discreet with what I have told you about William, but you may do with my *confession* as you see fit. I only hope . . ." He gathered himself. "I only hope that in time your sister might forgive such *deliberate* deception. There. That is all."

He gripped that pipe, waiting, a muted agony on his face. And what could I say? What did he expect from me? To forgive him? To make Mama forgive him? If he understood anything at all about Mama, he'd know she had few scruples about necessary deceptions.

"Madelyn?" said Mr. Dryfus.

I had nothing to say; nothing to say to Mama, either, even as she followed me, worried, out the shop door to the sidewalk, not with so many of my notions shattering in pieces around me.

"Maddy," she said. "Maddy," catching my arm. "You're not in trouble, are you?"

Mama's beautiful eyes searched mine. Over her shoulder, I could see Hanley and Mr. Dryfus, Little John in his arms, watching from the shop front, and I knew I'd never tell. About those letters, or Little John. What was I good for, after all, but keeping secrets?

"I'm not in trouble," I told her. Not the kind she meant, anyway.

35

The next morning, Miss Rose sent Mrs. Hardrow in the hansom to fetch William. She would need his blessing, now, to remain in the manor. I found myself in the library with Mrs. French, as usual, staring at a blank page. My mind was mush. I'd slept little, the house too quiet, my head loud with thoughts, the bed too big and empty without Lipman thrashing. When I gave up trying and came downstairs, I found Mrs. French bent over the same mountain of financial records she'd been scouring the night before. I don't think she slept at all.

"Mrs. French?" I asked, finally putting my pen aside. "What is probate?"

"Look it up," she said, without looking up.

I already had. "So this will. It might not be legal?"

"This has *what* to do with your assignment?"

Not a thing, but Mrs. French, eyes red behind her oculars, relented. She eased back in her chair.

"If the will was written under duress, or, if the testator, that is Mr. Werner, was not of sound mind at the time of the writing then no, it might not be legal. But, it is unlikely either of these conditions can be proven unequivocally. To do so would require considerable resources."

I thought about this. "Money?" I said. "You mean money don't you. Doesn't Miss Rose have money?"

"Does. Did." She plucked her oculars from her nose, rubbed the bridge. "To be perfectly honest, Madelyn, I don't know. She has been borrowing on speculation, against her inheritance." Then, seeing my blank expression, "Borrowing against the promise of her father's money." I nodded, though the clarification still outstripped my understanding. "I suppose I knew this. But I . . . Well, I didn't realize the extent. If I had known, I would have, what, reasoned with her?"

At the thought, an incredulous little laugh overcame her. She sobered. "Perhaps I didn't want to know." She pushed back from the table. "It would be better to come to terms out of court, but even if Mr. Stark is agreeable to some sort of compromise, I don't think there will be enough to cover her debts, and the nephews—"

The front door slammed. We felt a gasp of air. Heard voices in the entryway. The hansom had returned, Mrs. Hardrow with it, but no William. Miss Rose, poised by the staircase in one of her nicest walking dresses, puffed up so large I thought she might burst her stays.

"He said what? What did he say?"

Mrs. Hardrow could not meet her eyes.

"He said that if you wish to speak with him, you may come and see him in his studio."

"I may? Mrs. French did you hear that? *I may* come?" But as she turned to climb the stairs, I felt as much as saw the fear beneath that mask of amusement. "Are you coming, Mrs. Hardrow?"

When the two women reappeared a half hour later, Miss Rose again wore her mourning costume—black lace, black ostrich feather hat—and climbed into the hansom with a dignity so ferocious the gelding's ears stood rigid.

Mrs. French and I returned to the library. I pretended to make progress on my composition, but could hardly remember the assignment. Mrs. French turned pages, turned back. We did this for more than an hour until we heard carriage wheels on the drive. Violet rushed from the music room. Lizzette and Susan, their heads anyway, appeared one after the other like nervous pigeons from the second-floor balcony. The statues, the portraits, the very walls of the manor seemed to brace themselves as Miss Rose strode through the door. Taking in the room with one slow, forceful sweep of the head, she tossed her gloves and stole aside, ascended the stairs to her bedroom, and slammed the door.

MISS ROSE TOOK TO HER bed. Mrs. French went walking the river alone. That night Violet and I ate in the kitchen with Alby and Nettle; after dinner, Alby pulled me into the humid cave of the scullery. From her pocket she produced a tarnished object.

"That's a spoon, Alby," I said dismissively.

"It's a *silver* spoon," she said. "And there's three more sets in that armoire in the basement. You know how far west a few of these will take us?"

"No. And neither do you."

"What? You thinking about Miss Rose? Well, don't. Probably got buckets of money stashed somewhere, what with all those dead husbands. And what do I care about Miss Rose? Why do you care, Maddy, huh?"

I couldn't put words to why.

"Anyway," said Alby, "ain't Miss Rose's spoon, is it? Never was, was it? Maybe . . ." She poked me with the spoon.

"Stop."

"Maybe I'm stealing from your *luuver*. That it? Ah shit, Maddy. Lizzette saw you and Mr. Stark heading behind the garden shed during the funeral, and I seen your face after. Thought you was smarter than all that foolishness. What? Now you got nothing to say?"

Nothing. I couldn't say anything, for I knew then what I must have known all along. William's kisses had never meant anything. He had been protecting himself. Keeping me quiet. None of those touches had meant love.

"Alby!" cried Nettle in the kitchen. "Where'd you go off to?"

"Anyway," said Alby, "don't care do I, who it belongs to? Got to take care of myself. In my hand it belongs to me. And shoot me dead if you don't find more than a spoon under Lizzette's pillow by the end of the week. Might as well have it as Miss Rose, or Mr. Stark, or this Probate.

"Listen. You listening, Maddy? Cyrus found me a map west and I picked out a likely spot. South Dakota. Gold, Maddy." Her eyes lit, but there it was, a sharp smell of fear in the center of her optimism. "Go with me. I know enough to cook for a rougher sort. Go with me."

"Alby, I don't . . ."

"Well, I ain't going to wait on you forever. A bit. See how things go around here. But, I'm telling you. Ain't afraid of going alone." She stepped back, red hair catching a seam of white light through the ground-level window. "I ain't! I'll go without you. Don't think I won't."

She waited, holding her breath, for a response I couldn't give, then walked out. I slumped against the drying cabinet. Clean plates clinked. Flies thumped against the window.

Was Alby right? Could I just run off, leave Mama and Reliance, start over new in the West? I didn't want to think anymore. What was thinking worth anyway, when so much of my thinking turned out wrong?

WHATEVER ELSE TRANSPIRED IN THE exchange between William and Miss Rose, he allowed us to stay in the house. For a while, several weeks at least, life continued more or less as usual. Each morning I attended lessons with Mrs. French, and began to think (to hope, really) that she'd been wrong about Miss Rose's debts. I'd thought of Miss Rose's wealth as a physical thing, a high wall, nothing that could be lost or squandered—and thus far nothing in our routine suggested a breach.

I could almost convince myself everything would be all right. What did it matter if William hadn't written those letters about the river? Didn't mean he couldn't write letters just like them, if he wanted; write to me one day. I hated myself for trying, but I thought maybe, in time, I could forget Aileen, a nobody. Forget the baby. Then I'd sleep the night through without dark, formless dreams jolting me awake. Miss Rose's mood didn't help. Work on her memoirs stagnated. Every day I sat tense and watchful as she shuffled through those scribbled pages of disjointed memories, hundreds, piling the desk, mumbling, "Hopeless. Hopeless."

She blamed her block on Mr. Clemens for warning her away from structure, and on Mr. Stockwell, without saying why. And though she never blamed me, I felt the hulking weight of her judgment glaring from every angled reflection in the room. Each day I awaited her call with equal parts dread and longing, and each day found her lavender and rose scent growing thicker, stronger, like a last florid gasp of summer growth before decay. She was not well. Headaches came upon her often, and not even wigs and layers of fancy cloth could hide the diminished body beneath. Sometimes she'd forget herself, allow her manner to waver, her shoulders to slump, the old woman, bald and helpless, asserting herself.

"You are so lucky, Madelyn," she said as we stood before the vanity on one of those awful days. "To be spared beauty. And its abandonment. Look at yourself. So lucky."

A thin finger tracing my stain. Hot breath, sour in my ear; the word *lucky* like a curse. I didn't feel lucky, or, alluring either. I'd thought—Miss Rose had led me to believe—that becoming alluring would be like becoming educated, a capacity I might "by will and effort, attain." For a while, I could imagine the alluring part, inside me, might overgrow my stain. But I didn't anymore. It was one of the many things I desired that no amount of will or effort could give me. Alby was right. When people looked at me, they would see my stain first. I knew this wasn't my fault, but I still felt like a failure.

Then Miss Rose began calling Violet and me to recite poems and to say what we most loved about her, and I failed here, too. Among Violet's gifts was a talent for flattery I could not match. And anyway, how could I say that what I loved most was the bald head beneath Miss Rose's wigs, or the promises she had made me? I couldn't. Which was unfortunate, because daily the town's approval was shifting in favor of Mr. Stockwell, and Miss Rose's demand for our affections intensified.

Two weeks after the will had been read, Mrs. Drabney of the Wayward Home, always a demure and groveling presence, burst from the office.

"But you will produce your little plays? Miss Rose, am I right? Where, madam, are your priorities?"

Miss Rose, face bright as you please, but her voice full of thorns. "Why, you ungrateful leech."

"Rose." Mrs. French stepped between them.

"Not a shred of gratitude, not one shred for all I have done for her!" She shouted past Mrs. French after the retreating Drabney. "I always knew it. That presumptive insect!"

She raged for an hour, which, to be honest, put me more at ease than the cloak of forlorn composure she had been wearing. Things were not, and would not be, all right. Even as I tried once again to repair my idea of William, the effort was becoming exhausting. It was not just Aileen or the baby, but a whole ragbag of truths that, pieced together, made a picture of a man different from the one I'd invented to love me.

I knew, too, because Hanley told me, what people were saying about Miss Rose. Grumbles over her election scheme were flowering into declarations of impropriety. There was talk of bringing her to court for fraud, and now that word had spread about the will, people like Mrs. Drabney of the Wayward Home, with nothing ill to say of Miss Rose so long as she could depend on her patronage, now could say nothing good.

"Well, I don't feel sorry in the least!" said Nora, holding a yellow ribbon to Angela's hair in Mrs. Smith's dress shop. "That woman only came back to Reliance for the money, anyway. Serves her right! Putting on airs, I always said."

Mrs. Smith, who should have said a word in Miss Rose's defense, said nothing. "Why?" I demanded after they left, though I know why now. Successful shopkeepers are the world's most talented politicians. Loyal as she might be to Miss Rose's various causes, she knew better than to alienate paying customers.

Mama had slipped in the backdoor to the cutting room; Mrs. Smith motioned me to join her there.

"Maddy, someone told Mr. Stockwell about the womb veils. He found May Ann's. Rifled through her personal items until he found it.

"That's not all, Maddy. Listen. Are you listening?"

I was watching Mama. Mama in her stylish dress, Mama, a lady of business, who belonged here in this shop, on this street with Mr. Dryfus and Little John. Belonged making dresses, making money.

"I don't think Miss Rose is right about Stockwell getting that girl pregnant." Now I was listening. "I had a peek at May Ann's house ledger. That girl . . ."

"Aileen," I said. Mrs. Smith paused. "Her name," I said, a lump of remorse in my throat. "It was Aileen."

"Well, she left the Stockwell house last June, five months before she was found in the river." She paused. "Maddy, don't you see? If Mr. Stockwell . . . if he was the father, she would have been showing when they found her. They would have known she was pregnant. Tell Miss Rose, will you?"

I didn't tell Miss Rose about Aileen leaving the Stockwells' in June. I don't know who I was protecting, William, or myself from the kind of definitive knowledge such a revelation would demand of me. Instead, I told myself William was right, that Aileen's memory would suffer, that the truth wouldn't change what happened. That it didn't matter.

The womb veils probably wouldn't have mattered either, if the subject had been allowed to die quietly. You can be sure no one from the Benevolent Society, not even the snitch, whoever she was, would have stepped forward to confirm she'd ever procured, much less used such a device. But when Stockwell published his accusation against Miss Rose, she simply could not let the matter lie. She published this response:

If Mr. Stockwell believes such private matters to be of public note, then perhaps he should agree, also, that precautions against conception should enjoy public support, especially if such precautions protect the health of our daughters, wives, and mothers. The law, such as it is, considers a married woman's body the property of her husband. Would not a good husband take care of his property, promote her good health and longevity in any way he could?

And further down the page:

. . . I cannot help but reflect upon the tragic death, over a year ago, of Aileen O'Heaney, once in Stockwell's own employ. I have good reason to believe the poor girl was compromised and with child when she was found murdered in the river. We were all happy to assume her fate to be the work of a traveling rogue. Yet if the father of this tragedy lived and worked among us each day, how would we know? Her unfortunate death would mean he could easily conceal his conquest, and expect no repercussions at all . . . Perhaps the innocent maidens Mr. Stockwell so desperately wishes to protect would be better served if they possessed the means to guard against disgrace conferred upon them. I ask you, if conception alone is to be punished, then why not prevent conception?

"Tell me," demanded Mrs. French, walking late one night into dinner, holding the newspaper rolled into a club, "what you were hoping to accomplish with this?"

Miss Rose did not dignify the question with a response.

I felt a passing guilt for failing to tell her about Aileen's early departure from Oak Hollow, especially later, when Mrs. Smith came to speak to Miss Rose herself—until it was clear Miss Rose's opinion of Stockwell's guilt remained undamaged by Mrs. Smith's facts. She weathered the swift and damning responses her letter prompted with a kind of martyred pride, unshaken for a week, until Stockwell managed to raise another petition against her theater. On the night Violet debuted as Juliet, only a dozen people attended, most of them dockworkers, all of them drunk. And after the performance, as the hansom clattered to a stop before the manor, Violet's "Rose tone" finally cracked.

"It's all your fault," she whispered. I thought she was talking to me, until she said it again, louder.

"It's all *your* fault no one came to see me."

"Oh shut up, Violet." Miss Rose, head back against the cushion, closed her eyes.

"*You* didn't want anyone to see me. You want to be the star. It's all your fault and I hate you!"

Violet took a great gulp of air, her face pinched, all of her posturing affection replaced by a deep and vulnerable resentment, suppressed who knows how long. Miss Rose drew herself up as if to strike, but the force of the betrayal proved too much. She took to her bed. Violet locked herself in her room and would not come out the next day or the next.

"Will you go to her?" Mrs. French asked me. "Go to Violet."

"If she won't listen to you, she won't listen to me." But I knocked on her door anyway.

"Go away."

"Mrs. French thinks you should eat." The door was locked. "Violet." In spite of myself I felt pity rising. "Listen. It wasn't you. You were good." I thought her very good, in fact, but the admission was hard enough without such a qualification.

"I said go away!"

"She can stay in there and starve for all I care," I told Mrs. French. "She's scared, Madelyn. You don't mean that."

I thought maybe I did. I thought maybe Mrs. French was as wrong about me as I had been about William. I wasn't like her, wasn't intelligent or kind, didn't have any promise. Ordinary, except ugly. Extraordinarily ugly. She just couldn't see it. This was my fear: that she'd made up someone better than I'd ever be, and when she learned the truth, I'd lose her, too.

It was then late April, late afternoon, a Saturday. Usually we walked down the garden path to the river at this time, but Mrs. French turned the ankle she'd busted months ago and sat, captive in her bedroom, where I wasn't often welcome but always felt comfortable. Sparely furnished, with a long writing table beneath the window, plain drapes, a rag rug, an armchair, a canopy bed stripped of its canopy. Botanical paintings graced the wall, orchids mostly. No pictures or photographs or any other sign of the family she'd lost, which seemed so sad. A collection of Asa Gray's essays lay open next to the lamp on her bedside table. The window faced west.

I wonder now if the law was, in fact, Mrs. French's natural element. Such an active body and mind might have been better suited to physical explorations with books as aides but not the sole means of discovery. Where did her vigorous curiosity come from? What might *she* have become, given the opportunity?

None of these thoughts burdened me then, however.

Miss Rose called. I looked despairingly toward the door. For the time being, I replaced Violet at Miss Rose's beck and call, but didn't feel triumphant as I'd thought I might, didn't want to go, and didn't care if Mrs. French ignored me for the next four hours so long as she let me sit, quiet in the corner of that room, grounded in her presence.

"Ma-de-lyn!"

"I better go," I said, but hesitated.

"Mrs. French? You're not leaving, are you? You're not going to abandon Miss Rose?" *Abandon me*, I thought. "She is not well. She is getting worse, I think."

"I am not leaving, yet."

"Yet?"

She looked up, tapped her pen on her knee, put book and pen aside.

"I'm not sure either of us will have a choice, Maddy. There is no sense deceiving ourselves, however much"—her eyes gleamed; she pursed her lips—"however much we may wish things were different. One can only deny what one knows in one's heart for so long before the burden of self-deception becomes greater than the unpleasant truth. The lucky, perhaps, do not recognize the deception. But for the rest of us, Maddy, for you and for me, that needy denial, that deliberate blindness is a kind of poison. A self-imposed sickness. Do you understand what I am telling you?"

"That you're leaving," I replied, knowing this wasn't the only truth she was telling me. She, too, stayed in the manor with Miss Rose's blessing. Friend or not, with the paltry income from her writing, she was as dependent on Miss Rose as I.

"I may have no choice. We may not have a choice, Madelyn."

36

But just like that, it was the middle of May. A warm, damp wind from the south brought the scent of blooming orchards, and you could hardly see the river for the full gowns of new growth dressing the bluff. Summer was upon us. Violet, having given up sulking a week after she began, emerged withered and penitent to lay her head on Miss Rose's knee and weep her contrition. Miss Rose's mood and color improved. Her headaches eased. The snappish silence between her and Mrs. French relaxed, and they resumed their playfully competitive disagreements. William remained stranded in Reliance, penniless, until the lawyer untangled what was left of Old Man's finances. No servants had been let go, yet, and even Mrs. Nettle had fallen victim to a cautious optimism, brought on as much by the sunshine and sweet Virginia creeper climbing over the kitchen window as the light work.

It was only a lull, of course. Miss Rose knew the life we had been living was over. We would all have to leave the manor. There would be no choice. Her only choice, as she saw it, was how to make her exit—with a theatrical production of another kind.

"A masked ball!" she said one night at dinner, as if the extravaganza hadn't been ripening in her mind for the last month. "To be held on my birthday, June tenth."

Mrs. French, glancing up from her fish, was the only one alarmed. "Your birthday's in August, Rose." She paused. "And you have no money."

Neither fact made any difference to Miss Rose. In the coming weeks, her vitality returned, and with it a depth of voice and gesture. Not even the arrival of the appraiser, an exacting, mouse-faced man with a clipboard, seemed to concern her. Nor did the drawn look on Mrs. French's face each time a creditor came to the door or the mail arrived with a new batch of letters calling in debts. Nor did the closure of the River Theater after the third bust in a row. When men came with a train of wagons for the statues, leaving the gallery bereft of all but Daphne, she said, "Well, we must make room for dancing!"

By the last week in May, though no formal announcement had been made and no invitations sent, the ball had become public knowledge, the election (which had been ceded to Donovan) and Old Man's death all but forgotten in a wave of new speculations. There would be an ice sculpture, I overheard from one of the post-office gossips. A trio of Asian belly dancers, said a lady in the dress shop. Hanley heard there would be a live elephant in the garden, a layer cake as tall as a man, fireworks at midnight . . .

"Is it true?" he asked.

"Which part?" I didn't discount cake or belly dancers or fireworks (though I had no idea where the money would come from). But I knew there would be masks—hundreds of masks. I knew because I was to help make them from water, flour, and the piles of newspaper I'd been sent to the print shop to collect.

For the next two weeks, in fact, every free hand in the manor was drafted to make masks. Even Miss Rose took off her gloves and put on an apron to ply strips of gluey newsprint over cardboard molds while remembering aloud stories of costumes thrown together, stages erected with no budget, sets built from scratch on the day of a performance, the smell of wet paint still sharp when the house opened. When a batch of masks set, we painted them black. Each one covered the eyes and part of the nose and could be decorated as desired, then held like a lorgnette or attached by a strap behind the head. Four days in a row preceding the ball, Miss Rose sent Hanley and the bookshop owner's sons to tie masks with ribbons on doorknobs of households on Miss Rose's list. Two masks per household. Each mask an invitation.

I'd wager even those humbugs who swore they'd never attend checked their doors every morning. At any rate, Mrs. Smith told me, there weren't enough bonnets or bassinets to justify the amount of lace, wavy looking moiré, and ribbon she'd been selling. By the day of the ball, decorations in place, food arranged, anything in the world seemed possible.

WIND GUSTED THROUGH THE CONSERVATORY doors. Lavender streamers, draped from the second-floor balcony, bucked and thrashed. Laurel wreaths tacked along the front porch rail jerked free and rolled across the deck as clouds thundered into place. And then lightning, a glimmer in the gray, the acrid stink, and then rain, rising timpani, one minute, ten, and after twenty softened, stopped. Tree branches dripped. Leaves papered the newly swept drive, and when the clouds opened, the whole household breathed relief.

We should have known the storm wouldn't last; for all we knew, the storm, too, had been part of Miss Rose's script for the night's events. Certainly her demands had fallen as harshly and more persistently these last four days than that thundershower.

Every detail, every decoration, bouquet, and pastry had to pass her inspection. My dress, and Violet's, the servants' costumes and masks, the musicians' arrangement, the length of the lamp wicks—nothing escaped her authority. Why should the weather, which, after all, had doused the heat resting on the shoulders of the town for three days, and renewed the roses.

What concerned me more than the storm was that no one but Mrs. Hardrow, not even Mrs. French, whose concern first whetted mine, had seen Miss Rose since the storm passed.

"You think she's okay?" I asked Mrs. Nettle, sweating over her last batch of pies. "You think it's a headache? I think she's been working too hard."

"*She* has, huh?"

Raisin-fat flies writhed and buzzed over cheesecloths covering pies, tarts, and pastries lining cupboards and countertops. Already the tongue and the ham and the poultry were sliced and chilling in the ice house with the salads and jellies. There would be no elephant or belly dancers; the cake was not quite as tall as a man. But Rose had ordered marzipan fruits from the German baker; Nettle made ices, flan, and trifle. I stuck my head out the door to say hello to Alby and the hired girls. They sat three across beneath the kitchen awning, hair and dresses sodden with sweat, hands swollen from their labors. In silence we watched the thunderstorm sail away over the Missouri flats and threads of steam rise from the flowerbeds.

I felt like crying. Felt like crying all day, to be honest, and couldn't say why. Clocks, one after another, struck five. I went to the guest room to bathe and change.

"Look at you, Maddy," Susan said, holding the mirror so I could see the gathered twist of curls she'd arranged down my back. "You've got your dance card?"

The dress Miss Rose had ordered and Mama and Mrs. Smith had made was a dusty salmon pink with a long skirt and a bustle, which gave a swinging weight to my walk. A high, ribbed collar covered my mark but opened to reveal a padded bodice, generously enhanced. I wore cream-colored boots, kid gloves to match, and a little gold bracelet on loan from Miss Rose.

But it would be the mask that made me.

This, too, was Miss Rose's design. Pearl buttons formed a shimmering scale over the surface. Dyed red ostrich feathers, six of them, had been fixed to resemble a sideways S, one plumed extremity angling over my right temple, the other curling over my mark.

Susan slipped it into place, tied the straps, and hid them among my curls. It rested awkwardly on my nose, narrowing my vision but sharpening the sound of voices and carriage wheels on gravel, the smell of singed hair and gas lamps. Downstairs, the quartet, tuning for the past half hour, dipped into a slow gathering melody. My courage returned. I was not me. If not transformed, then anonymous, I made my careful way down the spiral staircase and saw I wasn't the only one to feel this way.

The first guests arrived in pairs, the men drab, carefully indifferent, the women like so many brightly colored birds beneath their masks. Roberts, the butler, took coats and hats. Mrs. Hardrow showed ladies to the dressing room. I hardly recognized Mrs. Bennett in yellow moiré. There was Mrs. Liederman with her husband, the tobacconist, a good-natured stub of a man ten years her junior, and Mrs. Smith with Emil Le Duc, arm in arm and equally mismatched.

Mama and Mr. Dryfus arrived moments later. Mama, lovely in a lilac-colored gown and a pink-sequined mask, didn't know me until I slipped my arm through hers and said her name: "Hello, Rebecca."

Still no Miss Rose. Her absence becoming a presence. Her name on everyone's lips. No William, either, though I didn't know if he was coming and wasn't sure I wanted him to. People gathered in small faceless islands. Music played. No one danced. I joined Mrs. French, but she, too, kept looking to the balcony where Miss Rose was to appear.

"She must make her entrance," I suggested.

Mrs. French didn't answer.

"Is she okay?"

"I think I'll go see."

A quadrille broke the dancers' reticence. Two, then four, then eight couples took the floor, relaxing behind their masks, giving in to the illusion of anonymity, their confidence contagious. People milled around the parlor and music room; a couple kissed in the conservatory; others strolled the garden. The day's last sunlight shrank behind the clouds. Lizzette lit the lamps and flung open the doors and windows, and the quartet reined their tempo to a slow waltz. Still no Miss Rose.

"And who have we here?" said a voice behind me in the conservatory where I stood watching the dancers. I paid it no mind. "Excuse me, Miss . . . ?" He was speaking to me? A young man, blond hair oiled and gleaming. It was his ears, large as flags on either side of his mask, that marked him as Mr. Sims, the young lawyer rooming with the Bennetts. And he was talking to me. "Do I know you?"

My cheeks flamed, but the mask hid all except my short dismissive shake of the head. He must have read my embarrassment as indifference, for as I looked past him to the dancers, he stepped into my line of vision, undeterred, perhaps even encouraged by my dismissal. Hanley ducked back through the door with lemon ices for both of us.

"A travesty," said Mr. Sims. "I was sure I had met every pretty young thing in this town."

He held out his hand, and I, still flabbergasted, looked at it.

"Your dance card is full, perhaps?" Mr. Sims said.

"Maddy?" said Hanley.

"Miss Maddy, is it?" said Sims. "You have not danced all night. I know. I have been watching. You are waiting for someone in particular to ask, perhaps?" He looked at Hanley. "Surely, he wouldn't grudge me one dance."

And so I entered that heated kaleidoscope of spinning skirts and danced as Miss Rose had taught me: one two-three, slow two-three. Mr. Sims's, hand upon my shoulder, talked and talked, about what I hardly knew, his breath tart, his teeth purple from red wine. When the music ended, another man marked my card, and then Elroy, a skinny, laughing fellow who clerked at the bank and sang in the German Choir. I danced, anonymous, alluring, almost forgot Miss Rose and William, until there he was at my side, linking his elbow with mine.

"Is that you, my apparition?" He raised my gloved hand, he kissed it, and slipped a letter into my palm. The eyes behind his mask asked nothing of me.

Had I a head for such perceptions at the time, I might have wondered about the story of the cave Mrs. French and I had read together. I'd imagined men with guns or knives had forced the prisoner from the comfort of his illusions. But what if it was not guns or knives at all that compelled him? What if what drove him was his own merciless curiosity?

I didn't have to know how wrong I had been about William. No one made me confront him about the dead girl, or Mr. Dryfus about the letters. I didn't have to know, and now I could not unknow.

"Don't read it now. Wait." He didn't say for what and I had no chance to ask because every eye in the room rose to the balcony above the gallery.

A man in a top hat and jerkin, wearing a ceramic mask with a bulbous nose and sneering pink mouth, glowered down at us. Holding Mrs. French's pointer under one arm, he turned and with stiff military posture descended the stairs, parted the crowd, and took the stage. With a slicing movement, he opened the pointer, raised it toward the servants' door, where a woman veiled in white satin appeared behind the houseboy, Tom. Tom wore his dress blacks. He carried a wooden pedestal. Slow, with ceremony, he preceded the woman to the stage, placed the pedestal, and helped the woman to stand upon it. Then with an exaggerated flair, he stripped her of the veil.

A woman beside me gasped. A plate clattered to the marble floor. There stood Violet in little more than a chemise, her bare arms aloft in heroic pose, nipples pert beneath the sheer fabric. She stared with a statue's blindness into the audience. And the man with the pointer—I realized as intrigue shuddered through the crowd—the man with the pointer was Miss Rose.

"Le Masque," she sang out, "by Charles Baudelaire." The oboe player began a soft moaning accompaniment. "Behold! This prize of beauties wholly Florentine. This luminous visage framed and veiled, whose every dainty feature boasts:"

"Lo!" cried Violet, raising one hand gracefully into the air. "Pleasure calls me and Love crowns my head!"

"This. This *creature*," Miss Rose sneered. "Vested with such majesty. See what tasty charms her mane suggests!" She lowered her voice. "Let us draw close to her beauty, tour around." Miss Rose toured. "O, yes. O, blasphemy of art! That body promising rapture rare transforms at the top into a two-faced freak."

Violet turned and a grotesque mask smiled hideously from the back of her head. The crowd shuddered.

Miss Rose rapped the mask smartly with her pointer; the audience came to order. Then, in the hush, Miss Rose turned Violet around again and pressed the tip of the pointer to the girl's bare forehead. "No! This . . . *this* is but a mask. A decorative snare. Poor visage lighted by a delicate grimace!"

Miss Rose paused. "But 'Why is it she weeps,' you ask?" No one said a word. "Why weeps she whose love brings mankind to his knees? What ill gnaws her athlete flanks?"

Miss Rose tucked her pointer beneath her arm. Both of them leveled their gazes to meet the masked faces of the crowd. Together they chorused: "She weeps for having lived, and for living, yet what makes her body tremble head to toe is that tomorrow she will have go on living, and all tomorrows after—like ourselves!"

Masks, for a moment forgotten, slipped from faces infant pink and raw with heat. Miss Rose bowed, held her hand for Violet, whose curtsy was as coy as her smile. Beautiful, vile Violet. The clock struck the quarter hour. The music began again, and then the dancing, and the warm breeze through the entryway chilled me.

He was gone. I didn't need to look. I felt him go, and turned now to see him slip for the last time out the conservatory door and drop his mask on the wicker table. I followed only as far as the table. Then tracing the feathered rim of my own mask, lifted it from my face and set it atop William's.

The cool air, a touch. The gardens opened, a panorama of backlit clouds and rustling sycamores, and near at hand the traipsing shadows of the dancers spilling with the lamplight across the porch planks. So clear, the smell of roses, the rumbled stomp of dancing feet through boards, and then Mama's presence in the doorway. I sat dry-eyed on the steps, hugging my knees. Mama sat down beside me. She said nothing. There was nothing to say. A reel. Laughter. Far below at the docks, the scream of the ten-o'clock steamer leaving Reliance; with it I felt the weight of false hope lifting, and the gasping ache rushing to fill its place was, frankly, a relief.

"Is that from William?" Mama asked. The letter, the only letter I would ever receive from him, was still in my hand.

"You want to read it? You want me to go?" A man and woman tripped, laughing across the lawn; Mama shifted as if to stand, but I held tight to her arm.

"No, Mama, please stay."

37

I already knew what that letter said and much of what it did not. I knew William cared for me, in his way, but not as much as he cared about protecting himself. I knew the baby had been his, and that Aileen had killed herself to escape the same disgrace that made me. I knew how guilty William must have felt. How after finding her dead, he'd committed the only kindness he could. He cut her throat. A kindness, yes.

I learned when Mr. Stockwell arrived the next morning with the constable that Georgiana had run away with William on the ten-o'clock steamer. I knew Miss Rose considered this desertion, as much as the masked ball, her victory over the man. And I knew, before I was beckoned to her bedroom later that week, and found her again a bald, old woman in an armchair, staring out the window at the river below, Miss Rose was leaving, too.

The japanned tallboy gaped open. Two wigs lay like slaughtered animals on the floor. Then I saw the pages of our manuscript curled brown in the fire.

"Miss Rose, what are you—"

"Leave it," she said.

"But."

"Leave it!"

Wind through the open window scattered white tufts of hair across her scalp. She looked so shriveled, so diminished as she watched the blackened pages dissolve to ash. Then I could see nothing for the tears in my eyes.

"I have heard the Mississippi called an old man." She pulled a raveled lavender string from her dressing gown, cast this, too, into the fire.

"But old men, have you noticed, become petrified in time. Only memories move them. And the fear of any change that might sully those memories. Their ears and noses grow larger as their minds shrink. Have you noticed? Every opinion is loosed as wisdom and truth, when it is no more than romance.

"What do you prefer, my dear?" She turned to look at me. "History or romance? Don't say. Romance. Rubbish. As soon as histories are properly told, there will be no more need of romances. And who will tell these histories? Who will tell my own? You? And what will you say then?"

I didn't know. I still don't know what to say about Miss Rose, what definitive opinion would please her, how to begin. Perhaps I never will.

I do know what people said when creditors came to gut the manor of its furnishings. Such extravagance. Such a shame. Serves her right, they said, even as the whole town turned out to see her board the *Geneva Queen*, with Mrs. French, Mrs. Hardrow, and Violet. Alby ran away without me two weeks earlier, with six silver spoons. The other servants had been let go.

But Miss Rose, her wig a towering masterpiece of braids and curls, let it be known she was on her way to Philadelphia for the

Centennial celebration, the nation's biggest stage, to argue for the franchise. Had Mrs. Stanton invited her to speak, as Miss Rose implied? Had she invited herself? I wasn't sure. I felt betrayed, abandoned, bitter, but no more so than when she stepped from the hansom to the steamer dock with Violet by her side.

I went back to the print shop, back to that little attic room. I learned to set type and walked with Hanley by the riverside, hung my feet in the cool black water of the millpond reading aloud the *Metamorphoses*. How crudely Ovid speaks of love and transformation. Each love a threat. Each transformation a death. Woman to tree. Woman to cow. Some salvation. I was nearly fifteen and distrusted any thought of the future. I held my stained face up, looked everyone in the eye, aware I was eddying purposeless. Until one day, Mama knocked on the composition-room door to say I had a visitor. William? But this habitual thought was no longer a desire. Mrs. French waited with her brisk posture and gray head, in a hired brougham.

This was late October, the weather changing, the air tart with the breath of winter. We passed the courthouse green and Oak Hollow and Millionaire's Row. Had I kept up with my reading? With my German and French? Why not?

"What are we doing here?" I asked her. "What do you want?"

The overgrown driveway, and then the abandoned manor rattled into view. A freshly carved sign, yet unpainted, hung on the wrought-iron gate: WERNER GIRLS' ACADEMY.

"I'm not done with you yet," she said.

"How did you? Miss Rose?"

"Miss Rose and William agreed."

The town had taken great delight in the flight of Stockwell's oldest with William. Stockwell blamed his wife as much as Miss Rose. She, too, soon left him to visit family in Chicago, an extended visit, it appeared, for she took Abigail, her heirloom quilt, and most of the money he'd married into. He accepted a position as postal inspector for the Western Society for the Suppression of Vice and moved to Saint Louis, losing four bids for state senate before declaring himself a man above political seats, a man seated in the moral authority of God.

If only he were the hypocrite Miss Rose believed him to be! It would have been so much easier to hate him for his intolerance. But he was merely a zealot, blind to the various shapes and colors of lives beyond his own. Too bad, really. He was hardly a worthy adversary for Miss Rose; he had simply been the only adversary on hand. Sure, he fancied himself a leader, a "good man," but when he died thirty years later, he died alone, forgotten.

But then, so did Miss Rose, though she spent the next four years touring the United States, giving readings and lectures on suffrage, contraception, motherhood, hydrology, the education of girls, even home economy—a grueling self-imposed schedule, the money only part of it. She needed the stage, the admiration of an audience far enough away to miss the careful movements of her head and the age lines trenching her eyes.

Over time, I would fill in a few more of the gaps in the glorious past she related to me. I learned of the libel suits, the annulments, the divorces. I learned she had had a child, a son, named Charles, but his father had taken him and divorced her, and the boy, now a senator in North Carolina, never acknowledged her. And when a letter arrived from Violet, five years after she left, Mrs. French and I learned that Miss Rose, too proud to ask for help, had died penniless and alone, in New Orleans.

Thanks to Hanley, I discovered, soon after she left, what had happened in New York before Miss Rose came to Reliance. Part of what happened, at least. He'd been picking through a long-discarded stack of newspapers in the print-shop attic when he saw an article in the *Times*, September 2, 1873, two inches long, one column wide. It announced the conviction of a young woman, Miss Floyd, a costume mistress in the Aurora Theater Company, owned by a Miss Rose Werner, for the murder of Senator Saulder.

"Miss Werner's claims that the senator, a much respected man in the state legislature, raped Miss Floyd, as well as other young ladies in the theater district, were never corroborated, and Miss Floyd was duly sentenced to death."

Miss Floyd, Mrs. French conceded, when I confronted her with this scrap, was Violet's older sister, her only living relative. Miss Rose promised her that she would take Violet in, but her efforts to overturn the verdict proved futile and costly.

"Is that why Miss Rose left New York?"

"One of the reasons."

Mrs. French never told me the others. Such was her loyalty. Such was her gratitude to the woman who gave her license to write and speak with her own voice, under her own name, and gave the manor, where Mrs. French was to live out her days, its new academic purpose.

Mrs. French raised money, designed curricula, and hired teachers—liberal-minded women who read novels, wrote articles, wore bloomers when it suited them, and encouraged their charges to do the same. She hired Hanley's sister, Muriel, to cook and clean. Before its reputation grew, the students were mostly wards of the Wayward Home, immune to the early gossip surrounding the place. The manor became a ghost of its former self, the accommodations spare but comfortable, as was the food, much of which we grew in the kitchen garden. I remained four years, first as a student and prefect of sorts to younger girls, who looked upon my mark as a badge of authority, and then as a teacher, hearing Mrs. French's phrases resurrected from my mouth. "If your convictions are to be taken seriously, Emily, you must state them with conviction." Sometime in that first year, I made myself a darkroom in the cellar and began taking portraits with the camera William left behind.

Miss Rose, Mrs. French, and this craft were the real gifts he gave me, though I persist even now in remembering him with a fond, youthful fancy. I have never entirely given up my infatuation. Watching my girls, I realize I'm not so different in this, not so unusual after all. Loving someone like that, or imagining you do, it's kind of a cockeyed way of learning to love yourself. I still wear his charm, though I like to think I do so in memory of a dead girl named Aileen.

I never went to university to study classics as Mrs. French wished, but I did finally go west. Mr. Edward Dargie offered Hanley the chance to run the Saturday edition of his paper in a place called Oakland. I went along to open my own photography studio, but alone there together, the fondness I'd always felt for him grew slow and strong into what I now call love. We married at city hall. Mama joined us to open a dress shop a few years later, after Little John went east and Mr. Dryfus passed (very soon after Clara). It was here, in our house on Harrison and Tenth, where, along with my first daughter, Sophie, the latent suffragette in me was born.

I have been called the Painted Lady and all kinds of suggestive and derogatory names that no longer rankle me as they do Hanley. Miss Rose was right, after all. I am a *Janus-faced fiend*. One face staring forward into the future I wish for my girls, the other forever looking back. The public face I put on now, rigid with confidence and purpose, and a private face Hanley sees when the mask becomes too heavy. Few others see this private face. My mark protects me. I have come to depend upon it, for I have never possessed the magnetic presence of Miss Rose, nor the raw, intuitive intelligence of Mrs. French. Instead, I have learned to speak to the washerwoman, the shopgirl, and the senator's wife, each in her own language, and have taught my girls to do the same.

That is Sophie I hear now as I write these last lines. Sophie slamming through the front door with her sister, Rose.

"Mama!"

Through my study window, I can see ladies, two dozen of the hundreds who will march today, Mama there among them, gathering amid the fallen leaves on Harrison Street, adjusting their suffrage sashes and hatpins, holding their banners strong in the breathless August heat.

Such enthusiasm saddens me some, yet as Rose—my dark-eyed, demonstrative Rose—pitches into the room and tugs my arm, I feel also the haunting presence of two women in the host who came before me. Look around you. Look back. This is what I want to tell my daughters, the message I wish to leave behind. Be grateful, but not too grateful for fragments of the rights due all persons. Remember, justice and change comes hard and slow. Remember, you will have many mothers in this life besides me, all of them flawed. Judge them, judge me, but not too harshly. Carry on, my girls, but guard yourself against the irrational defeats that may yet come.

But I don't say anything. I put down my pen, close the pages of my scrapbook. "Come *on*, Mama!" And I am filled again with a familiar, stubborn, and obligatory hope.

August 27, 1908

ACKNOWLEDGMENTS

On August 26, 1926, Gertrude Ederle swam the English Channel. What I call attention to is not the fact that she was the first woman to accomplish the feat, or that she did so in fourteen hours and thirty-four minutes, two hours faster than the fastest man. Nor is it my intention to paint a heroic solitary figure, head in a white cap, arms rising and falling with dogged regularity in choppy gray seas. Instead, direct your eye to the tug boat behind her, for it is full of the people who made such a mad attempt possible.

I don't claim to be, like Gertrude, the first or finest at anything. But I am a writer practicing the novelist's mad craft, and I too have a boat full of people behind me who have made this attempt possible and to whom I am endlessly grateful.

For time and space to work, thank you to the Vermont Studio Center and to Nancy Nordhoff for creating a place like Hedge-brook. Nancy, it was under the influence of your radical hospitality that this novel was reborn.

Thank you to scholars and writers like Andrea Tone, Donna Dennis, Barbara Goldsmith, Helen Lefkowitz Horowitz, Wendy Hamand Venet, Norma Basch, Richard Franklin Bensel, and Janet Farrell

Brodie, whose work brought the social concerns of the time alive for me. Any mistakes or liberties taken with history are entirely my own. Thank you to my students and colleagues at Saint Mary's College who continue to inspire and sustain me. For your honest and heart-felt responses to the work in progress, thank you to Chris Kilgore, Sandra Grayson, Rashaan Meneses, Michelle Dicinoski, Nicholas Leither, Nancy M. Williams, Koko Petitt, Stephanie Miller, Norman Partridge, Helen Bonner, Glenna Breslin, Casi Kushel, Bridget Hanna, William Newton, and Carol Lashof. Thank you to Naomi Schwartz who read and reread with such care and kept me writing when my faith deserted me.

Thank you to agent extraordinaire, BJ Robbins, and to the Squaw Valley Community of Writers for introducing us. Thank you to Bronwen Hruska of Soho Press for your patience and unwavering enthusiasm, and to my editor, Mark Doten, for his brilliant insights. Thank you to Rachel Kowal and the whole Soho team for your steadfast support. Special thanks to Cathy Volmer, my mom, my lending library, my first and last reader, my friend and guide in all things.

Most of all, thank you to my husband, Chris Jones, whose quiet support has been worth ten thousand words of encouragement.

NOTES

Reliance, Illinois, has never existed, nor have any but a few historical figures who appear in the novel. The rest of the characters, though fictitious, have been informed by real people and by a wealth of sources, some of which I cite below. A longer list of sources can be found on my website: www.maryvolmer.com.

In Chapter 2, Madelyn reads from Maria Susanna Cummins's *The Lamplighter* (John P. Jewett and Company, 1854) and later reads to Old Man Werner from a 1771 English edition of Ovid's *Metamorphoses*, translated under the direction of Sir Samuel Garth. In Chapter 6, William quotes Alfred, Lord Tennyson's "The Lady of Shalott." Samuel Clemens's thoughts on Henry Ward Beecher, voting rights, and the proper way to write an autobiography have been taken from a variety of sources, including *The Autobiography of Mark Twain* (University of California Press, 2010) and Justin Kaplan's *Mr. Clemens and Mark Twain* (Simon & Schuster, 1991).

Miss Rose quotes Shakespeare's "Sonnet 18" in Chapter 24. Her impressions of Hamlet's sanity are paraphrased from Sarah Bernhardt's *The Art of the Theater* (B. Blom, 1969); her assessment of her own unjust persecution are from Bernhardt's memoir, *My Double*

Life (State University of New York Press, 1999). Miss Rose's senti-
ments on voting rights closely resemble those of Elizabeth Cady
Stanton after the passage of the 15th Amendment. A number of her
arguments about the prevention of pregnancy are akin to those
of Emma Goldman and Margaret Sanger (who would have been
Madelyn's contemporaries). Miss Rose's dramatic recitation of
Charles Baudelaire's "The Mask" is a liberal adaption taken from
two published translations (by Jacques LeClercq and Richard How-
ard) and from the casual translations of two generous friends (Koko
Petitt and Catherine Marachi). Her final thoughts on history and
romance are courtesy of Walt Whitman.

Mrs. French's greeting, "Oh, you dear Big Livermore!" in Chapter
29 echoes Julia Ward Howe's greeting of that physically formidable
woman in Wendy Venet's *A Strong Minded Woman: The Life of Mary
A. Livermore* (University of Massachusetts Press, 2005). (Please don't
trust Miss Rose's unfavorable assessment of Mary Livermore. Read
Venet's book and discover this remarkable woman for yourself.)
"Mr. Knowlton's text," in Chapter 29, refers to Charles Knowlton's
The Fruits of Philosophy (though Mrs. French might well have used a
number of other controversial books and pamphlets on reproduction,
sexuality, and physiology). To ease Madelyn's fears in Chapter 30, Mrs.
French quotes one of my favorite poems, Rumi's "A Small Green
Island." Her insights on the slow pace of social change in Chapter 34
mirror those of 19th century Universalist minister Olympia Brown,
who said, "Reformers are often deceived by a kind of mirage. They
suppose victory at hand when . . . generations are yet to pass before
it can be realized." And, of course, the work is not yet done.